## "I DON'T WANT YOU TO KISS ME AGAIN, THE WAY YOU DID LAST NIGHT," SHE SAID TIGHTLY.

He trailed his hand down her neck and set the pad of his thumb over the pulse at the base of her throat.

"Are you afraid of me?" he asked softly.

"Certainly not!" Though it had been pride that dictated her quick answer, it was also the truth. She was frightened by the ease with which he could make her lose control, but she wasn't afraid of him. Somewhere inside, she knew he wouldn't hurt her. And despite her protestations to the contrary, she knew he wouldn't force her to do anything she didn't want to do. That was the problem. He could make her *want* to do things she shouldn't.

"Then why is your pulse beating so fast?" He was so close that she could feel his breath against her forehead. Lila stared into his eyes, mesmerized by their clarity. "Maybe the problem isn't that you don't want me to kiss you. Maybe it's that you do," he whispered.

*Also by Dallas Schulze*

THE WAY HOME

# GUNFIGHTER'S BRIDE

## DALLAS SCHULZE

A Dell Book

Published by
Dell Publishing
a division of
Bantam Doubleday Dell Publishing Group, Inc.
1540 Broadway
New York, New York 10036

ISBN: 0-440-21466-1

Printed in the United States of America

Published simultaneously in Canada

January 1996

10  9  8  7  6  5  4  3  2  1

RAD

# *Chapter 1*

*Happy is the bride the sun shines on.*

Lila watched dust motes floating through a beam of sunlight that had found its way through one of the high windows of the church. The thin swath of light fell directly in front of the minister, creating a tiny golden path on the polished wooden floor. If she slid her foot forward just a few inches, the sunbeam would fall across the toe of her satin slipper. Maybe that's all it would take to make the promise in the old saying true. Maybe if the sun was literally shining *on* her, she'd be happy, the way a bride was supposed to be.

A half smile trembled on her mouth. It was too bad things couldn't be that simple. When she was a child, a sunny day had been enough to make her happy. But she wasn't a child anymore and it would take considerably more than a little sunshine to put her world right. Like being able to turn back the clock.

Just three months ago, she'd been in this same church for another wedding. Her brother, Douglas, had been getting married, and Lila had watched the ceremony through eyes stinging with tears of joy. She'd been so happy for him, so pleased that he'd found someone to love. And she'd dreamed of her own wedding, seen herself in a veil of white lace, her family and friends filling the church behind her, her hand resting on a strong male arm.

Everything was just the way she'd imagined it. Her veil was made of bobbin lace so fine it seemed as if it must have been woven by faerie fingers rather than human hands. The fine white lace lay over the deep auburn of her hair like snow on fire. The small church she'd attended all her life was filled with family and friends, people she'd known since childhood. And the arm beneath her fingers was definitely male and solid as a rock. Yes, she had everything she'd dreamed of three months ago. The irony of that memory was so powerful that it was all she could do to keep from laughing out loud. She'd forgotten to wish for the one thing that would have given the picture real meaning.

She'd forgotten to wish for love.

"Marriage is a lifelong commitment," Reverend Carpenter was saying. "A man and a woman are joined together by God, bound by the vows of matrimony. Vows that will last the rest of their lives, making them one in the eyes of the Lord."

The words struck Lila with the force of blows. *A lifelong commitment.* That was what she was making. The rest of her life would be inextricably linked to Logan Sinclair, bound by the vows they were about to exchange. Panic swept through her.

Suddenly light-headed, she swayed. Reverend Carpenter's speech stumbled to a halt as Logan's arm came around her waist, steadying her. He lowered his head, his brown eyes dark with concern.

"Are you all right?" he asked quietly.

Was she all right? Lila felt a hysterical bubble of laughter rise in her throat. He, of all people, knew the answer to that question. But she knew what he was asking. She swallowed hard and forced her mouth to curve in a thin parody of a smile.

"I'm fine," she told him, the lie nearly choking her. "I just felt a little dizzy for a moment. I . . . didn't eat much breakfast."

She was aware of the barely audible buzz of concern and curiosity rising from the guests. In another moment, Douglas would be out of his seat and coming forward to see what the delay was, his green eyes, so like her own, dark with worry. And if that happened, Lila was afraid she'd throw herself into her brother's arms, confessing the whole wretched truth and begging him to make everything right, the way he'd always been able to do when she was a child. But she wasn't a child anymore and there wasn't anything Douglas could do to make things right this time.

"Please continue with the ceremony," she told the minister, forcing another smile.

*Please continue before I change my mind.*

Reverend Carpenter cleared his throat, his thin mouth compressed with irritation. He prided himself on his skill as an orator and he did not appreciate being interrupted in the midst of what he considered one of his better efforts. He cleared his throat again and cast Lila a disapproving look before continuing his one-sided discussion of the responsibilities of holy matrimony.

Lila tried to listen to what he was saying. After all, she was marrying Logan and she had every intention of being a good wife to him. She would do everything in her power to make sure that he never had cause to regret this day. She owed him that and more. Stealing a sideways look at his face, she felt a pang of regret for what she was doing to him. He deserved better than this. But she had no choice. She was doing the only thing she could.

She'd make it up to him, she promised herself. Focusing her eyes firmly on the minister's face, she tried to listen to what he was saying.

"Marriage is not about joy, though joy may be found within its bonds. But joy cannot be the solitary goal of a marriage. Nay, it *must* not be a goal at all," the reverend intoned solemnly.

*Well, they could meet that requirement,* Lila thought with a touch of hysterical humor. Joy was certainly not one of their primary goals in making this marriage.

"Marriage is about duty." The minister's voice boomed out sternly. "A man's duty to provide for his family. A wife's duty—"

But before he could tell the assemblage just what a wife's duty might be, there was another interruption.

The sharp thud of boot heels hitting the wooden

slats of the entryway was clearly audible. An instant later, the tall double doors were thrust open with force enough to knock them back against the walls on either side and sunlight spilled into the church. Heads craned as the guests gaped at the figure in the doorway. The bride and groom turned toward the disturbance and Lila's fingers suddenly dug deep into Logan's arm, her knees going weak under her.

Reverend Carpenter's speech came to an abrupt halt, and, for an instant, the church was quiet as a tomb. The silence stretched for the space of several seconds, giving Lila a chance to contemplate the magnitude of the disaster standing in the doorway. She wanted desperately to turn and run, to find a place to hide. But she could only stand there, clinging to Logan, her head swimming with shock.

"A late arrival, I see," the reverend said, recovering his equilibrium and anxious to assert his authority. "If you'll find a seat, sir."

But no one really believed that the man now walking up the aisle was simply a late arrival. The sunlight spilled into the church behind him, creating a brilliant golden path up the aisle, a path he strode like an avenging angel descending from heaven above. Lila wished that was exactly what was happening. Better an angel to smite her for her sins than the devil in dusty clothes walking toward her now.

There was a buzz of whispers as some of the guests recognized him and whispered to those who didn't. A man like Bishop McKenzie was not easily forgotten.

Booted and spurred and covered with dust, he looked as out of place in the tidy little Pennsylvania church as a wolf at a teaparty. The guests watched, breathless with curiosity as he strode up the aisle, looking neither right nor left. The air fairly crackled with the tension of a drama in the making.

Douglas Adams rose as Bishop neared the front of the church, stepping into the aisle to face the other man. A quick rush of whispers reminded those who might have forgotten that Bishop McKenzie had saved Douglas's life a few months ago, as well as that of his soon-to-be bride, Susan. As the story went, Douglas and Susan had been facing sure death at the hands of the ruffians who'd held up the stage in which they were riding. With the driver already dead, there had been nothing to stop the thieves from killing Douglas and doing something unspeakable to Susan when Bishop had suddenly appeared from out of nowhere. Some said he'd dispatched half a dozen of the murderers with an equal number of bullets, but there were those who claimed the cowards had simply fled upon finding themselves confronting an armed man.

Whatever the truth was, there was no doubt that a friendship had developed between the two men. It was an unlikely combination—Douglas Adams of the Philadelphia Adamses and Bishop McKenzie of nowhere in particular. But Douglas had invited Bishop to come East for his wedding and to stay with the family for as long as he liked, and Bishop had accepted the invitation. For the few days he'd been in Beaton, the tall westerner had been the source of considerable speculation. The word "gunfighter" had been mentioned, and there was something in the cool steadiness of his gaze that had given weight to the speculation. More than one female heart had beat faster at the sight of those broad shoulders and ice-blue eyes. There might even have been one or two foolish enough to set their caps for him if he hadn't left abruptly the day after the wedding. Everyone had assumed they'd seen the last of him.

But here he was, striding through the church and creating ripples of questions and speculation with every step.

"Bishop." Douglas's greeting held both question and confusion. "We weren't expecting you."

"I don't suppose you were." Bishop's eyes cut past him to Lila. She nearly whimpered aloud as that fierce blue gaze seemed to cut right through her. "I need to talk to your sister."

"Lila?" Douglas's bewilderment was reflected in his eyes but Bishop wasn't interested in offering explanations. Stepping past Douglas, he stopped in front of the bridal couple.

Lila stared up at him. All the color had drained from her face, leaving the green of her eyes to stand out in vivid contrast to the milk white of her skin.

"Call it off," Bishop told her quietly.

"I don't know who you are but I think you should either take a seat or leave." Logan's tone made it clear which of the two he'd prefer. He'd been in Europe three months ago and had missed Douglas's wedding so he hadn't met Bishop then.

"Stay out of this," Bishop said, barely glancing at the other man. His eyes pinned Lila where she stood. "Call it off," he told her again.

She was trembling like a leaf in a high wind but she managed to shake her head in refusal.

"What the devil do you think you're doing, Bishop?" Douglas had come forward, his open features darkening with anger. "This is my sister's wedding, for God's sake."

"I know what it is. She's not marrying him." Bishop jerked his head toward Logan, his eyes never leaving Lila. "Call it off. Now."

Dizzy with fear, her mind spinning with the implications of his arrival, Lila shook her head again.

"Go away," she whispered, knowing he wasn't going to do anything of the kind. She'd never, in her worst nightmares, imagined anything like this happening.

"Maybe we should talk about this somewhere less public," Susan Adams suggested as she joined the little group at the front of the church. "I think we've provided enough entertainment for one morning."

"No!" Lila's voice was choked. She felt hysteria rise inside her, like a bird beating frantic wings against the bars of a cage. "There's nothing to talk about. I'm getting married."

With an effort, she dragged her eyes from Bishop's and spun around to face Reverend Carpenter, who was staring at the sudden crowd in front of his altar in growing indignation. He was not accustomed to having his thunder stolen in his own church.

"Go on with the ceremony," she said, her voice high and tight. "Go on."

"I don't believe—"

But Bishop cut into the minister's angry words. "Call it off, Lila." His hand closed over her arm, turning her back to face him. "If you don't do it, by God, I will." His voice was low and hard, his eyes a sharp, angry blue.

Douglas spoke before she could say anything. "Have you lost your mind, Bishop?"

At the same time, Logan grabbed Bishop's arm,

jerking his fingers from Lila's arm. "Get your hands off of her!"

Bishop didn't so much as glance at him. His eyes remained locked with Lila's and what she read in them made her feel faint. He knew, she thought. She didn't see how it was possible, but he knew. Somehow he'd found out the truth, and he'd come East to stop her wedding to Logan.

"Please," she whispered, hardly knowing what she was asking. For him to leave, for time to spin backward, for the world to be the way it had been before she met him. "Please."

She thought she saw something flicker in his eyes— regret, perhaps. And for one tiny moment, she dared to hope that he was going to turn and walk away, that he'd leave her to put the pieces of her life back together in the only way she could.

"Who the devil *are* you?" Logan demanded.

The challenge in the other man's question made the hint of softness in Bishop's expression disappear, and Lila knew, with a feeling of despair, that he had no intention of walking away. He looked at her a moment longer, giving her one final chance to control what was about to happen, but she could only stare at him, her eyes begging him for a mercy she already knew he wasn't going to show.

When she didn't say anything, Bishop looked at Logan.

"You want to know who I am?" he asked, in a voice as cool and hard as his eyes. "I'm the father of the child she's carrying."

# Chapter 2

Though Bishop pitched his voice low, the minister stood too close to miss hearing what he'd said. In the stunned silence that followed the announcement, the hiss of Reverend Carpenter's shocked gasp seemed to echo like thunder. That small sound spelled a death knell for any hope Lila might have had of keeping her condition a secret. The good reverend's skill as an orator was easily outstripped by his talent for gossip. By the end of the day, the entire town would be buzzing with the news that Lila Adams was with child and that Logan Sinclair was *not* the father.

Lila would have given a great deal to have been able to die right there and then. Failing that, she would have settled for fainting. But neither blessing was granted her. She remained alive and painfully conscious.

Logan was the first to recover. His eyes flashed with hot rage. He took a quick step forward, his right hand lashing out. He was a big man, as tall as Bishop and nearly as broad through the shoulders. The punch he threw was backed by muscle and powered by anger. If it had connected, it almost certainly would have broken the other man's jaw. But Bishop had the reflexes of a cat. He jerked back reflexively and Logan's fist caught him a glancing blow, rocking him back on his heels and splitting his lower lip but doing no serious damage.

"Bastard!" Logan moved to continue the attack but Douglas stepped between the two men, catching his arm.

"For God's sake, man, remember where you are!" The reminder did nothing to soften the rage in Logan's eyes.

"If you knew what he did to Lila, it wouldn't matter where we were."

"Logan!" Lila's voice was shrill with panic. She hadn't thought things could get any worse, but she'd just realized that they could. Her fingers dug into the fabric of Logan's coat. "Please don't say anything more. It's not his fault."

"Not his fault?" Logan turned to look at her, his expression incredulous. "How can you say that?"

"I'll explain later."

"There's nothing to explain," he snapped. "After

what the bastard did to you, I can't believe he has the nerve to show his face here."

"One thing I've never been accused of lacking is nerve," Bishop said. He used the back of his hand to blot the thin trickle of blood from his lip, his icy blue eyes offering a challenge.

"Stop it, both of you!" Susan's hissed order was ignored.

Logan's arm was tight and hard under Lila's fingers. She could feel the rage in him and knew he was a heartbeat away from taking another swing at Bishop. She also knew, though she couldn't have said how, that Bishop wouldn't allow a second blow to go unanswered, and she had nightmare visions of a full-blown brawl breaking out right in front of the altar where she'd been baptized twenty-five years ago.

"Please," she whispered. Though she still held Logan's arm, it was Bishop's eyes she sought. "Please don't make it any worse."

"I don't see how it could get much worse," Douglas muttered, glancing over his shoulder at the assembled guests who were watching the remarkable scene at the altar with avid curiosity.

"I think we've provided enough entertainment for one day," Susan said briskly. She moved forward and slipped her arm around Lila's waist. "Let's move this into the vestry."

Lila was grateful for her sister-in-law's support as the oddly matched group moved toward the door leading to the vestry. Though she was careful to keep her eyes down, she could hear the whispers rising up around them. The sound made her stomach twist. Speculation would be running wild, everyone trying to guess what could have caused the scene that had been enacted before them. Once Reverend Carpenter spoke—confidentially, of course—to one or two of his closest friends, the truth would spread through Beaton, Pennsylvania, like floodwaters sweeping the town.

*Lila Adams in a family way? And the father that wild western friend of her brother's? Shocking! But, of course, she always was a wild one. Just look at her hair. Red—brazen, hussy red—it all but shouts Jezebel. Never mind that it's natural—the Lord doesn't give a woman hair like that without good reason. It was only a matter of time before her true nature was revealed. It's just as well that poor, sweet Margaret is gone. It would have killed her for sure to see her only daughter in such a fix.*

She'd never be able to stay here, Lila realized. No matter what happened now, her life in Beaton was over. Whether Bishop stayed or went, whether she married Logan or not, she'd have to leave her home. If not for her own sake, then for Douglas's. Her brother's political career might, just possibly, survive this scandal, but only if she was gone. As long as she was visible, the gossip would stay fresh in everyone's mind, doing irreparable harm to his future.

As the full extent of this new disaster sank in on her, Lila leaned more heavily on Susan's supporting arm. When she'd realized she was pregnant, she'd thought her life was over. But then Logan found out about the baby and offered to marry her, and she'd still been able to cling to the remnants of the life she'd always known. Now even that was torn from her.

They'd reached the vestry. The room was used for occasional meetings of the church council. It was plainly furnished with an oak table and chairs and a hideously ugly horsehair sofa that had been donated by one of the ladies of the church. Douglas pushed the door open and shepherded his wife and sister through. Susan led Lila over to the sofa, urging her down onto the unyielding surface. Bishop and Logan hesitated in the doorway a moment, their eyes clashing, and then Logan brushed past the other man. Bishop followed him into the room and Douglas started to close the door, but Reverend Carpenter was suddenly there, having followed them from the altar, drawn by the scent of juicy gossip.

"I know you'll wish my counsel and guidance," he said, his solemn tone at odds with the eager glitter in his eyes.

"Thank you, Reverend, but I think we'll handle this alone," Douglas said firmly, blocking the other man's entrance into the room.

"I think the situation calls for God's counsel," the older man said, trying to slip past.

"We'll call if we need you," Douglas said, not moving an inch.

"But—"

"He said we'll call if we need you." Bishop loomed up behind Douglas, his expression so coldly menacing that the minister actually took a quick little step back before catching himself and remembering that this was *his* church.

His face flushed with indignation. "Really, I—"

"Thank you, Reverend Carpenter." Douglas shut the door quietly, cutting off the man's gabbled protest.

There was a moment of deep silence and then Douglas turned to look at the room's occupants. His eyes touched on Logan and Bishop, each in turn, drifted over his wife, and then settled on his sister. Lila read the questions in his eyes and felt her stomach twist. Of all the things she stood to lose, her brother's respect and love was the most painful. Unable to sustain his look, she lowered her eyes to her lap. Her fingers smoothed an imaginary wrinkle in the heavy white silk of her gown.

"Would someone like to tell me what's going on?" Douglas asked, his tone deceptively mild. "Bishop?"

"Ask your sister," Bishop said shortly.

"You bastard!" Logan's voice vibrated with rage. Lila looked up in time to see him turn to face Bishop, his hands clenched into fists at his sides, his whole body rigid with anger. "You don't even have the guts to admit what you did to her. Maybe you've forgotten, but I haven't."

"Logan, no!"

But Lila's quick protest was drowned out by Logan's next words, spit out as he turned to Douglas. "He raped her!"

"Rape!" Bishop hadn't looked nearly as shocked when Logan hit him. He opened his mouth and then closed it without speaking. He glanced at Lila, and she physically winced away from the contempt in his eyes. His jaw flexed as if he were literally biting back words of denial.

"Rape?" The color drained from Douglas's face. He looked from Logan to Bishop, his expression stunned and disbelieving. "Bishop?"

Bishop met his friend's eyes squarely but said nothing, offering neither denial or defense.

"Lila?" Douglas looked at his sister. She met his eyes for a moment and then looked away.

If she said nothing, it would be as good as confirming Logan's accusation. She knew her brother well enough to know what his reaction would be then. Douglas was the most civilized man Lila had ever known, a staunch supporter of law and order. But when it came to his family, he was fiercely protective. He would never let such an attack go unpunished. Bishop would be lucky to get out of Pennsylvania alive.

*What do you care?* a small voice whispered. *Bishop McKenzie will be out of your life for good. Douglas will take care of you. He'll make everything right, just like he always has.*

But at what cost? At the cost of his political career? At the cost of her own self-respect?

"Lila?" he said again, asking her to confirm or deny. He'd believe whatever she told him, Lila knew. He'd never question her word.

"It wasn't rape." The words were dragged from her in a painful whisper, but they seemed to echo like thunder in the small room.

"It wasn't—" Logan stared at her in shocked disbelief. "But you told me that's what happened; that that was how you—"

"You assumed it and I let you believe it." Lila looked at him, feeling weary all the way to her soul, too weary to feel much pain at admitting to yet another lie, yet another betrayal. "I was ashamed to tell you the truth."

"You didn't have to lie to me." Logan's eyes darkened with anger. "I'd still have married you."

"I'm sorry," she said, knowing the words were hopelessly inadequate.

Logan clearly thought so too. "Dammit, Lila, you—"

"Leave her alone." Oddly, it was Bishop who gave the order. "And watch your language in front of the ladies."

"You're in a fine position to give lessons on how to treat a lady," Logan snapped, turning his anger and frustration on Bishop. "You apparently didn't give it much consideration three months ago when you—"

"That's enough, Logan." Douglas put his hand on the other man's shoulder. The two of them had grown up together, had been friends since boyhood. "I'm the one with the right to demand explanations."

"There's no point in explanations," Bishop said impatiently.

"I think I'm owed a few," Douglas snapped. "More than a few. When I invited you into my home, I didn't think it would be necessary to lock my sister away to keep her safe from you."

"It wasn't like that," Lila said. She could hardly believe that she was defending Bishop. But it seemed he was unwilling to defend himself. He just stood there, listening to Douglas's harsh condemnation, saying not a word, and she suddenly found that she couldn't let her brother's accusations go unanswered.

"This was my fault," Douglas said, his eyes anguished as he looked at her.

"No, it isn't."

"*I* brought him here. I allowed this to happen to you. You're young and innocent and he seduced you—"

Lila felt something snap inside her. She'd been living a lie for weeks, pretending that everything was going to be all right; that she could somehow patch the pieces of her life back together in some recognizable form. But that wasn't going to happen. There was no going back. She could only go forward, and she was suddenly, fiercely, determined that there were going to be no more lies.

"Stop it!" She stood abruptly, her heavy silk skirts rustling around her. "That's not the way it was at all."

"Lila." Susan had remained silent throughout the discussion, but she rose also and put her hand on her sister-in-law's arm. Her china-blue eyes were soft with concern. "You're upset. Don't say something you're going to regret."

*Regret?* Lila had to catch back a hysterical laugh. She had so much to regret. What was one more thing? Stepping away from Susan's touch, she faced her brother, her face porcelain pale, her eyes blazing green and filled with an angry pain.

"He didn't seduce me, Douglas. In fact, it was the other way around. I seduced him."

"That's enough," Bishop said sharply.

"Trying to protect my reputation?" Lila asked, shooting him a mocking look. "I think it's too late for that, don't you? I might as well tell the truth, if I can remember how. Why shouldn't Douglas know what happened that night?"

"It doesn't matter anymore," Bishop told her. "It's over and done."

"Of course it matters. That's why we're all here, isn't it? Because of what happened that night? Don't you think Douglas has a right to know why he's in the midst of a scandal? Don't you think he should know what kind of woman his sister is? That I'm nothing but a—"

Bishop moved with shocking speed for a man his size. One moment he was across the room, the next he was looming over her, his fingers wrapped around her arm in a grasp that stopped just short of being painful.

"Not another word." His voice was low and hard.

Lila stared up at him, reading the warning in his expression. Green eyes clashed with blue. Hers were the first to drop. She focused her gaze on the hard thrust of his chin, and it occurred to her that here was another example of how much she'd changed. The girl she'd been three months ago would have met the challenge in his eyes with one of her own. The woman she was now recognized a battle she'd surely lose.

"What happened is no one's business but our own," Bishop said in that same quiet tone. "It doesn't matter anymore."

Lila nodded slowly. "It doesn't matter," she whispered.

He smelled of dust and leather and horse, a distinctly masculine amalgam of scents. He was solidly muscled, overwhelmingly male, the reason her life was destroyed, and Lila wanted nothing more than to be able to lay her head against his shoulder and let him deal with everything and everyone.

The thought was so shocking that she stiffened and pulled away from him. He let her go and turned to look at Douglas.

"Lila and I need to talk."

"The way you 'talked' three months ago?" Logan asked, his mouth curling in a sneer.

"Logan!" Susan's shocked protest made him flush. Bishop stiffened but Douglas spoke first.

"That was uncalled for."

"You're right. I apologize." Logan spoke to a point somewhere between Lila and Bishop, his tone flatly polite, his expression rigid and as empty as his apology. "I don't really think I'm needed here. If you'll excuse me." He executed a stiff little bow before turning on his heel and walking out.

The door closed behind him and Lila felt her heart crack just a little more than it already had. She'd known Logan all her life, had counted him as a friend, almost as a second brother. Now he was gone, and she had the terrible feeling that she might never see him again. The repercussions of that one night seemed never ending.

"You'll marry her as soon as I can make the arrangements," Douglas said, breaking the taut silence left in the wake of Logan's exit.

"No!" Lila's gasp of protest was swallowed up in Bishop's response.

"Why do you think I came back?" he asked, sounding tired and angry.

"I don't know." The look Douglas gave him was sharp with dislike. "Apparently, I don't know you at all."

Bishop's jaw tightened but all he said was "Make the arrangements."

"Don't I have anything to say about this?" Lila demanded, feeling as if the jaws of a trap were closing around her.

"What is there to say?" Douglas asked. He jerked his head toward the door and the church that lay beyond. "Setting aside everything else, after the scene out there, I don't think you have much choice."

He was right. She knew he was right. Even if Reverend Carpenter didn't spread the news of her condition, Bishop's dramatic appearance would set the gossip mill in motion. It wouldn't take long for some clever soul to put the pieces of the puzzle together in more or less the correct order. She wouldn't be able to show her face in public without the whispers following her. And, even if no one guessed the truth, in a few weeks there would be no hiding it anyway.

"Besides, aren't you forgetting something?" Douglas glanced at her still-flat stomach, reminding her of the child she was carrying. As if she needed a reminder, Lila thought, swallowing against a wave of panic.

"Make the arrangements," Bishop said again when Lila didn't answer her brother. "Now I'd like to speak to Lila alone."

"I think that's a good idea," Susan said, rising from the sofa and shaking out the skirts of her pale-blue dress.

"Well, I don't." Douglas shot Bishop a look of acute dislike. "I'm not going to leave her alone with him."

"I'm not going to ravish her in a church," Bishop snapped impatiently.

"They need to talk," Susan put her hand on Douglas's arm. "We'll wait right outside."

Though he clearly wasn't happy about the idea, Douglas allowed himself to be shepherded from the room.

Their departure left behind a thick silence. For the first time since that night three months before, Lila and Bishop were alone.

"It's true then," he said. "You're pregnant."

Lila flushed. In polite society, no one used such blunt terms. If they referred to it at all, they might mention that she was in an interesting condition or in a family way. But considering the situation, it was probably a bit late to be worrying about polite conventions.

"I am with child," she said stiffly.

"Why didn't you write me?"

"How would I have addressed the letter? Mr. Bishop McKenzie, west of Pennsylvania?"

"Douglas knew where I was."

"Of course!" Lila widened her eyes in mock amazement. "Now, why didn't I think of that? All I had to do was ask Douglas for your address. And if he happened to ask me why I wished to contact you, I could have told him that I was sending you a receipt for strawberry jelly that you'd requested."

She was perversely pleased to see Bishop's jaw tighten at her tone. When he spoke, it was in the tone of a man nearing the end of his patience, and that pleased her too.

"Look, I've done a lot of traveling the last few days. There was a bridge down about twenty miles back and I had to buy a horse and then nearly rode it to death to get here. I'm not really in the mood to stand here listening to you sharpen your tongue on my hide."

"I didn't ask you to come here. Why *did* you come?" she asked, her eyes narrowing. When he'd first appeared, she'd been too stunned to question his presence. It had seemed as if the divine hand of justice had descended to punish her for her sins. But now that the shock was starting to wear off, it occurred to her that there was probably a more earthbound explanation. "How did you find out . . ." She let the question trail off, unable to say the words.

"That you were going to pass my child off as an-other man's?" Bishop asked, his voice sharp enough to make her wince. "Susan wrote me."

"Susan!" Lila stared at him in shocked disbelief. "I didn't tell her about—I didn't tell her anything. How did she know? And how did she know to contact you?"

"I don't know. But she did."

"She had no right! It was none of her concern." Her sister-in-law's interference felt like a betrayal.

"Maybe she thought it was *my* concern," Bishop said sharply.

"Why would Susan assume that you . . . That you and I . . . that we—" She flushed and looked away from him, her voice trailing off. "I didn't tell her. I didn't tell anybody."

"Well, don't look at me." Bishop ran his fingers through his hair, feeling weariness settle over him like a heavy cloak. "It's not something I discussed with anyone. Maybe she saw you sneaking out of my room."

"I didn't sneak!" Lila flared. "I just . . . left."

"Well, you must have done your leaving very quietly to avoid waking me."

"Considering how much you'd had to drink, I doubt anything less than a cannon blast would have roused you."

"I could say the same about you. As I recall, the champagne was flowing pretty freely that night."

"The last thing I want to do is recall anything about that night," she said tightly. "If I could, I'd forget it ever happened."

"I tried to see you the next morning. Your maid

said you weren't seeing anyone. I would have thought you'd make an exception for me."

Bishop had awakened the morning after Douglas's wedding with a mouth full of cotton, a pounding headache, and a sick feeling in his gut that had less to do with the amount he'd had to drink than it did with the vicious bite of his conscience. There had been no merciful period of forgetfulness, no whiskey-granted amnesia. His memories of the night before had been painfully clear. The feel of a woman in his arms, the uncertain eagerness of her response, the soft warmth of her body against him, beneath him.

"You were the last person I wanted to see," Lila said, pulling him away from the memories. "What was there to say? Unless you were going to offer to marry me?" When he said nothing, her mouth twisted in a mocking smile. "I didn't think so."

"I didn't think you'd want to spend the rest of your life paying for one mistake," he said. That was the conclusion he'd reached after a considerable amount of painful thought.

"How kind of you to think of me," she said with exaggerated gratitude. "But your efforts were in vain because here we are. It looks like we're both going to paying for that particular mistake for a long time to come. You should have stayed where you were. No sense in two people suffering where one would do."

Her mocking tone sparked Bishop's own temper. "Aren't you forgetting the man you were about to marry?" he asked. "Or is he so in love with you that playing father to another man's bastard was a small price to pay to have you?"

"Logan isn't in love with me. He's a friend. Nothing more."

"Seems to me he's carrying friendship a bit far," Bishop said sardonically. "Tying himself up for life."

"I was once engaged to his brother." Lila offered the explanation reluctantly. "Logan is like one of the family."

"What happened to the brother?"

"Billy was killed in a riding accident shortly before we were to be married."

"When was that?"

"Three years ago, though I hardly think it's any concern of yours." Her chin lifted, her eyes daring him to offer any sympathy. "Logan thinks of me almost as a sister. That's why he offered to marry me."

"Noble of him," Bishop said sardonically.

"I think it was. He's a true gentleman."

"If he's such a paragon, why didn't you tell him the truth about how you came to be carrying my child? Or didn't it bother you to lie to him?"

"I didn't lie to him."

"I forgot—he assumed that I'd forced myself on you and you didn't correct him." He didn't trouble to hide his contempt.

"It was easier that way," she muttered, her eyes avoiding his.

"I can imagine it was. I'm surprised you didn't let the lie stand. Douglas would have seen me dead, if Sinclair didn't beat him to it. That would certainly have simplified things."

"I wish I'd thought of it," Lila snapped.

"I bet you do," he said in a silken tone that had been known to make grown men pale. "Maybe, if you'd thought things through a little more clearly, you could have married your friend Logan. You managed to convince him it was rape when we both know I didn't exactly have to force you. With just a little effort, you could have had him believing the baby was his."

Lila felt a flash of rage so intense it was physically painful. It struck her that she hated Bishop McKenzie with a passion like nothing she'd ever felt before. She wanted to wipe that hateful expression from his face; wanted to see him lying dead at her feet. Without conscious thought, her hand came up. Whether she intended to slap him or to try to claw his damned, knowing eyes from his face, she didn't know. In that moment, causing him physical pain seemed the only way to ease the sick ache she'd been living with for the last three months.

But Bishop moved with the same easy speed that had surprised her before, his hand coming up, fingers closing around her wrist, halting her palm inches from his face. He used the hold to jerk her forward until they stood a heartbeat apart, the heavy silk skirts of her wedding gown rustling as they swirled against his legs.

Five feet eight inches in her stocking feet, Lila had grown accustomed to looking most men directly in the eye, a habit her mother had discouraged. *Keep your eyes modestly downcast, sweetheart. Gentleman always admire modesty in a lady. Too much directness makes them nervous.* Bishop didn't look the least bit nervous. But perhaps that was because he was a good seven inches taller than she was, forcing her to tilt her head back to look at him.

They stood there, eyes locked in a silent duel of wills. Pride kept Lila from struggling. Pride and the sure knowledge that she couldn't force him to release her until he chose to do so and she'd only make a fool of herself by pitting her strength against his.

This close, she could see the tiny flecks of gray that lightened the blue of his eyes. Unwanted, unwelcome, a memory came to her of those same eyes, heavy lidded with desire; of the softly scratchy brush of his mustache against her skin; of the warm rush of sweet pleasure that had followed on his every touch. The strength of that memory frightened her in a way that the anger in his eyes couldn't.

"Let me go."

"Not until you settle down. I've already been hit once today. I don't particularly want to make it twice."

"Settle down?" She repeated the phrase from between gritted teeth. "I'm not a fractious horse you're trying to break to saddle."

Bishop took his time in answering her. He'd spent three months trying to figure out what it was about Lila Adams that had made him abandon his common sense and betray his friendship with her brother. He'd told himself it was too much drink and the fact that seeing the way Douglas and Susan looked at each other had suddenly made him feel older and more alone than he had in his entire life. But looking at Lila, he was forced to admit that there had been more to it than whiskey and loneliness. She was fire and ice, all pale skin and big green eyes and temper. And he wanted her, the same way he'd wanted her the night of Douglas's wedding. The knowledge put an edge to his voice.

"Seems to me there's considerable similarity between a woman and a horse," he drawled. "They both need a firm hand on the reins to show them who's in charge."

Enraged beyond words, Lila forgot her determination not to struggle and tried to jerk away from him. Bishop's fingers tightened around her hand for a moment and then he released her, having made it clear that he was doing so because he *chose* to.

She took a quick step back. Only the weight of her skirts kept her from rushing from the room. That and her pride, which refused to give him the satisfaction of seeing her run.

"I won't marry you," she said. Despite her best efforts to sound calm and controlled, her voice shook with rage.

"You'll marry me."

"You can't force me."

"I don't have to. They will." Bishop inclined his head toward the door, reminding her of the church full of guests who'd witnessed his dramatic arrival, who had since dispersed to their homes to speculate on the truth behind the interrupted ceremony. *He was right,* she thought despairingly. She'd marry him because it was the only real choice open to her. The knowledge did nothing to soften her anger.

"I should have let my brother kill you," Lila hissed.

"Maybe. But it's too late now."

His calm response made her want to scream. She glared at him, her eyes stormy with frustration and rage. She was trapped. Because of one night of champagne and madness, she was going to be forced to join her life with that of the man before her, a man with whom she'd shared intimacies she could barely bring herself to remember and yet whom she knew not at all.

Bishop must have seen the acceptance in her eyes. His mouth twisted in a half smile that held no real humor. "I suspect Douglas's patience has stretched about as far as it's going to," he said, moving toward the door.

Lila hesitated a moment longer but there was no sense in delaying the inevitable. She couldn't stay in this little room forever. Bishop opened the door and then stood back politely to allow her to exit first. The guests were gone and the church was empty except for Douglas and Susan, who rose from one of the pews and came toward them. Seeing her brother's worried face, Lila was suddenly acutely aware of all that she was losing. If she'd married Logan, at least she'd have been able to preserve a piece of her life. Now it was all gone.

She glanced up, her eyes meeting Bishop's. "I wish you'd arrived too late," she said, her voice more weary than angry."If I'd already been Logan's wife, there would have been nothing you could do to change things."

Bishop smiled down at her, his eyes pale blue and cold as ice. "I could have made you a widow."

# *Chapter 3*

"We gather together in the sight of God and these witnesses to join this man and this woman in the bonds of holy matrimony," Reverend Carpenter intoned solemnly.

For the second time in a matter of hours, Lila listened to the same words. They didn't sound any more real to her now than they had earlier. Standing in the parlor of River Walk, her family's home for the last one hundred fifty years, she had the same feeling that she was standing outside herself, watching what was happening but not really a part of it.

The words were the same but everything else had

changed. There were no guests this time, only Douglas and Susan to act as witnesses. The elaborate white silk wedding gown with its rows of lace and fine pleated trim had been replaced with a simple dress of pale-gray muslin, its plainness relieved by touches of creamy lace at the wrists and throat. And instead of standing beside a man she'd known all her life, she was standing beside a man she didn't know at all.

The ceremony was mercifully brief. No doubt, given more time, the reverend would have come up with an oration appropriate to the circumstances, something laden with allusions to the wages of sin. As it was, he kept his commentary to a minimum. He conveyed his disapproval by the stern tone of his voice, but he couldn't hide the avid curiosity in his eyes.

Aware that everything she said and did was going to be reported over tea and cakes with the good reverend's friends, Lila struggled to present a calm façade. There was no sense in providing even more fodder for the gossip mill. Lord knew, this day had already given enough to keep the town talking for weeks.

"I now pronounce you husband and wife. You may kiss your bride."

Her feeling that she was observing everything from behind a glass wall was shattered as if a hammer had been applied to that same wall. She was only vaguely aware of the prim disapproval in Reverend Carpenter's eyes. All her attention was focused on the man standing beside her—the man who was now her husband.

Bishop felt Lila jump when he put his hand on her shoulder to turn her to face him. She stared up at him, her green eyes wide and dilated, swirling with a mixture of emotions he couldn't even begin to read. She was his. His wife. He was caught off guard by the gut-deep feeling of possessiveness that came with the thought. He touched her cheek. Her skin was cool and soft beneath his fingertips. His. Crazy as it was, considering the circumstances, there was an odd satisfaction in the knowledge.

She drew in a quick, sharp little breath as he lowered his head. He expected her to turn her face away, but she didn't. She watched him, her eyes smoky green and filled with a mixture of uncertainty and defiance. Bishop's mouth quirked. He should have known better than to think that Lila would turn away. If he'd learned nothing else about her, it was that she wasn't much inclined to turn away from a challenge.

Lila saw the flicker of amusement in Bishop's eyes but she had only a moment to wonder at its cause before his mouth touched hers. She'd expected nothing more than a brief peck on the cheek, a token gesture for Reverend Carpenter's benefit. Instead, his lips settled on hers in a kiss that was warmly caressing. Caught by surprise, her mouth softened, welcoming him. She lifted one hand and set it against his chest, her fingers curling into the fabric of his coat.

His mustache was softly rough against her skin, contrasting with the firm smoothness of his lips. She had a sudden memory of his mouth skimming down the length of her throat, the moist touch of his tongue against the pulse that beat at its base, of her own soft moan of encouragement as his mouth slid lower still.

Whether Bishop felt her stiffen or whether he'd never intended to draw the kiss out any further, Lila didn't know. He lifted his head, his eyes meeting hers for a long, still moment. She could read nothing in that look, no reflection of the memories that had crashed over her, no regret over the marriage they'd just entered into—not even resignation. His eyes were still, blue pools, revealing nothing.

"Lila." Susan's light voice was a welcome interruption. Relieved to have an excuse to turn away from her new husband, Lila stepped into her sister-in-law's embrace. "I wish you every happiness, my dear," Susan said as she hugged Lila.

"Thank you." If only all it took was good wishes, Lila thought, blinking against the sting of tears.

Stepping away from Susan, she turned to look at Douglas, her expression uncertain. Between the debacle at the church and the start of the ceremony here in the parlor, she'd made sure that there was no opportunity for a private talk with her brother. It had been enough to see the hurt in his eyes when he'd found out about her and Bishop; she couldn't bear to hear how he felt. Now she wanted desperately to see forgiveness in his eyes.

He looked at her. For a moment, she thought his expression softened and dared to hope that he might be able to forgive her for what she'd done. But it was too soon for that.

"I hope you'll be very happy," he offered stiffly. He gave her a perfunctory hug, stepping back so quickly that she wondered if he couldn't bear to touch her.

She turned away blindly and her gaze collided with Bishop's. Blinking against tears, she lifted her chin, daring him to notice her distress. His expression didn't change but he reached out, sliding one arm around her shoulders and drawing her against his side. She told herself that the only reason she didn't pull away was because she didn't want to make a scene, but that didn't explain why her body curved into his, why she leaned into his hard strength.

"Thank you," he said, speaking to Douglas and Susan as if they'd included him in their good wishes.

The muscles in Douglas's jaw knotted visibly, his expression tight and hard. Susan's eyes skittered uneasily from her husband to the newlyweds and then settled, almost gratefully, on the minister, who'd been watching the small scene with the expression of a hungry dog presented with a particularly juicy bone.

"Thank you so much, Reverend," she said. Her smile held no sign of the strain she must be feeling, and it struck Lila, not for the first time, that Susan was remarkably well suited to being the wife of a man with political aspirations.

"I'm always pleased to be able to be of service to this family," Reverend Carpenter said.

*Particularly when he was lucky enough to find himself in the midst of the juiciest scandal to hit Beaton since the blacksmith's wife ran off with a drummer who'd come through town selling musical instruments two years ago,* Lila thought cynically.

"You're welcome to stay for supper, if you'd like," Susan said, making the obligatory gesture.

"I wouldn't wish to intrude," he demurred, his eyes gleaming at the thought of a fine meal to go with the additional information he was sure to gather.

The thought of spending yet more time under the reverend's avid gaze made Lila want to weep. Unconsciously she leaned more heavily into Bishop's supporting hold, feeling as if she'd reached the end of her rope.

"It wouldn't be an intrusion," Susan said in a tone that struggled to conceal her dismay.

"Well, then . . ." The minister all but rubbed his hands together in anticipation.

Bishop spoke up unexpectedly. "It's been a long day and I think my wife is too tired to entertain guests."

Douglas, Susan, and Reverend Carpenter all gaped at him with varying degrees of surprise. It was hard to say what had surprised them most—the blatant arrogance of him rescinding Susan's invitation or hearing him refer to Lila as his wife. He returned their looks calmly. Lila knew she should be offended by his presumption, but all she felt was gratitude.

The minister's face crumpled like a child denied a favorite piece of candy. "But—"

"Perhaps you're right," Susan said, looking torn between annoyance at Bishop's presumption and relief at the thought of getting rid of the minister. "It really *has* been a very long day, hasn't it?"

Lila nodded and forced herself to smile at the reverend. "Perhaps another time, Reverend," she murmured, knowing it would never happen. No doubt Bishop planned to return West as soon as possible. It would take her a few days to pack, but then she'd be leaving her childhood home forever. She'd gladly have dined with the nosy minister if it meant that she didn't have to leave. But since it wouldn't change anything, it was a relief to see him go.

An hour later, Lila was starting to wonder if it might have been a good idea for Reverend Carpenter to have stayed. Surely nothing could be worse than the taut atmosphere that reigned at dinner. Tense silence was the rule, broken by brief intervals of stiff conversation, initiated by Susan and participated in, with varying degrees of cooperation, by the other diners. Years of social training forced Lila to try to support the façade of normalcy her sister-in-law was attempting to maintain. But no amount of social grace could gloss over the incredible awkwardness of the situation.

Though the staff served with their usual faultless elegance, Lila was acutely aware of the curious glances being cast at her and Bishop. She knew the servants, like everyone else in Beaton, were full of speculation about the abrupt change in the wedding plans. Arrangements of early spring flowers covered the sideboards and the center of the long polished table, remnants of the reception that had been planned to celebrate her wedding to Logan.

Staring at the fragile grace of an anemone, Lila tried to imagine how she'd feel if it were Logan sitting across the table from her now. She'd known Logan all her life, yet his image was blurred and out of focus. She closed her eyes, trying to picture him, but instead of golden blond hair and warm brown eyes, she kept seeing black hair, worn too long, a leaner, harder face, and eyes the pale blue of a winter sky and just as cold.

"Are you feeling all right, Lila?" Susan's concerned question broke her concentration. Lila opened her eyes and found herself looking directly into Bishop's cool gaze.

Bishop McKenzie. Her husband. Lila rubbed her thumb over the thick gold wedding ring he'd slipped on her finger. The plain band felt as heavy as iron shackles. In a sense it *was* a shackle—one that bound her to the man sitting across from her. It was the symbol of ties meant to last a lifetime.

"Please excuse me." Lila rose abruptly, her chair scraping across the polished floor in a way that would have made her mother wince. She left the room without waiting for a response, her skirts belling out behind her with the speed of her exit.

She left behind a silence thick enough to cut. Susan half rose from her chair as if to go after her, then glanced from her husband to Bishop and sank back down again.

Seeing her look and reading the worry in her eyes, Bishop almost smiled. She was obviously concerned about what might happen if he and Douglas were left alone. She was probably right to worry. He didn't doubt that there was nothing Douglas would like more than a chance to go for his throat. Not that he could blame him.

Bishop set his heavy linen napkin beside his barely touched plate. "I don't see much point in dragging this out. Unless one of you is dying for my company, I think I'll take a walk." When no one said anything, Bishop's mouth twisted in a wry half smile. He pushed his chair back and rose.

Susan spoke as he reached the door into the hallway. "Take a coat, Bishop. It's only April and the nights are cold."

Bishop turned to look at her, his smile gentling. Susan reminded him of his mother. She was a born caretaker, with a heart too soft and gentle for this world. "I'll do that."

"I hope the bastard freezes to death," Douglas snarled as they heard the front door close behind Bishop.

"Watch your language, Douglas." But there was no heat behind the reminder. Susan rose from the table. "You'd best get used to the idea that Bishop is Lila's husband now."

"I should have killed him." Douglas stood up, pushing his chair back with a barely controlled violence that nearly tipped it over. He threw his napkin down on the table. "I should have let Logan kill him in front of the whole blasted church."

"I understand your anger but he's a member of the family now, like it or not."

"I don't!"

"And you'd best learn to accept that," Susan finished, ignoring his interruption.

"He seduced my sister," Douglas reminded her angrily.

"Lila is a grown woman, and has a will that would be the envy of many men. If Bishop seduced her, it was not without her consent. Now, don't bite my head off," she added, raising one hand to forestall his furious response. "I'm not implying Lila is a woman of easy virtue, but even virtuous women sometimes make less than virtuous choices. Have you forgotten that we anticipated our own wedding night?"

Douglas stared at her, shocked by the blunt reminder. "That was different," he muttered. "We were planning to marry."

"So we were." Susan crossed the short distance between them and set one small hand on his sleeve, tilting her head back to look up into his eyes. "I'm not saying that what they did was right. But it can't be changed, and we—all of us—have to live with the consequences. Just don't forget that Lila is your sister. And Bishop is your friend."

*"Was,"* he corrected harshly.

"And now he's your brother by marriage. If you don't want to lose touch with your sister—not to mention your niece or nephew—you're going to have to accept that what's done is done."

"Bishop said the same thing this afternoon at the church."

"And he was quite right. Now I'm going to go see how Lila is." Susan rose on her toes to brush a kiss across his mouth. "Think about what I've said, darling."

She didn't wait for a reply but turned and left, leaving Douglas alone in the empty dining room.

Lila sat on the edge of a slipper chair upholstered in soft green silk. She'd fled the dining room in search of a place where she could forget the events of the day, at least for a little while. But it seemed she was not going to be allowed to forget, even for a moment. The first thing she'd seen when she entered her bedroom was a black portmanteau sitting at the foot of her bed. She'd stared at the unfamiliar case a moment before it struck her whose it was.

Bishop's. It was Bishop's case and the servants had put it in her room because he was now her husband and they assumed he'd be sharing her room. Her bed. The thought was so shocking that she'd all but staggered across the room to sink down on the edge of the graceful chair. She'd been sitting there ever since, bolt upright, her eyes glued to the case as if it contained a bomb set to explode if she looked away.

She hadn't given any thought to where Bishop would be spending the night. There hadn't been any time to think about it. When Logan had offered to marry her and claim her child as his own, he'd promised her that he'd make no demands. Bishop had made no such promises.

Despite the fire that burned on the hearth less than half a dozen feet away, Lila shivered. Surely Bishop didn't expect this to be a *real* wedding night. But she couldn't think of a single reason why he shouldn't. Not only were they married, but he had reason to know that she was no shrinking virgin. And he might also have reason to believe that she would not be completely averse to sharing his bed. She shivered again, remembering the abandoned response his touch had wrung from her three months ago. It frightened her to think that he might be able to draw that same response from her again.

The quiet knock on the door made her jump halfway out of her skin. She shot to her feet as if the smooth upholstery had suddenly caught fire. If it was Bishop . . .

"Lila? May I come in?" The sound of Susan's voice made Lila feel light-headed with relief. She didn't have to face her new husband. Yet. It was an effort to steady her voice enough to call permission for her sister-in-law to enter.

"I wanted to see if you were feeling all right," Susan said as she shut the door behind herself. Her eyes mirrored the concern in her voice.

"I'm fine," Lila told her. What was one more lie after having stood before a man of God, promising to love a man she neither knew nor liked?

"I was concerned when you left the table so abruptly. We all were."

"All?" Lila's dark brows rose. "Douglas can barely stand to look at me, and I suspect Bishop would be quite content to find I'd expired of some miraculously speedy illness."

"That's not true. Your brother needs a little time to get used to the situation. He'll come around. He loves you."

"Unlike my new husband."

A look of distress flitted across Susan's pretty features. "I know things are starting out . . . awkwardly. But, given time, I know the two of you will come to care for each other."

"Is that why you wrote to tell him about the baby? Because you thought we'd come to care for each other?" Lila asked, remembering what Bishop had told her about Susan contacting him.

Susan flushed but she met Lila's eyes without flinching. "I did what I thought was right."

"Did it occur to you that I already had things arranged quite satisfactorily? That I didn't need you to decide what was right?"

"Bishop had a right to know about his child," Susan said calmly.

"How did you know it was Bishop's child?" Lila demanded. "How did you know there was a child at all, for that matter?"

"I have eight younger brothers and sisters. I've seen the symptoms often enough to recognize them. As to how I knew it was Bishop's, I saw what was happening between the two of you three months ago. I saw you leave the ballroom not long after he did and when he left so abruptly the next morning, I had my suspicions."

"Suspicions?" Lila questioned incredulously. "You wrote to tell Bishop I was carrying his child just because you thought something *might* have happened between us? What if you'd been wrong?"

"I had more than suspicions." Susan's eyes shifted away, focusing on a delicate Meissan figure that stood on the mantelpiece. "After Bishop left that morning, I went to his room and found your maid stripping the sheets from his bed."

"Oh." It was Lila's turn to flush. She'd sent her maid to get the sheets so that she could wash them herself or burn them, if necessary—whatever had to be done to conceal the evidence of her lost virginity.

"Mary wouldn't say anything but it wasn't hard to guess what had happened. When I realized that you were with child, it seemed clear that Bishop was responsible."

"Did it occur to you to speak to me before taking it upon yourself to write to him?" Lila asked, anger flaring anew.

"I was going to but then you and Logan announced that you were getting married. Perhaps I should still have said something but you were so determined to rush the wedding through and I wasn't even sure I could reach Bishop."

"The problem was solved. I wasn't going to bring shame on the family by bearing a child out of wedlock. There wouldn't have been any scandal. I can't believe you prefer *this*!" Lila swept out one arm in a gesture that encompassed the whole situation, including the debacle at the church and the rumors that were surely racing through town with the speed of a wildfire, Reverend Carpenter's breath fanning the flames. "If you'd left well enough alone, no one would have known any of this. I had everything arranged. No one would have been hurt."

"What about Logan?" Susan asked quietly.

"I didn't lie to him."

"Didn't you?" Susan raised one delicately arched brow in question. The ugly word "rape" hung, unspoken, in the air between them. Lila flushed, feeling like a child caught out in a lie. Susan had the same gentle implacability that had characterized Lila's mother. She had the ability to make Lila feel like little more than a child. It was easy to forget that there was only four years difference in their ages.

"I didn't lie about the baby," Lila corrected herself sullenly. "Logan is a doctor. I *couldn't* very well lie to him, even if I wanted to. Which I didn't. Marriage was his idea, not mine."

"I'm sure it was. Logan cares for you." Susan frowned. "I am a little puzzled as to why you felt you could tell him about your . . . situation and yet you couldn't tell your brother and me the truth. Surely you know Douglas would never have turned his back on you."

"I know that." Lila smoothed her fingers over a crease in her dove-gray skirt. "I didn't intend to tell Logan about . . . about my situation." *Ridiculous that even now, she couldn't bring herself to say the words out loud!* "I didn't intend to tell anyone."

Susan's pale brows rose. "You surely didn't think you could keep something like that a secret for very long. There *are* signs when a woman is—"

"I'm not completely without sense, despite recent evidence to the contrary." Lila's tone was more weary than angry. "I had decided to go away. Someplace where no one knew me. I thought I could say I was a widow, perhaps find a job teaching. You needn't look at me as if doubting my sanity," she said in answer to the look in Susan's eyes. "I know it was a ridiculous idea. But it was the only thing I could think of. Obviously, I couldn't stay here in Beaton. I was trying to avoid a scandal." Her mouth twisted with bitter humor.

"Did you go to Logan for help with this idea of moving away? Is that how he found out?"

"Logan came by to see Douglas shortly after I'd realized that I was . . . that I had to do something. The two of you were in Philadelphia that week, and I'd had nothing to do but think of the situation in which I'd found myself. Poor Logan made the mistake of asking if I was feeling all right, and I burst into tears."

She'd never forget Logan's shocked expression. But he rallied immediately, drawing her into his arms and holding her as she cried. He didn't speak until the initial flood of tears had started to subside.

"Tell me what's wrong," he said quietly. And Lila, who had already determined that she could never, ever tell anyone what was wrong, found the truth spilling out. Not the whole truth, certainly. She'd refused to tell him who had fathered her child. And when he'd assumed she'd been forced, she'd been too weak to correct him. It hadn't seemed to matter at the time.

It had been such a relief to be able to talk to someone about it. Maybe it was the fact that Logan was a doctor that made it possible for her to tell him. Or maybe it was that, while he was nearly a brother to her, he wasn't actually her brother. Whatever the reason, she'd outlined her half-formed plans for moving away and seeking employment.

*"Don't be ridiculous,"* he'd snapped and Lila's eyes welled.

*"But I have to do something. The scandal...I can't...I have to leave."*

*"There's not going to be any scandal."* Logan caught her restless hands in his. *"And you don't have to go away, at least not for very long. You're going to marry me."*

Lila felt her eyes sting at the memory of his unselfishness. She'd argued with him. She couldn't let him sacrifice his life. There had to be another way. But there hadn't been another way, short of throwing herself in the river, and she was not quite ready for that. Logan's calm determination had overwhelmed every one of her protests. And maybe she hadn't protested quite as much as she might have, Lila admitted now. She'd wanted so desperately to be convinced that this was the right thing to do.

"I care for Logan," she told Susan now. "That's more than some marriages start out with. If you hadn't interfered, we would have been happy." She was uneasily aware that her words sounded more defiant than confident.

"Perhaps." Susan moved over to the fireplace. After lifting a log from beside the hearth, she set it on the fire, which had begun to burn down. Then, dusting her hands together, she turned to look at Lila, her expression pensive. "Did you give any thought to the idea that, when you married Logan, you were taking away his chance to find a woman who really loves him?"

Susan's tone was gently questioning, offering no reproach, but Lila found herself looking away. She had given a great deal of thought to what Logan might be giving up by marrying her. But she hadn't been able to see any other way out of her dilemma.

"If you were so concerned about Logan's future happiness, why didn't you simply tell Douglas the truth right away?" Lila asked, aware that her tone verged on sullen.

"I didn't know if my letter would reach Bishop in time."

"You mean, you didn't know if he'd care that I was having his child."

"I knew he'd care. I knew he'd get here if he could. If I couldn't reach him, marrying Logan was certainly better than the alternative."

"You have a great deal more faith in Bishop than I do," Lila said.

"I think I know him a good deal better." Susan moved away from the fireplace. Her skirts rustled around her as she sat down on the edge of the bed. She tilted her head, her mouth quirking in a half smile. "That may sound odd, considering... well, considering the situation, but I think it's the truth."

Lila didn't doubt that it was. No one could know Bishop *less* well than she did.

"Why don't you sit down, dear," Susan said, patting the bed beside her.

"I'm quite comfortable standing, thank you."

Susan sighed but didn't repeat the invitation. "Last summer, when your brother and I met, it was on a stagecoach traveling through Arizona Territory. It's hardly a pleasant way to travel to begin with but, to make matters worse, our stagecoach was set upon by thieves. They killed the driver outright and would probably have killed Douglas and me also, if it hadn't been for Bishop McKenzie. He—"

"I know what he did," Lila interrupted. "He rode

out of the desert like some knight on a white charger and dispatched the villains in a hail of bullets.''

That story had been a big part of what had attracted her to Bishop in the first place. When he'd arrived for the wedding, she'd been prepared to offer him her gratitude for having saved Douglas's life. But instead of the half-tamed ruffian she'd been expecting, she'd found herself being introduced to a man who made her heart beat faster with nothing more than a look. The cool disinterest in his eyes had been a challenge. She was not accustomed to having a man—any man—look at her as if he barely saw her. She'd set out to make him notice her. And she'd certainly succeeded, she thought with bitter humor.

"I'm aware of the debt of gratitude this family owes him for saving your lives," Lila said flatly. Linking her hands together in front of her to conceal their trembling, she met Susan's eyes. "Douglas told me the whole story when he returned home."

"Did he?" Susan looked thoughtful. "Did he tell you that, once the villains were driven off, the three of us were left alone in the middle of the desert with only Bishop's horse between us? If it hadn't been for Bishop's knowledge of the desert, the land would have accomplished what the thieves had failed to do. It took us nearly a week to walk to the nearest town."

"That's when you and Douglas fell in love," Lila finished impatiently, beyond caring that she was behaving like an ill-mannered brat. She wasn't in the mood to hear a rehash of old history. The china clock on the mantel seemed to be ticking louder than it ever had, reminding her that time was passing. At any moment, Bishop might knock on her door—if he bothered to knock at all.

"That's when Douglas and I fell in love," Susan confirmed, ignoring Lila's rudeness. "But I also had a chance to get to know your husband."

Lila flinched at the word. Despite the wedding band that weighted her finger out of all proportion to its size, she couldn't even begin to think of Bishop as her husband.

"I don't mean to be rude." Another lie. She seemed to be telling a lot of them today, Lila thought bitterly. "But I'm really not in the mood to hear what a wonderful man I've married and how terribly happy we're going to be. I'd really like to be alone, if you don't mind."

Lila half expected Susan to depart on a wave of indignation, and she would almost have welcomed it. She was not in the mood for sympathy or reason. But if Susan was annoyed by her blatant rudeness, she didn't let it show—another way in which her sister-in-law reminded her of her mother. Margaret Adams had considered strong emotional displays the essence of bad manners. *A lady is always restrained. It's up to us to set an example for the stronger sex. No matter how upset you are, you must show a calm façade to the world.* Lila had spent her whole life trying—and failing—to live up to her mother's ideal of ladylike behavior, an ideal that seemed to come effortlessly to Susan.

She rose, shaking out the china-blue silk skirt of her dress. Her expression reflected nothing but compassion for the younger woman. "I know the circumstances are less than ideal, but I think you and Bishop could have a good marriage. You must have been attracted to one another. He's a good man, Lila. He may seem hard and unapproachable but there's a gentleness inside him. And a strength you can lean on, if you'll let yourself."

The last thing Lila needed or wanted was a recitation of Bishop McKenzie's wonderful qualities. Not when all she could think of was that he might be climbing the stairs at this very moment, expecting to spend the night with his bride.

"If you were so taken with him, I'm surprised you didn't marry him instead of Douglas," she snapped, making no effort to conceal her anger.

There was a brief, uncomfortable silence and then Susan sighed. "I'll leave you alone. Just think about what I've said."

Lila stayed where she was, staring unseeingly at the delicate china clock. The door closed quietly behind Susan and Lila's shoulders slumped. She'd behaved badly. She knew it, knew also that she owed her sister-in-law an apology. No matter how upset she was about Susan writing to Bishop, she could have handled it better. *There's never an excuse for bad manners.* How many times had she heard her mother say that? Apparently it hadn't been enough.

She half turned toward the door, thinking to go after Susan, but she'd taken no more than a step when her glance fell on the bed. She stopped, the need for apologies forgotten.

Bishop. Just what did he have in mind for tonight?

Bishop inhaled one last lungful of smoke before dropping the cigarette on the ground and grinding it out with the toe of his boot. The night air was chilly and he was grateful for the warmth of the coat Susan had suggested he take. Remembering the scene in the dining room, he smiled. Trust Susan to worry about whether or not he was warm enough, no matter what the circumstances. She was a born mother hen. Even in the midst of the desert, with their odds of survival somewhere on a par with that of a snowball in hell, she'd fussed over him and Douglas.

At the thought of Douglas, Bishop's smile faded. In his entire life, he'd known only a handful of men he was willing to call friend. Douglas Adams had been one of them. If he'd given some thought to that friendship three months ago, things might have turned out considerably different. But Douglas had been the last thing on his mind that night.

Turning back the way he'd come, Bishop saw the big house laid out at the bottom of the hill. He pushed his hands into the pockets of his trousers, his eyes narrowing in memory. The house had blazed with light that evening. It had been full of light and laughter. Everyone had been delighted to celebrate Douglas and Susan's wedding. He'd been pleased for them too but, as he'd watched them swirl across the dance floor, their faces alight with happiness, he'd been aware of a soul-deep loneliness. And then Lila had been standing in front of him, her eyes sparkling with challenge, all but daring him to ask her to dance.

He'd accepted the challenge, drawing her into his arms and waltzing her onto the ballroom floor. And, for a little while, the loneliness was gone, driven away by the flirtatious mischief in her smile. From the moment of his arrival a few days before the wedding, she'd made no secret of finding him intriguing. Under other circumstances, Bishop might have been inclined to give in to temptation and take her up on the invitation in her eyes. But beneath the invitation, there was an innocence he couldn't ignore, even if she hadn't been Douglas's sister.

He'd left the ball soon after that dance, retreating to his room with a bottle of whiskey he had every intention of draining. He'd worked his way just far enough down the bottle to be feeling no pain when Lila knocked on the door. She'd said that she wanted to make sure everything was in order. With the servants so busy with preparations for the reception, she was afraid they might have missed some item necessary to his comfort. But there had been something in her eyes that said that it wasn't concern for his comfort that had brought her to his room.

He'd reached for her and she'd come into his arms as if coming home. In some distant part of his mind, he'd known that he should stop. They'd both had too much to drink. He had about as much business making love to Lila Adams as he did jumping off a cliff and expecting to fly. But the taste of her had drowned out the small voice of reason. For a little while, he hadn't felt so alone.

Bishop shook his head and started back to the house. He was paying a hell of a price for a few hours of not being alone. They both were.

He'd stayed outside longer than he'd realized, and, by the time he got back to the house, most of the lights were out. He'd assumed that everyone had gone to bed but, as he stepped into the foyer, the butler rose from a chair that sat in one corner.

"Were you waiting up for me, Thomas?" Bishop asked, feeling a twinge of guilt. "You shouldn't have. I can find my own way around."

"I'm sure you can, sir." An elderly black man with

the erect carriage of a general and an arrogance to
match, Thomas had been with the Adamses all his
life, taking over the position of butler from his father.
On Bishop's last visit, Thomas had treated him with
a fatherly warmth, reflecting his gratitude for Bishop's
saving Douglas's life. Now the chilly disapproval in
Thomas's voice was palpable.

"Allow me to take your coat," he said, coming forward to take the garment as Bishop shrugged out of
it.

"Thank you. Do you know where my bag ended
up?"

"Certainly, Mr. McKenzie. I had it put in Miss Lila's room."

"Lila's room?" Bishop's head jerked around in
shock, his eyes meeting Thomas's.

"Mrs. McKenzie, I suppose I should have said."
Thomas draped Bishop's coat over his arm.

"Does she know it's there?" Bishop asked, his
mind boggling as he tried to imagine Lila's reaction
to finding his things in her bedroom.

"I wouldn't know but it seems likely that she saw
it when she went up to her room."

"I guess she would have," Bishop murmured, looking up the broad staircase.

"I'll say good night then, Mr. McKenzie. Unless
you need me to show you to Mrs. McKenzie's room."

Bishop winced at the subtle sarcasm that infused
the last sentence. Obviously, the servants had a pretty
good idea of why Lila had started out to marry one
man and ended up married to another.

"I'm sure I can find it," he told the butler.

"Then I'll say good night, sir."

"Good night."

Bishop waited until Thomas had disappeared toward the back of the house before he started up the stairs. *Mrs. McKenzie.* It wasn't going to be easy to get used to hearing Lila referred to that way. It had been a long time since he'd heard that name used. Which brought up another problem, he thought uneasily. His unexpected marriage could solve almost as many problems as it was causing, although it was doubtful that Lila would see it that way. He'd have to talk to her tomorrow before he left. There were things she needed to be told.

Bishop reached the top of the stairs and turned down the hall that led to west wing of the house. He was not nearly as familiar with Lila's room as Thomas had assumed but, as it happened, he didn't have to rely on his memory to find it. His steps slowed when he saw the familiar black bag sitting in the hallway.

He stood in the hallway a moment, staring down at his bag and feeling his temper edge upward. Knowing it was a waste of time, he reached out to try the doorknob. Locked. Bishop drew a deep breath and considered his options.

He was tired. He'd been traveling for days. He'd been punched, lost a good friend, and married a girl he barely knew and wasn't at all sure he even liked. He hadn't had a whole lot of time to contemplate what the future might be like, but he'd always thought that it was a good rule of thumb to start as you meant to go on. And one thing he knew for sure was that he did not intend to let his new wife have everything her way. He had the distinct feeling that she'd already had more of that than was good for her.

He knew, as surely as if he could see through solid wood, that Lila was wide awake and staring at the door, wondering what he was going to do. Reminding himself that it had been a difficult day for her as well, Bishop grabbed a firm hold of his temper and tapped on the door.

"Open the door, Lila," he said in as level a tone as he could manage.

There was a lengthy pause and he wondered if she was going to pretend to be asleep, but then she spoke, her voice muffled but audible.

"Go away."

Without giving it a second's thought, Bishop smashed the heel of his boot against the door. The lock yielded and the door flew open, slamming back against the wall with an echoing crash. He stepped into the doorway.

Lila was sitting up in bed, her green eyes huge and startled in her pale face. Before either of them could speak, a door down the hall opened and Douglas and Susan ran out of their room.

"What the devil do you think you're doing?" Douglas demanded.

Ignoring him, Bishop strode to the foot of the bed, his eyes on Lila's face. She watched him with the expression of a rabbit facing a diamondback, her fingers wrapped around the covers, her knuckles white with the force of her grip.

He let the silence build. Lila could feel her heart pounding in her chest. When she'd put his bag outside the door, she hadn't given much thought to his reaction; she simply hadn't been able to bear having it in her room a moment longer. The last thing she'd expected was that he'd kick in her door and stride into her room as if he had every right to be there. The frightening thing was that he did have the right.

He loomed at the foot of the bed, huge and dark and angry. She was suddenly, frighteningly, aware that, a few hours ago, she'd given herself, body and soul, into his keeping. If he chose to beat her, the law would say he had the right. Not that she thought he'd beat her. Not really.

He leaned toward her and she flinched back from the blazing heat in his eyes. How could she ever have thought they were cold?

"Don't ever lock a door against me again," he said.

The soft order sent a shiver up Lila's spine. She swallowed, trying to think of something to say, something that would show him that he couldn't intimidate her. But Bishop didn't wait for her response. Turning, he strode back out into the hallway, nodding to Douglas and Susan as he scooped his bag off the floor. Lila heard his footsteps going down the stairs and then silence.

# Chapter 4

It took every ounce of courage she possessed for Lila to come downstairs for breakfast the morning after her wedding. She had lain awake into the early hours of the morning, her mind replaying the events of the day, particularly the final scene with Bishop. She kept thinking of things she could have said or done to show him what she thought of his barbaric behavior, to make it clear that he couldn't intimidate her. Except he had intimidated her—quite thoroughly. Not even in her imagination could she conjure up a picture of herself standing up to the man who'd loomed so menacingly over her bed.

Feeling an uneasy mixture of bravado and trepidation, she entered the dining room, prepared to greet her new husband with a show of calm. But Bishop was not there, and Lila refused to acknowledge that there might be a trace of disappointment mixed in with her relief. Douglas and Susan were seated at one end of the table. They looked up as she entered, their self-conscious expressions giving Lila a pretty clear idea of what they'd been discussing. Douglas, and Susan, and everyone else in Beaton, she thought with a twinge of wry humor.

"Good morning." She was pleased to hear how normal she sounded.

"How are you this morning?" Susan asked, her expression anxious.

"I'm fine." Lila lifted her brows in faint surprise, as if she couldn't imagine why Susan was asking. Thomas slid her chair out for her and she sat down at the table, casting him a quick smile. "Are there any muffins left or did Douglas hog them all, as usual?"

"I think Cook held back one or two just for you, Miss Lila." Thomas's smile was affectionate.

"See if you can sneak them in past my brother, please, Thomas." They'd had variations on the same conversation many times over the years.

"He doesn't have to sneak them past me," Douglas protested automatically. "You'd think I stole the food right off your plate, the way you talk."

"Well, I did notice you eyeing my bacon this morning, dear," Susan said.

The light conversation was strained. Too much remained unspoken for it to be otherwise, but Lila was grateful for its normalcy. For a little while, it almost seemed possible that she'd imagined everything that had happened—that yesterday had never happened.

But the fragile illusion was destroyed a moment later when Bishop walked into the room. Lila didn't need to see the sudden stiffness in Douglas's expression to tell her that Bishop had arrived. Even with her back to the door, she knew he was there. She could feel him, as if something in the very air changed when he entered a room. There was a tense moment of silence, broken by Susan.

"Good morning, Bishop."

"Morning." Bishop nodded to Douglas before walking to the sideboard to pour himself a cup of coffee. He'd spent a damned uncomfortable night sleeping on a sofa in the library, and his mood was about as warm as the ache in his neck. At that, it was warmer than the atmosphere in the dining room.

He leaned one hip against the sideboard and studied the three people before him. Douglas was wearing a dark, tailored suit, sober as a judge and about as friendly. Susan, in a dress of her favorite soft blue, was casting worried looks from him to Lila, who seemed to be utterly fascinated by the floral pattern on her plate.

"Good morning, Lila." For a moment, he thought she was going to ignore him, but he should have known better. Hearing the soft challenge in his voice, her chin came up, her green eyes meeting his coolly.

"Bishop." She nodded her head as regally as a queen greeting a subject—a not terribly important subject, at that, Bishop thought.

He was torn between annoyance and admiration, a combination that was rapidly becoming familiar. He took a swallow of coffee, watching Lila above the rim of the cup. She was studying her plate again, her head tilted slightly downward, revealing the soft curls that fell against her nape. The sunlight that spilled in through the tall windows turned her hair to pure fire and highlighted the milky softness of her skin.

Bishop wondered idly if he would have found her easier to deal with if she hadn't been so damned beautiful. She was wearing another gray dress, this one a deep, dusty charcoal, trimmed with ivory lace at the neck and wrists. A row of buttons marched down the front of the gown with military precision. The effect was austere, aggressively restrained. The severity of the garment all but shouted at a man to keep his distance. Yet Bishop found himself wondering how long it would take to open that prim little row of buttons.

Not that he was likely to get a chance to find out. She'd made it pretty clear that she had no intention of letting him close enough to touch her buttons—or anything else. The thought did nothing to improve his mood.

"I'll be leaving this afternoon," he said, directing the comment at no one in particular.

Lila's head came up, her eyes startled. "I can't be ready that soon. I'll need at least a week to pack."

It was Bishop's turn to look surprised. "Pack for what?"

"To go . . . wherever we're going. Where *are* we going?"

Bishop stared at her a moment. "*I'm* going to Colorado. *You're* not going anywhere, at least not with me."

"Of course I am. I'm going with you. Where else would I go?"

"You'll stay here."

"Here?" Lila felt as if the wind had just been knocked from her. He expected her to stay here? After the scene in the church yesterday? Had she made him so angry that he felt the need to punish her so cruelly? "I'm going with you."

"No, you're not."

"Yes, I am. You're my husband." Funny, how easy that word was to say all of a sudden. "My place is with you."

"Your place?" Bishop's dark brows shot up in surprise at this sudden display of wifely devotion. Lila flushed but she wasn't going to give in. She couldn't.

"I won't stay here," she said flatly.

"Maybe he's right," Douglas said, though it clearly cost him to agree with anything Bishop said. "Maybe you should stay here. You don't know what it's like in the West, Lila. It's no place for a lady, particularly one in your delicate condition." He cleared his throat, uncomfortable at having to refer to her pregnancy.

"I'm sure women don't stop having babies just because they're living west of the Mississippi." Lila struggled to sound calm and reasonable, not an easy thing when what she wanted to do was stamp her feet and shriek that she wasn't going to stay and nothing they said could make her. "I'm sure there are doctors in the West."

"Not many," Bishop said. "And none to speak of in Paris."

"Paris? As in Paris, France?"

"Spelled the same but that's about the only resemblance. The miner who laid out the town was French and he had big plans for the place. It's just a mining town. The closest thing we've got to a doctor is Zeke Doolin, who's the barber. He can do a pretty fair job of pulling a tooth or setting a broken bone, but I don't know about delivering a baby."

"There must be women in this town," Lila said, trying not to show how much his words frightened her.

"There's women."

"And they must have babies."

"A few," he admitted reluctantly. "But—"

"I'm going with you. There's no sense in arguing about it because I've made up my mind." She tilted her chin and looked at him, hoping she looked calmly determined rather than just mulish.

Bishop met her look, his expression unreadable. He was wearing the same clothes he'd worn to the church the day before—a plain white shirt and black trousers tucked into a pair of knee-high black boots that had clearly seen plenty of wear. The men Lila had known all her life would have looked awkward and under-dressed in such casual attire. But Bishop looked right at home. All he needed was spurs and a gun on his hip and he could have stepped right off the pages of a dime novel.

"I think Bishop is right," Douglas said. "Clearly you'll be better off staying here where you can receive the proper care."

"I'm not staying here." Though Lila spoke to her brother, she looked at Bishop. Much as it galled her to admit it, the final decision lay with him. If he refused to take her with him, there wouldn't be much she could do about it. But she wouldn't beg. "If it's a matter of money, I can purchase my own ticket."

She was perversely pleased to see the quick flare of anger in Bishop's eyes. "*If* you were going with me, I would buy your ticket. But you're not going with me."

"I think Lila is right." Susan spoke for the first time. "I think she should go."

"You can't mean that!" Douglas gave his wife a look of disbelief. "You've been out there. You remember what it was like. You can't seriously think that a woman in Lila's delicate condition belongs there."

"I watched my mother carry eight children to term and I can assure you that a woman in Lila's condition isn't nearly as delicate as men like to believe. I'm sure she'd be just fine."

"I don't want her out there with no one but a . . . barber to take care of her."

"I understand your concern but you're not looking at the whole picture, Douglas," Susan said calmly. "After the scene in the church yesterday, gossip will be running wild, and we both know that Reverend Carpenter is not noted for his discretion. Think about what it will be like for her if she stays here."

Bishop went still, his cup frozen halfway to his mouth as he pictured exactly what Lila's life would be like if she stayed here. He didn't know Beaton, Pennsylvania, but he knew small towns—east or west, they all had some things in common. He finished lifting the cup and took a drink, swallowing a curse along with the coffee. He'd had plenty of time last night to figure out exactly how things would work, and taking his bride to Colorado with him hadn't been part of the plan.

"The gossip will die down after a while," Douglas said, looking less certain than he sounded. "The primary concern must be Lila's safety. The West is no place for a lady, let alone one who's in the family way."

"I'm not staying here," Lila repeated, looking directly at Bishop.

It was crazy to take her. She had no idea what she was asking. But she did know what life would be like if she stayed here. And so, unfortunately, did he.

Bishop's mouth thinned with irritation. "You've got until tomorrow to pack whatever you want to take."

Lila felt relief well up inside her. Whatever awaited her in the vast and unknown West, it couldn't be worse than what she knew she'd endure here. For a moment, she felt almost warm toward her new husband. But then the full import of his words sank in.

"Tomorrow? I can't be ready by then. I'll need at least a week."

"Tomorrow." Bishop tilted his head back and emptied his cup.

"Four days," she bargained. "I can have the rest of my things shipped later, but I can't possibly be ready in less than four days." That was fair, she thought, reaching for one of the muffins Thomas had just carried in. She'd meet him halfway. He couldn't possibly expect more.

"Tomorrow. If you aren't on the train with me, you'll have to find your own way to Colorado." Bishop set his cup down on the table, nodded to

Douglas and Susan, and strode out of the dining room before Lila could say anything more.

"He can't be serious," she said when she'd regained the breath that shock had knocked from her.

"He looked very serious to me," Susan said mildly.

"He can't just leave without me." Lila spread butter on a muffin, wielding the knife with such force that the delicate little roll broke apart in her fingers. She dropped it onto her plate but her fingers remained clenched around the knife. The glitter in her eyes suggested that it was a good thing Bishop was no longer in the room. "If he thinks to frighten me into rushing through my packing, he can think again. He can wait until I'm ready to leave."

"You don't have to leave at all," Douglas said. "I think you should stay here."

Susan's eyes locked with Lila's across the polished table. A moment of silent communication passed between them.

"We can pack the basic necessities and ship everything else," Susan said as she pushed back her chair. Lila followed suit and the two women hurried from the room, leaving Douglas sitting alone with the remnants of the half-eaten meal.

The remainder of the day passed in a blur of sorting and packing. Trunks were dragged down from the attic, dusted off, and filled in record time. By the time Lila fell into bed, she was too tired to wonder where Bishop might be spending the second night of their marriage.

The next morning, she was standing in the turmoil of what had been her bedroom, giving the maids some last-minute instructions on the items to be packed and shipped later when Thomas knocked.

"You have a visitor, Miss Lila," he said when she answered the door.

Lila gave a harassed look over her shoulder at the clock on the mantel. In less than an hour, she was supposed to be ready to go to the train station. She didn't doubt that, if she wasn't ready, Bishop would make good on his threat to leave without her.

"I'm very busy, Thomas. Who is it?"

He lowered his voice. "It's Mr. Sinclair, miss."

"Logan?" Her head jerked around and she stared at him in surprise. "Logan is downstairs?"

"He's in the rose parlor, miss."

"Thank you, Thomas." She brushed past him, the packing momentarily forgotten. She hadn't expected to see Logan again. Even if there had been more time, she'd assumed that he wouldn't *want* to see her, after what she'd done. Picking up her skirts in a way that would have horrified her mother, she flew down the stairs. Slipping into the rose parlor, she turned and slid the pocket doors shut behind her. She didn't want anyone to interrupt them.

Logan had been standing in front of one of the windows, looking out at the rose gardens, but he turned as she entered the room. They looked at each other across the width of the room. But the real distance between them were the events that had happened in the last forty-eight hours.

Lila clasped her hands together in front of her. She longed to go to him and throw herself into his arms. Aside from Douglas, he was the person who meant most to her. There had never been a time when Logan wasn't a part of her life—Douglas's best friend,

Billy's older brother, her own dear friend. Looking at him now, she was struck by how differently things had turned out from the way she'd always imagined they'd be.

"I wasn't sure you'd see me," Logan said stiffly.

"I didn't think you'd *want* to see me ever again. Not that I blamed you. I used you abominably. I was going to write and tell you how sorry I was."

"Yes, well..." Logan looked away. "It was something of a shock to find you'd lied to me."

"I'm so sorry." Unable to bear the distance between them anymore, Lila walked to him. Reaching out, she caught one of his hands between hers, looking up at him pleadingly. "I never meant to hurt you, Logan. And I didn't mean to lie to you, either. But when you assumed I'd been ... forced, it was so easy to let you believe it."

"You could have told me the truth, Lila. I would still have married you."

"I know." She blinked back tears. Her fingers tightened around his hand. "I've always been able to count on you. I was just so ashamed. I don't have any right to ask it, but can you forgive me?"

Logan looked down at her. In his eyes, she saw the years of memories they shared. He'd seen her grow from a freckle-faced child to a woman. It had been Logan who'd told her about his brother's death; Logan who'd held her, urging her to cry out the pain of a hurt that went too deep for tears. He'd always been there for her—more than a friend, not quite a brother—one of the constants in her life. Other than Douglas, there was no one on earth she wanted less to hurt. And no one she had hurt more.

His hand was not quite steady as he touched his

fingertips to her cheek. His dark eyes were serious and there was a rueful twist to his smile. "I never could stay mad at you, brat."

Lila felt as if a great weight had been lifted from her soul. She smiled at him through tears of joy before stepping into his arms. With her cheek pressed against the soft wool of his jacket, the world seemed to settle in place again. "Oh, Logan, you're my best friend in the world."

She felt Logan stiffen and wondered if he'd changed his mind about forgiving her. But when she looked up at him, he was looking over her head, his expression so still and hard that she knew exactly what she'd see when she spun around.

Bishop stood just inside the door, watching them. Lila could see the scene as if through his eyes—she and Logan alone in the parlor, the doors shut to insure privacy and her in the other man's arms. A damning picture, to say the least. Remembering his cool comment about making her a widow if he'd arrived too late to stop the wedding, Lila felt her heart thump with sudden fear. Though he wore no gun, it didn't seem to lessen the danger Bishop projected.

"It's not the way it looks," she said quickly. She moved toward him, careful to keep herself between the two men.

Bishop let the silence stretch a moment longer, his gaze shifting from her to Logan and back again.

"It looks like you're saying good-bye to an old friend," he said calmly. He reached out and caught her hand, drawing her to his side. His arm settled around her waist. His touch was light but there was no mistaking the possessiveness of it. He nodded to Logan. "Sinclair."

"McKenzie."

If Bishop heard the dislike in Logan's tone, he didn't acknowledge it. "It's almost time to leave for the station," he said, looking down at Lila. "You'd better finish your good-byes."

He released her, nodded again to Logan, and turned and left the room, leaving Lila to stare after him in shocked disbelief. Clearly she had a great deal to learn about the man she'd married.

As the train pulled away from the station, Lila strained for one last glimpse of her brother's tall figure. Saying good-bye to Douglas had been one of the most difficult things she'd ever had to do. The strain that lay between them hadn't made it any easier. He'd hugged her and wished her a safe journey but, beneath the love and concern, she'd seen the pain she'd caused him, not only with her actions but with her lies. It was going to take time to completely heal the rift between them.

A curve in the track put the station—and Douglas—out of sight. Lowering her head to conceal the sudden moisture in her eyes, Lila tugged at the reticule in her lap but the strings were twisted together and resisted her efforts to open the small bag. She fumbled with them, blinded by tears. A large hand came into her line of vision. She blinked and stared at the snowy white handkerchief being offered.

Bishop. She'd been so wrapped up in her grief at saying good-bye to her brother that she'd almost managed to forget that she wasn't alone. Stupid, really, considering the fact that, if it hadn't been for the man seated across from her, she wouldn't have had to say good-bye at all.

"It won't bite," he said. The hint of dry amusement in his voice made Lila realize that she was staring at the handkerchief as if she didn't recognize its purpose. Flushing, she took it from him.

"Thank you," she muttered without lifting her head. She'd never in her life met a man who could annoy her so easily. It was her misfortune to find herself married to him. The thought was enough to bring on a new rush of tears. She buried her nose in his handkerchief and let the tears fall.

She slept. And as she slept, she dreamed.

The ballroom was a glittering rainbow of color and laughter. Planning and organizing her brother's wedding reception had been Lila's final task as Douglas's hostess. After tonight, entertainment at River Walk would be Susan's responsibility. As she watched the guests swirl around the dance floor, Lila was pardonably proud of the results of her efforts. Everything had turned out just right. The flower arrangements were exquisite, the food was delicious, and the champagne was marvelous. Lila knew the latter for a fact since she'd consumed two glasses of it herself. Everyone looked as if they were having a wonderful time.

Everyone but him.

Lila's eyes settled on the tall, broad-shouldered figure across the ballroom from her. Her smile faded slightly.

*He* didn't look as if he was having a wonderful time. Bishop McKenzie surveyed the ballroom with a detached air that could have signified boredom or simply a total lack of interest in the scene before him.

Her mouth tightened a little. It wasn't the first time she'd gotten the impression that Douglas's western friend was unimpressed with the civilized East. In fact, she was starting to wonder if anything ever impressed Mr. McKenzie at all.

Lila continued to study him, her eyes taking on a stormy tint as she considered Bishop's tall figure. She couldn't put her finger on just what it was about him that annoyed her so. He was polite certainly. She couldn't fault his manners.

And it wasn't as if he was hard to look at. Far from it. In fact, if she were to be completely honest, she'd be forced to admit that the man was much too handsome for her peace of mind. Hair the color of a raven's wing, strong, even features, and a thick black mustache that gave him a vaguely dangerous air and sent an annoying little shiver of awareness up her spine. His shoulders were broad, his legs long and lean—though no lady would ever notice a man's lower limbs. All in all, he was handsome enough to set a girl's heart to beating just a little faster.

Not that her own heart had done anything so foolish. And even if it had, Mr. McKenzie had made it quite clear that the feeling was *not* mutual. He hardly seemed to know she existed. Lila's fingers tightened on her fan, endangering the delicate ivory sticks. She didn't think she was particularly vain, but, having been courted and flattered from the time she was old enough to let her skirts down and put her hair up, she would have been very foolish indeed to remain unaware of her own attractiveness to the opposite sex. It was more than a little annoying to find Bishop McKenzie so completely indifferent to her charms.

His opinion did not matter a whit. Still, there was something about being so completely ignored that pricked her pride. Particularly tonight, when she knew, without vanity, that she was looking her best. Her dress was of sea-foam green silk that draped low across her bosom and left her shoulders nearly bare. The pointed bodice dipped into a skirt cut slim across the front before gathering in luxurious folds in the back. Silk roses in ivory and green decorated the sides of the gathers. Long gloves covered her arms to the elbow. Silk stockings and satin slippers dyed to match the dress completed the ensemble. It wasn't conceit to see that the gown complemented her pale skin and made the most of her thick auburn hair.

Not that *he'd* seemed to notice.

As the orchestra paused between songs, Lila made her way across the ballroom. Her progress was delayed by the necessity of pausing to speak to friends and acquaintances; to nod and smile and agree that Susan was a delightful young woman and Douglas was lucky to have found such a charming bride. She liked her new sister-in-law very much, but her thoughts were turned in another direction entirely.

"You're not dancing, Mr. McKenzie."

Bishop turned to look at her and Lila felt a little breathless from the impact of those cool blue eyes. She'd never met a man who could make her feel breathless with just a look.

"I assume you do have music out West," she continued when he didn't speak.

"We do. Though not many full orchestras." He nodded to the formally attired musicians who sat on a raised dais at the far end of the room. "Our dances tend to be a little more informal than this."

"But you do dance," she pursued.

"Sometimes."

"You're not dancing now."

"Should I be?"

"As your hostess, I'm concerned that all of the guests have a good time. You neither dance nor mingle, Mr. McKenzie. It gives a hostess some concern." She opened her fan and waved it idly in front of her, aware that the motion drew attention to her low décolletage.

"I certainly wouldn't want to give you any concern, Miss Adams," Bishop said solemnly. His eyes flickered downward and then back up to meet hers, and Lila felt her skin flush with sudden heat.

"I'm sure you wouldn't mean to do so," she said, aware of an almost imperceptible breathlessness in her voice.

"Tell me what I can do to ease your mind," he asked.

Lila pretended to consider, allowing her brows to draw together in a delicate frown. She was flirting with him. The very idea should have shocked her into more sober behavior. Behavior more befitting of Lila Adams of River Walk, grieving fiancée of Billy Sinclair. The thought of Billy brought with it a twinge of guilt, followed by a champagne-assisted flare of defiance. She had loved Billy but she hadn't died with him, despite what everyone else seemed to think. Billy had been known and loved by everyone in Beaton, and for three years she'd been treated with the circumspection usually reserved for widows of great war heroes. Though she would always mourn Billy's death, lately she'd begun to feel as if she were suffocating beneath the weight of his memory.

But Bishop McKenzie neither knew nor cared that she'd once been engaged to Billy Sinclair. When he looked at her, he saw only her, not her fiancé's ghost.

There was something dangerously appealing about that thought.

"Perhaps, if you asked a lady to dance, I might be reassured that you're enjoying our hospitality," she said finally.

One corner of Bishop's mouth quirked upward but his tone remained solemn. "What if she were to refuse? Think how humiliated I'd be."

"I doubt a lady would refuse if you asked politely, Mr. McKenzie." She peeked up at him from under her lashes, feeling like a girl of seventeen again. It had been so long since she'd enjoyed a gentle flirtation with a man. Behind her, she heard the scratchy sound of violins being tuned and knew the orchestra was about to start the next tune. Bishop glanced over her shoulder at the dance floor, his expression considering. Lila knew, as clearly as if he'd spoken out loud, that he was debating whether to ask her to dance. And she suddenly wanted, more than anything in the world, to dance with him.

"Miss Adams, will you do me the honor of granting me this dance?"

"Perhaps this dance is already taken. I'll have to check my dance card." She widened her eyes innocently and fluttered her fan a bit.

"If it's already taken, then why are you trying to get me to ask you to dance?" Bishop asked coolly, one black brow raised in question.

Lila gasped as if someone had just tossed cold water in her face. He wasn't suggesting that she . . . Never mind that she'd intended . . . He couldn't think . . .

Before she could decide whether to slap him for his gross impertinence or simply turn and walk away, Li-

la's eyes met Bishop's. In his look, she read both humor and a challenge. He was waiting to see how she'd
react to his baiting question, daring her to surprise
him. She felt excitement flutter in the pit of her stomach. She swallowed a bubble of laughter and formed
her mouth into a prim line.

"Really, Mr. McKenzie. It's most impolite to suggest that a lady would try to manipulate a gentleman
into an invitation to dance. Not to mention the implication that she'd need to resort to such measures."

"My apologies, Miss Adams." He gave her a shallow bow. "I certainly didn't mean to imply that a lady
as beautiful as yourself would have to browbeat a
guest into dancing with you."

"Browbeat! Really, Mr. McKenzie, you have the
most appalling manners."

"You're not the first to mention it, Miss Adams,"
he admitted without concern. "May I have this
dance?"

"How could I refuse such a gracious invitation?"
Lila set her gloved hand on his arm as the orchestra
struck up another waltz.

Though she'd spoken in jest when she asked if they
had dances in the West, she wouldn't have been at
all surprised to find that Bishop's skill on the dance
floor was rudimentary. She'd been willing to have her
toes trod upon in order to get a closer look at her
brother's enigmatic friend. But she realized almost
immediately that her toes were in no danger. Bishop
moved with a grace at odds with both his size and his
rough appearance.

He whirled her around the floor, making her feel
as light and dainty as thistledown. The hand clasping
hers was firm and strong. Where he touched her

waist, his fingers seemed to burn through the layers of clothing, making her skin tingle with awareness.

For the first time in her life, Lila was vividly aware of the more erotic aspects of the dance. The rhythmic dip and swirl of the movements; the way her skirt swung out to brush against his legs as they turned. Though she'd danced with dozens of men over the years, she'd never before been so aware of being close to a man. When she inhaled, she could smell the sharp tang of soap on his skin, the smooth bite of bourbon on his breath.

She looked up, ready to say something light and amusing, something to ease the odd tension that seemed to have sprung up between them. But whatever she'd intended to say died unspoken. He was watching her and the look in his eyes stole her breath. Hunger.

She'd always thought of blue eyes as being cool, but Bishop's eyes were pure heat. With nothing more than a look, he made her vividly aware of her femininity, of an emptiness somewhere inside her that ached to be filled, of a loneliness that went soul deep. In a heartbeat, she was made aware of the differences between man and woman. They moved in rhythm to the waltz, dip and sway and turn, but Lila no longer heard the music.

There was a sudden tightness in her stomach and heat washed under her skin, making her feel flushed and feverish. It was suddenly hard to breathe and her lips parted as if to draw in more air. The movement brought Bishop's eyes to her mouth, and it was as if he'd touched her. As if he'd kissed her.

She'd never felt such a connection to another person in her life, as if she breathed only in rhythm with him. His hand tightened over hers. He drew her an inch closer, his fingers shifting against the curve of her waist. Lila swayed toward him, their surroundings forgotten, everything forgotten but the need to be closer to him, to find out if what she felt was truth or illusion.

And then the dance was ending. He brought them to a halt, his hand lingering against her waist in a way that had nothing to do with propriety and everything to do with the awareness that still swirled between them. Lila kept her eyes on his face, waiting for something, though she couldn't have said just what. Something had just happened between them, something too deep, too profound to go unacknowledged. He'd felt it too. She knew he had. It was in his eyes. It was—

"I believe this is my dance." The vaguely plaintive comment shattered the tension between Bishop and Lila like a hammer striking a pane of glass.

Lila blinked and turned her head to look at the speaker. Though she'd known Eustace Smith all her life, it took her a moment to attach a name to his thin, pockmarked face. It was as if she'd been somewhere very far away and was having a hard time returning to the here and now.

"I'm not—" She started to tell Eustace that he was mistaken in thinking this was his dance, though she knew perfectly well that he was right. But she couldn't possibly dance with him, not when she and Bishop—

"Thank you for the dance, Miss Adams." Bishop interrupted her refusal. Lila's eyes jerked back to his but he didn't meet her look. With a shallow bow, he turned and walked away, leaving her standing in the middle of the dance floor with Eustace Smith. Lila's eyes followed his tall figure, her companion forgotten even as he led her into the dance.

For the rest of the evening, Bishop kept his distance. In Lila's experience, no matter how large the crowd at any gathering, as a rule, you saw the same people over and over again. And she certainly saw Bishop quite often. But only from across the room. Several times she saw him on the edge of the dance floor as she swept by in another man's arms. And more than once she thought she saw him watching her. But he didn't approach her and Lila's pride wouldn't let her approach him. She'd already teetered on the edge of brazenness once tonight; she wouldn't do it again.

She drank champagne and chatted with her brother's guests as if she hadn't a care in the world. But in the back of her mind, she kept remembering those moments on the dance floor. She couldn't put a name to what had passed between them, but she knew she hadn't imagined those moments of awareness. That sense of connection was like nothing she'd ever known before.

It made no sense, of course. She told herself as much as she sipped a glass of champagne. It was ridiculous to think that she had some special, mystical connection to Bishop McKenzie. No matter how well he managed to don the veneer of civilization, the man was essentially a ruffian. Certainly he was nothing like her dear, sweet Billy.

The thought of her dead fiancé made Lila's fingers tighten around the stem of her glass. A familiar tangle of emotions rose up inside her—love and grief; anger that he had died; guilt that she was still alive. And, more recently, a deep resentment that, alive or not, her own life seemed to have ended with his.

Lila swallowed the last of the champagne in her glass. She was aware of a not-unpleasant buzzing sensation in her head. Setting the glass down on a table, she turned to survey the ballroom, her eyes automatically seeking Bishop's tall figure. The big doors that led into the foyer had been pushed open to allow the party to spill into the rest of the lower floor and Bishop stood in the open doorway. But even as she saw him, he turned and left the ballroom.

He was leaving. Lila knew it as surely as if he'd told her so. He wasn't just slipping out to smoke a cigarette or joining the card players in the library. He was leaving the party. And tomorrow he was leaving River Walk, going back to wherever he'd come from.

It took Lila a moment to recognize the emotion surging up inside her. Fear. When he left, she'd be alone again. Enclosed in the glass cage that was Billy's memory, forever barred from life by his death. A small voice inside whispered that she was being ridiculous but it was drowned out by the conviction that Bishop held the only key to that cage.

Driven by that conviction, Lila moved toward the doors through which he'd disappeared. Her progress was slowed by the necessity of exchanging light conversation with half a dozen acquaintances on the way. By the time she was finally able to slip into the foyer, at least thirty minutes had passed since Bishop left the reception, but her sense of urgency had not diminished. She hurried across the foyer, her skirts rustling with the quickness of her pace.

It wasn't until she'd reached the second floor and was moving down the hallway toward the room

Bishop had been given that it occurred to her that she didn't have the slightest idea what she was going to say to him. She could hardly expect him to understand something she didn't understand herself. But that didn't stop her from knocking on his door.

When there was no immediate response, she wondered if he'd gone outside after all. She sucked in a quick breath when the door opened abruptly and Bishop stood framed in the opening. He'd discarded his jacket and tie and wore only trousers and a white shirt, the top three buttons of which were undone, exposing the strong column of his throat and an intriguing wedge of skin dusted with black hair. He looked even bigger than he had in the ballroom. Bigger, darker, more dangerous. Lila stared at him, her thoughts scattered.

"Miss Adams." Just a statement of her name, without inflection.

Lila swallowed and tried to summon up a calm smile, not an easy thing to do when a dozen butterflies seemed to be fluttering frantic wings in the pit of her stomach.

"I wanted to assure myself that the servants had seen to your needs," she said, grabbing the first—and only—thought that came to her.

There was a moment of dead silence and then Bishop's brows rose in slow comment. Lila flushed but forced her expression to remain serene. She was his hostess, after all. At least until tomorrow when Susan would be his hostess. Unless, of course, one considered Susan his hostess from the moment she'd exchanged wedding vows with Douglas. Lila frowned a little as she tried to work her way through the social rules governing this particular situation.

"An odd time to be checking up on the servants, isn't it?" Bishop asked.

*Of course it was.* "Not at all," she said calmly. "You'll be leaving us tomorrow and I just wanted to make sure your stay had been pleasant."

He looked at her, his blue eyes hooded and unreadable. Lila fought the urge to fidget with her fan and returned his look calmly, as if there were nothing unusual about a young, unmarried woman leaving a party to knock on a gentleman's door in the middle of the night. Bishop seemed to come to some conclusion because he stepped back from the door and gestured to the room behind him with one hand.

"Everything is in order but you're welcome to see for yourself."

Lila hesitated a moment, aware of warning bells going off somewhere inside. Something told her that a step through that door was fraught with hazards she hadn't considered. Her life might never be the same again. It was that thought that made the decision for her. Because, no matter what else, the one thing she knew was that, if her life remained the same, she wasn't going to have a life at all.

She stepped into Bishop's room, hearing the door shut behind her as if closing out the world. She turned toward Bishop. He reached for her, drawing her into his arms, and she went willingly.

# Chapter 5

Lila came awake with a start, her heart pounding. So powerful had been the dream, which was not really a dream but a memory, that it took her a moment to separate the past from the present. She'd tried so hard to forget that night, had blamed her incredible behavior on the champagne, on the heat in the ballroom. On Bishop.

Bishop. She closed her eyes as her memory rushed back with unwelcome speed and clarity. The endless journey by train with him sitting silent and uncommunicative across from her, their arrival at the hotel in St. Louis last night and her immediate collapse into bed.

She opened her eyes and stared at a hairline crack in the plaster ceiling. Sunlight poured into the room through the open curtains. From the pale quality of the light, she guessed that it was still quite early. Bishop hadn't told her how long he planned to stay in St. Louis, which was no surprise, considering he hadn't told her anything else either. The thought of getting on a train again made Lila shudder. If she was lucky, they'd be stopping over here for a few days. If she was extraordinarily lucky, her new husband would be content to keep his distance, the way he'd been doing.

She sat up—or tried to. Her head had barely come off the pillow before something caught at her hair and tugged her back down. Startled, Lila turned her head to discover the source of the problem and found herself staring into Bishop's sleepy blue eyes.

Loose, her hair fell almost to her hips. Normally she braided it before she went to bed, but she'd been so tired last night that she hadn't bothered. Now it spilled across the pillows and sheet in a tumbled wave of deep auburn. Following the path of that wave, she saw it disappear under Bishop's shoulder. He was lying on her hair. She'd never given a thought to the possibility of such a thing happening. But then, that was understandable, since, aside from that one night she'd tried so hard to forget, she'd never shared a bed with someone. There was something shockingly intimate about the sight of her hair caught under his shoulder—his *bare* shoulder.

Lila swallowed hard, her eyes widening as she considered the implications of what she was seeing, which was a great deal more than she wanted to see. Bishop was lying on his side, one arm thrown over the top of the covers, which were shoved down almost to his waist. His chest was bare and she gaped at the mat of black, curling hair that covered the solid muscles there. Though she struggled not to, she couldn't help but remember the crisp feel of that hair beneath her fingers, against her breasts. Breathing just a little too fast, she slammed a door on that memory. If his chest was bare, what about the rest of him?

Lila jerked her eyes back to his face, too shocked to speak. He looked back at her, as if . . . as if there were nothing extraordinary about his presence in her bed. As if he had a right to be there. As if he planned to stay there.

"Let me up." She grabbed a handful of her hair and tried to jerk it out from under him, almost frantic with the need to put some distance between them.

"Hold still," Bishop ordered sharply. "You're going to end up bald as an egg if you don't stop struggling."

"Let me go!" There was a razor edge of panic in her voice. She had to get away.

"Give me a second," he snapped.

He sat up. The covers fell around his hips and Lila saw nothing to reassure her about his state of undress. She swung her feet off the edge of the bed and then stopped. When she got up, he'd see her in her night-gown, an intimacy she had no intention of permitting. A quick glance told her that her robe was draped over the arm of the room's one thinly padded chair, well out of reach.

"Close your eyes," she snapped, clutching the covers against her chest.

"Close my eyes?" Bishop repeated the question on a note of disbelief. "We're married and you're pregnant with my child and you're asking me to close my eyes?"

"Close your eyes," she said between gritted teeth. She didn't need to be reminded of the situation.

"There's enough cloth in that thing you're wearing to make a blasted circus tent."

"Don't curse. And a gentleman should never refer to a lady's intimate apparel."

"Intimate apparel?" Lila looked over her shoulder in time to see Bishop arch one dark brow derisively. "I've seen nuns wearing less. And I never claimed to be a gentleman."

"You certainly couldn't do so with any truth." But her sarcasm was perfunctory. She swallowed, fighting down a sudden wave of nausea. Not now. Oh, please, not now. This had been happening sporadically for the last month, this sudden violent illness that hit as soon as she set foot out of bed. Please, not this morning. But beads of sweat were breaking out across her forehead. Her stomach rolled and she swallowed. Bishop must have seen the color drain from her face.

"What's wrong?"

Lila was beyond appreciating the sharp concern in his voice. She swallowed again, trying desperately to delay the inevitable. Her stomach twisted and, with a groan, she lunged from the bed, her state of dishabille forgotten as she ran for the dresser and the china bowl on it. She just made it, dropping to her knees with the bowl on the floor in front of her as her stomach heaved again.

Bishop was beside her in an instant. He caught her hair in one hand, holding it back from her face and wrapping his arm around her shoulders, supporting her trembling body.

"Go away," Lila groaned between heaves. "Please go away."

"Don't be an idiot," he told her, his impatient tone at odds with the gentleness of his touch. "I've seen people throw up before."

"I don't care what you've seen. I want you to go away." She'd never been so humiliated in her entire life. Being ill was bad enough, but to have him there made it ten times worse.

Ignoring her, Bishop held her until her stomach had finished its tantrum. By the time the bout had passed, Lila could only lean weakly against his knee with her eyes closed. She wanted to order him to leave again, and, at the same time, she wanted to turn into his arms and sob like a child.

"Rinse your mouth."

Lila opened her eyes to find the china pitcher in front of her. "I can't drink out of that," she protested automatically.

"It's clean. Rinse your mouth."

His tone was so matter-of-fact that Lila forgot her embarrassment. Too weak to argue, she did as she was told.

"Do you want to go back to bed?" Bishop brushed wisps of damp hair back from her forehead.

"I want to die," she muttered.

"Not today," he said heartlessly. He stood, drawing her up with him.

Lila leaned against him, gathering her strength for the trip back to bed. But when she swayed, he slid one arm under her knees and lifted her off her feet, carrying her as easily as if she were a child. At five feet eight inches, it wasn't often that she felt small and helpless, but Bishop made her feel almost fragile.The fact that she rather enjoyed the sensation did nothing to improve her mood.

"I can walk," she said crossly.

"You'd fall on your face." He held her with a gentleness at odds to the cool tone of his voice.

There was something oddly comforting about the feel of his arms around her, the broad muscles of his chest pressed against her arm. Lila had to resist the urge to press her cheek against his shoulder, close her eyes, and just give herself over into his keeping. She couldn't deny a small—very small—twinge of regret when he reached the bed and lowered her onto it.

He stepped back and she was relieved to see that he was wearing a pair of woolen drawers. It was better than if he'd been naked, but they rode distressingly low on his hips. Lila found her eyes tracing the dark line of hair that arrowed across his stomach before disappearing beneath the waist of the drawers. She jerked her eyes away, her cheeks flushing.

"Put some clothes on, for heaven's sake. A gentleman would never appear before a lady in such a state of undress."

Bishop studied her for a moment. He'd never in his life met a woman quite like her. She sat there, her hair tumbled around her shoulders and her skin the color of skimmed milk. He'd just spent five minutes holding her while she puked her guts up yet she still managed to sound as haughty as a queen handing out decrees to the peasants.

He crossed his arms over his chest. "Seems to me a lady wouldn't notice a gentleman's state of undress."

"I can hardly help but notice it with you standing there in your . . . your underwear." She flicked her fingers in his direction but kept her eyes resolutely turned away.

"Why, Lila, I do believe you've just made a reference to my intimate apparel."

She glared at him, her eyes bright green against the pallor of her face. "Just put some clothes on," she said between gritted teeth.

"Always happy to oblige a lady."

He put just a touch of mocking emphasis on the final word, and Lila's fingers curled into the covers as she struggled with the urge to hit him. He was the most exasperating man she'd ever met. Though she was determined not to look, she found it impossible to ignore him as he walked around the foot of the bed and bent to pick his clothes up from the floor.

The room had been dimly lit the night she'd come to him and her impressions of his body had been more tactile than visual. Seeing him now, in broad daylight, she found it difficult to take her eyes from him. He was all smooth muscles and hard angles. She was suddenly vividly aware of the differences between male and female. Even more distressing was the odd little twinge in the pit of her stomach, a twinge that had nothing to do with her recent sickness and everything to do with the way the muscles rippled across Bishop's back and shoulders as he stepped into his pants.

Lila looked away, ashamed of the effort it took. There was something shockingly intimate about having a man dressing in the same room with her. Now that she was a married woman, she supposed it was the least of the intimacies to which she was going to have to become accustomed. The thought sent a shiver up her spine, a shiver she was determined to believe was caused by dread rather than anticipation.

"I'll have them bring up some dry crackers for you," Bishop said as he finished buttoning his shirt.

"I don't want anything." The thought of food of any kind made Lila's stomach twist uneasily.

"They'll settle your stomach. Eat them slowly." He shrugged into his jacket. "I'll have them bring up a pot of tea too."

"I don't want any tea," she said, feeling as cranky as a child.

"It will help your stomach."

"Since you know so much about what will make me feel better, it's a shame you aren't the one having the baby," she snapped.

Bishop grinned, his teeth a slash of white beneath his dark mustache. "That would be an interesting trick."

Lila's mouth twitched but she refused to grant him a smile. She preferred it when he wasn't being pleasant. It was easier to keep her distance then.

"Where are you going?" she asked when he picked up his hat.

"I've got some things I have to do. I'll be back in a couple of hours. We can have lunch in the dining room downstairs."

Lila shuddered. "I don't think so."

"You'll feel better once you get something in your stomach."

She didn't bother to dignify that with a response. She didn't particularly appreciate his certainty that he knew her stomach better than she did.

He grinned again, as if he knew what she was thinking and found it amusing.

"Don't miss me too much," he said as he pulled open the door.

Lila barely restrained the urge to stick out her tongue.

"If you'll wait here, Mr. McKenzie, I'll tell Mr. and Mrs. Linton that you're here."

As if they didn't already know, Bishop thought cynically but there was no sense in saying as much to the maid. "Are Gavin and Angelique here?"

"Yes, sir. They're upstairs."

"Tell them to come down."

The maid looked uncertain. "I don't know as how I should do that, Mr. McKenzie. Mrs. Linton, she said they was to stay upstairs until—" She stopped abruptly, as if she'd just realized she was about to say something unwise.

"Until I left?" Bishop asked.

She flushed. "I'm sure she didn't mean it, sir."

Bishop didn't doubt that Louise Linton had meant exactly what she'd said. He gave the maid a shallow smile. "Tell the children I'm here and that I want to talk to them. I'll deal with Mrs. Linton."

"Deal with me, Bishop?" Louise Linton's sharp voice preceded her into the room. "That sounds very much like a threat."

Bishop was struck, as always, by the amazing amount of presence she carried with her. She was a small woman, barely five feet tall, with a reed-thin body that gave her a delicate, almost birdlike appearance. But if Louise Linton had been a bird, it would have been a hawk, not only because of the fierce intelligence in her pale-blue eyes but because of the sheer ruthlessness with which she dealt with anyone unfortunate enough to enter her circle.

She wore a black silk gown trimmed at wrist and neck with fine white lace. The effect was both elegant and daunting. No one looking at her would ever suspect that she'd been born Louise Pervy, illegitimate daughter of a tinker and a Tennessee mountain girl. George Linton had been a simple shopkeeper when she married him. With her pushing him, he'd made a small fortune supplying the emigrants and miners heading west along the Oregon Trail and now owned a good portion of St. Louis.

With money behind her, Louise had obliterated all trace of her dirt-poor beginnings. She'd become more elegant and refined than anyone borne into money would have needed to be. No one who knew her now would ever have guessed her hardscrabble background. The fact that Bishop knew exactly where she'd come from was the one thing she could never forgive.

"Are you threatening me, Bishop?" she asked, as she came farther into the room. Though he could have snapped her neck without effort, there was no concern in her eyes. Rather there was a challenge, almost a dare.

"I came to see the children," Bishop said, ignoring her question.

"I'm not sure that's a good idea."

"Either the maid can go get them or I will." He didn't raise his voice but his tone was pure steel.

"You do not give orders in this house."

"Then you give the order. One way or another, I will see them."

"Perhaps it would be best if we sent someone up to get them." George Linton had entered the room behind his wife. Of medium height and rotund build, he nevertheless seemed to disappear into her shadow in some way that Bishop had never completely understood. He gave Bishop an apologetic smile. "After all, he is their father."

Louise's thin features tightened. "Since that is the reason our daughter is dead, I hardly think the reminder is necessary."

A tense little silence followed her comment. Bishop knew he was expected to fill it by offering some defense on his own behalf. He said nothing, letting the silence stretch until George felt compelled to break it.

"Yes, well, Isabelle's death was a terrible tragedy, of course. But Bishop is still the children's father, my dear." He cleared his throat and glanced uneasily from his wife to Bishop and back again. "I'm sure Isabelle would want everyone to let bygones be bygones."

"Isabelle was an idiot," Louise snapped. "If she hadn't been an idiot, she would have married someone worthy of our position in society instead of throwing herself away on this . . . this shootist. I warned her no good would come of it but she wouldn't listen. See where it got her!" There was a certain bitter satisfaction in her voice at having been proven right, even at the cost of her only child.

"Now, my dear, you mustn't upset yourself so. Isabelle has been gone these past five years now.

There's no sense raking over old coals. Mary, go tell the children that their father is here to see them."

Mary looked at Louise. It was clear that she knew who ran the Linton household. Louise hesitated a moment and then flicked one hand in the direction of the door. "Bring them down."

The maid hurried out, patently relieved to be gone. She left behind a silence thick enough to touch. Bishop stood with his back to the fireplace. There was a small fire on the hearth, but the heat it produced was not adequate to combat the chill emanating from Louise's stiff figure. The woman could put frost on the devil's horns. Bishop liked to think she'd get the chance to try.

George cleared his throat again, his eyes flickering between the room's other occupants. He pulled a linen handkerchief out of his jacket pocket and dabbed at his forehead. He put the handkerchief away and cleared his throat again. No one spoke. He shifted from one foot to the other like a nervous child at a grown-up's party.

Briefly Bishop considered saying something to ease the older man's discomfort, but he discarded the idea. There had been a time when he'd have said that George was a good man who had the misfortune to be married to a woman stronger than he was. But, over the years, he'd lost patience with George's passivity in the face of his wife's ambitions. While Louise ran roughshod over everything and everyone in her path, George stood by and did nothing. It was not a trait likely to earn a man much respect.

"I've married again," Bishop said, speaking to both of them but looking at Louise. "As soon as my wife and I are settled, I'll be sending for the children to join us."

It was nearly worth all the trouble his marriage had caused just to see Louise Linton momentarily slack-jawed with shock.

"Married again. Well, that's good news," George said, too heartily. "Isn't that good news, dear?" From his tone, it was difficult to tell whether he was asking her to confirm his assessment or begging her to agree.

Louise didn't spare him so much as a glance. Her attention was all for Bishop. "What makes you think we'll allow you to take the children?"

"What makes you think you can stop me?" Bishop asked coolly.

Before she could respond, they were interrupted by the arrival of the children. Mary barely waited until they'd entered the room before making her own escape. Not that Bishop blamed her. Given a choice, he'd have cut a wide path around any place that Louise was. But he didn't have a choice, at least not quite yet. And the reasons stood just inside the parlor doorway, looking at him with varying degrees of uncertainty.

It had only been six months since he saw them, but he was struck by how much they'd changed. Gavin had to have grown at least an inch. At twelve, he was all arms and legs, his lanky body showing promise of matching his father's height. With his black hair, blue eyes, and strong jaw, he was the spitting image of Bishop at the same age. Angelique, on the other hand, with her pale blond hair and soft blue eyes, was very like her mother. Looking at her, Bishop could imagine that, in another fifteen years, looking at her would be like looking at Isabelle's ghost.

"Hullo" Angelique offered him a shy smile but hung back, edging a little behind her older brother. Her mother had died giving birth to her. In the nearly five years since then, Bishop had seen so little of her that he doubted if she had any real idea of who he was.

Not so Gavin. He knew exactly who Bishop was. And, from the wariness that marked his expression, he wasn't overwhelmingly happy to see his father.

"Hello," he said, nodding in Bishop's direction.

"Your father has married again," Louise said, without giving Bishop a chance to return their greeting. "He says he plans to send for you when he's settled. I haven't decided yet whether I should allow you to go. What do you think, children?"

Bishop's jaw knotted with anger. Damn the woman! He should have insisted on seeing the children alone.

"Why ask us?" Gavin asked in a sullen tone. "You don't care what we think. You're going to do what you want, just like always."

Bishop felt a twinge of admiration for the boy's courage. There weren't many adults who'd have risked drawing Louise's wrath.

"Of course we care," George said hastily. "Don't we, my dear?"

"Not in the least," she said with icy indifference. "Why would I care about the opinion of an ungrateful boy such as yourself?"

Gavin shifted so that he faced his grandmother more directly. "Why should I be grateful? You only keep us 'cause *he* doesn't want us." A jerk of his head indicated Bishop. "And you figure people would say bad things about you if you didn't take us in."

The bitterness in his son's voice made Bishop wince. It had been a mistake to leave the children here. He'd known it at the time but, after Isabelle died, he hadn't known what else to do with them. He had no family of his own. He rarely stayed in one place more than a few weeks or months. He'd had no way to care for an infant and a seven-year-old boy. So, when Louise had offered to take them in, he'd gone against his better judgment and agreed.

"Go to your room," Louise told the boy in a chillingly calm voice. "I'll deal with you later."

"Wait." Bishop spoke for the first time since the children entered the room. He stepped forward and set his hand on Gavin's shoulder, turning so that he faced the old woman. "You'll *deal* with him? Now who's issuing threats?" he questioned softly.

"As long as he is under my roof, I will deal with him as I see fit. As I told you once before, you do not give orders in this house. Gavin, go to your room."

Gavin's shoulder was rigid with tension beneath Bishop's hand but he didn't say anything. It was clear that he expected no help from his father. It struck Bishop suddenly that, when he'd been Gavin's age, he'd been able to turn to his own father if he found himself in a situation he couldn't handle. Looking down, he saw Angelique creep forward and slip her hand into her brother's, saw Gavin's fingers close almost convulsively over hers.

"Go to your room and pack your things," he said. "Get Mary to help you. You're both coming with me."

Gavin's head jerked around and he stared up at his father, his eyes round with shock. "Do you mean it?"

"I mean it."

And God help him when Lila found herself a stepmother to two children she hadn't even known existed.

Lila finished pinning the heavy mass of her hair into a roll at the back of her head. The simple hairstyle wasn't particularly fashionable, but it was neat and tidy. Surely one of the benefits of being a married woman was the freedom to choose comfort over fashion, at least occasionally.

Standing back from the mirror, she studied her reflection and was reasonably satisfied with what she saw. The gown was one of her favorites. The Prussian blue muslin was simply but elegantly cut, close-fitting through the bodice with the back of the skirt gathered into elegant folds that dropped to a hem trimmed with crisp, knife-edge pleats. The color suited her, making the most of her eyes and hair. Though she would have died before admitting as much, she wanted to look her best when Bishop returned. Considering the bedraggled creature he'd left behind, her pride demanded it.

She gave one last pat to her hair before turning away from the mirror. She was feeling in better charity with her husband than she would have believed possible. Not only had he sent up the tea and crackers he'd insisted she have, but he'd also arranged for bath water to be brought to her. The tea and crackers had settled her stomach, though she'd certainly never tell Bishop that. But it was the bath that had made her feel as if she just might live to see another day. She was even feeling a bit hungry, which was something of a miracle considering how she'd felt a few hours ago. Lunch in the hotel dining room sounded quite pleasant. Bathed, freshly gowned, and properly coiffed, she could face the thought of dining with her new husband with equanimity.

As if in answer to her thoughts, Lila heard the sound of a key in the lock. She turned toward the sound, aware of a feeling of anticipation. Bishop pushed open the door and stepped inside.

"I was starting to think you might have forgotten me," she said lightly. She'd determined to try to put their relationship on a more pleasant footing than it had so far enjoyed.

Bishop didn't respond immediately. He simply stood in the open door, a rather odd expression on his face. "I have something to tell you."

Lila raised her brows. "Is something wrong?"

"No." But he didn't sound too sure.

Before she could question him further, he shifted to one side and gestured two children into the room— a boy of about twelve, with thick black hair and vivid blue eyes, and an exquisitely beautiful little girl of four or five with hair the color of newly minted gold. Her eyes were blue also but they were a softer, gentler shade. The children stood next to Bishop, looking at her—the boy with a wariness older than his years, the little girl with the kind of open curiosity possible only in the very young. Lila looked back at them, wondering who they might be and why they were with Bishop. The boy looked familiar, though she was sure she'd never met him before.

She looked from them to Bishop. He opened his mouth—to offer an explanation? But before he could say anything, the little girl tugged at the hem of his coat.

"Who's that lady, Papa?"

*Papa?*

When she was a girl, Lila had been thrown from a horse and had hit the ground with force enough to knock the breath from her. She had a similar feeling right now.

"This is Lila," Bishop told the child without taking his eyes from Lila's face. "Lila, these are my children. Gavin and Angelique."

"Your children?" Lila repeated blankly. He had children? She was still struggling to absorb that idea when Bishop dropped his next bit of news.

"They're going with us."

# Chapter 6

"Going with us? To Paris?" She must have misunderstood him, Lila thought. He couldn't have said that these were his children. And, most especially, he couldn't have said that these same children were going to be traveling with them, which meant—Good Lord, did that mean the children were going to be *living* with them?

"I've arranged for another room for the children," Bishop said, dispelling any hope that she'd misunderstood. "We'll be leaving on tomorrow's train."

"Oh." Lila struggled to adjust her thinking. She looked at the children. They looked as bewildered as she felt, and Lila's heart went out to them. Whatever was going on, it wasn't their doing. She knew exactly where the blame lay, and she'd deal with *him* later. She conjured up a smile, hoping it didn't look as false as it felt, and moved forward.

"Well, Gavin and . . . and Angelique, I'm very pleased to meet you. I'm Lila, your . . . father's new wife." She couldn't quite manage the word "stepmother." Not yet. She held out her hand to Gavin, who took it after a slight but perceptible hesitation.

"Pleased to meet you," he mumbled in a tone so lacking in sincerity that Lila's smile became genuine. Clearly he was versed in the polite forms but young enough to lack the guile to project false emotions. It was too bad his father didn't share his son's honesty. She shot Bishop a dark look before turning her attention to the little girl.

"And you're Angelique. That's a very pretty name."

"Angel," the child said. She was holding her brother's hand, her eyes reflecting uncertainty.

"Angel?" Lila questioned.

"She means her name is Angel," Gavin clarified. "She can't say Angelique so everybody calls her Angel."

"I've never seen a lady with hair like yours before," Angel said, curiosity overcoming her shyness.

"Like mine?" Lila lifted one hand to her hair.

"It's looks like it's on fire."

"Does it?" Lila smiled, thinking that it was her temper rather than her hair that was burning. "Well, I've never seen a real, live angel before, so this is a first for both of us, isn't it?"

"I isn't an angel," the little girl said, giggling. "That's just my name."

"My mistake. But you look so much like an angel, how was I to know?"

Angel giggled again and hid her face against her brother's side. When Lila straightened, she caught Gavin's eye. Though his expression couldn't be termed friendly, he seemed a little less wary. It was easy to see that he and his sister were close. If she wanted to win him over, she'd obviously have to win his sister over first. And heaven help her, it looked as if she were going to need to win them both over.

"How could you?" Lila leaned across the table, glaring at Bishop. "How could you just show up with those children in tow and announce that they were going with us?"

"I didn't have much choice." Bishop lifted his cup, wishing it contained something stronger than coffee.

They were sitting in the hotel dining room, the remains of their barely touched meals on the table in front of them. It had been his suggestion that they have lunch as planned even though the plan hadn't originally included Gavin and Angelique. The four of them had eaten in near silence.

Lila's efforts to draw the children out had met with limited success. Angel was willing to be friendly but Gavin was uncommunicative to the point of being sullen. He spoke only when addressed directly and, even then, his responses were monosyllabic. At that, he spoke more than his father.

When the children had finished their meals, Bishop gave Gavin a quarter and told him to take his sister to the emporium across the street and get them both some candy. From Gavin's expression, it was clear that he recognized the gesture for exactly what it was—an excuse to get him and his sister out of the way so the adults could talk. But he took Angel's hand and did as he was told.

From across the table, Bishop had felt Lila's simmering anger. On the rare occasions that their glances crossed, her eyes had promised retribution, but she hadn't, by word or deed, done anything to make the children feel unwelcome.

"I appreciate your kindness to the children," he told her.

"What did you expect me to do? Tell them the truth, which was that I didn't even know they existed until you walked in the door with them?"

"I hadn't planned on doing things this way." He signaled the waiter for another cup of coffee. "I was going to send for them later, after the baby was born. I thought that would be easier for you. But they couldn't stay where they were anymore."

"How kind of you to consider me," she said in a tone of sweet insincerity. "And just where were they? I don't have a great deal of experience with children, but I don't believe it's customary to store them away like old trunks. Someone must have been taking care of them."

Bishop's jaw tightened at her sarcasm but he couldn't deny that she had ample justification for her anger. "They've been with their grandparents."

The waiter arrived just then to refill Bishop's cup and Lila waited until he'd left before speaking again. "Would that be your parents? Or their mother's? And where *is* their mother? I do hope you're not going to surprise me again by telling me that you already have a wife. Surely Douglas would have mentioned that, even if the children slipped his mind."

"Douglas doesn't know anything about the children or their mother. Isabelle died giving birth to Angelique," he said shortly. "They've been staying with her mother and father since her death. But it was no longer a . . . suitable arrangement."

Lila stared at him, at a loss for words. None of her mother's many lessons in deportment and manners had dealt with the proper response to a situation like this. Was she supposed to express her regrets for his first wife's death, a wife she hadn't even known existed until barely an hour ago? Was she supposed to smile graciously and tell him that she was delighted to find herself stepmother to a little girl—and a half-grown boy who was clearly no happier about the situation than she was?

Not that what she said was important. Obviously, nothing was going to change his mind. The children were going with them and that was all there was to it. She was just going to have to get used to the idea, right along with being married to a man she didn't know and carrying a child she wasn't prepared for. To her dismay, Lila felt her eyes burn with sudden tears. She was not, ordinarily, a woman who cried often. But lately she'd found herself feeling weepy over nothing at all. And this certainly qualified as more than nothing. She forced the tears back with sheer willpower.

"It seems everything has worked out quite nicely, hasn't it?" she said evenly.

"What has?"

"I had wondered why you came back," she continued as if he hadn't spoken. "After all, if you'd stayed away, no one would have known what had happened between us."

"I came back because you were carrying my child and I wasn't going to let another man raise it."

"Why? Someone else was raising the two children you already had." She was pleased to see the impact of her words in his eyes.

The room was filled with other diners. The sounds of their voices and the clink of silver against china lapped against the sudden silence that fell between Bishop and Lila.

"That was a mistake," Bishop said, his voice low and grating.

"A mistake?" Lila widened her eyes and gave him a patently false smile. "And now you've been able to use me to rectify that mistake. Isn't that nice?"

Without giving him a chance to reply, she pushed her chair back from the table and rose. Her intention was to sweep out of the dining room and leave Bishop sitting alone, not a genteel action but a thoroughly satisfying one. But his fingers clamped around her wrist before she could take so much as a step.

"Sit down." Bishop spoke quietly but there was an undercurrent of pure steel in his tone.

Lila tilted her chin and looked down her nose at him. "I'd prefer to leave."

"Sit. Down." The two words were separate and distinct. His eyes were clear blue and hard as ice.

Lila debated her options. She was aware of the other diners casting them curious glances. Though they hadn't raised their voices, it must have been obvious that there was more than a simple conversation going on between them. She could still pull away from Bishop and walk out. Surely he wouldn't risk causing a scene by trying to stop her. As if in answer to her thoughts, Bishop's fingers tightened subtly around her wrist.

"Sit down, Lila," he said almost gently. "Now."

She sat.

He should have let her go, Bishop thought as he released her wrist and sat back in his chair. And he would have, except he couldn't shake the feeling that he owed her an explanation. Obviously, Lila agreed.

"I didn't plan on taking the children with us," he said.

"Then perhaps you shouldn't have bought them tickets for the train," Lila suggested with sweet sarcasm.

Bishop ground his teeth together and grabbed for his temper. Never in his life had he known anyone with the ability to make him so angry with so little effort.

"I went to see them today to tell them that I'd be sending for them in a few months."

"When did you plan to tell me about them? When they arrived on the doorstep?"

"I would have told you before then."

"The way you told me about them before you brought them here this morning?" Lila's huff of disbelief came perilously close to being an unladylike snort.

"I didn't have a chance to tell you this morning." Bishop thrust his fingers through his hair. Drawing a deep breath, he spoke in a tone of strained reason. "I know this came as a shock but I couldn't leave them there."

"Why not?"

*Why not?* Bishop stared at her. It was a reasonable question but that didn't make it any easier to answer. How was he supposed to explain what he'd felt when he'd heard Gavin say that his father didn't want them, seen the weary acceptance in the boy's eyes?

"They were unhappy," he said simply.

Lila stared at him. What was she supposed to say now? That he should have left the children with their grandparents anyway? That she didn't care if they were unhappy as long as she didn't have to deal with them? Feeling suddenly very tired, she sighed. "I hope they're not poor travelers."

She had assumed that the children would make the long, arduous journey even more difficult, but that expectation was not met. They endured the confinement and boredom with more grace than she could have imagined possible. Considering the way their lives had been turned upside down, Lila would not have been at all surprised if they had been fussy and ill-tempered. Heaven knows, she was feeling more than a little cranky about the abrupt changes in her own life. But Gavin and Angel showed no sign of missing their grandparents and the home they'd had with them, which gave credence to Bishop's statement that they had not been happy there.

Though the idea of being a stepmother terrified Lila, it turned out, at least in the beginning, to be not nearly so difficult as she'd expected. The children were remarkably self-sufficient. Gavin, in particular, seemed old for his age. He appeared to expect nothing from the adults around him, either for himself or for his sister. And, from the way Angel turned to him for companionship, it seemed she shared his lack of expectations.

But there was an edge of sullen resentment in Gavin's attitude that was lacking in his little sister. Angel seemed to live up to her name. Lila had never met a more sunny-tempered child. When they first boarded the train, Angel settled into her seat and pressed her face to the window to watch the hustle and bustle of the station. Though Gavin pretended indifference, Lila noticed that he was not completely immune to the excitement.

For a while after leaving St. Louis, the children were content to watch the passing countryside. Lila divided her attention between them and the book she had open in her lap. Susan had given her the book— a novel detailing the highly improbable adventures of a young woman who seemed to have more hair than wit, in Lila's opinion. Not that she had the right to throw stones in that regard, she admitted with an inaudible sigh. Certainly her own judgment had not been above reproach in recent months.

She stole a quick glance at Bishop. He was looking out the window at the farmland they were passing through. Seeing his attention elsewhere, Lila took the opportunity to study him. He really was a remarkably attractive man. His thick black hair was neatly combed and worn just long enough to brush the collar of his plain black coat. His features were even, handsome by any standards. The heavy black mustache gave him an air of danger that was undeniably appealing, and the sharp, vivid blue of his eyes added the final, lethal touch.

She certainly wasn't the only woman to find him attractive. More than one feminine glance had been cast his way as they made their way through the station. She couldn't deny feeling a certain satisfaction, maybe even a touch of possessiveness, that he was walking next to her.

"Something wrong?" Bishop's question startled Lila into a realization that she'd been caught blatantly staring at him. She cursed her fair skin as she felt color run up under it. She must look like a guilty schoolgirl, caught mooning over a handsome tutor.

Lifting her chin, she scrambled for something intelligent to say. "I was just thinking that Gavin looks very like you."

Gavin's head snapped around, his eyes startled. His gaze shot from her to his father. Lila thought she read something that might have been pleasure in his expression, but it was gone so quickly she couldn't be sure. His eyes chilled and he looked suddenly older and harder than seemed possible for a boy his age.

"Grandmother always said that blood would tell, especially if it was bad," he said, his calm tone holding a bitter edge that made Lila catch her breath in shock.

Bishop's face was an emotionless mask as he met his son's look. The muscle that ticked in his jaw was the only sign that he'd understood Gavin's meaning. They stared at each other for the space of several heartbeats, involved in some silent, masculine duel that transcended age and relationship. In that moment, the resemblance between them was striking. From the color of their hair, to the solid strength of their jaws, to the ice blue of their eyes, it was like looking at daguerreotypes of the same person, man and boy. It was Angel who broke the tense exchange.

"I think Gavin and Papa are very pretty," she said, giving them both a sunny smile.

"Pretty?" Bishop repeated, looking less than flattered.

"Boys can't be pretty," Gavin told his little sister firmly. Lila was amused to see that he was blushing and suddenly looked very much like a twelve-year-old boy.

"You're pretty," Angel repeated firmly, showing a stubborn streak beneath the soft blue eyes and pale-gold curls. "So's Papa."

Gavin and Bishop exchanged looks. There was no challenge this time, only mutual dismay.

"There's no sense in arguing with her when she takes that tone," Gavin said, sounding disgusted. "It'll just make her say it more."

Lila smiled. Whatever the conflict between father and son, at least they agreed on something.

Afterward, Lila remembered the trip as being one long, dusty blur. She tried, on several occasions, to engage Bishop in conversation, but, though he was polite, he was not particularly communicative. She managed to pry out of him the fact that he was the sheriff in Paris but not much else. The news that he was in law enforcement filled Lila with mixed emotions. On the one hand, it was certainly a respectable calling. On the other, it seemed a somewhat uncertain profession. And wasn't there a certain amount of danger inherent in it?

The thought made her suddenly very aware of her dependence on him. Not only hers but the children's. If something happened to Bishop, she could always turn to Douglas. Despite the distance that had been between them when she left, she knew he would always be there if she needed him. What about Gavin and Angel?

Lila felt her heart sink at the realization that they were now her responsibility. As their stepmother, it would be up to her to see that they were cared for, to raise them—alone, if something should happen to Bishop. The thought was overwhelming.

The children occupied the seats opposite her and Bishop. Outside, all was darkness. Inside the coach, lanterns had been lit. They cast a thin light over the passengers. Angel was stretched out across two seats, her head in her brother's lap, a battered rag doll clutched in one arm. She looked like her namesake, her sweetly rounded face flushed with sleep, her lashes creating shadowy crescents on her cheeks. Gavin slept also, one arm in his lap, the other flung across his sister. In sleep the wariness that usually marked his expression disappeared, leaving him looking very young and very vulnerable.

Lila tried to imagine herself raising the two of them alone, but her imagination boggled. And it wouldn't be just Gavin and Angel, she thought, remembering the child she carried. In a few months she'd have a brand-new baby to care for, someone smaller and even more dependent than Angel.

She touched her fingers to her still-flat stomach, trying to imagine the child inside her. Would it be a boy or a girl? Would it have red hair or black? Her green eyes or Bishop's blue? Other than the disruption it had created in her life, Lila hadn't given much thought to the child she carried. In some odd way, it hadn't seemed quite real to her. She'd been too busy worrying about other things to think of the child as anything more than an enormous complication. But looking at the sleeping children, she was suddenly aware of the life she carried as something apart from both herself and Bishop. Feeling someone watching her, Lila turned her head and met Bishop's eyes.

He'd been watching her for several minutes, watching the expressions flicker across her face in the thin light from the lamps, wondering what she was thinking. When she set her hand against her stomach, he'd realized that she was thinking about the child she carried—his child. The thought filled him with a restless hunger. He wanted to see the changes his child had wrought with her body. If he set his hand over hers, would he feel a new curve to her stomach? Were her breasts fuller now? More sensitive?

Those were the thoughts passing through his head when Lila looked up and saw him watching her. She was startled by the raw hunger in his gaze. Since he'd seemed in no hurry to consummate their marriage, she'd assumed that whatever desire he'd felt for her three months ago was gone. But from the way he was looking at her now, she couldn't have been more wrong. The depth of hunger in his eyes was almost frightening. Even more frightening was the echo of that same hunger within herself. She had only to look at him to remember what it had felt like to lie in his arms, to feel him kissing her, touching her, loving her.

Lila wrenched her gaze away from his, aware that she was breathing too quickly. It was wrong to feel the way that she did. Wrong to feel this desire for a man she didn't love. Married or not, without at least affection between them, what she felt could only be called lust. And wasn't it lust that had gotten her into this situation in the first place?

Bishop thought he saw an echo of his own hunger in Lila's eyes, but then her expression stiffened and she looked away. He let his own gaze linger on the smooth curve of her cheek, the determined thrust of her chin. Her hair seemed to catch and hold the light, glowing as if with its own inner fire. He wanted to reach out and tug loose the pins that held it, warm his hands in the silken fire of it.

He'd almost certainly draw back a bloody stub if he tried, he thought with a quick stab of black humor. She'd made it clear that she was in no hurry to become his wife in fact as well as in name. Last night she'd slept in the same room with Angel, leaving him to bunk with Gavin.

But once they arrived in Paris, she wouldn't find it so easy to use the children to keep him at a distance. Sooner or later, she would be his wife, in every sense of the word.

# Chapter 7

At first sight, Paris, Colorado, was far from impressive. Nor did a second and third look uncover any hidden splendors. It had started out as a gold mining town, founded during the rush of '59. When the gold played out, the town eked out an existence until the discovery of silver brought it new life. Situated in a valley in the middle of the Rocky Mountains, it survived because of its location at the end of a branch rail line that brought supplies to the miners as it labored its way up the mountain from Denver City and, on its return down the mountain, transported ore back to the city.

Though she'd known it was foolish to do so, Lila had let the town's name influence her expectations. But as the four of them disembarked from the train, she saw immediately that it had been even more foolish than she'd realized. Paris, the small mining town in Colorado, bore no resemblance to the great city from which it took its name. There were no tree-lined streets, no ancient buildings and soaring cathedrals. Instead, plain wooden buildings, most with false fronts, lined a single dirt street. To Lila, accustomed to the older, more established towns of the East Coast, the lack of brick or stone buildings gave the town a temporary feeling, as if it were made of building blocks, ready to be knocked down at the whim of a child.

The businesses were much the same as those to be found in any town, east or west. There was a general store, a restaurant bearing a hand-painted sign proclaiming Fine Home Cooking, a barbershop with a newspaper office above, a small butcher shop, a livery and blacksmith shop combined, a bank, and two saloons. Not exactly a metropolis, Lila thought, looking down the dusty main street from her vantage point on the platform.

While Bishop was making arrangements for their luggage, she forced down her dismay. No matter how unimpressive it looked, this was to be her home for the foreseeable future. One thing about traveling with a man who rarely strung more than two words together at a time and two children who were better at entertaining themselves than she could ever hope to be was that it had given her plenty of time to think. Her marriage vows had been taken for better or worse. It was going to be up to her to see to it that there was more of the former than the latter in her marriage. She was going to make the best of things, and she might as well start now.

If the town itself was unimpressive, the same could certainly not be said for its setting. The Rocky Mountains rose up on all sides, like the fingers of a giant hand in the palm of which rested the town. She'd had plenty of opportunity to admire the Rockies as the train huffed and puffed its way upward between Denver City and Paris. The splendor of the mountain peaks was such that not even Gavin had been able to conceal his awe. Certainly no man-made cathedral could match nature's offerings.

"We'll walk to the hotel," Bishop said as he joined her and the children on the edge of the platform.

"The hotel?" Lila raised her eyebrows in question. "Is that where we'll be staying?"

"Until I can make arrangements to rent something for us. I've been sleeping in a room at the jail until now." His glance ran over his newly acquired family. "I don't think we'd all fit."

The dry humor caught Lila by surprise. She smiled at him, the first natural smile she'd given him since his sudden appearance at her wedding to Logan. "Even if we could all fit, I don't think a jail is a suitable place for the children."

There was a teasing light in her eyes that reminded Bishop of the girl he'd met three months before, the one who'd sparkled so brightly that he'd been drawn to her like a moth to a flame—with results almost as destructive. He gave her a half smile in return.

"Then I guess we'll have to make do with the hotel.

It's not far." Setting his hand against the small of her back, he guided her down the platform steps and into the street. Gavin followed, holding Angel's hand.

Though the sun was shining down out of a pale-blue sky, the temperature was cool enough to make Lila glad for the protection of the light wrap she wore over her dove-gray traveling dress. It was the middle of the afternoon and there weren't many people about, but those in evidence stared at their small party with open curiosity. Lila was grateful that they'd spent the night before in Denver City before boarding the train to Paris. It had given her a chance to take a bath and change her clothes so that she didn't have to make her first appearance in her new home looking like a filthy ragamuffin.

Bishop returned one or two greetings but didn't stop to introduce Lila. Within the hour, word would have spread through town that the sheriff was back with a woman and two kids in tow. Speculation would be running wild. It struck Lila as ironic that she'd fled Pennsylvania to escape gossip and here she was smack in the middle of it again.

The hotel was a boxy two-story building with no pretensions to great beauty on the outside. Nor did it have any on the inside. The rug that covered the lobby floor was so faded that the original colors could only be guessed at, and the furnishing were neither elaborate nor expensive. But Lila was relieved to see that it appeared clean and tidy. If the rooms were as well cared for as the public areas, then she could offer no objection to staying here.

"Afternoon, Sheriff. Good to have you back." The man who stood behind the registration desk was short and balding. He'd carefully combed his few remaining strands of dark hair over the top of his head where they presented the appearance of thin brown stripes against his pink scalp. His eyes were brown also, and they darted from Bishop to Lila with quick curiosity. "What can I do for you?"

"I need two rooms, Mr. Lyman," Bishop said. "One for myself and my wife, one for my children."

"Your wife?" Mr. Lyman's voice rose on a squawk of surprise. His eyes darted from Lila to Gavin and Angel. "Children?"

"That's right." Bishop drew Lila forward. "Lila, this is Clem Lyman. This is my wife, Lila."

"I'm pleased to meet you, Mr Lyman," Lila said with a smile.

"Pleasure's mine, Miz McKenzie." Mr. Lyman ducked his head in her direction. He still looked dazed. "Didn't know you was married, Sheriff. Let alone had kids."

"We were married when I went East a few months back," Bishop said casily. "Gavin and Angel are my children from my first marriage. Now, how about those rooms?"

The other man pushed the register toward him without speaking, apparently struck dumb by this spate of information. Lila hoped he'd attribute her flush to shyness rather than to her embarrassment at the lie Bishop had just told about their wedding date. Obviously he was thinking ahead to the time when her pregnancy started to show and making sure that, when people began counting on their fingers, the answer they came up with wouldn't shame her. She appreciated his foresight, even as she resented the necessity for it.

Bishop signed his name to the register and collected two keys from Clem Lyman, who couldn't seem to take his eyes from Lila and the children. It was a relief to have an excuse to move away from his fascinated gaze. She followed Bishop up the stairs, glancing over her shoulder to make sure the children were following. As they reached the landing, she heard Mr. Lyman's voice echo below.

"Dot! Dot, come quick!"

"Dot is his wife," Bishop said as he turned in to the upstairs hallway. "She's also the second biggest gossip this side of Julesburg."

"Oh." Lila wasn't exactly thrilled by the information, but it wasn't as if their marriage was a secret. "Who's the biggest gossip?" she asked.

Bishop bent to set their bags down in front of room five. As he straightened, his eyes met hers. "Clem Lyman," he said dryly.

"Oh." That was certainly something to keep in mind, Lila thought as he unlocked the door. She'd have to be careful not to give the Lymans any more grist for the gossip mill than her mere presence had already supplied.

The rooms were as simply furnished as the lobby had been. A bed, a wardrobe, and a small dresser with a mirror atop and an uncomfortable-looking wing chair sitting stiffly in one corner. The decor was so plain, it bordered on the stark, but everything was clean and neat as a pin.

Bishop set the bags down at the foot of the bed in one room. Looking at Lila and the children, he felt a sudden sense of unreality. A couple of weeks before, he'd been a single man with no one to worry about but himself. Over the years, he'd managed to convince himself that the children were better off where they were, and he'd never expected to marry again. Yet here he was with a wife, two children, and a third on the way. The thought was enough to make his head spin.

"I need to check in with my deputy," he said, looking at Lila. "I've been gone awhile and I'll have some catching up to do. Will you be all right if I leave you and the children here?"

"I think we'll be fine." Lila glanced at Angel, who was leaning tiredly against her older brother, her blue eyes heavy with sleep. "I know at least one of us could use a nap," she said with a smile. "And there's plenty of unpacking to do."

"I'll be back around six and we can go down to dinner. Dot may only be second best when it comes to gossip, but nobody sets a better table, at least not around here."

"That sounds nice," Lila said dutifully. The truth was, now that she'd reached the marginal sanctuary of the hotel room, she wasn't sure she had the courage to leave it again.

"Well, then, I guess I'll be on my way."

As Bishop moved toward the door, Lila was struck by an unexpected urge to grab hold of his arm and beg him not to leave her alone. He suddenly seemed like the only familiar thing in her world, the only tie to her old life. The absurdity of that thought stiffened her spine. She'd never been the sort to cling to a man, and she wasn't going to start with this husband she barely knew.

"We'll see you later," she said as he opened the door. Bishop glanced back at her, touched his fingers to the brim of his hat, and stepped out into the hall. The door shut behind him with a quiet click. Lila looked at Gavin and Angel and swallowed against a wave of panic as she realized that she was alone with them for the first time.

"Well, looks like it's just the three of us. Isn't this nice?" she said with forced cheer.

Neither of the children offered a response to that. As well they shouldn't, Lila thought, disgusted with herself. She'd sounded about as sincere as a snake oil salesman extolling the virtues of his product. Gavin was looking at her with the wariness that seemed to characterize all his dealings with adults. And Angel simply blinked sleepily in her direction and then yawned.

One thing Lila remembered from her own childhood was her utter contempt for insincerity. And no one could recognize insincerity faster than a child could. She sighed and looked at her stepchildren. Angel yawned again.

"Let's get you into bed," Lila said, using a normal tone this time.

"I'm not sleepy." The token protest was punctuated by a yawn, and the child offered no real protest when Lila took her hand and led her to the bed.

"You don't have to go to sleep," Lila assured her. "Just lie down for a little while." It was a stratagem she remembered her own mother using on her when she'd protested that she didn't need a nap. It seemed to work with Angel as well as it had with her. Angel climbed up on the edge of the bed. Yawning, one hand clutching her rag doll against her chest, she stuck out her feet for Lila to unbutton her shoes.

"You and I will sleep in here," Lila said as she unhooked the buttons and eased the little shoes off.

"Your brother and Papa will have the room next door."

"He said one room was for us and the other was for the two of you," Gavin said from behind her.

Lila cursed the accuracy of his memory as she worked the buttons that marched down the front of Angel's olive-drab dress. Over the last few days, she'd noticed that, while the children's clothing was well made, it was also dull and nearly bare of trim. "After we're settled, we're going to have to see about getting you some new dresses," she said, hoping to avoid Gavin's comment. "Something bright and pretty."

"I heard him tell Mr. Lyman that he wanted one room for him and his wife and the other for us," Gavin said again.

"Did he say that?" Lila swept Angel's dress off and draped it over the foot of the bed. The petticoats came next. Wearing her chemise and drawers, Angel crawled under the covers Lila turned back for her.

"I'm not sleepy," she insisted, her eyelids already drooping.

"Fine. You just rest your eyes a bit and then you can get up." Lila knew the child would be asleep almost as soon as her eyes closed. She brushed a golden curl back from Angel's forehead, smiling a little at the innocence of her face. It was going to be very easy to love Angel, with her sunny temperament and sweet personality.

"You know that's what he said."

Gavin, on the other hand, was not going to be as easy to deal with. Lila straightened away from the bed and arranged her expression into a pleasant smile before turning to face her stepson.

"I believe your father did say something like that, but I think this is a better arrangement. Now, why don't we take your things into the next room?" Without giving him a chance to argue, she picked up Bishop's bag, scooped the key off the dresser, and headed out the door. She heard Gavin come up behind her as she was unlocking the door to the room next door and felt a sense of relief that he hadn't simply ignored her. The relief was short-lived, however.

"You're going to have a baby, aren't you?"

Bishop's bag dropped from Lila's suddenly nerveless fingers, hitting the floor with a thump. She turned to look at the boy.

"What?"

"I heard him tell Mr. Lyman that you got married months ago. Only you didn't, did you?" His eyes were steady on her face.

If Bishop had to have two children, why couldn't they both have been Angel's age? Lila wondered distractedly. Why did one of them have to be this boy with his watchful blue eyes and his uncomfortable questions? She could lie to him, of course, but he'd probably recognize it for what it was.

"Your father and I were married recently," she admitted carefully.

"Are you going to have a baby?" he asked, pursuing his line of thinking with the ruthlessness characteristic of members of the Inquisition and the very young.

"Yes." There was no sense in denying something that would soon be obvious to anyone who cared to look.

"Is that why you married him? Because you were going to have a baby?"

Though Lila had seen the question coming, it still knocked the breath from her. Her first impulse was to tell him that he was mistaken, that her pregnancy had nothing to do with her reasons for marrying Bishop. But looking into those blue eyes, so like his father's in both color and expression, she knew that it would accomplish nothing to lie to him. Not only would he recognize it for what it was, but it would damage any chance she might have of gaining his respect, let alone his friendship.

"I don't think my reasons for marrying your father are any of your business," she said, choosing her words carefully. "What's important is that we are married and the four of us are a family now."

Gavin appeared to consider that, his expression thoughtful. Standing there, in his dark suit, his black hair mussed from taking off his hat, he looked like any other twelve-year-old boy, until she saw the maturity in his eyes. She remembered what Bishop had said about the children being unhappy with their grandparents and wondered what had happened there to make Gavin so much older than his years.

"Angel likes you," he said thoughtfully.

"I like her."

"She looks like our mother."

"Does she?" Lila felt as if she were picking her way over a sheet of thin ice. "Your mother must have been very pretty."

"She was. Angel doesn't remember her but I do."

"You must miss her," Lila said.

"Sometimes." Gavin shrugged but, for just a moment, his eyes revealed a stark grief that tore at Lila's heart. The expression was gone in an instant but she knew it hadn't been her imagination.

"I lost both my parents a few years ago. They were killed in a carriage accident. I miss them all the time."

He shot her a quick look, his eyes guarded, but his only response was another shrug.

"You're lucky to still have your father," she said, knowing that she was treading on very thin ice and curious to see his reaction. It came in the form of a quick flash of emotion, gone too fast for her to identify. Rage? Hatred?

"*He* doesn't care about us."

Lila noticed the emphasis he put on the pronoun and realized that she'd yet to hear him refer to Bishop in any other way. Angel called him Papa as easily as if she'd been living with him all her life, but Gavin referred to him only as "he." That the boy was bitter, she'd already known. But it was obvious that the gap between father and son was much wider than she'd realized.

"Did you know that your father didn't plan to bring you with us right away?" she asked him. "He'd planned to send for you later, after the baby was born. Do you know why he changed his mind?"

Gavin shrugged again, keeping his gaze on the floor between them. Lila wasn't fooled by his apparent indifference.

"He told me that you were unhappy and that was why he didn't leave you with your grandparents."

Gavin's head jerked up, his eyes wide and startled.

"Sounds to me like he cares," Lila added softly. She wasn't sure why it mattered to her whether Gavin knew that his father cared. The boy hadn't, thus far, done anything to endear himself to her, unless it was with his meticulous concern for his little sister. She just knew it was important that the boy know his father cared.

"Maybe." He looked away again, apparently unimpressed by her words, but Lila had seen the hunger in his eyes and was unimpressed by his indifference.

"I'll leave you to unpack," she said, judging it best to give him time to digest her words. "I don't know about you, but I'm almost as tired as Angel. I'm going to lie down for a little while. You might like to do the same."

She walked to the door without waiting for an answer. She had her hand on the knob when Gavin spoke from behind her.

"You're not my mother and I'm not going to call you that." There was challenge in his voice, and it was echoed in the set of his chin when she turned to look at him.

Was there no end to the problems associated with being a stepmother? Was she going to spend the rest of her life involved in diplomatic discussions with Bishop's children? She chose her words with care.

"I'm not really old enough to be your mother," she said lightly. "And I'm certainly not foolish enough to try to take her place."

Gavin looked at her uncertainly. She guessed that he'd been expecting an argument, perhaps even wanted one, and, when she didn't give it to him, he wasn't sure how to react.

"Angel is little, she may want to call you mother," he said, probing for her reaction.

"Why don't we leave that up to Angel?" Lila's mind reeled at the thought but she kept her tone casual.

"Okay." Gavin looked down, studying the toe of his shoe. Sensing that the conversation was not over, Lila waited. It didn't take him long. He looked up at her, his eyes, so like his father's, curious and not quite as wary as they had been. "What do I call you?"

Good question, Lila thought. It was something she should have considered before now.

"I guess you could call me Stepmother," she said slowly. She wrinkled her nose. "That's a bit of a mouthful, isn't it?"

Gavin nodded.

"And Mother Lila is even worse. Besides, it makes me sound like someone who should be carrying a cane and wearing thick shoes, doesn't it?"

Gavin nodded again and she caught the merest hint of a smile teasing the corners of his mouth. It was the first time she'd seen him smile at anyone other than his sister.

"Why don't we keep it simple for both of us? There are those who won't approve, but I think you should just call me Lila."

"Okay." He shrugged to show how little it mattered but she'd already seen his eyes widen in quick surprise and caught a glimpse of that almost smile again. He was going to break hearts when he was older, she thought. Just like his father.

Not that she had any intention of letting Bishop break *her* heart, she assured herself as she stepped out into the hall.

# *Chapter 8*

It seemed as if half the town's population had been struck by a sudden urge to sample Dot Lyman's cooking. Bishop hadn't thought it possible to get so many people into the hotel's dining room but, with some chairs dragged in from the lobby, a little determination, and a willingness to eat without moving their elbows, every table was filled to capacity and a bit beyond. Most of the diners made a show of being there to enjoy the food, but the more honest among them gave scant attention to the meal and concentrated instead on the real reason they'd abandoned hearth and home, which was to take a look at the sheriff's brand-new family.

Bishop shifted in his seat, uneasy at finding himself the center of so much attention. The only time he'd ever had so many people staring at him at once was in the aftermath of a shooting. Unconsciously he reached down to loosen his gun in its holster, only to remember at the last minute that he wasn't wearing a gun. Irritated, he reached for his coffee cup. Curiosity wasn't a shooting offense, he reminded himself. But he was starting to think it ought to be.

"Frowning isn't going to do any good," Lila said without looking up from the task of cutting up Angel's meat.

"The way they're acting, you'd think they'd never seen anybody eat a meal before," he muttered.

"What they've never seen is you with a family," she told him. She handed Angel her fork and checked to make sure the child's napkin was in place before looking across the table at him. "You must have known they'd be curious."

He *should* have known, Bishop thought. He'd lived in enough small towns to know that one characteristic they had in common was an unending curiosity about anyone or anything new. Six months ago, he'd come to Paris to take the job as sheriff and, for the first few weeks, every time he walked down the street, he'd been aware of people sliding sidelong glances in his direction. There had been whispered speculation about whether he was as fast with a gun as they'd heard, some half hoping they'd get a chance to see for themselves. He knew there'd been some disagreement about whether to hire him. There were those who thought that hiring a man like Bishop McKenzie would help to curb the lawless element in town and those who feared that his reputation actually would draw trouble.

As the weeks passed and he'd provided them with no spectacular displays of his skill with a gun, the townspeople had gradually lost interest. He should have realized that he couldn't expect to return from his abrupt trip East with a wife and children in tow without touching off a whole new round of interest. Well, they could be as interested as they liked, as long as they kept their distance.

"So, this is why I'm so overworked tonight," a soft voice trilled next to the table. Bishop winced. He should have known. Dot Lyman was not only a world-class gossip and a good cook, she was the only person in town who'd dared to ask him if his reputation was exaggerated and, if not, just how many gunfights had he been involved in. She'd taken his blunt refusal to answer in stride, offering neither apology nor excuse for her interest. Short and plump, she resembled her husband so much that it would be easy to think them brother and sister. Despite her predilection for minding other people's business, there was not an ounce of malice in her. She was almost childlike in her belief that everything and everyone in Paris was her personal business. It was only natural that she'd be the first to risk approaching the table.

"I didn't think it was just my cooking that was drawing a crowd," she said with a soft giggle. "Don't sit there like a bump on a log, Sheriff. Introduce me to your family."

Bishop set his napkin by his plate and rose politely. "Lila, this is Dot Lyman. Dot, this is Lila McKenzie, my wife."

"I didn't think she was one of your children." Dot giggled again and cast Bishop a teasing look. "She's pretty as a picture, Sheriff. Where have you been hiding her?"

"I've been in Pennsylvania, Mrs. Lyman. Not hidden at all," Lila said, smiling at the other woman.

"Well, this husband of yours didn't say a word to anyone about getting married when he went East a few months ago. In fact, I didn't even know he'd been married before, let alone that he had two beautiful children. And if I didn't know it, no one did," she said with simple pride. "What are their names?"

Bishop turned to perform the introductions and was surprised and pleased to see that Gavin had risen from his seat. He should have guessed that the one thing his former mother-in-law would have drummed into the children was good manners.

While Dot expressed her amazement over how tall Gavin was and how much like his father and exclaimed that Angel was the most beautiful child she'd ever seen, Bishop became aware of the sudden silence that had seized the room. Not a single fork clinked on a single plate. No one spoke. It seemed as if they barely breathed as every ear strained to hear what was being said at the corner table. Not that they had to worry about missing anything, Bishop thought cynically. Anything that was said to Dot would soon become common knowledge.

"So I understand you and Bishop were married in February when he went back East." Dot fixed Lila with a bright-eyed look, apparently deciding enough pleasantries had been observed and that it was time to get to the heart of the matter.

"That's right. He came to Pennsylvania for my brother's wedding. That's when we met."

Dot's eyes widened. "He wasn't gone more than a couple of weeks. You met *and* married in that little bit of time?"

"I swept her off her feet," Bishop said. His eyes met Lila's and he wondered if she was remembering the way he'd literally swept her off her feet the night he carried her to his bed. He thought he saw color warm her cheeks, but the light was such that it was difficult to be sure.

His comment drew Dot's attention back to him. "Oh, do sit down, Sheriff. I can't think with you looming over me like that. You too, young man." She waved a hand in Gavin's direction. She waited until they both sat and then returned her attention to Lila.

"Seems odd, you marrying in such a hurry and then staying in Pennsylvania and letting him come back to Paris alone."

"Unfortunately, there was an illness in my family that necessitated my staying in Beaton. It was not our preference, of course, but we had no choice." She spoke with such grave sincerity that Bishop found himself halfway believing her.

Dot prided herself on the delicate nature of her sensibilities, and her eyes shone with sympathetic tears. "Oh, it must have been terrible, having to part so soon after finding each other."

"It was difficult," Lila admitted. She forced a brave smile and gave Bishop such a fond look across the table that he nearly choked on the coffee he'd just swallowed. "I was fortunate to marry such an understanding man."

"Yes." Dot looked at Bishop, who tried to look understanding. He was relieved when she returned her attention to Lila. "I hope whoever was ill made a good recovery?"

"Oh, yes." Lila gave her a sunny smile. "Uncle Duke is almost good as new."

This time Bishop did choke on his coffee. Duke was the name of Douglas's favorite horse, an ill-tempered gelding who'd tried to attack a stablehand the day before the wedding and had managed to tear his own shoulder open on an exposed nail in the process. The gouge had been deep and ragged, and there had been some concern about the animal's recovery. His eyes met Lila's across the table. She returned his look with one of such bland innocence that he nearly laughed out loud. For the first time since the wedding, they were completely in charity with one another.

Dot was called back to her kitchen soon after that, but, as if she'd broken through some invisible barrier that had been keeping everyone at bay, others began to approach the table, asking to meet the sheriff's new family. After the easy way she'd handled Dot, Bishop knew Lila didn't need his help, so he made the introductions and then sat back and watched his wife charm everyone who came near.

He shouldn't have been surprised by her easy handling of the situation, he thought. After all, she'd acted as Douglas's hostess from the time she was old enough to let her skirts down and put her hair up. Douglas had once told him that, if he made it to Congress, it would be thanks in no small part to Lila's ability to charm even the crustiest of politicians. Watching the way she dealt with the citizenry of Paris, Colorado, Bishop could believe it.

This was the girl he'd met three months ago, the one whose eyes had sparkled with such invitation that all thoughts of honor and friendship had faded before the need to possess her. She'd been wearing green that night too, he remembered. That gown had been cut low across the bosom, the dark silk a potent contrast to the milky whiteness of her skin. He remembered the sound of the delicate fabric tearing beneath his impatient fingers and the sound of Lila's breathless laugh as he stripped the gown from her.

Bishop shifted uncomfortably in his seat and forced his thoughts back to the present. The poised woman sitting across from him seemed a far cry from the spoiled girl he'd met three months ago. Which one was she? Was she the girl who'd bewitched him or the woman sitting across from him dispensing charm with easy grace?

Whichever it was, he wanted her, had wanted her from the moment he'd seen her. Now she was his. No matter what the circumstances of their marriage, she was his wife now. And tonight they'd make their marriage real in every sense of the word.

"You did what?" Bishop watched in disbelief as Lila shooed Angel through the door ahead of her and then turned to face him. They'd finished their meal and come upstairs to their rooms. This was the first time he'd heard about the distribution of those rooms.

"It seemed the best arrangement," she said calmly. "I put Angel in my room and Gavin in yours."

"That wasn't what I had in mind."

"Perhaps we should discuss this in the morning," Lila said, acutely aware that Gavin stood listening, his too-old eyes knowing.

"We'll discuss it now." Bishop's eyes cut to his son. "Go to bed."

The boy cast one last look in Lila's direction, but the light wasn't strong enough for her to tell whether there was sympathy or a simple I-told-you-so in his eyes. She waited until the door closed behind him before speaking to Bishop.

"This is the arrangement we had in St. Louis and again last night in Denver City."

He was silent for a moment, his eyes shadowed and watchful on her face. Lila did her best to look unperturbed. She'd known this moment was coming, but that didn't mean she felt ready for it. Bishop was an unknown quantity. She didn't know what to expect from him. The silence stretched until she could stand it no longer.

"Angel isn't old enough to take care of herself yet. Do you want to help her undress for bed?" she asked, arching one slim brow in question.

"Help her . . ." Bishop glanced past her at the door, which she'd left open a crack. Help that fragile-looking little girl undress for bed? He'd rather skin a live rattlesnake. "No, I don't."

"I didn't think so. And I doubt if you want to help her get dressed in the morning or supervise her baths either." Lila's mouth quirked with humor at the look of horror that passed across his face. "It's not fair to expect Gavin to do it. That's why Angel and I are in one room and you and Gavin are in the other."

Bishop stared at her, frustrated but unable to argue with her reasoning. He hadn't given any thought to the fact that a child as young as Angel was going to need care beyond the basics of seeing that she had something to eat and a place to sleep. This wasn't the way he'd planned to end the evening. Reasonable or no, he knew there was more to this arrangement than practicality.

"I'll see about renting a house tomorrow," he said, giving grudging approval to the arrangements.

"That will be lovely," she said with bright insincerity.

Looking at her, Bishop nearly groaned with frustration. He didn't plan on spending the rest of his life sharing a room with his son. And he sure as hell didn't plan on this marriage being one in name only, even if Lila seemed content to keep it that way. Maybe it was time to remind her of what it was that had gotten them into this situation in the first place.

Lila had already started to turn away, and she squeaked with surprise when Bishop's hand closed around the back of her neck, turning her back toward him. She caught a glimpse of his vivid blue eyes, their expression mixing cool determination with a warm hunger that made her stomach clench with sudden awareness. She put her hands to his chest but then his mouth came down on hers and she forgot to push him away.

She'd spent weeks telling herself it had been the champagne that had made her forget all about right and wrong, that had made her go to his room on a trumped-up excuse to satisfy her curiosity. Just once in her life, she'd wanted to know what it felt like to kiss a man like Bishop McKenzie—someone wild and dangerous; someone who didn't think of her as Douglas Adams's sister or Margaret Adams's daughter or Billy Sinclair's fiancée. She'd convinced herself that it was champagne and curiosity that had caused her downfall.

With one kiss, Bishop proved her a liar. She might have had too much champagne that night and she'd certainly been curious, but what had driven her to follow him to his room had been something more elemental than either of those things.

The gentle scrape of Bishop's mustache was an intriguing contrast to the softness of his mouth. She was going to push him away, of course, Lila told herself. But she didn't have to hurry. Safe in the knowledge that, with Angel waiting, this could go no further than a kiss, she allowed herself to feel the hunger that was slowly uncoiling in the pit of her stomach.

He slid his hand upward from her nape, his fingers burrowing into her hair, wreaking havoc with the heavy knot into which she'd labored to wind it before dinner. His other hand flattened against her lower back. Lila's skirts rustled as he drew her close against his body. He changed the angle of the kiss, his mouth hardening over hers. She felt her knees go weak as his tongue stroked across her lower lip, demanding a response she was helpless to deny. With a soft sigh of surrender, she opened her mouth to him, welcoming the demanding thrust of his tongue, hungry for the taste of him. Her fingers curled into the crisp white fabric of his shirt front, clinging to him as the world dipped and spun around her.

This was what she'd tried so hard to forget. Not just the passion but the feeling of completeness, as if a part of her that had been missing all her life had suddenly been found. The feeling was as exhilarating as it was terrifying.

She was all but melting in his arms when he broke off the kiss. He stepped back as she opened her eyes and stared at him, feeling almost dizzy at the abruptness of his withdrawal.

"You can't hide behind the children forever," he told her, his voice holding a ragged edge.

Lila watched, dazed, as he turned and walked away. She was still standing there when the door to his room shut with a quiet click.

# Chapter 9

Lila shepherded Gavin and Angel through the lobby of the Lyman Hotel, nodding to Clem Lyman who stood behind the desk watching their departure with unabashed interest. She was careful not to pause long enough for him to engage her in conversation. The last thing she wanted to do was get involved in a conversation with the hotelkeeper. She had too many secrets in her life to be comfortable talking to the "second biggest gossip" in town. The sooner Bishop found a house for them, the better.

Although that was hardly without its hazards. Her cheeks warmed as she remembered the night before and the incendiary kiss they'd shared. Standing in a public hallway of all places! If anyone had seen them ... The thought was enough to make her shudder. She'd had a mostly sleepless night to consider what had happened, and she still couldn't understand how she'd so far forgotten herself as to kiss him back. Not only kiss him but to cling to him like ivy to a wall.

"I don't see why I have to go to some stuffy old store." Gavin's complaint provided a welcome distraction from her thoughts.

"Because it's the best place to meet people," Lila told him as they stepped onto the boardwalk in front of the hotel.

"I don't want to meet people." Gavin was very definite about that.

"Yes, you do." Lila unfurled her parasol as protection against the bright spring sunshine. "If Paris is going to be our home, it behooves us to make the acquaintance of the people among whom we'll be living," she told the boy. She'd decided that the best way to handle her stepson was to treat him like the adult he seemed to so nearly be. She certainly wouldn't get anywhere treating him as a child. "We need to make a place for ourselves, perhaps make a few friends."

"I don't need friends," he muttered, scowling out at the nearly empty street.

"Nonsense. Everyone needs friends. You must have had some friends back in St. Louis. Boys you went to school with? Perhaps you visited their homes or they visited yours?" She was probing deliberately, trying to get a picture of what their life had been like.

"I had a tutor. Grandmother wouldn't have let us bring anyone home anyway. Nor visit them. She said she didn't want to risk us coming in contact with the wrong sort of people and exposing our bad blood." The look he gave her was defiantly casual, but there was a flicker of pain in the back of his eyes.

Lila's fingers tightened over the handle of her parasol until it was a wonder the finely polished wood didn't crack under the pressure. She'd been taught to respect her elders. It was a tenet she certainly expected to pass on to her own children and, inasmuch as she'd found herself in charge of Bishop's children, she intended to teach them the same. But there were limits.

"Your grandmother sounds like a remarkably stupid woman," she said crisply. "If I believed in bad blood, which I do not, I would have to say that the only bad blood you should be concerned about is what you might have inherited from her. I count it as a great pity that I'm not able to give her a piece of my mind."

Gavin's eyes grew round with shock, and he stared at her as if seeing her for the first time. No doubt she should feel guilty for corrupting an innocent young mind, Lila thought, but she couldn't conjure up any feeling of guilt. Louise Linton sounded like a positively horrible woman, and she was suddenly, quite fiercely glad that Bishop hadn't left the children with her.

She fixed Gavin with a stern look. "I don't ever want to hear mention of bad blood again. Do you understand me?"

He goggled at her a moment longer in silence and then swallowed hard. "Yes, ma'am."

"Good. Now, let's go see what this town has to offer. The mercantile is generally a good place to start. Not for merchandise so much as for information and for meeting people."

"I don't see why you expect to meet people at a store," Gavin said.

"Because people tend to gather in such places. Besides, I want to purchase some ribbon to brighten up your sister's gowns." Glancing down at Angel, Lila frowned at the starkly simple dress the child wore. The robin's egg blue muslin certainly suited her delicate coloring and the quality was above reproach, but that was all the gown had to recommend it. "They're much too plain for a child her age."

"I like ribbons," Angel said, giving Lila a smile of dazzling sweetness.

"Do you?" Lila brushed her free hand over the little girl's golden curls. If Gavin presented something of a puzzle, Angel was simplicity itself. Lila couldn't imagine a child who was easier to love.

"Red ribbons," Angel suggested. "And some for Cassandra too." She held up the simple rag doll that was her constant companion.

"Red?" Lila winced at the thought of trimming the blue dress with red ribbons. "How about red ribbons for Cassandra and maybe some rosy pink ones for you?"

Angel's delicate chin firmed. "I like red," she said, showing the streak of stubbornness that Lila had seen a time or two before.

"We'll see what they have," she said diplomatically. Hopefully she'd be able to persuade Angel to accept a more suitable color. If not . . . She shuddered at the image of red ribbons on robin's egg blue. "Come along now."

She took Angel's hand in hers as they stepped off

the boardwalk and into the dusty street. This second view of Paris was no more impressive than the first. The Frenchman who'd named the town must have been unbearably homesick or remarkably optimistic. This collection of frame buildings fronting onto a dirt street bore no resemblance to the famed City of Lights that she could see.

There was a bell over the door of Fitch's General Store, and its cheery jangle announced their entrance. Lila paused just inside to let her eyes adjust. After the crisp sunlight outside, the interior of the store seemed dim. Fitch's looked much as she'd expected. It wasn't as polished and tidy as the mercantile back home nor was it as organized. Stacks of canned goods mingled with bolts of cloth and a display of men's hats similar to the one Bishop wore. There was a potbelly stove in the center of the store. No fire burned within it today but she guessed that, during the colder months, it would offer much-needed warmth. Winters in these mountains must be difficult, she thought, repressing a small shiver.

Also as she'd expected, there were a goodly number of customers in the store. There was a man paying for his purchases at the counter, two elderly gentlemen hunched over a checkerboard next to the cold stove, and three women standing beside a table that held bolts of fabric stacked in colorful disarray. Behind the counter was a tall, thin man of indeterminate age.

A profound silence followed the bell's announcement of their arrival. All eyes turned toward the door, and the newcomers were examined in minute detail. Lila felt Gavin edge a little closer to her and bit back a sympathetic smile. As the daughter and sister of politicians, she was somewhat accustomed to being the focus of all eyes. But even for her it was not comfortable. For a child who'd never even attended school, it must be an alarming experience. But apparently not for Angel. Looking around the store and finding all eyes on her, she blessed her audience with a singularly sweet smile.

"I want a red ribbon," she announced, confident that everyone else would find this information as interesting as she did.

Lila couldn't have come up with any better way to break the ice if she'd planned it. The laughter that followed her announcement put an end to the awkward moment. Mr. Fitch, for that's who was behind the counter, assured her that he could provide her with all the red ribbons she could possibly want. The two old men gave rusty-sounding chuckles and then returned their attention to their checker game, and the burly man who'd been paying for his purchases immediately added a handful of stick candy to his order and presented it to Gavin and Angel. "With your permission, ma'am," he said, looking at Lila.

"It's very kind of you," she said, smiling at him. She was not yet accustomed to having people look to her to make decisions regarding the children. With time, she would surely lose the urge to look over her shoulder to see to whom they might be speaking.

As Gavin and Angel went to the counter to get their candy, the three women abandoned the yard goods and approached Lila. She immediately recognized Dot Lyman, her plump figure wrapped in a heavily decorated gown of rose-colored muslin. The garment sported so many rows of tucking and so much lace and ribbon trim that she looked like nothing so much as an animated notions counter.

"It's good to see you again, Mrs. McKenzie," she said as they neared. The genuine pleasure in her greeting made Lila feel guilty for her uncharitable thoughts. "I hope you're well rested? Traveling is so tiring, isn't it? Though how just sitting can tire one out is something I've never understood."

"I slept very well," Lila assured her untruthfully. After all, her lack of sleep had nothing to do with the accommodations. "Thank you for asking. Your establishment is very comfortable."

"Thank you," Dot actually blushed with pleasure at the compliment. "Clem and I do our best. Of course, we can't compete with the fine hotels back East. Not that there's much call for that kind of thing here. Most of our clientele asks for nothing more than a roof over their heads and a reasonably clean bed. But we—"

"Really, Dorothy, I doubt Mrs. McKenzie is interested in hearing about the problems of running a hotel." The woman who spoke was nearly as tall as Lila but outweighed her by at least forty pounds. The extra weight did not make her look plump and cuddly the way it did Dot Lyman. Instead, it gave her a certain imposing presence, an impression accentuated by the elegant severity of the steel-gray dress she wore. The contrast between its stark simplicity and the fussiness of Dot's gown was almost painful to see.

"Of course she's not." Dot's fair skin flushed painfully. "I don't know what got into me that I should ramble on like that. I guess it's just the surprise, you know. Having Sheriff McKenzie turn up with a family when we didn't even know he'd been married, not just once, but twice. I don't usually forget myself like that and ramble on about nothing," she said, oblivious to the fact that she was doing just that.

The woman who'd spoken before drew a sharp breath, no doubt preparatory to blasting poor Dot for her foolishness, but the third woman spoke first.

"Don't worry about it, Dot. Your rambling makes for pleasanter listening than some folks' careful speeches." Traces of Ireland gave a lilt to her voice, and her hazel eyes were a warm and friendly contrast to the first woman's icy displeasure. "Remember, Sara, patience is a virtue. Besides, it's not as if Mrs. McKenzie is going to disappear on us, now is she? There's plenty of time for introductions."

The gentle reproach made Sara's mouth tighten into a thin line, but it was the fact that she accepted the reproach that Lila found interesting. Calmed, Dot was able to perform the introductions with laudable economy.

The tall, dark-haired woman with the cold eyes and tight mouth was Sara Smythe. "With a 'y,' " she clarified in icy tones. Her husband was Franklin Smythe—also with a "y," Lila presumed. He owned the Bank of Paris, Dot said in tones of proper respect. Aware of Sara's watchful eyes, Lila did her best to look impressed.

The other woman was Bridget Sunday. She was barely five feet tall and so fine boned that she looked as if a strong wind might blow her over. Until you looked at her face, that is. There was so much life in her expression, so much laughter in her eyes that any impression of fragility immediately vanished. Her hair was unabashedly carrot red, and there was a smatter-

ing of frankly unfashionable freckles across her nose.
There was a kind of earthy charm about her that
made it hard to picture her as the wife of a minister,
but that's what she was.

"Minister Sunday," she said, wrinkling her freckled
nose. "Can you imagine it? I told Joseph that it was
downright embarrassing to have a name like that and
go into the ministry. Better to be a bank robber, I
said, but he didn't listen to me. So here we are."

Lila chuckled, delighted by the other woman's
sense of humor. Sara's mouth tightened further still,
something Lila wouldn't have believed possible.

"A calling to the ministry is a gift from God," she
said repressively. "I hardly think one can compare it
to robbing banks."

"I've no doubt there are bank robbers who consider their profession something of a calling," Bridget
said imperturbably. "Isn't that why we've hired Sheriff McKenzie? To protect us from folks with that kind
of thinking?"

"Humpf." Sara's snort was a masterpiece of genteel
disdain. "I never did approve of hiring a gunfighter.
Seems to me there's a risk of finding you've asked the
fox to guard the henhouse. No offense meant, Mrs.
McKenzie," she added with barely perfunctory concern.

Lila had known more than a few women like Sara
Smythe. They frequently organized charitable com-
mittees, a laudable occupation in itself but one they
took on more to allow them to exercise their bullying
personalities than because of genuine civic concern.
It had been her experience that it was better to set
them back on their heels at the outset rather than to
let them think they could run roughshod over you.

Not to mention that she hadn't been raised to stand idlly by while someone insulted her husband.

"What is it I shouldn't be offended by?" Lila asked, arching one dark brow in question. "The reference to my husband being a gunfighter or the implication that he might have criminal tendencies?"

It was said with such a pleasant smile that it took a moment for the other women to realize what she'd said. Out of the corner of her eye, Lila saw Dot's mouth drop open and saw Bridget's eyes widen in surprise, but she kept her attention solely on Sara. The older woman couldn't have looked more shocked if a lamppost had addressed her.

"I . . . Well, I simply meant that . . . I didn't mean to imply . . ." Sara caught herself in midsputter. Taking a deep breath, she drew herself up to her full height, which was still an inch or more shy of Lila's. "Naturally, I didn't mean to suggest that Sheriff McKenzie's ethics weren't above reproach," she said with careful dignity. "If I implied otherwise, I sincerely apologize."

She knew exactly what she'd implied, Lila thought. What's more, she'd meant every word of it. Whether she actually believed Bishop was less than honest was another question, but, at the very least, she'd hoped to make Lila uncomfortable. Lila wondered how much Sara liked finding the shoe on the other foot. Under other circumstances, she might have nodded coolly and made her departure. But this was her home for the foreseeable future, and, in a town this size, it would be foolish to begin a feud the day after her arrival.

She softened her smile and allowed the chill to fade

from her eyes. "Perhaps I'm overly sensitive," she said. "We've had so little time together and you know how new brides can be."

Her response gave Sara a way to save face, which was more than she deserved. Lila could see that knowledge in her eyes, along with a new wariness as the other woman considered the idea that she might have underestimated her. There was a moment's silence as the two of them weighed and measured each other. It was Sara who looked away first.

"I really must be going," she said, glancing at her companions. "I have a great many things to do today. It was a pleasure meeting you, Mrs. McKenzie. We must have tea together."

"That would be lovely," Lila said, sounding so sincere that she nearly believed it herself.

"Lovely." Sara's thin mouth twitched in a smile that didn't reach her eyes.

"I'll go with you," Dot said. She nodded to the other two women, eyes darting nervously across Lila's face as she hurried after Sara. The door shut behind them with a crisp jangle of bells.

Lila looked uncertainly at Bridget Sunday, wondering if she'd offended the minister's wife. To her relief, Bridget's eyes sparkled with amusement.

"I didn't think I'd live to see the day when someone would set Sara Smythe back on her heels."

"That wasn't my intention," Lila said, a little uneasy now that the moment was past.

"Not to worry." Bridget waved one small hand in airy dismissal. "She earned it. And I've no doubt it did her a world of good into the bargain. She's a tendency to run roughshod over anyone who'll let her.

It won't do her any harm to be brought up short. As my husband would say, a bit of humility never hurt anyone."

"I'm not sure Mrs. Lyman agrees," Lila said, remembering the uneasy look Dot had given her as she departed in Sara's wake.

"Don't you be worrying about Dot. She'll come around. She's a good soul but she's been playing fart catcher to Sara for so long, it's hard for her to think on her own. Oh, my!" She slapped one hand to her mouth, her eyes rounding with horror above it as if she'd just realized what she'd said.

Lila stared at her, shock warring with amusement. "I don't believe I've ever heard that particular phrase before," she said, struggling to keep her tone level.

"It's a horrid old saying my granda used to use." Bridget pressed her hands to her cheeks as if to cool their heat. "If Joseph knew I'd said such a thing, I'd never hear the end of it. Though it is true," she added, with a quick spurt of mischief. "I swear, Dot hardly dares to take a breath without asking Sara's permission. And you can be sure that she tells Sara every bit of rumor she hears so beware what you say to her."

"Bishop said she was the second biggest gossip this side of Julesburg and that her husband was the biggest."

Bridget's chuckle was warm and rich, seeming almost too big for a woman her size. "I always knew Sheriff McKenzie was a man of great sense. And he's confirmed it by marrying a fine, sensible woman such as yourself." She linked her arm through Lila's in an impulsive gesture of friendship. "Introduce me to these two children of his. I've heard tell the little girl's as pretty as her name and that the boy is the spittin' image of his da. I'd have thought the good Lord would be breaking the mold after making a handsome devil like your husband. He certainly should have anyway, to be protecting vulnerable female hearts."

Lila allowed herself to be led over the counter where the children were waiting after having selected their candy. Though it should have been too soon to tell, she knew she'd found a friend in Bridget Sunday.

Nearly a week after her arrival in Paris, Lila was reasonably pleased with the progress she'd made toward establishing a place for herself and the children in the little town. She was still considered an outsider, of course. That was something only time would change. But she'd made the acquaintance of most of the townspeople and had been, for the most part, welcomed. She had even managed to have tea with Sara Smythe without either of them saying a single sharp word to the other—a not-insignificant accomplishment, considering their first meeting.

Not that they were ever likely to become friends, Lila thought as she walked past Fitch's General Store. But they might manage to remain civil acquaintances, as long as they didn't spend too much time in each other's company.

Just as she might have guessed, Sara was the driving force behind the Women's Charitable Fund of Paris, an organization that seemed to be dedicated less to dispensing charity than it was to sponsoring the aggrandizement of the small mining town. At the moment, the fund was trying to raise money to install marble pillars in front of the Bank of Paris. The absurdity of attaching a pseudo-Greek façade to the squat little building apparently escaped Sara, who'd solemnly explained that beautification of one's surroundings was an important step toward improving the moral tone of a community. The fact that her husband happened to own the bank didn't seem to strike her as a conflict of interest, but the idea might have occurred to others because, after three years, the charitable fund was still woefully short of having the required amount. Sara had admitted as much in the disgruntled tone of a great leader whose followers were proving annoyingly slowwitted.

Thinking of it two days later was enough to make Lila's mouth curve in a smile as she stepped through the door of the hotel. She paused to allow her eyes to adjust to the dimly lit lobby.

"Afternoon, Miz McKenzie." Clem Lyman greeted her from his usual post behind the lobby desk. Lila couldn't imagine what he found to occupy his time. Certainly the hotel was not so overrun with guests as to require his presence at all times. On the other hand, the lobby, with its big windows fronting onto the street, offered as good a place as any to keep tabs on the town's comings and goings.

"Good afternoon, Mr. Lyman." Lila's greeting was friendly. Despite their predilection for gossip, she'd come to like both the Lymans. There was something almost childlike about their eagerness to know—and share—everyone's business. "It's a lovely day, isn't it?"

"It is, at that," he agreed with a smile. "You're looking lovely yourself, if you don't mind my saying so."

"Have you ever known a woman to mind being told she was lovely?"

His smile widened into a grin. "Now that you mention it, can't say that I have. Where are the children?" he asked, looking past her as if expecting to see them dawdling behind.

"They're at Mrs. Sunday's. They were having such a nice time playing with her children that she offered to let them stay."

"Gives you a bit of a break, doesn't it?"

"It does that." Lila struggled to keep from sounding too appreciative of the break but it wasn't easy. She'd become very fond of Angel this past week and she thought that Gavin was even starting to thaw toward her a bit, but she couldn't deny that the thought of a few hours alone sounded like sheer heaven. And Bridget knew it, God bless her. Her offer to keep the children had been as much for Lila's sake as theirs.

"With my five, two more won't make a bit of difference," she'd insisted. "They'll have a splendid time and it'll give you some time to yourself. If you can't make use of it, then you're not as smart as I think you are."

Lila knew exactly how to make use of this unexpected gift of privacy. One thing she'd learned about children was that they made long, hot baths a near impossibility. She just didn't have that much time to herself. "If it wouldn't be too much trouble, Mr. Lyman, I'd like to have a bath brought up to my room."

He pondered her request a moment, his round face thoughtful. Just when she was wondering if begging would help, Clem nodded his head.

"I reckon we could manage that. Take a little time to heat the water, but, if you don't mind waiting, I'll see to it."

"I don't mind waiting," she assured him, trying not

to look too pathetically grateful. "Mrs. Sunday has invited Mr. McKenzie and me to join her family for dinner tonight and she's keeping the children until then, so I have plenty of time." She was turning away from the desk as she spoke, eager to go to her room and make preparations for her bath.

"That reminds me, the sheriff was here looking for you a little bit ago."

"Was it anything important?" Lila asked, turning back to look at him. Bishop hadn't exactly been seeking out her company these past few days. Other than dinner each night in the hotel dining room, they'd barely seen one another, which suited her just fine. She wasn't sure who was avoiding whom and didn't really care as long as they were successful. He created too many conflicting emotions, made her feel things she didn't want to feel, remember things she didn't want to remember.

"Didn't say what it was about," Clem admitted with obvious disappointment. "But he seemed a bit perturbed when he couldn't find you. Said to tell you to wait for him here."

"He did, did he?" Lila's eyebrows rose. *Wait for him here?* Was there no limits to his arrogance that he thought he could simply ask someone else to pass on his instructions and she'd jump to obey? Her first impulse was to march right out of the hotel. Never mind that she didn't have anywhere else to go, she simply didn't want to be there when Bishop arrived.

"Still want that bath?" Clem asked, apparently reading something of her thoughts.

"Of course." Lila forced a surprised smile. She wasn't going to let Bishop spoil her little treat. No doubt there'd be other opportunities to make it clear that he couldn't expect to snap his fingers and have her jumping to obey. In fact, she was willing to bet that there would be frequent opportunities for such demonstrations. "Just bring the water upstairs when it's ready."

And if the water wasn't hot enough, she probably could set it steaming all on her own, she thought as she climbed the stairs. She'd give Bishop a piece of her mind just as soon as she saw him. He needed to understand that there were some things she simply would not tolerate.

# Chapter 10

He was going to have to explain to Lila the way things were around here, Bishop thought as he stalked down the hallway. Checking back at the hotel had been his last stop before he started tearing the whole damned town apart to find her. For the last few days, he'd kept an eye on her as she made the town's acquaintance. Since the jail was located in the center of the main street, it hadn't been difficult to track her comings and goings.

This afternoon, for example, he'd glanced out the window in time to see her and the children go into Fitch's. Since he was sitting at his desk doing paperwork, it would have been simple enough to keep an eye out and see where she went from there.

Or it would have been if he hadn't been called to settle a dispute between two of the patrons of the Red Lady Saloon. The disagreement had begun over the worn favors of one of the girls who worked the upstairs rooms. It had started with harsh words and soon advanced to an exchange of blows, an event that wouldn't have been brought to his attention if it had ended there. But when it escalated to knives, the bartender had sent someone to get the sheriff.

By the time Bishop arrived on the scene, one of the men had his opponent pinned to the floor and was about to cut his throat. If he hadn't felt it necessary to pause to enjoy the terror in his victim's eyes, he would have succeeded. But his delay gave Bishop time to rap the butt of his pistol up against the side of his head, ending the fight in a summary manner. He'd hauled both men to jail and tossed them in a cell to give them time to contemplate the error of their ways.

Incidents like this were common enough that they hardly rated a mention in the *Paris Examiner*. Bishop wouldn't have thought anything of it if it hadn't been for the fact that, while he was dealing with the quarrelsome miners, Lila had managed to disappear.

This wasn't Pennsylvania, where she'd been able to do whatever she liked. This was a mining town in the midst of the far-from-tamed West. There were dangers here she probably couldn't even imagine. Not the least of those dangers was his own desire to shake her until her teeth rattled, he thought grimly.

After unlocking the door of the room Lila and Angel had been using, he pushed it open and stepped inside. At first glance, the room seemed empty. The bed was neatly made, one of Lila's dresses laid out across it; a pair of Angel's tiny shoes sat next to the single chair, the toes turned at drunken angles; but there was no sign of the room's occupants. But Clem had said Lila was there so, unless she'd slipped down the back stairs to avoid going through the lobby, she had to be there. That being the case, there was only one place to look, he thought, fixing his attention on the screen that blocked off one corner of the room. He started toward it.

Bishop had heard it said that cleanliness was next to godliness. He didn't feel qualified to speak to the holiness of it, but there was certainly something to be said for the sheer beauty of a naked woman sitting in a tub full of water. Even if her eyes were spitting fire.

"You!" Lila put more venom into the single word than most men could put into a string of profanity.

"Were you expecting someone else?"

"When I heard the door open without the courtesy of a knock, I didn't know what to expect," she said pointedly. "I assumed it was a criminal of some sort."

"And you figured the best place to greet him was in the tub?" He lifted one booted foot and set it on the edge of the tub for emphasis.

"I thought it best to remain quiet and hope the ruffian would go away," Lila said stiffly.

"Didn't work, did it?"

"Obviously not."

Using the side of one thumb, Bishop tipped his hat back on his head and let his eyes roam over as much of her as was visible, which was not nearly as much as he would have liked. The tub was not long enough to allow her to stretch out, and her updrawn knees concealed most of her upper body from him. Only her shoulders and the creamy upper slopes of her breasts were visible. Still, it was enough to set a man to thinking.

"Didn't it strike you as odd that this 'ruffian' had a key?" It was an effort to drag his gaze back to her face. She was glaring at him.

"Certainly. But it didn't seem likely that a gentleman would enter a lady's room without so much as a knock."

"I think I told you once before that I never claimed to be a gentleman. And, in case you've forgotten, we *are* married. I'd guess that gives me the right to open a door without knocking now and again. You *do* remember that we're married, don't you?"

"Of course." Lila had to swallow to get the words out. There was something about the way he was looking at her that made it difficult to speak. She was suddenly, vividly aware of the vulnerability of her position. "If you don't mind, I'd like to get up now."

She realized immediately that she'd said the wrong thing.

Bishop's crooked grin confirmed it for her. "I don't mind a bit. Want me to hold a towel for you?" he offered obligingly.

Lila closed her eyes for a moment, her teeth grinding together. It was a wonder the water didn't start to boil around her. But it didn't. In fact, it was rapidly going from tepid to downright chilly. She opened her eyes and looked at him. His elbow rested on his knee as he leaned toward her, and he didn't look as if he had any intention of going anywhere. With his hat tipped back, the faintest hint of a smile visible beneath his dark mustache, and his blue eyes gleaming with amusement—at her expense!—he was wickedly attractive. Damn him.

"What I want is for you to go away and allow me to get dressed in privacy," she said, her tone stiff with annoyance.

"I guess that would be the gentlemanly thing to do, wouldn't it?" Bishop drawled.

"Yes, it would."

There was a moment's taut silence while their eyes warred with one another. She couldn't force him to do as she asked, and he knew it. Legally and, some would say, morally, he had every right to stay where he was and watch her rise stark naked from her bath. Lila's stomach clenched at the thought. She told herself it was anger and resentment, but she couldn't deny a tiny thread of dark excitement at the thought of standing naked before him.

"Don't take too long," Bishop said, just when she thought he was never going to speak again. He straightened, dropping his foot from the edge of the tub, and disappeared around the other side of the screen, leaving Lila sitting in her cold bath, telling herself that what she felt was relief, not disappointment.

He was a fool, Bishop told himself as he listened to the splashing sounds coming from behind the screen as Lila left her bath. A damned fool, he amended as she whisked the soft linen towel from where it had been draped across the screen. He should have scooped her out of that tub and carried her to the bed and put an end to this waiting once and for all. She'd been hiding behind the children long enough.

"Where *are* the children?" he asked.

"Bridget Sunday is looking after them this afternoon," Lila's voice came from behind the screen. "She has children their age. They've invited us to have dinner with them this evening. I told them we'd be delighted to join them."

"At the minister's house?" Bishop considered that idea. He had a nodding acquaintance with Joseph Sunday and his family, but he'd certainly never pictured himself sitting down to dinner with the man. He'd generally found it more comfortable to keep a bit of distance between himself and men of the cloth. They had a nasty tendency to want to lecture him on the error of his ways. "Is that where you disappeared to this afternoon?"

"I didn't disappear. I met Bridget at Fitch's and she suggested that the children and I spend the afternoon with her family. We've become quite good friends." Lila's voice was a bit breathless, as if she were busy doing something that took a bit of effort. Drying herself perhaps? The thought of her running a linen towel over her soft skin made Bishop's mouth go dry, and it took him a moment to hear the rest of what she said. "They're nice people and I think it's a chance for the children to make friends. According to Gavin, that wasn't something their grandmother encouraged. She actually told them that she didn't want to risk them coming into contact with someone who might bring out their bad blood."

The anger in her voice made his mouth twist in a half smile even as he felt a renewed pang of guilt for having left Gavin and Angel in his mother-in-law's not-so-tender care.

"I told them, if they were going to worry about bad blood, it should be hers," Lila said, sounding defiant and just a little guilty. "I probably shouldn't have spoken ill of her but, really, any woman who would tell two innocent children such absolute rot doesn't deserve to have them respect her. I'm just sorry I won't have the opportunity to tell her so to her face."

Bishop found himself more than a little sorry too. That would have been something to see. He had a feeling that Louise would have found she'd met her match in Lila Adams McKenzie.

"You've been very good with the children," he said slowly. The acknowledgment was overdue.

Lila had been tying the belt of her robe but her fingers abruptly fumbled in the simple task. There was something approaching warmth in his voice, something she hadn't heard much of in their brief acquaintance. The sound of it melted the last traces of her anger at the way he'd intruded on her bath. It was difficult to stay angry with him when he was thanking her.

"If I let . . . circumstances affect my behavior toward them, I'd be no better than their grandmother." She finished belting her robe and patted her hand over her hair to make sure it was still confined in the loose knot on top of her head. She would have preferred to be fully dressed before facing him again, but her clothes were on the other side of the screen and she didn't think it wise to ask Bishop to leave the room so this would just have to do. The robe covered everything her dress would have done, she told herself.

"They're very nice children," she said as she came around the screen. "It isn't hard to be—good heavens, what on earth are you doing with those?"

Bishop had been standing to one side of the window, watching the activity on the street below. He responded to the shock in Lila's voice more than her words, spinning away from the window to see what was the matter. He scanned the room quickly but there was nothing out of the ordinary. Nothing but her standing next to the screen looking at him as if he'd suddenly grown horns and a tail.

"What's wrong?" he snapped.

"Those things." She pointed an accusing finger at him. "Why are you wearing them."

"My guns?" Bishop asked incredulously. His right hand dropped to the butt of the Colt.38 he wore on his hip. "Is that what you're talking about?"

"Yes. Why are you wearing them?"

"I usually wear them."

"I've never seen you do so," she said flatly. She gave the weapons a look of acute distaste.

That didn't seem possible. The Colts were as much a part of what he wore as his boots and his hat. But when Bishop thought about it, he realized that she probably hadn't seen him with his guns on. He always took them off before taking her and the children down to dinner, and, apart from that one meal each day, they'd barely set eyes on each other. But even if this was the first time she'd seen *him* wearing guns, that didn't mean it was the first time she'd seen *anyone* wearing them.

"Most of the men in Paris wear guns," he said.

"I had noticed that and I thought it was extraordinary that you allowed them to do so."

"Allowed them?" Bishop's brows rose.

"Yes, allowed them." She jerked her belt tighter with a quick, nervous gesture. "You're the sheriff.

Why don't you tell them they can't go around wearing guns?"

"I could, I suppose," he said slowly. "Of course, I'd probably find myself on the wrong side of a lynching party."

"You can't be serious!" Lila's eyes widened in disbelief. Her shocked reaction reminded Bishop of why he'd come here in the first place and rekindled the anger he'd felt when he hadn't been able to find her earlier.

"This isn't Pennsylvania. Things are different here."

"I don't believe they're so different that grown men need to arm themselves in order to walk down the street."

"Whether they need to or not, there's no law that says they can't, and it would be more than my life is worth to try and tell them otherwise," he said bluntly. "This is Colorado, and the people walking the streets out there aren't the shopkeepers and businessmen you used to know in Beaton."

"I don't see that they're all that different." Lila restrained the urge to sniff in disbelief. She'd heard so much about how "different" things were in the west, first from Douglas and Susan and now from Bishop. But as far as she could see, other than being dustier and somewhat less endowed with cultural amenities, Paris wasn't all that different from Beaton. People were much the same, no matter what part of the country you were in. "Mr. Fitch doesn't seem that different than Mr. Miller who ran the mercantile in Beaton."

Bishop saw the stubborn set of her chin and knew

she still didn't understand. "What do you think your Mr. Miller would do if two men tried to rob his store? Give them what they wanted and then call for the law to deal with them?"

"I can't speak for Mr. Miller but it seems a reasonable reaction," Lila said stiffly.

"Six months ago, two miners came down out of the hills." Bishop spoke rapidly, hoping to make her understand. "They hadn't made the big strike they thought they deserved and they were feeling a little out of sorts. They did some drinking at the Lucky Dragon and decided they'd probably just missed hitting the mother lode. One more try and they'd strike it rich. Only problem was, they didn't have any money for supplies. I guess it must have seemed like a good idea to rob Fitch's. They could get the supplies they needed and disappear back up into the mountains. Either they didn't know Fitch sleeps in a back room at the store or they figured one skinny old man wouldn't cause them much trouble."

Interested despite herself, Lila prompted him when he paused. "What happened? Mr. Fitch wasn't hurt, was he?"

"Fitch wasn't hurt. He came at them with a sawed-off shotgun. One of them lost the use of an arm. We buried the other one."

"That nice old man?" Lila gaped at him in shock. The story was all the more shocking for its flat delivery. She wouldn't have thought the tall, thin storekeeper capable of anything more violent than swatting a fly. "When I took the children to his store today, he was so nice."

"That 'nice old man' was trapping beaver in these mountains long before either of us was born," Bishop told her. "He was at the first American Rendezvous in '25. Not long after that, he took a Crow wife and lived with her people for a few years. When she died, he went to work for the army as a scout. And when he got tired of that, he did a little mining before deciding to settle down and run a store."

"Mr. Fitch?" Lila's voice rose high on a note of disbelief. She simply couldn't connect what he'd just told her with the man she'd met.

"Quite a few people in this town could tell similar stories," Bishop told her. "Folks don't come west because they're settled, stay-at-home types. More than a few of them were known by another name; some have a price on their heads in other parts of the country. Most are good enough people but not all of them, not by a long shot. This town isn't like the places you know. If it was, they wouldn't have hired someone like me to keep the peace. I don't want you disappearing again the way you did this afternoon."

"I didn't disappear," Lila snapped. She was shaken by what he'd told her, but that didn't mean she was going to let him dictate to her. "I was at the minister's house. I hardly think I was in danger there. Unless you're about to tell me that he's really a wanted killer in three states or is secretly head of a murderous gang of rustlers."

Despite himself, Bishop felt his mouth quirk at the testy edge to her voice. One of the things he admired about her was her spirit. She'd tackle hell with a hand bucket if it suited her. Maybe he had overreacted a bit when he'd realized that he didn't know where she was. This wasn't Pennsylvania but it wasn't exactly San Francisco's Barbary Coast either. He just wasn't used to having anyone to worry about besides himself. Finding himself abruptly a family man again might have made him a little touchy.

Besides, it was hard to hold on to his anger when she was standing there wrapped in nothing but a robe. The sapphire-colored silk covered her from her throat to the delicate arch of her feet. She would hardly have been more modestly covered if she'd been fully dressed. But there was no chemise beneath the heavy silk, no layers of petticoats and drawers—nothing between his hands and her soft skin but that one layer of fabric.

"As far as I know, Joseph Sunday isn't wanted for anything," he said absently, trying to pull his attention back to the conversation.

"That's certainly a relief," Lila said with heavy sarcasm.

"That's not the point." His eyes drifted to where the fabric of her robe clung to the full curves of her breasts. He could see the peaks of her nipples pushing against the dark silk, and he suddenly remembered the pebble hardness of them pressed into his palms.

"Just what is the point, then?" she asked impatiently.

Damned if he could remember. Damned if he could think of anything but the fact the she was standing in front of him wearing next to nothing. But she was looking at him impatiently, waiting for his response.

"The point is that things are different here," he said, aware that it wasn't exactly the commanding finish he'd originally envisioned.

"I'll keep that in mind." She gave him a slightly puzzled look, as if the conversation hadn't gone the way she'd expected. "Did you burst into my room just to tell me that?"

"I didn't exactly burst," he pointed out, but he was losing interest in the conversation. "How long are the children going to be with Mrs. Sunday?"

"She said they were welcome to stay until we join them for dinner at six. I suppose I should have consulted with you before accepting her invitation," she admitted grudgingly.

"That's fine," he said absently, more interested in the here and now. He'd worry about dinner with the parson later. "So we're alone for the next couple of hours."

Like a doe scenting sudden danger, Lila stilled. While they were talking, she'd nearly forgotten the intimacy of their situation. Now Bishop's soft-voiced comment reminded her that this was the first time they'd been completely alone since the children joined them. Her wide green eyes met his and what she read there had her heart suddenly beating much too hard. Even more frightening than the hunger she saw in his eyes was the echo of it she felt in the pit of her stomach.

What was it about him that brought out this . . . wantonness in her? Did marriage take away the sin of feeling such powerful desire for a man she didn't love?

With an effort, she turned away, her fingers tugging once more at the belt of her robe. She suddenly felt woefully underdressed.

"Maybe you'd better go," she said, her voice not quite steady.

"Maybe I shouldn't." Bishop's fingers closed around her arm, turning her back to face him. "It occurs to me that we've yet to have a wedding night."

"It's broad daylight," she reminded him, scandalized. "You can't possibly mean to—"

"Why not?" His thumb brushed the inside of her wrist and Lila's pulse was suddenly beating much too fast. "There's no law that says a man can only make love to his wife in the dark."

She was going to pull away, she told herself. She wasn't going to allow this to continue. But she stayed where she was, hypnotized by the rhythmic stroke of Bishop's thumb against her skin, the searing blue of his eyes.

"I want to see you," he said, his voice low and husky. "I want to watch your face when you take me inside you. Remember?"

Lila felt as if she'd just had the breath knocked from her. She'd never even imagined the possibility of anyone saying something so shockingly intimate. And worse than what he'd said were the memories that rushed back over her, memories she'd spent three months trying to suppress. *Remember?* She hadn't been able to forget.

"I think—" she began breathlessly.

"You think too much," he said as he slid his hand from her wrist up her arm, pulling her closer.

"This is wrong." He was so close that she could feel the heat of him, smell the crispness of soap and sunshine that clung to him. He set one hand against the small of her back, his boot sliding between her bare feet. Looking up at him, Lila was suddenly conscious of his size and strength. In contrast, she felt small and vulnerable, not a feeling to which she was accustomed.

"It's not wrong," he contradicted. "You're my wife

and I want you. I'm your husband and you want me. There's nothing wrong with that."

"But I don't want—"

"Yes, you do." And he proceeded to prove it by threading his fingers through her hair, tilting her face upward, and closing his mouth over hers with ruthless sensuality.

He didn't ask her for a response, he demanded it. There was no slow, easy build to passion. Instead, he let the full force of his hunger sweep over her. For half a heartbeat, Lila remained stiff against him, telling herself it would be wrong to give in to the heat already uncoiling itself in the pit of her stomach Surely it was a sin to want him so much when she didn't love him.

"Open your mouth," Bishop whispered against her lips. He slid his tongue across the sensitive flesh inside her lower lip in a gesture that coaxed even as it demanded.

Lila opened her mouth—to protest—surely that was the reason. It certainly wasn't to comply with his sensual command. But whatever her reason, Bishop was quick to take advantage of the opportunity. His tongue slid between her teeth, laying claim to the vulnerable softness beyond.

Lila's resistance collapsed with shameful speed. She'd raised her hands to push him away, but her fingers were suddenly curling over the edges of his coat, clinging for support as his tongue ravaged her mouth. This was the way it had been before—he'd only had to kiss her and she'd forgotten everything she knew of right and wrong, forgotten everything but the need to belong to him. She simply wasn't strong enough to fight her own hunger as well as his, and she let her body curve into the hard strength of his.

Feeling her surrender, Bishop gave a low murmur of encouragement against her mouth and pulled her so close that not even a shadow could slip between them. Locked together from breast to knee, they kissed with the deep hunger of lovers too long apart, with an urgency caused by needs too long denied.

His fingers burrowed into her hair, loosening the pins that held the heavy coil in place. An instant later, fiery curls tumbled over his hands and arms, falling past her hips in a wild, luxuriant tangle. Lila's knees weakened when his tongue traced the delicate shell of her ear, his teeth worrying the lobe a moment before his mouth found the sensitive skin along the side of her neck.

She felt Bishop loosening the belt of her robe and, for an instant, panic swept over her. She didn't have a stitch on beneath the robe. If he removed it she'd be completely naked. It was broad daylight. She couldn't let him—Bishop's mouth was suddenly on hers, swallowing her incoherent murmur of protest, making her forget everything but his kiss.

Keeping his mouth on hers, Bishop slid his hands beneath the heavy silk, slipping the robe off her shoulders until it slithered to the floor, pooling around her feet—a brilliant splash of blue against the pale wood. He could feel the tension beneath Lila's surrender and guessed that a wrong move could make her bolt. He should move slowly, coaxing and soothing her every step of the way. But he'd been hungry for so long. For three months she'd haunted his thoughts. Whatever sin he'd committed that night, he'd surely been punished for it since their wedding.

Having her close but always out of reach had been the most refined of tortures. His self-control had been strained to the limits and beyond. He simply didn't have enough left to begin a long drawn out seduction of his own wife. But maybe he didn't have to. She was all but melting in his arms, her slender body warm and pliant.

Lila let her head fall back as Bishop's mouth left hers. His lips trailed downward, tasting the sensitive arch of her throat, exploring the pulse that beat raggedly at its base. Eyes closed, hands clinging to his shoulders, she let herself fall into the pleasure he was offering.

The softly scratchy feel of his mustache brushing against the upper curve of her breast made her eyes fly open. Bishop had dropped to one knee in front of her, and she stared in shock as he opened his mouth over her breast, laving the sensitive tip with his tongue. He'd done the same thing the last time they were together, and the memory had haunted her most secret dreams. But his room had been dark that night and her memories had been limited to those of touch and scent and sound. Seeing his face at her breast, the sharp contrast of his black mustache with the creamy pallor of her skin was shockingly erotic. She felt the tug of his mouth against her breast, a drawing pressure that was echoed deep inside her, spreading outward until her entire body throbbed in rhythm to his suckling.

*This couldn't be happening,* she thought wildly. It was broad daylight, for heaven's sake. She couldn't be standing there, letting him do this to her. She had to stop this before it went any further, had to stop him.

Bishop turned his attention to her other breast, dragging the edge of his teeth across the puckered nipple before soothing the sensitive flesh with his tongue. She whimpered out loud, her fingers digging into his shoulders as her knees buckled under her.

He caught her as she sagged, lifting her in his arms as he rose. Lila turned her face into his shoulder, her hair streaming over his arm, a deep auburn curtain trailing almost to the floor. He set her down beside the bed, one arm circling her back, offering much-needed support as he stripped the covers back. Lifting her as easily as if she were a child, he lay her on the bed. The linens felt almost unbearably cool against her sensitized skin.

Looking at her, Bishop felt a hunger like nothing he'd ever known before. It was gut deep and almost painful in its intensity. In some distant part of his mind, he knew there was a danger in a need this powerful. There was a hazard in wanting her so much, in the raw hunger he felt. But the warning voice was drowned out by the drumming of his pulse. If it had meant his life, he couldn't have walked away from her at that moment. He shrugged out of his jacket and reached for the buckle of his gun belt.

Lila closed her eyes only to open them again almost immediately, curiosity winning out over modesty. Years ago, just before the war, she'd walked over to the Sinclair house one hot, summer afternoon. Cutting through the fields between the two houses, she'd passed by the pond. Billy had been swimming there and was just getting dressed.

She'd ducked behind a tree before he saw her and had stayed there, hardly breathing, until she heard him start for home, whistling cheerfully to himself. As soon as he was gone, she'd run for home lifting her skirts in a way that would have earned her a sound scolding if she'd been caught. She'd run straight to her room, throwing herself on the bed and closing her eyes, the better to remember that single quick glimpse of Billy's bare chest. The memory had been enough to make her cheeks flush and her heart beat double time.

Though she was years removed from that young girl, she'd never forgotten seeing her soon-to-be fiancé's body and the way it had made her feel. From that day to this, she'd kept that image in her mind of the way a man's body looked. Now, looking at Bishop as he stripped his white shirt down over his arms, she realized how foolish she'd been. Billy had been seventeen, hardly more than a boy. Bishop was very much a man. His muscled body was a far cry from Billy's narrow chest and slim arms.

Forgetting discretion, Lila stared at him. Dark, curly hair covered his broad chest, emphasizing the solid muscles there before tapering to a thin line that arrowed downward across his flat stomach before— Lila jerked her eyes away, her checks warming, as his hands dropped to the waist of his pants.

Bishop was grateful for her sudden attack of shyness. Having her watching him, those wide green eyes filled with curiosity, had put considerable strain on his somewhat tenuous self-control. He already wanted her so much that he felt like he was sixteen again. He stripped off the rest of his clothes, letting them fall to the floor.

Lila started as the mattress dipped beneath his

weight. With a muffled sound of panic, she grabbed for the covers. Bishop's hand was there before hers, catching her fingers in his.

"Leave them," he ordered, his voice low and husky.

"I'm cold."

"I'll warm you," he promised. He pressed her hand back against the pillow beside her head. She left it there, even when he released her, her fingers curling into her palm. Satisfied with her compliance, he lowered his head, planting a series of soft kisses along her collar bone.

Shivers of awareness worked their way up her spine. Bishop's hand closed over her breast, his thumb brushing across the acutely sensitive peak. Lila was shocked by the sound of her own whimper of pleasure. Looking at him, she saw that he was watching what he was doing to her, his attention completely focused on the tiny bud of her nipple as he caught it between thumb and forefinger, plucking it gently. The sensation was so acute that it hovered on the knife edge of pain. She arched her back, not sure whether she was pleading for more or begging him to stop. But Bishop knew exactly what it was she needed. He lowered his head, taking her swollen nipple into his mouth.

In some distant part of her mind, Lila was shocked to find her fingers sliding into his hair, pressing him closer, all but begging him to continue his sensual assault. Closing her eyes, she gave herself up to the pleasure, so absorbed in the feel of his mouth at her breasts that she was barely aware of his hand moving downward, stroking the inward curve of her waist, the soft flare of her hip. And then he flattened his hand on her stomach, just above the curling triangle of hair that guarded her most feminine secrets, and she was jerked out of the sensual haze.

"No!" She grabbed his wrist, her slender fingers falling well short of circling it. She tugged but his hand didn't move.

Bishop lifted his head, his eyes meeting hers. "It's all right."

"No." But the protest sounded weak even to her own ears. It was hard to think when he was looking at her, his blue eyes holding both promise and demand.

"Let me," he whispered.

Mesmerized by the heat of his gaze, she released her hold on his wrist, surrendering the last fragile remnant of her resistance, giving herself over to him.

His mouth caught her soft cry of surprise as his fingers slid through the soft thicket of curls, finding the damp heat of her.

Bishop felt the slick moisture of her arousal against his fingers and groaned softly. She was incredibly responsive, like a fine instrument tuned to his touch. The lightest stroke of his fingertip had her arching against him, a whimper of pleasure leaving her throat. It was like holding a flame in his hands, her skin burning to his touch. She whimpered again and his control snapped.

He lifted himself over her, his legs sliding between hers, opening her to him. His arousal pressed against the silken nest of auburn curls and Lila went still, her green eyes staring up at him, wide and full of sudden uncertainty. Every nerve in his body screamed for him to complete their union, but he forced himself to stillness. Though she carried his child, she was far from experienced. Bracing his weight on his elbows, he wound his fingers into her hair, his eyes holding hers.

"Look at me," he said.

As if she could do anything else, Lila thought dazedly. He filled her vision. Lost in the brilliant blue of his eyes, she forgot how to breathe, forgot how to think. Forgot everything but the slow, steady pressure of him easing into her body. This was what it had been like before—the sensation of emptiness filled, of being completed, made whole in a way she'd never known possible. This was what she'd been afraid to remember.

Her body gloved him as if made for him alone, Bishop thought as he sheathed himself with her. He closed his eyes for an instant, gathering the tattered threads of his control. This was the way it had been the first time, this feeling of coming home to the place he'd always been meant to be. It had haunted all too many of his dreams and filled him with a sense of loss he hadn't been able to shake.

Lila's hands clung to his back, feeling the dampness of sweat and the ripple of muscles as he began to move over her. Instinctively she echoed that movement, her body arching to welcome each thrust. The soft drag of withdrawal was an exquisite torture only partially soothed when he filled her once again. Tension coiled within her, growing tighter and harder each time the pattern was repeated.

Her entire world was reduced to this room, this bed, this man. Her vision was filled with Bishop's face, with the searing blue of his eyes. Layers of sensation built one upon the other, each more exquisite than the last, each adding to the tension spiraling inside her. Her movements took on a frantic edge, her breath coming in soft little pants. She was striving toward something, something she had to have, had to have now.

"Please." She couldn't have said what she was asking for but she knew it was within his power to give it to her. "Please," she whispered again.

Looking down at her, Bishop felt a purely masculine sense of triumph. Her face was flushed as if with fever and her eyes were a deep, smoky green, unfocused and looking inward as her slender body strained toward the peak that lay just beyond her reach. At another time, he might have slowed the pace, drawing out the moment. But he'd spent too many months thinking about her, too many nights wanting her. His patience was gone, his self-control stretched thin.

He slid one hand beneath her bottom, tilting her to receive him more fully. He thrust once, twice. Her eyes widened, the breath catching in her throat as she reached the goal toward which she'd been striving. Bishop felt her body tighten around his, delicate contractions gripping him, dragging him into the maelstrom of her climax. With a groan, he gave into his own burning need. His body arched into hers, shuddering as the heavy pulse of completion took him.

Joined together, they tumbled headlong into pleasure. Bishop's only coherent thought was that she was his. Finally and completely his.

# Chapter 11

Lila stepped out of the hotel and onto the board-walk. Twilight pulled a dusky veil over the town, softening the harsh edge of reality and lending an air of solidity to the false-front buildings that daylight refused to grant them.

"You seem to be in something of a hurry," Bishop said as he stepped through the door behind her.

"It's impolite to be late." She pretended to be absorbed in arranging the strings of her reticule just so around her wrist.

"It's no more than five minutes away, even if we crawl."

"That would make something of a spectacle, don't you think?" It was a humorless response to his light comment, but she wasn't in the mood to be amused. At least not by anything her husband had to say. And he was her husband in every sense of the word, she thought, memories of the afternoon sweeping over her. She'd been quite thoroughly made a wife, not just once but twice. Worse than that was the fact that she'd been an eager participant both times. And as if that wasn't enough, there was the fact that Clem Lyman had come looking for Bishop and found him in her room.

"Are you still upset about me answering the door when Clem knocked?" Bishop asked, reading her thoughts with disturbing accuracy.

"I don't know what he must have thought, finding you in my room like that," she muttered, still fussing with the strings of her reticule.

"I doubt he thought much at all. I was dressed. And even if I hadn't been, I don't think he'd have been too shocked. We *are* married," he pointed out.

As if she could forget, Lila thought. There wasn't an inch of her that didn't bear the stamp of his possession. She was tender in places she'd been taught not to think about, aware of her body in a way she'd never imagined. After he'd left in response to Clem's summons, she'd taken a sponge bath, using her cold bathwater, but it would take more than soap and water to wash away the memory of his touch. And her own passionate response.

"Considering you're the one who told me about Mr. Lyman's propensity for gossip, I should think you'd be more concerned with his reaction to finding you in my room," she said, aware that her tone verged on prissy.

She jumped when Bishop caught her chin in his hand, tilting her face up to his. Even in the dusky light, the vivid blue of his eyes was clearly visible. "You're the only one who thinks my presence in your room is news. If anything is likely to excite comment, it's the fact that we're in separate rooms. If you're so concerned about the possibility of gossip, maybe we should put the children in my room and I could move into yours," he said softly. He brushed his thumb across her mouth, which was tender and slightly swollen from his kisses. "Then you wouldn't have to worry about what Clem would think if he found us in the same room. Or in the same bed."

There was an unmistakable sensual threat in the words. His touch was a reminder of how little she'd objected to his presence in her bed just a few hours ago. Lila stared up at him, mesmerized by the look in his eyes, her entire being concentrated on the light pressure of his thumb against her lower lip. She felt herself leaning toward him, her body going soft and pliant as hunger stirred deep inside. It took a conscious effort to drag her gaze from his and turn her face away from his touch.

"I don't think it would be a good idea to change our arrangements," she said breathlessly. "The children are nicely settled. There's no sense in moving them around."

It was a thin excuse at best but, to her intense relief, Bishop accepted it without argument. "We'll be moving soon enough" was all he said.

"Good," Lila said without conviction. Living in the

hotel meant that her every move was under the scrutiny of Clem and Dottie. But moving into a house would mean sharing a room with Bishop. After this afternoon, that was a prospect fraught with even more hazards than she'd realized. It was one thing to resist his desires, something else altogether to resist her own. She didn't like the fact that, with little more than a look and a touch, he could make her forget everything but the need to have him hold her. She'd never felt that way before, not even with Billy. And she had loved him.

They didn't speak again during the walk to the Sundays'. They passed a few people on the street but no one showed any inclination to stop and talk. Most of the businesses had closed for the day, except the saloons, and it would be a couple of hours before they hit their full stride. The town was quiet, at peace. Lila wished she felt the same.

The minister's home in Paris was a far cry from the elegant stone rectory occupied by Reverend Carpenter back home in Pennsylvania. The white paint had begun to fade and one of the green shutters hung at a drunken angle, courtesy of Bridget's oldest son who'd attempted to climb onto the roof using the shutter as a ladder.

Reverend Carpenter had taken considerable pride in the beauty of the gardens surrounding the rectory. They had been started by one of his predecessors and had been admired even before he took over the ministry, but he'd taken it upon himself to improve upon them, installing a sunken rose garden and an elegant allée of maples leading up to the rectory itself. All for the glorification of the Lord, of course, he'd insisted modestly.

Joseph Sunday was also a plant lover, but he preferred to study them in their natural element. Spring through fall, he spent a great deal of his spare time tramping through the local mountains, sketching the native plants and observing their growth habits. Bridget had proudly shown Lila some of his drawings. She'd been impressed by his ability to re-create every detail of leaf and bud, making the black-and-white sketch seem almost alive. But he wasn't much inclined toward planting and tending gardens of the traditional sort. The closest the Sunday home came to a formal garden was a somewhat scraggly rosebush that occupied pride of place next to the front gate, and that was Bridget's doing.

The rose was the offspring of cuttings Bridget's mother had brought all the way from Ireland. Bridget, in her turn, had hand-carried cuttings from Boston to brighten her home in the untamed West. The rose's survival in its harsh new environment made Lila feel better about her own chances. Since Bridget had told her the story of how the rose had come to be where it was, Lila had felt a certain kinship with the shrub and had made it a point to bestow a fond smile on it whenever she passed by.

But tonight she barely glanced at the plant. Tonight her attention was all for the man at her side. Bishop pushed open the gate and stood back to allow her to enter first. Lila walked past him, trying not to allow even her skirt to brush against him. If he was aware of her attempt to keep distance between them, he ignored it, setting his hand against the small of her back as the gate swung shut behind them.

The light touch seemed to burn right through the layers of her clothing, making her skin tingle with awareness. She was grateful when, just as they reached the front step, the door burst open and two children tumbled out. One of them was Bridget's only daughter, Mary. The other was Angel. Mary was five, and with her red hair and sparkling hazel eyes, she was the spitting image of her mother. She looked like a mischievous sprite next to Angel's golden curls and soft blue eyes.

Lila used the children as an excuse to step away from Bishop's touch, bending down to hug Angel. The child returned her hug with gratifying enthusiasm and Lila felt some of her tension ease. In the confusing tangle of her life, Angel was a bright and shining exception. She'd grown to love the little girl as if she were her own. Gavin kept her at arm's length and viewed her with, at best, a certain wary acceptance. And Bishop . . . Well, she couldn't even begin to define her relationship with her husband. But Angel had accepted her new stepmother completely, treating her with a sweet affection that was impossible to resist.

"Did you have fun today, Angel?" Lila asked as she straightened.

"Yes." Angel nodded enthusiastically. "Mary and me played with dollies."

"Mary and I," Lila corrected as she brushed a stray curl back off the child's forehead.

Angel frowned in confusion. "But you wasn't there."

"Weren't there, darling. You *weren't* there." Lila straightened the sash on Angel's russet-colored dress.

"I was too there," Angel said, giving her stepmother a look that suggested doubts about her intelligence.

Bishop's snort of laughter made Lila decide that the grammar lessons could wait for another time.

"Of course you were there," she said briskly. "And I'm very glad you had a good time this afternoon."

"I did." Angel gave her a solicitous look. "Did you have a good time too?"

It was a perfectly innocent question but remembering how she'd spent the afternoon, Lila felt her cheeks flush. She was careful not to look at Bishop but she couldn't shut out the sound of his voice.

"Did you, Lila? Have a good time this afternoon?" His tone was full of wicked amusement, as if he already knew the answer. And he undoubtedly did, blast him. Considering he bore the marks of her nails on his back, she could hardly pretend that she didn't know what he was talking about. There was no safe answer to his needling question so she chose the only reasonable option and ignored him.

"Let's go see if we can help Mrs. Sunday with anything," she said, holding out her hand to Mary.

"Mama told us to scat from the kitchen," Mary said, taking Lila's other hand with the friendly confidence of a child who knew she was well loved. "She said we were a pair of pestulant pests and that, if we didn't get out of her kitchen, dinner wasn't going to be done until breakfasttime."

"What's a pestulant pest?" Angel asked, her blue eyes wide and questioning.

"I guess it's what you and Mary are," Lila said. "Why don't we see if we can find something useful for the two of you to do?"

Bishop had never been a churchgoer. He didn't have any quarrel with the Lord, he simply didn't feel the need to formalize his relationship with Him by attending church. The last time he'd set foot in a church, he'd been younger than Gavin. He'd found a frog on the way to the service and put it in his pocket for safekeeping. The creature had escaped sometime during the service and made its presence known by jumping onto the piano keys just as Mrs. Cleary was beginning the second chorus of "Bringing in the Sheaves." The resulting chaos had been caused more by her hysterical screams than by anything the frog did, but pointing this out had not saved him from a trip to the woodshed.

The minister, a humorless man who viewed all humanity as a seething cauldron of sin and Bishop as a proof positive of that theory, had visited the McKenzie household the next day. He demanded—and got—an apology from Bishop. He also demanded the right to punish the boy personally and publicly. Bishop's parents had refused and the sermon that followed had detailed the wages of sin and the dangers of allowing them to go unpunished. His parents had stood firm and the minister had departed, casting dark glances in Bishop's direction.

He'd learned several lessons from the incident: that the seat of his pants was no protection against a firmly wielded piece of hickory; that he wasn't cut out to be a churchgoer; that being a man of God did not necessarily give a man a charitable nature; and never to bring a frog to church.

Finding himself sitting down at a minister's table twenty years later, he had to restrain the urge to check his pockets for stray frogs. He felt as out of place as a bull in a china shop or a sinner in church, for that matter. Glancing around the table, he half expected to catch a disapproving look or two but the only glance that crossed his was his hostess's.

"Another biscuit, Sheriff?" Bridget asked, lifting the bowl and offering it to him.

"No, thank you, Mrs. Sunday."

"A mite more stew then?" Bridget suggested. "There's plenty more on the stove."

"I don't—"

"Leave the poor man alone," Joseph ordered mildly. "He hasn't had a chance to eat what he has." He glanced at Bishop, his dark eyes holding a smile though his mouth remained solemn. "My wife believes that all the world's ills could be solved if everyone ate more."

"You'll not be trying to deny that hunger is at the heart of a great deal of the troubles in the world today, now will you?" Bridget asked her husband. "A man can't be content when his belly's empty, that's a certainty. And a man who's not content is a man likely to go looking for trouble. And *that's* always easy enough to find if you're looking."

"Well, you certainly don't have to worry about anyone getting up from your table and looking for trouble," Joseph told her, his eyes sparkling with laughter. "The only thing you have to worry about is whether they'll be able to get up at all."

"You can laugh all you want." Bridget sniffed. "But I don't recall seeing you turn down a second helping in the last fifteen years."

"Guilty as charged," Joseph admitted, chuckling. "I can certainly offer myself as evidence of the benefits of a full stomach making for a contented man. But that doesn't mean that our guests want to find themselves as well stuffed as a Christmas goose, my dear."

Listening to the light exchange between the other couple, Lila wondered wistfully if she'd ever find that kind of ease in her own marriage. Would there come a time when they could laugh with each other the way Bridget and Joseph did? It was difficult to imagine such a thing. She stole a glance across the table at Bishop and found him looking at her. Their eyes locked for a moment. There was something questioning in his gaze, something that made her wonder if his thoughts had been running along a path similar to her own. Did he look into the future and wonder about their hasty marriage?

A loud squeal broke into her thoughts and drew her attention to the end of the table where Bridget sat. George, the youngest of the five children, sat next to his mother. At not quite a year old, he was plump, rosy-cheeked, irresistible, and quite well aware of his charm. Perched on a stack of books, with a dish towel looped around his torso, under his arms, and tied in back of the chair, he waved his spoon with the enthusiasm of a medicine man holding a bottle of snake oil and repeated his squealed demand for attention.

"Heavens above, George, where are your manners?" Bridget scolded softly. "You'll have our guests thinking I'm raising a wild Indian, yelling at the table that way."

Delighted at finding himself the center of attention, George laughed, a fat chuckle that made it clear that he didn't take his mother's scolding seriously.

"He seems like a very happy baby," Lila commented, watching Bridget dexterously maneuver a spoonful of mashed potatoes into his mouth.

"He's a spoiled young man, is what he is. Aren't

you, my pet?" Bridget mopped potato off his chin and returned his messy grin with a loving smile.

Beneath the table, Lila touched one hand to her still-flat stomach. It still didn't seem possible that she was carrying a child. In a few months, she'd be a mother. From the beginning, the idea had terrified her. Looking at George, for the first time she felt a twinge of anticipation. There was something enormously appealing about the way his eyes crinkled almost shut when he smiled. She wasn't foolish enough to think that babies were always smiling cherubs, but still . . .

Angel, who had been sitting quietly next to Lila, chose that moment to speak up, apparently reading her stepmother's thoughts with devastating accuracy.

"Lila's going to have a baby," she said cheerfully.

Lila flushed as all eyes turned in her direction. There was nothing embarrassing about Angel's announcement, she told herself. It wasn't as if she could keep her condition a secret for much longer. But she couldn't shake the idea that Bridget and Joseph had only to look at her to read the truth—that her child had been conceived out of wedlock. Angel continued before anyone could offer any comment.

"I like babies," she said, filling the silence before it could become awkward. "I'm going to have a hundred of them when I grow up."

Her extravagant claim caused the adults to chuckle. "I'll offer up a prayer for your husband, then," Joseph told her. "He's going to have his hands full with such a houseful."

"I'm going to marry Joey," Angel said calmly. She bestowed a sweet smile on Joseph, Jr., who turned crimson with embarrassment. At twelve, he had his mother's red hair and his father's quiet nature. From the moment she'd been introduced to him, Angel had viewed him as her personal property.

There was another round of laughter but, looking at her stepdaughter, Lila found herself wondering if perhaps young Joseph shouldn't start looking for a way to earn sufficient money to support a large family. If there was one thing she'd learned about Angel, it was that, underneath her sweet exterior, was a will of solid iron. In fifteen years, if she still had her eye on Joseph, Lila wouldn't be surprised if she got him.

The potentially awkward moment was past and the conversation continued without anyone mentioning Lila's pregnancy again. The rest of the evening passed without incident. Lila insisted on helping Bridget clean up after supper. Though she'd grown up with servants and had always assumed she'd one day have servants of her own, her mother had made sure that Lila was capable of running a household without them. She might not have washed many dishes but she knew how to go about it, just as she could wash clothes, mop a floor, and, if necessary, make her own soap to do those tasks.

She and Bridget worked companionably, talking as easily as if they'd known each other for years rather than a matter of days. Bridget's friendship, new as it was, had helped to ease the homesickness Lila had felt at finding herself abruptly transplanted two thousand miles away from family and friends. By the time the evening ended, she was feeling relaxed and at ease.

The walk back to the hotel was enlivened by Angel's recitation of her day's adventures. She'd spent most of her time playing with Mary, but Lila noted the number of times the name Joey was mentioned and guessed that she'd managed to make herself known to her future husband in no uncertain terms. Gavin, as usual, had little to say. When questioned directly, he lifted one shoulder in a shrug and said that he liked the Sundays well enough. Coming from her taciturn stepson, that was high praise.

Though she was vividly aware of Bishop's presence, as long as the children were with them, Lila felt safe. He'd already agreed to leave their room arrangements as they were. She'd simply make sure that they didn't find themselves alone again the way they had this afternoon. She had no intention of being caught off guard that way again, not until she'd worked a few things out in her own mind.

Bishop was just as glad that the children were with them too. Though a part of him wanted nothing more than to be able to take his wife back to bed, another part of him found the very strength of that desire something of which to be wary. There was a danger in wanting something so much. It could make a man vulnerable.

They parted outside Lila's door, each acutely aware of the other, neither willing to let it show.

"The house has been empty for six months," Bishop said as he unlocked the door. "Pete Moreton built it when he struck a vein of silver. He was planning on bringing his girl out from Boston but, when he sent for her, she wrote back to tell him she'd married somebody else. No one ever lived here."

"What happened to Mr. Moreton?" Lila asked as

she stepped across the threshold, lifting her skirts a little to keep them clear of the dust on the floor.

"He got drunk, lost his mine in a poker game and left town, heading for Nevada." He left the door open behind them, letting sunlight spill in across the dusty room.

"The poor man. He must have loved her very much."

"He was a fool," Bishop said flatly. "He hadn't even seen her in almost ten years."

"So he was a fool to still love her?" Lila slanted him a questioning glance.

"He didn't love her. After all those years, he didn't even know her any more. He was in love with a memory."

"Perhaps. But perhaps not. I think real love can withstand a great deal, including time apart."

There was a wistfulness in her tone that made Bishop suddenly remember the boy she'd been engaged to, the one who'd died. Was she thinking about her dead fiancé?

"I guess this wasn't real love then, was it? Lucky for us, Pete built the house before he found that out."

Lila looked a little startled by his tone or perhaps by his callous dismissal of the other man's loss. Bishop turned away from the questions in her eyes, crossing the room with brisk strides to push open a window, letting in a wave of crisp air. He turned and gave the room a critical look.

"He furnished the place for her too. Had all this stuff hauled up the mountain from Denver."

"That will certainly make things simpler," Lila said. She ran her finger through the layer of dust on a small end table. "Who owns this place now?"

"The bank does. They gave Pete a mortgage based on what the mine was worth. When he left town, he left Frank Smythe holding the mortgage. There's not much call for houses this size in Paris so it's been empty since. Not many miners have families with them."

As he spoke, Lila was flicking back the corner of the sheet that covered an upholstered wing chair, studying it critically. Watching her, Bishop was acutely aware that this house, while nice by local standards, was a far cry from what she'd grown up with. He wouldn't be surprised if she turned her nose up at the idea of living here, he thought as he watched her move from room to room. She was, after all, Lila Adams of the Philadelphia Adamses. Changing her name to McKenzie couldn't change who and what she was.

"Is the furniture included in the rent?" she asked as she returned to the front room.

"Yes."

She tugged the sheet completely off the sofa, dropping it on the floor while she stood back and surveyed what she'd uncovered. Bishop looked at the sofa and thought about the exquisite heirlooms that furnished River Walk. The comparison was painful.

"Not exactly Queen Anne," he said.

"Since I'm not particularly fond of Queen Anne, I consider that to be in its favor." She finished her study of the sofa and turned on her heel, giving the room one last inspection before looking at him.

"Is the rent reasonable?"

"It's reasonable," he said, surprised by the practicality of the question. He'd been expecting her to reject the house out of hand.

"It needs a good cleaning, of course." She glanced critically at the dusty surfaces and grimy windows. "But all in all, I think it will do quite nicely. Mr. Moreton may have been a poor judge of females but he did quite nicely when it came to houses. When can I start cleaning?"

"Anytime." Bishop was stunned by her easy acceptance of the house. She actually looked pleased with it!

"Good. I'll need to get some things at Fitch's," Lila said, thinking out loud. "A little furniture wax and some fresh curtains on the windows and you'll hardly recognize the place."

He stared at her, thinking that he knew her even less than he'd realized.

It was while she was cleaning the house that the idea came to Lila. Pete Moreton had either planned on having a family right away or he'd believed in building for the future. In addition to the parlor and large kitchen, there were four rooms of varying sizes that would certainly function as bedrooms. The largest bedroom was furnished with a rather elegant maple bedframe, with a matching dresser and wardrobe. Angel immediately claimed the smallest room as her own because she liked the view of the mountains through the single window. Gavin professed indifference to his sleeping quarters so Lila gave him the room next to his sister's.

That left one room empty. Since it wasn't furnished, she had no way of knowing what purpose the departed Mr. Moreton might have had in mind for it, but its position right next to the large bedroom seemed to cry out for it to be a nursery. If she narrowed her eyes a bit, she could envision how it would look with soft gingham curtains hanging at the windows, a cradle against one wall, with perhaps a rocking chair beside it.

She pressed her hand against her stomach, her mouth curving in a wistful smile. This baby was starting to seem more real every day. She could almost see herself sitting in that rocking chair, cradling a child in her arms. The image was fuzzy around the edges but it was much clearer than it had been even a few days ago. She shook her head, forcing her mind back to the matters at hand. It would be several months yet before they had any need of a nursery. For the moment, the room could remain empty.

Lila was halfway out of the room when the idea came to her. She stopped short and turned around, looking at the sunny room through new eyes. A quick mental refurnishing and her mouth curved in a smile. It was perfect. And practical. Her smile faded a little as she considered whether Bishop would agree with her. But if she presented it to him a fait accompli, surely he wouldn't offer any argument. Well, not much of an argument.

Her jaw setting with determination, she spun on her heel, her skirts swishing against the newly waxed floor, and hurried from the room. Bishop had told her to do what she wanted with the house, that he didn't have any opinions about furnishings and such like. She was simply taking him at his word.

Bishop was amazed by the transformation Lila had worked. With just a few days' work, she'd taken the empty house and turned it into a home. The floors were covered with a fresh coat of wax, new curtains hung at the windows, and every surface was dust free and gleaming. The big stove had received a new layer of blacking. A cast-iron Dutch oven sat on one of the burners, filling the room with the rich scents of meat and potatoes. Dishes were neatly stacked on shelves, and there was even a handful of wildflowers tucked into a glass jar and set in the middle of the table.

It had been a very long time since he'd lived in a house where there were flowers on the table. His first wife had liked to have flowers in the house, but her tastes had run to roses in a crystal vase. He couldn't imagine Isabelle picking wildflowers and setting them in a jar of water. Considering her upbringing, he would have expected Lila to feel the same. Yet there the flowers were, taking pride of place in the middle of the kitchen table.

Obviously, he had a lot to learn about his second wife.

He went looking for Lila. He'd brought her trunks over earlier today and he could see that she'd been busy unpacking. Lacy doilies decorated every surface. Antimacassars covered the backs of the sofa and chairs. A china clock with richly curving sides sat on the mantel in the parlor, flanked by a pair of silver candlesticks. There were new curtains in here, simple muslin drapes, drawn back to allow the late-spring sunshine to spill across the newly polished floor, picking out the grain in the wood and making it gleam golden.

Feeling more and more as if he didn't belong there, he found his way down the hallway that led to the bedrooms. Lila was in the largest one, leaning over the bed, smoothing a linen sheet across the mattress. Bishop paused to admire the view. Though he didn't make a sound, she turned suddenly, as if sensing his presence.

"You startled me!"

"Sorry." He came farther into the room, setting his hat on top of the tall chest of drawers. "I wasn't trying to sneak up on you."

"That's all right. I was thinking of other things."

Her dress was plainly cut and trimmed only with the merest touch of lace at the wrist and throat. In a soft, buttery shade of yellow, it looked like the personification of springtime. Late-afternoon sunlight slanted through the window behind her, turning her hair to pure fire. She lifted one hand to tuck a stray curl back from her forehead. He knew it wasn't her intention, but the gesture drew attention to the full curve of her breast and the gentle indentation of her waist. She was beautiful, desirable—and his.

"I didn't hear you come in," Lila said, smoothing one hand over her skirts. Though she was modestly covered, there was something in Bishop's eyes that made her feel suddenly naked and vulnerable. "Supper's in an hour. I was just finishing up a few things."

"You've worked hard. The house looks good."

"Thank you." Had he moved closer or had the room gotten smaller? She shifted back a little. "I put your things away. I wasn't sure how you wanted them arranged."

"It doesn't matter. Where are the children?"

"They're outside. Gavin said he'd look out for Angel." He *was* closer. He was much too close, in fact, and it was suddenly hard to breathe. She inched back only to feel the bed come up against the back of her legs. That was *not* where she wanted to be.

"So we're alone."

He hadn't touched her but her skin tingled as if he'd just run his hands over her. She swallowed. "They could come in any time."

"True." He lifted one hand, brushing his fingertips across the curve of her cheekbone.

Lila felt the light touch all the way to her toes, weakening her knees, softening her resolve. It would be so easy to melt into him, to forget the children; forget her determination to have a marriage that was grounded in something more than mutual attraction; forget everything but how good it felt to be in his arms. She stared up at him, losing herself in the clear blue of his eyes. His head lowered. He was going to kiss her. Panic fluttered in her chest. If he kissed her, he'd make her forget all about the plans she'd made. She'd forget everything but how good it felt to be in his arms.

"My things are in the room next to this," she got out, her voice quick and breathless.

"What?" Bishop lifted his head to look at her.

"I want us to have separate rooms."

# Chapter 12

Dead silence followed her announcement. Hearing the echo of her blurted words, Lila winced. This wasn't the way she'd pictured it. She'd planned to wait until after the children were in bed and then the two of them would sit down in the parlor or the kitchen—as far from a bed as possible. He'd be well fed, perhaps in the mood to appreciate some of the less . . . basic benefits of a marriage. She would calmly explain that she didn't feel ready to make their marriage real in every sense of the word. She'd point out that, since she was already expecting a child, the most obvious reason for them to share a bed was not a factor. When she pictured the scene in her mind's eye, she'd been so reasonable, her arguments so inarguable that he'd immediately agreed with her.

But it hadn't been part of her plan to blurt it out like a frightened child.

"You want what?" Bishop's tone was even—too even?

Lila took a deep breath. "I want us to have separate rooms." She stepped sideways and away from him. He didn't try to stop her. She wanted to believe that was a good sign, but she suspected it was because he was still reeling from shock. "It makes sense," she said as he turned to look at her.

"Does it?" With the window at his back, his face was in shadow, his expression unreadable.

"Certainly." She struggled to inject a faint air of surprise into her response.

"Why?"

The flat question threw her momentarily off balance. Of course there were any number of reasons why, and she'd expected to have to point at least a few of them out, but there was something about the way he asked.

"I think we should take some time to get to know each other before we . . . become intimate."

"You're carrying my child. That seems pretty intimate to me."

The dry sarcasm of his response struck a spark off her temper. She drew a deep breath, reminding herself that no good would come of getting angry.

"That was an . . . accident," she said carefully. "That doesn't mean that we really know each other the way a husband and wife should."

One corner of Bishop's mustache curled in a

sneer. "I suppose what happened a few days ago was an accident too?"

"It was a mistake," Lila said evenly. She'd expected him to bring that up and she had an answer ready. "It was a case of circumstances and . . . and propinquity leading to—"

"No."

"N-no?" *No to what?*

"No separate rooms," Bishop said flatly, answering the question she hadn't quite asked. "You're my wife. Like it or not, we'll share a room. And a bed."

"I don't like it," she snapped, infuriated by his dictatorial tone. "I don't like it at all."

"You should have thought of that before you married me."

"I don't recall that I had much choice," she said bitterly. "You made sure of that when you strode into the church like some conquering warrior and announced to all and sundry that I was carrying your child."

Bishop leaned toward her, his eyes hard as sapphires and just as blue. "I don't recall making any announcement. But I do remember you telling your good friend Logan that I'd raped you so that he'd marry you."

"He didn't know it was you." Lila felt the same mixture of anger and guilt she always did when she remembered the lie she'd let Logan believe.

"And he would have married me even if he'd known the truth."

"And do you think he'd have been willing to have separate rooms?"

"Of course." Lila lifted her chin, her eyes flashing

with righteous indignation. "Logan is a gentleman. He'd never have asked me to do anything I didn't wish to do."

"Well, like I said before, I never claimed to be a gentleman," Bishop said in an infuriating drawl. "But I think your good friend Logan might not have been so eager to sacrifice himself to save your honor if he'd realized that you expected him to spend the rest of his life celibate."

"Stop calling him 'my good friend Logan,' " Lila ordered, her temper soaring. "And I never said anything about it being for the rest of your life."

"Oh?" Bishop's dark brows went up, nearly disappearing into the heavy black wave of hair that had fallen onto his forehead when he took off his hat. "So you had some specific length of time in mind? Would it be too ungentlemanly of me to ask what it is? When do you think we might know each other well enough to share a bed as well as a name?"

"I can't predict that." She turned away from him, crossing the room with quick, nervous steps. This was a weak point in her argument and she knew it. How could you put a time limit on something like this? How could she say that in three months or six months or even three years she'd be able to give herself to him without reserve? It wasn't possible to know ahead of time.

"So you want me to just wait and see when your mood changes?"

"It's not a mood!" She spun to look at him, frustration and anger turning her eyes a smoky green. "I'm just asking for a little time. Everything has happened so fast. We hardly know each other. And if you mention what happened in my room the other day or the fact that I'm carrying your child, I won't be responsible for my own actions," she warned him. "That's not what I mean and I think you know it."

The hell of it was that he did know it, Bishop thought, feeling more than a little frustrated himself. She wasn't talking about the physical aspect of their marriage. Inexperienced as she was, she had to know that *that* wasn't in need of work. What she was talking about was something else, something not so easily defined. It was the kind of thing that women set store by and that most men could happily ignore in favor of the simpler and more easily grasped pleasures of the flesh.

"No separate bedrooms," he repeated and saw her eyes flare with quick anger. He waited for the explosion but she caught herself with a visible effort. When she spoke, her tone was painfully level.

"I'm not asking for that much. Perhaps just until the baby's born. That's not much to ask, is it?"

It damn well was, Bishop thought, feeling a gut-deep sense of frustration. He seemed to see a wavery image of Isabelle superimposed over Lila. Isabelle, with her pale gold hair and soft blue eyes. *It's just until the baby's born. Please, Bishop, let me go home to St. Louis. I'm afraid to have a baby out here. I'll come back as soon as the baby is born. I promise.*

Only she hadn't come back. When he'd gone to St. Louis after Gavin's birth, Isabelle had begged him to let her stay longer. The baby was so small, she'd said. Why put him at risk by taking him into the untamed West? When he was a little older, it would be better. He'd given in to her pleas. To tell the truth, his tiny, helpless son had scared the hell out of him. And despite the mutual dislike he shared with his mother-in-law, she was certainly in a better position to see to Isabelle and Gavin's care.

Time had passed and his trips to St. Louis had grown farther apart. Gavin was two when Bishop realized that, if he didn't get his wife and child away from her mother, he was going to lose them forever. So he'd turned a deaf ear to Isabelle's tears and moved his family as far from St. Louis as he could get them. He took a job guarding gold shipments on the journey from the gold fields to San Francisco and settled Isabelle and Gavin in a small house in the city.

Isabelle had tried. God knows, she'd tried. But, never a forceful woman, she seemed to have lost all ability to make a decision on her own. She'd simply given over control of her life to her mother. Without Louise to tell her everything from what to wear to how to think, she'd been lost. She'd looked to Bishop for the guidance she couldn't seem to live without. By the time Angelique was conceived, he'd begun to feel more like her father than her husband.

Maybe if she hadn't become pregnant again, things would have been different. Maybe Isabelle would have gotten stronger, more independent. But when she found out she was carrying another child, she'd begged him to let her go home. He could have pointed out that "home" was supposed to be wherever he was, but he hadn't. Something had told him it was too late, that she was lost to him. He took her back to St. Louis and left her there to await the birth of her child. And never saw her again.

"Bishop?" Lila's questioning tone dragged him back to the present. "Just until the baby's born? That's not asking too much, is it?"

"No separate bedrooms."

Without giving her a chance to continue the argument, he turned and strode from the room, sweeping his hat off the dresser on the way out.

"We're not through talking about this," Lila said, following him into the kitchen.

But she might as well have been talking to the wind. He strode out, leaving the back door to bang shut behind him. Lila glared after him, her hands clenched into fists at her side. He was the most annoying, obnoxious, frustrating man she'd ever known. After stamping over to the stove in a most unladylike fashion, she jerked the lid off the pot simmering there. Then she snatched up a wooden spoon and stirred the stew with vicious force.

Life would have been much easier if Bishop hadn't come back to Pennsylvania. She could have married Logan and been perfectly content with him. He would have treated her like a gentleman should treat a lady. He wouldn't have been so infuriating. With just a cock of his eyebrow, Bishop could set her temper soaring. Logan would never have *dreamed* of cocking an eyebrow at her. And he would have understood her desire to have separate rooms. Lots of couples had separate rooms, even if they'd married for the usual reasons. It was a perfectly civilized thing to do. But if she said as much to Bishop, he'd probably say that he hadn't claimed to be civilized any more than he'd claimed to be a gentleman. Lila jabbed at a potato, shoving it under the bubbling juices. She should have married Logan, she thought again. He wouldn't have upset her like this.

The door opened behind her and she spun, ready to deliver a blistering diatribe about people who walked out in the middle of arguments. But it wasn't Bishop who entered. It was Gavin and Angel. Lila told herself she wasn't disappointed. She'd be just as happy if Bishop never came back at all. She forced a smile for the children.

"Supper's almost ready. Why don't you two get washed up?"

Bishop could eat alone if and when he bothered to return. Better still, he could go hungry. It was the least he deserved.

Dinner was eaten largely in silence. Gavin was never talkative but Angel could usually be counted upon to fill any awkward gaps in the conversation. Tonight, tired out by the excitement and turmoil of their move from the hotel into their new home, she barely stayed awake long enough to get through her meal. Without her friendly chatter, the big kitchen seemed painfully quiet. Lila looked up several times to find Gavin watching her. His blue eyes, so like his father's, seemed to hold a question. But each time their eyes met, he looked away without speaking and Lila simply didn't have the emotional energy to pull whatever it was out of him.

This wasn't at all the way she'd envisioned the first evening in her new home. Bishop was conspicuous by his absence. Angel was practically falling asleep in her plate. Gavin was watching her with those eyes that were much too old for a boy of twelve, and she was caught between the urge to track her husband down and take an unladylike but satisfying swing at his arrogant nose and the desire to put her head down on the table and howl like a baby.

Lila might as well have been eating sawdust for all she tasted her food. She was relieved to see the meal end, relieved to be away from Gavin's watchful eyes and the empty plate at the end of the table. Pushing her chair back, she came around the table and scooped Angel up into her arms. She balanced the sleepy little girl on her hip to carry her to bed.

"Take the lantern and bring in some wood for morning, please, Gavin," she asked over her shoulder as she left the room.

He didn't respond but she knew he'd do as she asked. That was another way in which he was too adult for his age. There was none of the rebelliousness she remembered in herself at that age, none of the irritating whining she'd inflicted on anyone foolish enough to listen to her. If he'd been a meek or shy child, she wouldn't have questioned his acquiescence. But she didn't believe there was a meek bone in Gavin's body. Beneath his quiet exterior was solid steel. Not unlike his father.

The McKenzie men were enough to drive a sober woman to drink, she thought as she set her stepdaughter down on her bed and began undressing her. It was too bad they weren't more like Angel. Not that the child didn't have a will of her own— Lila remembered in particular a certain soft blue dress that was currently trimmed in bright red ribbons—but Angel had the courtesy to wrap her determination in a soft package, which made it much easier to swallow.

Angel was asleep almost as soon as her head hit the pillow. Lila lingered next to the bed, watching the sleeping child. How had the child's mother known what to name her? Bishop had said that his first wife had died soon after giving birth. Had she looked at her newborn daughter and seen the sweetness in her even then? Or had she given her the name Angelique as a kind of prayer for the child she'd known she wasn't going to be there to watch over?

Lila touched her hand to her own stomach. Thinking of the life growing there, she offered up a prayer that she'd be able to see her own son or daughter grow to adulthood. But there was no sense worrying about that now. Or any other time, for that matter. It was in God's hands and she had to trust that He would take care of her and the child she carried. With a sigh, she turned and left the room, pulling the door almost shut behind her.

Gavin had just finished filling the wood box when she entered the kitchen. She saw at a glance that he'd brought in a good mix of small and large pieces, along with plenty of kindling to make it easy to get a fire going in the morning.

"That looks fine, Gavin. Thank you."

She expected him to mumble an acknowledgment and leave the room. Though she liked to think that he was starting to feel trust, if not yet affection, for her, he was not much inclined to seek out her company. But tonight he surprised her by lingering in the kitchen. Lila gave him a questioning look as she began to clear the table, but whatever was on his mind, he didn't seem in any hurry to bring it up. Reminding herself that patience was a virtue, she continued with what she was doing, leaving him to decide when he was ready to speak.

She drew enough hot water from the reservoir in the stove to fill a dishpan. There weren't many dishes so washing them was the work of just a few minutes. All the time she worked, Lila was acutely aware of Gavin's presence. By the time the dishes were rinsed and set to dry and he still hadn't said anything, her patience had run out. Drying her hands on a soft linen towel, she turned to look at him.

"Are you going to tell me what's on your mind?" she asked.

"Nothing."

"Nothing?" She arched one brow in disbelief. "You just wanted to watch me wash the dishes?"

He shrugged and looked down at the floor. Looking at him, Lila was struck by how young he was. He acted so much older than his years that it was easy to forget that he was still a child.

"What is it, Gavin?" she asked quietly.

He shrugged again and she thought he might not answer, but then he spoke without looking at her. "I saw him leave."

"Your father?" She'd yet to hear Gavin refer to Bishop as anything other than "him" or "he."

"Yeah. He looked angry."

"He might have been a little . . . upset," she temporized. Lord, she didn't know anything about being a mother. How was she supposed to handle this? Nothing in her past had given her any idea of what to say to him. As far as she knew, her parents had never exchanged so much as a harsh word with each other. What if he asked her why Bishop was upset?

"Is he coming back?" His tone was casual but there was nothing casual about his eyes when he looked at her.

"Coming back? You mean tonight?"

"Ever."

It took Lila a moment to realize what he meant. When she did, she was horrified that he should think Bishop might leave for good.

"Of course he's coming back! Why on earth would you think he wasn't?"

Again that casual shrug but she had no trouble seeing through it to the fear beneath. "He didn't come back before."

"Before? You mean when he left you with your grandparents?"

"Yeah. And when Mama was going to have Angel and he left us there. He didn't come back then."

Lila stared at him, at a loss for words. How could she have missed seeing how Gavin felt? Had she been so absorbed in her own fears and uncertainties that she'd failed to see his?

"Sit down, Gavin." She pulled a chair out from the table and sank into it, gesturing him to another. He hesitated a moment before obeying. He sat rigidly upright in the chair, his eyes wary as he looked at her. "Your father was upset tonight. We . . . disagreed rather strongly about something. But that doesn't mean he isn't coming back."

"How do you know?"

The stark question revealed a deep vulnerability that broke Lila's heart. "Because he wouldn't leave us like that. I don't know what happened before.

But I do know that he wouldn't just walk out on the three of us—four," she added, touching her stomach. "I don't know why he left you and your mother in St. Louis but I'm sure there was a good reason. Did you ever ask your mother about it?"

It was a risky question. For all she knew, Bishop's first wife had had nothing good to say about her husband.

"I asked once. She said I wasn't to blame him for going—that she'd sent him away. She said he was a good man who'd made a bad choice. I didn't know what she meant but she started to cry so I didn't ask anything else. She said it was her fault he wasn't with us."

*A bad choice? In his choice of wife, perhaps?* Lila wondered. She filed the idea away for later consideration.

"Didn't you believe her?"

"I don't know. Maybe." Again that carefully indifferent shrug, as if they were discussing a topic that held little interest for him.

Lila sought a way to allay his fears that Bishop might disappear from his life again. "Do you remember what I told you? About the reason your father decided to bring you and Angel with us right away instead of leaving you in St. Louis until after the baby came?"

Gavin lifted one shoulder in a shrug, his eyes focused on the floor between them. "Yeah."

"It was because he thought you were unhappy, remember?"

"That's what you said." Clearly, he wasn't ready to commit himself to believing her.

"That's what your father said," she corrected him.

"If he cares enough about you to bring you along with us, to get us this house to live in, it doesn't seem likely that he'd just walk out on us, does it?"

"I don't know." Gavin was not so easily won over, but she could see that he was considering what she'd said.

"Your father is a good man, Gavin. And he takes his responsibilities seriously. You don't have to worry about him leaving."

"I guess." He shifted restlessly. "Can I go to my room now?"

"Of course." Lila was amused to find that he'd apparently forgotten that he was the one who'd started the conversation. "Good night."

"Good night." He shot to his feet as if fired from a cannon.

"Gavin?" Lila's voice caught him in the doorway. He paused, his reluctance almost palpable as he turned to look at her. "If something ever happened to your father, I'd still take care of you and Angel. You don't ever have to worry about that."

"Why would you take care of us?" he asked, his eyes wide with surprise.

"Because we're family now. And family takes care of each other."

Bishop backed silently away from the door. He'd come back, all set to lay down the law to his wife. Instead, he'd nearly stumbled into the midst of her conversation with Gavin. He'd heard it said that eavesdroppers never heard good of themselves. That might be true, but it was certainly a surefire way to get a new perspective on things.

He moved into the shadows near the door. Hunching his shoulders against the chill in the air, he stared out at the dark bulk of the mountains that loomed against the night sky. Above them, the moonless sky glittered with stars, sparkling like diamonds against black velvet. From the direction of Paris, he could faintly hear a piano playing in one of the saloons, the sound made tinny by distance. In the near distance, a timber wolf howled, a lost and lonely sound.

*We're family now. Family takes care of each other.* Lila's words ran through his mind. A few weeks ago, she hadn't even known his children existed. And since their abrupt appearance in her life, Gavin at least had done little to endear himself to her. Yet she'd offered the boy the reassurance that she'd care for him, no matter what. It was more than he himself—the boy's own father—had offered, Bishop admitted with bitter self-condemnation. And more than his mother could have given him. Isabelle hadn't been capable of caring for herself, let alone her children.

It was a mistake to compare the two women. With her moonlight-pale hair and fine-boned beauty, Isabelle had been as delicate and fragile as a china figurine. Lila was sunlight and fire. Where Isabelle had been frightened of life, Lila faced it head on. From her response to him in bed, to her refusal to back down from an argument, she was the opposite of Isabelle in every way.

She'd taken his children into her heart, taken this house and turned it into a home, met every challenge with her chin up and her eyes clear. She was strong without being unfeminine, tough without losing her softness. Maybe a woman like that was worth making a few compromises for. Stepping away from the house, he headed for town, his expression thoughtful.

Now was as good a time as any to take one last look around.

Lila slid her needle through the fabric, using her thumbnail lightly to push the bead into place. Needlework was the one field of feminine endeavor in which she excelled. Her singing voice could make dogs howl. Her piano playing was atrocious, and her talent for watercolors was nonexistent, but, at anything involving a needle and thread, Lila had soon far outstripped her mother's own efforts, a fact her mother had pointed out to friends with considerable pride.

Though she was proficient in most kinds of needlework, when she was working purely for pleasure, she preferred embroidery in wools or silk. She'd been working on this particular piece for several months, though she hadn't found much time for it in recent weeks and none at all since her marriage to Bishop. The lambrequin, with its elaborate pattern of scrollwork and flowers, done in wools and beads, originally had been intended to decorate one of the mantels at River Walk. She wasn't sure what she'd do with it now. It would look rather foolish on the modest mantel in this room. But that was something she'd worry about later. Right now, it was enough to take pleasure in seeing the work come to life under her hands.

The sound of the back door opening shattered the fragile peace she'd found. Bishop was home. After the way he'd stalked out earlier, she'd half expected him to stay out all night. Her whole body went rigid, her fingers almost cramping around the needle. She lowered the work to her lap and lifted her head as he entered the parlor.

"There's stew, if you're hungry," she said, determined not to let him see how shaken she was.

"No, thanks." He'd taken off his hat in the kitchen. Now he shrugged out of his jacket and ran his fingers through his hair. He sank down into the wing chair, draping his coat over its back. He looked tired, she noted reluctantly. She didn't like seeing anything that made him seem human. "Are the children in bed?"

"Yes. Angel all but fell asleep at supper. Gavin went to his room not long after."

He nodded. "They seem to be settling in well enough."

"Children are adaptable," Lila said by way of agreement. "They have to be since they're at the mercy of adults."

"I guess so."

There was a brief silence and she was surprised to realize that it wasn't entirely uncomfortable. Wherever he'd been since he walked out, his mood seemed to have softened. He leaned forward in the chair, bracing his elbows on his knees and fixing those piercing blue eyes on her.

"I could make you change your mind," he said without preamble.

Lila didn't have to ask what he meant. Their earlier conversation was vivid in her mind. She felt color slide into her face but she refused to lower her eyes. "I know you can make me . . . respond. But that just makes it worse—that I can respond like that to a man I barely know."

"A lot of people are strangers when they marry," he said.

"I suppose so." She looked down at the embroidery in her lap, stroking the tip of her finger over the

shading in a leaf. She chose her words with care, trying to make him understand how she felt. "But my
parents' marriage was one based on affection and
trust. It was a blessing they died together in a way
because I don't think one would have survived long
without the other. I always thought my own marriage
would be the same, that I'd marry a man I loved."

"Like Logan's brother? Did you love him?" Bishop
asked, not sure he wanted to hear the answer.

"I loved Billy," Lila said, more easily than he
would have liked. She continued without lifting her
head. "Did you love your first wife?"

"Isabelle?" Bishop hesitated, caught off guard by
having his own question turned around on him. He
wasn't sure how to answer. Had he loved Isabelle? "I
thought I did," he said slowly.

"Then perhaps you can understand something of
what I'm feeling. I'm not asking for that much—just
a little time."

Bishop was silent, though he'd already made his
decision. Damn but marriage was a lot more complicated than anyone ever admitted.

"I won't agree to separate rooms," he said. Lila's
head jerked up, her eyes bright with temper. He lifted
his hand to halt the torrent of angry words he could
sense hovering on her lips. "We'll share a room and
a bed but I won't touch you."

"You won't touch me?" Lila repeated question-
ingly.

"I'll give you the time you want," he said, feeling
suddenly very tired.

"How much time?" she asked, still dazed by his
proposal.

"We can talk again after the baby is born."

She looked down at her embroidery again, considering his words. It certainly wasn't what she'd hoped for. Sharing a bed with him wasn't what she'd had in mind. But it was undoubtedly more than many men would have offered. He would be well within his rights to demand that she accept him as her husband in the fullest sense of the word. Even those who might sympathize with a maiden's uncertainties would look askance at her reluctance considering the intimacies they'd already shared.

"If we're not going to be . . . intimate, wouldn't it be simpler to just have separate rooms?" she asked him.

"No."

The flat denial left no room for argument. Lila's mouth tightened in annoyance. He was the most irritating man. And she'd have been more than happy to tell him as much, but caution won out over temper. He hadn't given her what she wanted but he was willing to compromise. She didn't want to goad him into changing his mind.

"Very well," she said. "We'll share a room."

# Chapter 13

Lila was in bed, the covers drawn up to her chin, when Bishop entered the bedroom. He didn't bring a lantern with him so he was only a silhouette against the darkness—a large, masculine silhouette. She considered pretending to be asleep but, since she'd come to bed only minutes before, it didn't seem likely that he'd believe that. Besides, she was determined to handle this situation in a mature fashion. She wasn't going to let him see that this ridiculous arrangement of his bothered her.

"I was going to leave your nightshirt out for you

but I couldn't find it," she said, pleased by her casual tone.

"I don't wear one." He shrugged out of his shirt and Lila swallowed hard.

"You don't wear one? What do you sleep in?"

He turned toward the bed and she thought she could almost see the glitter of his eyes. "Nothing."

She was so busy trying to show how undisturbed she was that it took her a moment to realize what he'd said. *Nothing?* What did he mean, nothing? He couldn't mean he slept . . .

"You don't sleep . . . You can't expect to . . . You have to wear *something!*"

"I don't."

"That's barbaric!"

"It's comfortable." His voice held a shrug, as if he couldn't understand her concern.

"But you can't sleep that way now. Not when I . . . we. . . . You said you wouldn't touch me!"

"What does one have to do with the other?" he asked, his tone full of exasperation. "I sleep this way when I'm alone too."

"But you're not alone and you can't just get into bed like that. With me." She clutched the covers so tightly that her fingers ached.

"If it bothers you, don't look," he said, and she saw his hands drop to the waist of his pants.

With a gasp, Lila closed her eyes. She didn't open them until she felt him lift the covers and slide into bed next to her. His foot brushed against her calf and her eyes popped open. She stared up at the ceiling, hardly breathing, but other than that initial contact, he didn't touch her. Still, just having him lying next to her was enough to have her heart beating double time.

She lay there, staring up at the ceiling, her body stiff as a board, her breathing light and shallow as she struggled to avoid doing anything that might make him notice her. She had no idea how many minutes passed that way before Bishop moved.

Lila heard him sigh as he rolled toward her. Supporting his weight on one elbow, he caught her chin in his fingers and tilted her face to his. Her protest was reduced to a squeak as his mouth closed over hers. She brought her hands up to push him away but her traitorous fingers curled into the mat of hair on his chest instead.

He kissed her thoroughly, his mouth plundering hers with a ruthless sensuality that swept aside her determination to keep a distance between them. If he'd chosen to make love to her, she wouldn't have so much as whispered a protest. He kissed her until she was limp and clinging, willing to give him anything he wanted. Her breath left her on a soft sigh as he lifted his head and looked down at her, the glitter of his eyes faintly visible in the dim light.

"Now go to sleep," he told her, his voice husky. He released her, rolling away, turning on his side so that his back was to her.

It took Lila several seconds to realize what had just happened. *Go to sleep?* Stunned disbelief slowly gave way to fury. How *dare* he do this to her? Of all the infuriating, arrogant . . . male things to do. Obviously he'd set out to prove that she didn't have to worry about him losing his self-control and ravishing her in the middle of the night. And the fact that he had proved it was thoroughly annoying for some reason she couldn't quite put her finger on.

*Go to sleep?* Ha! There wasn't much chance of that. She was too annoyed for sleep. She'd probably never sleep again. At least not as long as *he* was in the same bed with her.

Bishop was gone when Lila woke, only the imprint of his head on the pillow to prove that she hadn't slept alone. She felt a spark of self-directed annoyance at the fact that she'd not only gone to sleep but had slept well. If she'd tossed and turned all night, maybe he would have felt guilty. She smiled suddenly, realizing how absurd the thought was. Talk about cutting off her nose to spite his face.

She shook her head as she swung her feet off the bed. It was a new day, her first full day in her new home, and she wasn't going to spoil it with spiteful thoughts—though she couldn't suppress the faint hope that Bishop hadn't slept a wink. It would have served him right after the shameful way he'd behaved last night.

Lila reached for her wrapper, which had been draped over the footboard, and shrugged into it as she padded, barefoot, across the room to the dresser. After lifting the china pitcher that sat there, she poured water into the matching bowl. The water was icy cold, of course, but it would serve to wake her up. Dampening a cloth to wash her face, she considered Bishop's sins.

First he'd refused her perfectly reasonable request that they have separate rooms. True, he'd come up with a compromise, even if it was only marginally acceptable. But then there'd been the shock of finding that he slept in the nude and had every intention of continuing to do so. *That* was something she certainly intended to see changed. And last, but far from least, was the way he'd kissed her. He'd said he wouldn't touch her and then had immediately broken his word. Still, he could have pursued his advantage and he hadn't. Heaven knew, she wouldn't have stopped him. *That* was something she had no intention of thinking about right now. It could wait for another time, when she was feeling a little more able to deal with all the emotions her husband so effortlessly stirred in her.

Her face washed and dried, she reached for the heavy braid that confined her hair. She studied her reflection as she loosened it. She remembered overhearing her mother talking to some of her friends, commenting on someone of their acquaintance who was expecting a child. They'd all seemed to agree that pregnancy was flattering to a woman, giving her a special beauty that shone from within. At the time, Lila had thought it an absurd idea. How could a woman possibly look beautiful when she was growing fat with child? But she had to admit that, now that the morning sickness seemed to be a thing of the past, her hair did seem to shine a little more and her skin seemed to glow in a way it never had before.

Had Bishop noticed? She threaded her fingers through her braid, loosening her hair as she picked up the silver-backed brush that had been a sixteenth-birthday present from her parents. Tracing the pattern on the back of the brush, she thought about the love that had existed between her par-

ents, so real it could almost be touched. She and
Bishop might never achieve that kind of closeness,
but she wanted to believe that they could develop a
respect to go along with the undeniable physical attraction between them.

She was uneasily aware that no stretch of the
imagination could put Bishop in her father's shoes,
but she shoved the thought aside. According to arti-
cles in *The Lady's Journal of Home & Hearth,* it
was up to a woman to set the tone of a marriage. It
was her responsibility to guide her husband by gentle example.

*A lady is at all times pleasant and soft spoken.
There are few things less attractive than an aggressive
female. Never forget that your husband is your lord
and master in the eyes of God and man. But it's
equally important to remember that it's a woman's
gentle, civilizing touch that protects men from their
baser instincts.*

There. No less an authority than *The Lady's Journal of Home & Hearth* endorsed her actions. Bishop
might not appreciate it now, but she was confident
that this arrangement was best for both of them. It
needed a little refinement, perhaps, she admitted,
thinking of that kiss. But she was sure they could
straighten out any small problems that might come
up.

Bishop was seated behind his desk when the
door of the jail opened. Since he hadn't heard any
shots and noon was a bit early for even the most
belligerent of the miners to be starting a fight, he
didn't look up right away. But then his deputy, who
had been sprawled in a chair reading a stack of

wanted posters, scrambled to his feet so quickly that he sent the chair skidding.

"Ma'am."

Even before he saw her, he knew who it was. It wasn't just Bart Lewis's awestruck tone that told him Lila had entered. It was the subtle smell of lavender that drifted in with her. The sweet seduction of that scent had haunted him for months. Lying beside her last night, it had filled his head, teasing him with memories of her silky hair spilling through his fingers, her soft skin under his hands. He'd had plenty of time to consider the wisdom of the arrangement upon which he'd insisted. Sharing a bed with his very attractive wife and not touching her was likely to make sleep an elusive goal.

"A-afternoon, Miz McKenzie," Bart stammered, sounding as awestruck as if he were speaking to Queen Victoria. Not that Bishop could completely blame him, he thought as he looked at her. Lila was wearing a dress in warm shade of rose that brought out the fire in her hair and highlighted the creamy softness of her skin. A matching hat was perched on top of her upswept hair, tilted at a demurely rakish angle over her green eyes. She was, Bishop admitted, considerably more impressive than the pictures he'd seen of England's short, plump little queen.

"Good afternoon, Mr. Lewis." She bestowed a smile on the lanky deputy that made his Adam's apple bob up and down. "It's a beautiful day, today, don't you think?"

"Yes, ma'am. I can't recollect last time I seen a day this pretty."

Bishop's mouth twitched with amusement. He was willing to bet that Bart would have said the same thing if a blizzard had been sweeping down out of the mountains.

"I've come to see my husband," Lila said.

"He's here," Bart assured her earnestly, as if she might have overlooked Bishop.

"Why don't you take a break?" Bishop suggested to his deputy as he came around his desk.

"A break?" Bart gave him a blank look as if he couldn't quite remember who Bishop was.

"Go have lunch," Bishop clarified.

"I ain't hungry." Bart's gaze had returned to Lila.

So much for subtle hints, Bishop thought, not sure whether to be amused or annoyed. The kid was clearly on the verge of complete infatuation. He might have been more amused if it hadn't suddenly occurred to him that the "kid" was twenty-four, only a year younger than Lila.

"I want to talk to my wife," he said, abandoning subtlety for bluntness.

"Oh!" Bart's thin face flushed a painful shade of red. "Sorry, Bishop. I wasn't . . . I mean, I . . . I think I'll go see what they're serving at the boardin' house." He snatched his hat off the rack beside the door, nodded in Lila's direction, and shot out the door as if a pack of wolves were nipping at his heels.

"He seems like a nice young man," Lila said into the silence that followed his departure.

"He'll do."

The laconic response didn't encourage further discussion of his deputy but, since she hadn't come here to discuss Bart Lewis, that was fine with Lila. She'd come to discuss something much more important, and it seemed to her a stroke of genius to have the conversation here. The small jailhouse was about as far from intimate as it was possible to get. Built of solid stone, the walls were enlivened by wanted posters. The furnishings consisted of a battered wooden desk, a potbelly stove, and a glass-front cabinet that held an impressive array of guns. The windows were small but fronted onto the street, and since anyone could walk in at any time, it was the next best thing to a public location. It should be possible to have a calm, rationale discussion, no matter how annoying he was.

"Angel is with Bridget. And William Smythe and Joseph Sunday offered to show Gavin his favorite fishing hole."

"The banker's son?" Bishop arched one dark brow. "I'm surprised Sara Smythe is willing to risk her son coming in contact with Gavin. She's not exactly an admirer of mine."

"There aren't many boys around for William to play with," Lila pointed out with careful honesty.

"That's true. I bet she'll have some sleepless nights, worrying about what a terrible influence Gavin might be." He didn't sound particularly concerned by the thought of Sara's insomnia, nor by her low opinion of him.

"That's possible," Lila agreed. She didn't care about Sara Smythe any more than she had about Bart Lewis. She cleared her throat. "I was hoping I could talk to you for a moment."

"I'm listening." Unfortunately, he was also watching her with those cool blue eyes that made it so difficult to think.

Lila looked away, fidgeting with the strings on her reticule. It had seemed so simple when she thought about it earlier. But nothing was ever simple when Bishop was standing so close.

She met his eyes, trying to look and sound coolly confident. "What happened last night, when you kissed me, I mean. It—it can't happen again."

Bishop raised his brows. "Are you telling me I can't kiss you?"

Something in his soft tone made her uneasy but she lifted her chin. "It wasn't part of our agreement."

"The only thing I agreed to do was give you some time. I didn't say anything about not kissing you."

"I thought you were a man of your word," she snapped, forgetting her determination to remain calm at all costs.

"I am. I gave you my word that I wouldn't make love to you until after the baby's born, unless you ask me to. And I won't. That doesn't mean I won't kiss you now and again."

"Against my will?" The implication that she might *ask* him to make love to her was infuriating. It would be a cold day in hell before *she* asked *him* for anything, let alone that.

"I don't recall you begging for mercy when I kissed you," Bishop drawled. His own temper was visible in the tightness of his mouth, a warning she chose to ignore.

"You didn't give me much chance to protest, did you? You just . . . pounced on me like a . . . an uncivilized brute."

"Pounced? Uncivilized brute?"

To Lila's chagrin, amusement replaced the anger that had been simmering in his eyes. While it hadn't been part of her plan to make him angry, she preferred that to knowing that she'd amused him.

"You know what I mean," she muttered.

"Like I said, I don't recall you begging for mercy last night. Nor a few days ago when I made love to you, for that matter." He grinned wickedly. "Now that I think about it, I do seem to recall you begging then, but it wasn't mercy you were asking for."

Goaded beyond endurance, Lila swung at him. He moved with that speed that always surprised her, catching her hand in his and using the hold to jerk her up against his chest. He'd held her like this once before, she remembered. In the church right after breaking up her wedding to Logan. She'd felt the same frustrated anger then that she did now.

"You tried that once before," he said, making it clear that he hadn't forgotten either. "You should learn to control your temper."

"I didn't have a temper until I met you," she snapped.

"Bring out the best in you, do I?"

Lila bit back the urge to scream at him. Remembering her mother's strictures about acting like a lady, she struggled to regain control.

"I don't want you to kiss me again the way you did last night," she said tightly.

He didn't respond right away, at least not verbally. He brought his free hand up to her face. His fingertips slid gently over her cheeks and traced the rigid line of her jaw, leaving tingling awareness everywhere they touched. He trailed his hand down her throat and set the pad of his thumb over the pulse at the base of her throat.

"Are you afraid of me?" he asked softly.

"Certainly not!" Though it had been pride that dictated her quick answer, it was also the truth. She was frightened by the ease with which he could make her lose control, but she wasn't afraid of him. Somewhere inside, she knew he wouldn't hurt her. And despite her protestations to the contrary, she knew he wouldn't force her to do anything she didn't want to do. That was the problem. He could make her *want* to do things she shouldn't.

"Then why is your pulse beating so fast?" He was so close that she could feel his breath against her forehead. Lila stared into his eyes, mesmerized by their clarity. "Maybe the problem isn't that you don't want me to kiss you. Maybe it's that you do," he whispered outrageously.

It took a second for his words to sink in. When they did, Lila forgot all about ladylike decorum. Her eyes flashing with rage, she jerked her arm away from him and took two quick steps back. It was infuriating to know that he was letting her go. She glared at him, her hands clenched into impotent fists at her sides. She would have given a great deal to take another swing at him, but it would have been a futile effort.

"If my pulse is beating quickly, it's because you make me so angry," she told him.

Bishop appeared unmoved and with a sound that could only be described as a snarl of frustration, she spun around and wrenched open the door. Slamming it behind her, she took off down the boardwalk, sure that steam must be rising from her person.

She was almost to Bridget's house when it occurred to her that Bishop hadn't agreed to a single thing she'd asked.

# Chapter 14

Lila's temper was still simmering when she got to Bridget's. She'd never known anyone who could make her so angry with so little effort. With nothing more than a lift of his eyebrow, Bishop could make her forget everything she'd ever been taught about proper behavior. She'd gone her whole life without ever striking anyone—although she had kicked Douglas in the shins a time or two when he was particularly annoying—yet within a matter of weeks, she'd tried to slap Bishop not once but twice. And the fact that she hadn't succeeded didn't make her feel any better.

If she was completely honest with herself, she'd have to admit that she felt only regret at her failure.

She nodded a greeting to Mr. Fitch as she swept past his store. His answering smile was almost shy, and Lila found herself remembering the things Bishop had told her about him. If they'd come from someone else, she would have thought them lies, but, while Bishop might be a despicable excuse for a human being whose main purpose in life was to annoy her, she didn't think he was a liar. A fiend from hell perhaps, but not a liar.

Lifting her skirts a modest inch, she stepped off the boardwalk onto the dirt, turning off the main street. Her mood had improved only marginally when she let herself through the gate in front of Bridget's house, but she paused to admire the rosebush. A sprinkling of slender buds decorated some of the canes, a promise of beauty to come. Somewhat soothed by the sight, she continued up the walkway and knocked on the door. Bridget's voice called out from inside, inviting her to enter.

"I'm in the kitchen." Lila made her way through the house, hearing the sound of children laughing somewhere outside. The big kitchen was filled with the rich scent of baking bread. Half a dozen finished loaves were lined up on one end of the big oak table. Crisp, tan crusts peeked from beneath the edges of flour-sack covers. An earthenware bowl sat in the middle of the table, the dough it contained starting to press up against the towel that covered it. Bridget was shaping another mound of dough into loaves, setting them in waiting pans.

"Are you going into the bakery business?" Lila

asked as she set her reticule down and lifted her arms to unpin her hat.

"A bakery wouldn't be able to supply this family," Bridget said without pausing in her work. "The way they eat bread, you'd think it grew on trees. The Lord provides, Joseph tells me, but He's getting a good bit of help from me when it comes to feeding this family."

"Men generally neither understand nor appreciate a woman's point of view," Lila said, setting her hat on a chair.

Bridget glanced at her, one sandy red brow raised in question. "Had words with the sheriff, did you?"

Lila flushed with embarrassment at having allowed Bridget to guess as much. "I don't know what gave you that impression," she said stiffly.

"It's a subtle thing," Bridget said as she shaped the last of the dough and set it into a loaf pan. Straightening, she wiped her hands on the apron tied around her slender waist and gave Lila a considering look. "I think it might have been the fact that your hair seems a mite redder than it did when you left the little one here."

"My hair?" Lila put her hand up to touch the carefully pinned twist into which she'd confined the heavy mass that morning.

"I was thinking it might be a good idea to have a bucket of water handy, just in case it actually burst into flames." Her hazel eyes twinkled with laughter.

"That's ridiculous," Lila said, torn between amusement and embarrassment that she'd allowed her anger to show. In the best of all possible worlds, a lady didn't feel strong emotions but, if she *did* feel them, she certainly didn't reveal them. "My hair doesn't look any different."

"Maybe not," Bridget conceded. "But there's no denying the sparkle of temper in your eyes. Had a tiff with him, did you?"

"We . . . disagreed," Lila admitted uneasily.

"Don't take it so much to heart." Bridget tossed a towel over the loaves she'd just shaped. "Your husband has kept himself pretty much to himself since he came here so I don't know him as well as I might, but he strikes me as a man with a bit of a stubborn streak."

"He has the temperament of a mule," Lila said before she could stop herself.

Bridget laughed. "The best of them do. It seems that strong men are generally blessed with more than a small helping of will."

"I think Bishop got more than his fair share," Lila said.

"Could be." Bridget set a cast-iron tea kettle on the stove. "I've always found a cup of tea is a good way to soothe the temper after having a run-in with one of the stubborn creatures. Is this the first time the two of you have had words?"

"Not exactly," Lila admitted uneasily. Bridget seemed so matter-of-fact about discussing something Lila had been brought up to believe shouldn't even be mentioned.

"Well, it won't be the last time," Bridget said comfortably as she got out cups and saucers. "My advice to you is to try not to take it to heart. Every couple has their quarrels now and again."

"My parents never spoke a single harsh word to each other."

Bridget's eyebrows lifted. "Did they love each other?"

"Very much!"

"Then they had their quarrels. They just kept it to themselves." She spooned tea into a sturdy brown china teapot. "Loving someone doesn't mean you agree with them on all things. In fact, I think the more you love someone, the more likely you are to disagree with them. At least that's the case with Joseph and myself."

Lila thought that she and Bishop were proof positive that a couple didn't have to be in love to disagree, but that certainly wasn't something she could tell Bridget, no matter how good a friend she was.

"You don't always agree with him?" she asked, fascinated by this glimpse into her friend's marriage. She'd never seen her mother utter a word of disagreement about anything her father said or did. And even if Margaret Adams *had* disagreed with him, Lila couldn't imagine her admitting as much to anyone else.

"Always agree with him?" Bridget's chuckle was rich with humor. "I don't even always agree with myself! My mother used to say I'd argue with St. Peter himself. I don't know about that but Joseph and I have had our fair share of quarrels."

"You have?" Lila tried to imagine the soft-spoken minister quarreling with anyone but the picture wouldn't come clear.

"Oh, well, I suppose if I told the strict truth, I'd have to say that *I* quarrel and Joseph allows it. If I want someone to speak back, I'd do just as well to be addressing myself to a piece of furniture." Bridget shook her head in apparent disgust. "The fact is, the man has the disposition of a saint—a fine trait for a man of the cloth but a source of some frustration in a husband. Not that I'd change a thing about him," she added, as if the love in her eyes hadn't already made that clear.

While Bridget poured boiling water over the tea leaves, Lila considered what she'd said. The idea that her parents might not always have agreed was novel but, thinking about it, she thought Bridget was probably right. Her mother had been a firm advocate of ladylike behavior, but she had certainly not been an opinionless cipher. There must have been times when she'd disagreed with her husband. They'd simply kept such disagreements private.

It occurred to Lila that she'd retained a somewhat childlike view of her parents. She'd been relatively young when they were killed in a carriage accident. At nineteen, she'd not yet begun to view them through an adult's eyes. When they died, her perceptions of them had been frozen in place and she was still thinking of them as that nineteen-year-old girl.

"Now that we've agreed that men can be provoking creatures, tell me how you're settling in," Bridget said as she removed the porcelain strainer from the teapot and set it on a plate.

Before Lila could respond, there was a brisk knock on the front door. Bridget clicked her tongue in annoyance. "That will be Sara. She said she'd be coming to get young William about this time. As if the boy couldn't walk home on his own. As protective as she is, you'd think William was next in line for the throne of England, with kidnappers lurking behind every bush, ready to jump out and snatch him away."

"His father does own the Bank of Paris," Lila

pointed out in a dry tone. "Perhaps she's concerned that, as heir to the Symthe fortune, William is at risk."

Bridget snorted with laughter as she circled the table. "That's probably it. The Smythe fortune." She paused beside Lila, lowering her voice as if afraid Sara might be able to hear her through the entryway and door that separated them. "If gambling weren't a sin, I'd bet you two solid bits that her name is plain old Smith and not a single 'y' in sight."

Lila chuckled as Bridget left the kitchen. She was fortunate to have met Bridget. Her friendship had made everything much easier than it would have been otherwise. Sniffing the air, she thought that maybe the time had come to repay a bit of that friendship. When Bridget and Sara entered the room, Lila was just setting the first loaf of bread from the oven on a thick towel she'd placed on the table.

"They were starting to smell a little brown," she said as she pulled the second loaf from the big oven and set it down.

"I'd forgotten all about them!" Bridget exclaimed. "Thank you. Of all the silly geese! How could I forget them when I'm standing not three feet from the stove? Here, let me do that. You don't want to spoil that pretty dress."

She hurried forward and took the folded towel Lila had been using as a hot pad. "Since it seems I've already put you to work, perhaps you wouldn't mind getting out a cup for Sara and pouring us all some tea."

"Perhaps we should repair to the parlor," Sara suggested. Though her tone was polite, there was no mistaking the distaste in her eyes as she glanced around the kitchen.

"If you don't mind, I'd rather we stayed here. That way I can tend to my baking." Bridget set the last loaf pan on the table. "And it's easier to keep an ear out for the children," she added, nodding toward the back of the house where their voices could be heard. "Of course, here I am assuming you've time for tea, Sara. Do you need to be taking William and rushing home?"

Lila wondered if she was the only one who heard the faintly hopeful note in the question. But Sara's sense of her own importance was too great to allow her to entertain the idea that her company was not devoutly desired.

"I can stay for a short while," she allowed graciously. Taking a lace-edged handkerchief from her reticule, she pulled a chair out from the table and dusted off its seat before sitting down. "William has his piano lesson this afternoon but we've a little time before that."

"Is there someone in town who teaches piano?" Lila asked, thinking Angel might enjoy lessons when she was a little older. While Bridget was sliding new loaves into the oven, she got out a cup for Sara.

"*I* am teaching William," Sara said. "Unfortunately, we do not have anyone in Paris capable of teaching the finer arts. Not that a piano teacher would have much work here since I own the only piano in town. Franklin had it brought up from Denver when I expressed concern that William was not getting a well-rounded education."

"How nice for William," Lila said politely.

"I think it's important for children to have contact with the finer things in life, don't you? Just because we're living on the frontier is no reason to forget that we are civilized people. And music is one of the hallmarks of civilization, don't you agree?"

"I'm quite fond of music." Lila set Sara's cup in front of her. For one wistful moment, she allowed herself to consider how undignified the other woman would look with a lap full of hot tea. "I'm sure William appreciates the effort you've gone to on his behalf."

"You know, it's not strictly true, Sara, to say that you've the only piano in town." Bridget shut the oven door and turned, wiping her hands on her apron. "There's a piano in the Red Lady Saloon."

There was a moment of dead silence. Sara could not have looked more offended if she'd just discovered a dead mouse in her teacup. Lila glanced at Bridget and then looked quickly away, afraid that she'd laugh out loud at the look of innocence on her friend's face.

"I certainly wouldn't know what might be in such a place," Sara said tightly.

"I should think you might have heard it when you walked by," Bridget suggested as she sat down at the table.

"I make it a point to cross the street to avoid places of that sort."

"Of course," Bridget murmured. Her eyes met Lila's across the table and Lila knew they were thinking the same thing, which was that, considering the number of saloons in Paris, Sara must spend a great deal of time zigzagging across the street to avoid walking in front of any of them. Her amusement was short-lived, however.

"I understand congratulations are in order, Lila," Sara said. She lifted her teacup, her little finger crooked at precisely the right angle.

"Congratulations?" Lila raised her eyebrows in question.

"William tells me that your stepdaughter told him that you're expecting."

*Good Lord, was Angel making announcements on a regular basis?* Lila smiled at Sara. "That's right."

"When is the blessed event, if you don't mind my asking?"

Since she'd already asked, it seemed a bit late to be asking if she minded, but Lila resisted the urge to point that out.

"My baby is due in October."

"So soon?" Sara's thin, dark brows climbed toward her hairline.

"It can't be soon enough for me. I'm quite anxious to hold my child."

Lila was a little surprised to realize how much she meant it.

"Of course you are. I was just surprised to hear that you were expecting so soon. After all, you just arrived in our little town. But then I believe Sheriff McKenzie did say you'd been married quite some time, didn't he? When was your wedding?"

Lila kept her smile in place with an effort. It was obvious what the other woman was wondering. And the fact that her suspicions were accurate didn't make her questions any more palatable.

"We were married in February. We met at my brother's wedding and were married just a few days later."

"So it was love at first sight? How romantic." Sara's tone of voice made it clear that she thought it tawdry and ill-bred. "Franklin and I were engaged for nearly five years before we were married."

*Probably took the poor man that long to get up the courage to tie the knot,* Lila thought viciously. "More tea?" she asked.

"Thank you." Sara lifted her teacup. "I'll admit that poor Franklin got a teensy bit impatient, but I wanted to be sure we were suited to one another. After all, choosing a life partner is such an important step for a woman. I think you were very courageous to know your mind so quickly."

"Some people recognize love right away," Bridget said, her eyes bright with temper.

"Yes, but love can be quite ephemeral. True compatibility is much more difficult to determine," Sara said, with the air of one dispensing wisdom to the ignorant. She stirred a quantity of sugar into her cup, apparently oblivious to the silence that had greeted her last remark. "So you've been married just a few months and are already expecting your first child. Franklin and I had been married several years before we were blessed by William's arrival. It seems certain he'll be an only child. You'll probably have a large family."

Her tone made the words something less than a compliment. The woman's arrogance was amazing, Lila thought, torn between laughter and irritation.

"I wouldn't mind that. Of course, with Gavin and Angel, we've a good start on a family already."

"That's true." Sara took a sip of her tea. When she spoke again, she changed the direction of her catechism. "Since you were obviously so much in love, it must have been difficult for you to stay behind when your husband returned to Colorado."

"An illness in the family necessitated my remaining behind," Lila said, her calm tone belying the knot in her stomach.

"An aunt, was it?" Sara asked, her dark eyes sharp and questioning. "I do hope she made a full recovery."

"An uncle, actually. And he's doing quite well, thank you."

"I'm so glad to hear that." Sara looked anything but glad. She looked acutely disappointed at having failed to trip Lila up.

Even from across the table, Lila could feel Bridget's simmering anger and knew she was barely restraining the urge to tell Sara exactly what to do with her questions and her superior attitude. Though she would have given a great deal herself to be able to give Sara Smythe-with-a-y a piece of her mind, Lila knew it would do more harm than good. Nothing would delight the other woman more than to provoke an angry reaction. Bland indifference was not only the safest response, it was probably the most frustrating.

She was relieved, however, when the back door banged open and the room was suddenly filled with children. They brought with them loud voices and the smell of dirt and sunshine, not to mention a shaggy black-and-white dog the size of a small pony. Instant chaos followed on their heels, and it was several minutes before Bridget managed to convince her son that Patch did not belong in the house, despite the fact that he was the best dog in the whole wide world. That this was not the first time this argument had raged around the dog was evident by his guilty expression and his willingness to leave without protest.

Once the dog had departed, Bridget was able to sort the children out and get them settled around the table with an efficiency that Lila found somewhat awe-inspiring. Balancing Angel on her lap, she watched Bridget slice and butter a loaf of bread. Its quick disappearance offered support to her earlier comments about the pace at which her family consumed bread.

Lila had met Sara's son before but this was the first time she'd spent more than a moment with him. Though he was a year older than Gavin, he was at least two inches shorter and considerably lighter. Franklin Smythe was a slightly built man of medium height. William had obviously inherited his father's build rather than his mother's taller, sturdier bone structure. Dark-haired and dark-eyed, he was politely spoken, with a sweet smile that probably would melt female hearts when he was older.

Glancing from him to his mother, she was struck by the way Sara's face softened when she looked at her son. The change was startling. Whatever else could be said against her, there was no doubt that Sara loved her son a great deal.

The presence of the children precluded any serious conversation. Angel and Mary were full of excitement because the three older boys had promised to build them a tree house that was, as Angel put it, "at least a hundred miles up a tree." Both Lila and Bridget looked less than thrilled with the idea. Even making allowances for exaggeration as to the proposed location, a tree house didn't sound like the safest place for two small girls.

"A hundred miles?" Lila repeated dubiously. She glanced at Gavin, who gave his sister a disgusted look.

"It's not more than six or seven feet," he said as he reached for his third slice of bread. Lila made note to increase her estimate of what a twelve-year-old boy could eat.

"That's almost a hundred miles," Angel said, unperturbed by the correction.

"You'll have to talk to your father about it, Joseph," Bridget told her son. "Make sure he thinks it's safe enough. He'll want to see the place you've got in mind."

"I'm sure Bishop will want to see it, also," Lila said. She caught Gavin's doubtful look and made up her mind that Bishop would inspect the site of the proposed tree house if she had to get him there at gunpoint.

"I certainly don't want William involved in anything that might be at all dangerous," Sara said. "You'll have to build this tree house without his assistance."

"It's not dangerous, Mama," he assured her. "And we'd be careful. It'll be fun. Please let me help."

Sara hesitated, clearly torn between the urge to give her beloved child anything he wanted and the desire to keep him safe from all possible harm. For a moment, Lila found herself almost in sympathy with the other woman. But it was only for a moment.

"No. I'm sorry, William, but you must defer to my

judgment in this matter. It's not just the danger. You must remember who you are. It's not as if you're going to be a common laborer when you grow up. When you inherit your father's bank, you'll need skills other than those learned by cobbling together a tree house."

Sara appeared oblivious to any possibility that her words might have offended anyone. William was not so unaware. A flush began at the base of his throat and worked its way upward, flooding his face with embarrassed color. Though the younger children were unaware of the insult, implied or otherwise, Lila saw Gavin's eyes flash with anger, but he didn't speak. Bridget appeared on the verge of an explosion. It was left to young Joseph to find the right words to smooth over the awkward moment.

"We could sure use William's help in figuring out how to build it, Mrs. Smythe. He's better than anybody at figuring out how to do things."

Sara's chest swelled at the compliment. Lila could see exactly what went through her mind. Joseph's words had transformed William's position from that of a common laborer to something in a more supervisory capacity. Permission was graciously granted.

Sara and William made their departure soon afterward. Gavin and the other Sunday boys went back outside. It was midafternoon and time for the little girls to lie down for their naps. Angel offered only a token protest when Lila told her they were going home. Yawning, she trailed off with Mary to get her wrap.

"I swear, it's difficult to keep Christian charity in mind when it comes to that woman," Bridget snapped as soon as the two little girls were out of earshot. After taking the towel off the bread she'd set to rise earlier, she punched down the mound of dough with considerably more force than necessary. "How she ended up with such a pleasant son is a mystery to me."

"He does seem to be a nice boy and it's plain to see that she loves him."

"Worships him is more like it." Bridget thumped the dough onto the table and began dividing it into loaves, her small hands moving with quick efficiency despite her annoyance. "Don't you let her snooty tone spoil your pleasure in this baby," she said, looking up from her task to fix Lila with a stern look. "Though she's never dared say as much, I know she thinks it isn't decent that Joseph and I have five children—thinks it's too lusty for a minister to have a large family." She pounded a loaf into shape and plopped it in the pan. Setting her hands on her hips, she looked at Lila, her hazel eyes still bright with anger. "All I can say is that if I were as prune-faced and nasty as she is . . . Well, it's no wonder she and that husband of hers only have the one child. Poor man probably had to close his eyes and think of God and country just to do his duty long enough for that!"

"Bridget!" Lila was torn between laughter and shock.

"There now. You see what she's made me do." Bridget flushed with embarrassment. "I'll have to say an extra prayer for saying something so uncharitable. That woman never fails to bring out the worst in me."

Despite the unpleasantness with Sara, Lila's mood was lighter when she left Bridget's than it had been when she arrived. Bridget's natural optimism never failed to make her feel better. The basket she carried held two loaves of bread, and Bridget had promised to teach her how to make it herself. She was very lucky to have found such a friend.

"I like Mrs. Sunday," Angel said, as if reading her thoughts.

"So do I." Lila glanced down at the child. "I like her whole family."

"Me, too. Mary's my best friend." She looked up at Lila, her china-blue eyes solemn. "I never had a best friend before. It's nice."

The simple summation made Lila's eyes sting with sudden tears. Forcing them back, she smiled at Angel. "I'm glad you and Mary are friends."

"Me, too." Angel looked pensive for a moment. "Next to Mary, I'm most glad I met Joseph 'cause I'm going to marry him when I grow up."

"I'm starting to believe you," Lila murmured. She laughed softly. "And heaven help poor Joseph."

"Ma'am?"

Lila came to an abrupt halt to avoid running into the man who'd stepped in front of her. He was a large man with a head of wild black hair and a bushy beard that looked vigorous enough to have a life of its own. If it hadn't been broad daylight, she might have been frightened. But despite his ferocious appearance, there was nothing threatening in his expression.

"Yes?" She shifted so that Angel was partially concealed behind her skirts.

"Pardon me, ma'am." The giant swept his hat off his head and twisted it between his hands. "I know it ain't exactly proper, me stoppin' you on the street and all, but I just got back to town after spending the winter working my claim. You're the first female I seen in a long time and the prettiest one I seen in even longer. I was wondering if you'd be willin' to just let me look at you awhile."

Lila stared at him, at a loss for words. She'd never heard of anything quite like it. He wanted to *look* at her? There was nothing threatening in his stance. In fact, other than the sheer size of him, he looked quite harmless. But that didn't mean that she was going to stand there on the boardwalk in front of the offices of the *Paris Examiner* and let a complete stranger stare at her.

"I really don't think—"

"Is there a problem?" Despite the way they'd parted earlier in the day, Lila had to admit that the sound of Bishop's voice was not unwelcome. Apparently he'd seen what was happening from across the street and come to her rescue. Not exactly a knight in shining armor, Lila thought, viewing his plain black coat and pants. The brim of his hat cast a shadow across his upper face, leaving just his mouth and chin exposed. To tell the truth, he looked considerably more dangerous than the miner standing in front of her.

"I'm not causing any trouble," the other man said as Bishop stepped onto the boardwalk next to Lila.

"That so?" Though the question was directed to Lila, Bishop kept his eyes on the miner.

"He was . . . perfectly polite," Lila said truthfully. Something told her that it wouldn't be a good idea to tell her husband why the man had stopped her.

"I don't want no trouble," the miner said. Though he was as tall as Bishop and outweighed him by at least thirty pounds, he seemed anxious that Bishop not misunderstand him. "I didn't mean any harm to the lady. Or to the little one," he added, casting a quick glance at Angel who was watching the proceedings from behind the shelter of Lila's rose-colored skirts.

"The lady is my wife," Bishop said softly. There was nothing overtly threatening in his tone, but the bigger man actually paled. At least Lila thought he did. It was difficult to tell when his face was covered by so much hair.

"I didn't know. I heard tell you had yourself a wife but I didn't know she was it."

"Now you do," Bishop said quietly.

"I didn't mean no harm, ma'am," the miner said, throwing Lila a quick look.

"I believe you," she assured him. She actually found herself feeling sorry for the man. He seemed so anxious to reassure her.

He bobbed his head nervously then turned and hurried off down the street, suddenly looking much smaller than he had only minutes before.

Bishop turned his head to look at her. Though his eyes were in shadow, she could guess their expression. And he didn't have to say anything for her to know that he was thinking of the discussion they'd had about the differences between Paris and the towns she'd known. Certainly she'd never been accosted by a man who just wanted to look at her nor could she imagine such a thing happening in Beaton, but, strange as the incident had been, no harm had come of it. Nor was she convinced any harm would have come, even without Bishop's intervention.

"I was handling things just fine on my own," she told him, forgetting how grateful she'd been to hear his voice. "He was really quite harmless."

"And you recognized that right away?" he asked. She saw one black brow lift in sardonic question. "It must have been his civilized appearance that reassured you."

Despite her desire to remain annoyed with him, Lila couldn't prevent her mouth from curving in a reluctant smile. "Civilized wasn't quite the word I would have used. But he was polite and I could have discouraged him without your help."

"Maybe," Bishop conceded. "But you'll be safer if everyone knows you're mine."

"Yours?" She bristled at that.

"Mine," he repeated without apology.

"I'm surprised you don't just slap a brand on me," she muttered.

"Don't tempt me."

Before she could respond to that, Angel interrupted them. Releasing her hold on Lila's skirts, she held up her arms to Bishop. "I'm tired. Carry me."

Lila held her breath, wondering what Bishop's reaction would be. She remembered making similar requests of her own father but the situation was hardly the same. She didn't doubt that Bishop cared for his children—their presence in Colorado was proof of that. But he didn't have much contact with them.

He looked surprised and disconcerted but he hesitated only a moment before lifting Angel up. He balanced her against his hip with an awkwardness that Lila found oddly appealing. He always seemed so completely in control of every situation. It was amusing to see him thrown off balance by a five-year-old child.

Her earlier annoyance with him forgotten, she walked home feeling almost in charity with him.

# Chapter 15

It would have been impossible to say whether Lila
or Bishop was more surprised to find the first
few days in their new home passing quite peace-
fully. Lila had assumed it would take her some time
to adjust to living with Bishop, let alone to become
accustomed to sharing a bed with him. But it was
pleasantly easy to accept the new arrangements.

After that first night, he waited to come to bed until
after she was asleep. Lila didn't know whether this
was out of consideration for her or a matter of personal preference. Either way, it made life easier for
her. And since he was always up and gone when she

woke, it was almost as if she had the bedroom to herself. Still, it was a little disturbing to wake and see the imprint of his head on the pillow and know that she'd slept soundly with him there.

When she thought about it, she told herself that she was adapting to her new life with relative ease because there had been so much change in her life these past few months that she was numb. The problem with that theory was that she didn't *feel* numb. She actually felt more alive than she had in years. She was filled with energy.

Perhaps it was some mysterious effect of being pregnant. Or maybe it was that, after so many months of uncertainty, things had finally settled down. Her life might not be exactly the way she'd once imagined it would be. She couldn't *possibly* have imagined all that had happened in the past few months. But good, bad, or indifferent—and there was a bit of each— things were settled, at least for the time being. There was a certain relief in that.

She preferred that theory to the possibility that she actually *liked* being married to Bishop. Though, aside from his flat refusal to have separate rooms, he had not been difficult to live with. There was the matter of his sleeping attire—or lack thereof. She'd purchased a nightshirt for him. Buying such an intimate piece of male apparel at Fitch's had been one of the most embarrassing experiences of her life. But she would be severely remiss in her duties if she allowed her husband to continue his barbaric habit of sleeping in the nude, not to mention that itwould add considerably to her peace of mind to know that he was decently clothed.

She hadn't said anything to him about her purchase, thinking it better to just set the nightshirt and matching nightcap out for him. According to *The Lady's Journal of Home & Hearth*, it was best to lead a man into proper behavior by gentle example rather than by confrontation. *It's never a good idea to demand that a man do anything, even when it's clearly the right choice. Their natural inclination to direct can sometimes lead to a certain balkiness when thus approached. Better to gently point them in the proper direction and allow their feet to take the right path of their own accord.*

Lila wouldn't have applied the word "balky" to Bishop. Pigheaded and stubbornly unreasonable were the phrases that came to mind. Still, the advice seemed sound. Surely, when he saw the nightshirt, he'd realize that civilized people did *not* sleep in the nude. The first night she put the nightshirt out, she went to bed pleased at having found a simple solution to a tricky problem. The next morning she found the nightshirt and cap, still neatly folded and obviously unused, on top of the dresser.

Some women might have accepted this as a sign of defeat. But Lila was made of sterner stuff. Given time, Bishop would see the error of his ways. Every night since then, she placed the nightshirt and cap on his pillow. Every morning she found it, still folded, on the dresser. The only variation in the pattern was the morning she found the nightshirt on the dresser and the nightcap in the trash. Though her mouth tightened a little, she took it as a positive sign. He could have thrown them both out.

Other than that ongoing conflict, she was reasonably content with the pattern of her life, at least for the moment. Considering the rocky start of her marriage, things were better than she had any right to expect. She was starting to get used to the whole idea.

Bishop couldn't imagine ever getting used to the idea of himself as a husband and father. Though he'd been married to Isabelle for almost a decade, they'd lived together for a total of less than two years. During that time, she'd wanted him to be all father—to her as much as to the children.

Lila showed no sign of needing him to be a father to her. Of course, she didn't show much interest in him being a husband, either, Bishop admitted ruefully as he let himself into the kitchen through the back door. The house was dark and quiet. Though it had long been a habit of his to make one last circuit of the town after dinner, the last few nights, he'd been lingering over that last stroll, giving Lila plenty of time to be in bed and asleep before he got home. He didn't know what interpretation, if any, Lila put on his absence every night. Maybe she was too relieved to care. Maybe she thought he was doing it out of consideration for her. But the truth was, he delayed his return home for purely selfish reasons.

Sleeping with Lila without touching her was difficult enough without lying next to her knowing that she was awake and as aware of him as he was of her. If he waited until she was asleep, the torture was not quite so acute. A man with more sense and less stubbornness might have been willing to admit that the idea of sharing a bed yet keeping a distance between them was not as good as it had at first seemed. Bishop's mouth tilted in a self-deprecatory smile as he silently shut the door behind him. He'd certainly have gotten more sleep if he'd agreed to Lila's request that they have separate rooms, but he was damned if he'd back down now.

The smell of roasting meat lingered in the air, along with the slightly earthy scent of biscuits. He winced a little at the memory of those biscuits. He hadn't expected Miss Lila Adams of River Walk to have spent much time in a kitchen, so he'd been surprised when she turned out to be a more than decent cook. Her stews and roasts were as good as any he'd ever eaten, but her biscuits were another story. Bridget Sunday was teaching her to bake, and he sincerely hoped there were more lessons on biscuit making. The ones she'd served tonight had looked fine but the golden brown exterior had been a trap for the unwary. The interior had been the color of old glue and roughly the same consistency.

"I think these biscuits are much better than last night's," Lila had said as she pried one open.

Bishop's eyes met Gavin's across the table and a rare moment of communication passed between them. Without a word being spoken, they agreed to lie through their teeth.

"Much better," Bishop said. If he put enough honey on the biscuit maybe he wouldn't notice that it was only half cooked.

"They're good," Gavin said, managing to look as if he believed it.

Angel poked a finger into the doughy center of her biscuit. She gave her father and brother a dubious look but refrained from comment.

Bishop shook his head as he hung his hat on one of the hooks beside the door. A few months ago, he'd had no one to answer to but himself. Living in a room at the jail, his life had been relatively simple. He did his job and kept to himself with no one expecting anything more of him. Now he was lying about biscuits and avoiding nightshirts and having dinner with the minister's family.

Looking around the tidy kitchen, Bishop had to remind himself that he lived here. After so many years of living in rented rooms when he had money or sleeping under the stars when he didn't, he felt oddly out of place in this homey atmosphere. He'd been too long without roots to feel completely at ease with the idea of putting them down now. He'd already been in Paris longer than he'd stayed anywhere in more years than he cared to think about. His peripatetic ways had been a matter of necessity as well as preference.

One disadvantage of having acquired a reputation for being a fast man with a gun was that, if he stayed in one place too long, it was all but guaranteed that some kid would show up, packing a brand-new Colt, anxious to prove himself faster than Bishop McKenzie. He'd avoided the fights he could and handled those he couldn't. A combination of skill and luck had kept him alive this long, but he knew that the day would come when he'd be a little too slow or the luck would turn against him and he wouldn't be the one walking away. Over the years, he'd found it easier to move on before the next kid had time to show up and get himself killed.

He'd been drifting for so long that he'd forgotten what it was to stay in one place. He'd always assumed that he'd just keep moving on until a bullet found him. But a man with a wife and children didn't drift from town to town, blowing where whim and wind took him. A family meant putting down roots, making plans for the future.

A future. Hell, who would have thought he'd even have one? He was suddenly aware that he'd been standing in the kitchen for several minutes, staring at nothing in particular. Shaking his head, Bishop walked through the silent house. He must be getting old. He was spending too damned much time thinking these days.

Bishop had gotten into the habit of lingering over his coffee on Sunday mornings. *That* was where he'd gone wrong, he saw now. If he hadn't had that second cup of coffee, hadn't taken time to savor an unaccustomed feeling of contentment, he would have been out of the house before Lila and the children were up. As it was, he'd been a sitting duck.

Seeing him sitting at the kitchen table, Angel ran up up to him, her face lighting with that easy affection that he found so disconcerting. He'd done nothing to earn that affection, but that didn't seem to matter to her. She leaned against his knee and smiled up at him.

"We're going to church," she told him.

"Are you?" Looking at her was like looking at a miniature replica of Isabelle. The same china-blue eyes and pale skin, the heart-shaped face and cupid's bow mouth. But the chin was not her mother's. Isabelle's chin had been as soft and gentle—as weak— as the rest of her features. Purely feminine and as delicate as the rest of her, Angel's chin showed promise of stubborn determination. For her sake, he hoped it wasn't a false promise. The world had sent Isabelle running back to the smothering security of her childhood home. He didn't think this child of theirs would run from anything.

Either of their children, he amended as Gavin came into the kitchen just ahead of Lila. God knew, his son would probably stand toe to toe with a grizzly if the mood struck him. He felt a sense of pride at the thought, a feeling so unfamiliar that it took him a moment to recognize it for what it was.

"How come you're not dressed?" Angel's question dragged Bishop out of his unaccustomed introspection.

"Not dressed?" He glanced down at his black pants and white shirt, confused by the question. "Dressed for what?"

"For church," she clarified, giggling with amusement at what she deemed a silly question.

"Church?" he repeated blankly. *Church?* "I don't go to church."

"But aren't you going to go with Lila and Gavin and me?"

"I haven't gone the last few weeks, have I?" he said, hoping that would be answer enough.

"That's 'cause we wasn't settled into a house," Angel told him, looking surprised that he didn't realize that himself. "That's what Lila said when I asked how come you weren't going with us."

"She said that, did she?" He glanced at Lila, who was busy putting together a cold breakfast for the four of them. She met his look but offered no help. He returned his attention to Angel.

"I haven't been to church in quite a while," he said, stalling for time.

"Don't you *want* to go to church so you can go to

heaven?" Still leaning against his knee, his daughter looked up at him, her big blue eyes questioning.

Now, how was he supposed to answer that one? He could hardly tell Angel that he didn't believe going to church guaranteed your ticket to heaven, anymore than he believed not going guaranteed your ticket to hell. Church was good enough for most folks and certainly he wanted his children to be raised with a respect for the Lord's teachings. But he didn't feel the need for it himself.

Unconsciously he glanced at Lila for help, but she was busy spreading butter on the slices of bread she'd just cut. Though she said nothing, something in the set of her spine told him that she was waiting for his response. He looked back at Angel.

"I haven't really given going to heaven much thought," he admitted.

Her eyes widened and her mouth formed a perfect O of surprise. "You should always think about heaven, Daddy. Grandmother said it was never too soon to start worrying 'bout your immoral soul."

"Your *immortal* soul," Lila corrected briskly. Her eyes met Bishop's for a moment. "Though I suppose, in some cases, either word would suffice."

"But don't you *want* to go with us?" Angel asked. Her voice held an edge of hurt that went straight to Bishop's heart. But go to church?

"I—"

"Of course he wants to go," Lila said, setting a plate of sliced and buttered bread in the middle of the table. A jar of jam hit the table with a militant thud. Though her words were directed to Angel, her eyes were on Bishop's face. "Your father wants to set a good example for you and your brother."

Bishop felt the jaws of the trap closing about him. He could still refuse, of course. He was master in his own house, wasn't he? And he certainly didn't have to go to church unless he chose to do so. He glanced at Gavin and caught the knowing look in his son's eyes. Clearly, Gavin didn't believe for a minute that his father gave a hoot in hell about setting a good example for his children. The boy was too damned old and too damned cynical for his age. Bishop's jaw knotted with irritation as the trapped clanged shut over him.

"I'll change clothes," he said.

So here he was, sitting on a pew that felt as if it had been carved of solid granite, listening to a sermon intended to save his immoral soul, as Angel had put it, and he still wasn't quite sure how he'd come to be here. Worse, he had the feeling that, by coming to church today, he'd set a precedent of some kind and that he'd be expected to spend every Sunday morning in church, courting entrance to heaven.

He glanced at Lila and the children, who were seated to his left. Angel sat next to him, her hands clasped in her lap, her small face still as she listened to the minister's words. Gavin was on her other side. Though his expression was as still and calm as his sister's, Bishop could feel the restlessness in the boy. When he was Gavin's age, he'd have thought it a sad waste of a nice spring day to be spending it inside a church. His mouth curved in a sympathetic half smile before his gaze shifted to Lila, who was seated on Gavin's other side.

Bishop's smile faded, his breath almost catching in his throat at the sheer beauty of her. A sunbeam had found its way through one of the narrow windows that perched high up on the church walls. Where the light fell across her hair it seemed to catch fire. In contrast, her profile was as pure and graceful as an ivory cameo. Wearing an elegant dress of deep-gold silk, her hands neatly clasped around a prayer book, her green eyes intent on the minister, she looked untouched and untouchable. Only the sensual fullness of her mouth belied the purity of the image.

Bishop thought suddenly of the last time he'd been in a church, the day he'd stopped Lila's wedding. She'd looked exquisite that day, also. The cobweb-fine lace veil had skimmed over her fiery hair, falling almost to the floor, a fragile frame for her slender body. Clad all in white, she'd looked as pure and virginal as a nun. For a moment, he'd thought that Susan's letter had been wrong, that his own memory was mistaken. He couldn't possibly have touched this woman, have held her in his arms and felt her come apart with pleasure beneath him. But then he'd seen the remembrance in her eyes, the guilty knowledge—and the plea that he not do anything to tumble her world into chaos.

There had been an instant, hardly more than a heartbeat, when he'd considered turning and walking away—out of the church, out of her life. But even as the thought occurred to him, it had been drowned out by a wave of possessiveness so powerful that it had been a knife in his gut. She was his. He'd been the one to feel the fragile surrender of her maidenhead; it was his child she carried within her. She was his by right and he had to claim her. Looking at her now, he knew that he'd make the same choices again. No matter what the cost, now or in the future, he had to have her.

Discomfited by the intensity of his own thoughts, Bishop was relieved to realize that the service had come to an end. He rose with the rest of the congregation, aware of the attention he was attracting. Most of the glances were simply curious—after all, it was the first time the citizens of Paris had seen their sheriff set foot inside the church—but a few of the looks coming his way held more than a touch of indignation, and he knew the Lord would be taken severely to task by some for not striking him down with a bolt of lightning the moment he dared set foot on hallowed ground. After all, everyone knew he'd broken more than his fair share of the Lord's rules, starting with thou shalt not kill. And would probably do as much again, if it came right down to it. The fact that the town had hired him precisely because of his skill with a gun was not excuse enough, according to some.

Bishop's shoulders shifted uneasily. He didn't give a tinker's damn what the townspeople thought of his sudden religious leanings, but he'd never much cared for finding himself the center of attention. He was more comfortable staying in the shadows. He was startled to feel Angel slipping her hand into his. Glancing down at her, he saw her giving him a concerned look, as if she'd picked up on his uneasiness and was trying to reassure him. The idea of *her* trying to reassure *him* startled a smile out of Bishop that surprised several people who thought they knew him.

Progress down the aisle was slowed by the necessity of everyone stopping to greet the minister, who stood on the step outside the doors. Bishop watched as Joseph pressed Lila's hand between his, his face lighting in a smile. His liking for her was plain to read. It seemed that, in the short time she'd been in Paris, she'd made more of a place for herself than he had in all the months that had gone before.

Joseph shook hands with Gavin, who looked as uncomfortable as his father felt and then leaned down to say hello to Angel, who returned his greeting with such adult composure that it was hard to remember how young she was. Then Bishop was face to face with the minister.

"It's good to see you, Bishop," Joseph said as they shook hands.

"And you, Joseph." He could say that honestly enough. He liked Joseph Sunday. It was the man's profession that caused him a bit of uneasiness.

"I believe this is the first time you've joined us."

"I've never been much of a churchgoer," Bishop admitted uncomfortably.

"Your wife is a strong-willed woman," Joseph said, his eyes twinkling with laughter. Obviously, he was under no illusions about Bishop's religious leanings.

Bishop glanced to where Lila stood talking to some other women. When he looked back at Joseph, his expression was rueful. "That she is."

Lila saw Sara Smythe making a beeline for her across the church yard. A quick glance around told her that there was no graceful escape route open. Bishop had been waylaid by Clem Lyman. The two of them stood talking near the church steps. She could hardly leave without him. Besides, living in a small town, her path was bound to cross Sara's regularly. She could hardly make it a habit to run every time she saw the other woman. Forcing a welcoming smile, she moved forward, taking Gavin and Angel with her.

"Sara, how nice to see you. And what a lovely dress."

"Thank you." Sara glanced down at her deep-blue silk gown with its discreet pleated trim and touches of lace at collar and cuffs. The simple style suited her ample figure. A glance at Lila's elegant gold silk gown, softly draped across the front and trimmed with a row of jet buttons, made her mouth tighten. "I think restraint in dress is the hallmark of a true lady, don't you?"

Lila wondered if she was being subtly accused of flashy dress. "I believe I'd put kindness and good manners ahead of dress," she commented.

"But the way one dresses is a reflection of one's true nature," Sara stated in a tone that brooked no argument.

"It seems to me it's more frequently a reflection of the contents of one's purse."

Sara's mouth tightened and her dark eyes flashed with irritation but she allowed the subject to drop. "I was quite surprised to see your husband here," she said, glancing to where Bishop stood talking to Clem Lyman.

"Were you?" Lila raised her brows in question. She followed Sara's eyes and saw that a couple of other men had joined them. She wondered if it was her imagination that Bishop looked surprised and a little uneasy to find himself a part of the small group.

"Well, he hasn't exactly been a regular member of the congregation," Sara said with delicate sarcasm. "In fact, I believe this is the first time he's attended a service at all."

"Really?" Lila laughed indulgently. She would

have given a great deal to be able to wipe that smirk off Sara's face, preferably with the flat of her hand. She reached down to twitch one of the ribbons that held Angel's flaxen hair in place. "You know how bachelors are. They're inclined to be careless about such things. Obviously, now that he has a family to consider, things have changed. I'm sure you can understand his concern that his children have a proper upbringing."

"Naturally." Sara cast a fond look at William who stood off to the side, talking to Gavin and young Joseph. "Nothing is more important than making sure one's children receive the proper guidance when it comes to the Lord's teachings. Still, I can't deny that I'm more than a bit surprised by his presence at the services today."

"Whose presence surprised you?" Bridget asked as she joined them. Dot Lyman was with her.

"Sheriff McKenzie's," Sara said. "I was surprised, as I'm sure we all were, to see him attend the services."

Dot's head nodded in agreement, just as it always did whenever Sara made a pronouncement.

Bridget shook her head in disagreement. "If you mean because he hasn't been before, you should have taken into account that the man has a family to consider now. He'd be wanting to set an example for his children, of course."

Lila could have hugged her right then and there. She barely restrained the urge to shoot a childish look of triumph at Sara. "So I was just saying."

"Children or no, one doesn't expect to find a man of his profession attending church."

"Why not?" Lila's brows shot up. "It seems to me a lawman has more need than most to speak to the Lord."

"I didn't mean the position he currently holds," Sara said in a repressive tone.

"She means because he's a gunfighter," Dot explained when Lila continued to look blank.

"A gunfighter?" Lila arched one brow. Bishop? She'd heard the rumors, of course. When he attended Douglas and Susan's wedding, there had been a great deal of talk. Several people had claimed that Bishop McKenzie was a famous gunfighter. She'd dismissed the rumors then and she dismissed them now. People were inclined to foolish exaggeration. Before she could say as much, Bishop and Clem Lyman joined them.

Bishop set his hand against the small of her back. The casually possessive gesture sent a not-unpleasant shiver up Lila's spine, a tingle of awareness that she would have given a great deal not to feel.

"Ladies." Clem's greeting included all of them. "I'm sorry to have to break up your pleasant gathering, but Dot and I have to get back to the hotel. We've guests today."

"It's a sin to work on the Sabbath," Sara pronounced, her disapproval plain.

"I'm afraid our guests would consider it more of a sin if we let them go hungry," Clem said, his good cheer undented.

"I've no doubt the Lord understands that an innkeeper can't take a day of relaxation like the rest of us," Bridget said. Her hazel eyes dared Sara to disagree, and Lila was amused to see the other woman back down.

Before Clem and Dot could take their leave, the small group was expanded by the arrival of Frank Smythe and Joseph Sunday. Greetings were exchanged, there were several compliments given on the service, Clem mentioned the possibility of rain before nightfall, and Dot said that Mr. Fitch had told her he was getting a new shipment of dress goods in all the way from St. Louis.

There was a lull in the conversation, broken by Bishop. "If you'll excuse us, I've things to see to. The Lord will have to add lawmen to the list of those who work on the Sabbath," he said, with a bland look in Sara's direction. The pinched line of her mouth was her only response.

Franklin Smythe cleared his throat. "Before you go, Sheriff, I had a letter from an associate of mine in Santa Fe a few days ago. He made mention of something I thought might be of interest to you."

"What was that?" Bishop's voice came from behind Lila. His fingers shifted against her back and she had to control a shiver of awareness.

"He mentioned that Dobe Lang has been asking around about you."

"Has he?" Bishop's tone was casual but Lila felt the sudden tension in him and knew he wasn't as indifferent to the banker's words as he sounded.

The other man cleared his throat again. "I . . . ah . . . thought you'd like to know Lang was interested in your whereabouts."

"Thank you." Again, Bishop's tone expressed only mild interest, but Lila knew she wasn't imagining the change in him. And it wasn't just Bishop. The mood of the small gathering seemed to have taken a grim shift.

"Who is Dobe Lang?" she asked. She turned her head to look at her husband. "And why would he be asking about you?"

"He's no one important," Bishop said, his eyes cool blue and empty of emotion. "He's rumored to have robbed a few banks but he's never been caught."

"They say he's faster than greased lightning." William's voice was high with excitement. The adults turned to look at him, unaware until that moment that he and Gavin and young Joseph had joined them. "They say he's killed better'n a hundred men and that he's faster'n greased lightning when he draws his gun. He's supposed to—"

"William!" Sara's shocked tone cut off her son's recitation of the skills of Dobe Lang. "Where on earth do you hear such things?"

"I read about them in the paper. I read about you, too, Sheriff," he told Bishop, his dark eyes bright with excitement.

"I wouldn't believe everything you read in the paper," Bishop said lightly. But the hand against Lila's back was stiff with tension.

"They say you was faster with a gun than anybody. They said you killed Augie Lang in a fair fight and then paid for his funeral. That's why Dobe Lang is looking for you, isn't it? 'Cause you're the one that shot his brother. They said you was cool as a cucumber about the whole thing, as if it was all in a day's work and didn't bother you a bit."

A taut little silence fell in the wake of his words. The people around them were staring at William with varying expressions of surprise, dismay, and, in the case of his mother, outright horror. There was no mistaking the worshipful expression in the boy's eyes. Clearly, he was smitten by a severe case of hero worship and his only intention was to flatter the object of his worship. Behind her, Lila could feel Bishop's rigidity as he stood next to her.

"Really, William, I—" Sara's sharp tone was drowned out by Bishop's quiet voice.

"Let me tell you something," he said, leaning forward to pin William with a brilliant blue gaze. "The day it doesn't bother you to take another man's life is the day you stop being human. And anyone who says otherwise is a damned fool."

Such was the power of his quiet words that no one even thought to offer a protest at his use of strong language when ladies were present. Lila felt a chill go down her spine. For a moment, it seemed as if a cloud had drifted across the sun, stealing the brightness of the spring day.

"I won't hear any more talk about killing," Sara said, breaking the stillness that had gripped them all. She gave Bishop a look that placed the blame for the turn the conversation had taken squarely on his shoulders. "Such a discussion on the Sabbath and standing in the church yard! I'll speak my mind frankly and say that I never did approve of hiring a man of your reputation, Mr. McKenzie. Now see what's come of it. Gunfighters descending on our quiet town and children talking of killing as if it were a game."

"If Paris was a quiet town, we wouldn't have had need of Sheriff McKenzie's talents," her husband reminded her.

"You have to admit that things have been much

quieter since he's been here," Dot said, unexpectedly coming to Bishop's defense. "Why, there hasn't been a single killing in almost two months!"

"I still say that trouble attracts trouble," Sara said adamantly. "No offense meant, Mr. McKenzie."

"None taken, Mrs. Smythe." Bishop tilted his head, his face completely expressionless.

"Mark my words, no good will come of it. Come along, William. Franklin." The Smythes departed with a look of disapproval from Sara, vague apology from her husband, and pure hero worship from William.

The Lymans said hasty farewells and disappeared in their wake, leaving a pregnant silence behind them.

"I know it's the Sabbath and I shouldn't be havin' such uncharitable thoughts," Bridget said, her Irish accent thickening a little with emotion. "But I don't believe I've ever met a woman more in need of a good, solid kick in the—" She broke off, glancing at Angel, Gavin, and Joseph, who were all listening with unconcealed interest. "—conscience," she finished stiffly.

"I believe you'll have to take your place behind me," Lila said tightly. Really, the nerve of that woman, criticizing *her* husband.

She was so intent on glaring after Sara that she missed the startled look Bishop shot at her. If it wasn't such a foolish idea, he'd have said she was angry on his behalf. He rolled the idea over in his mind, only half hearing Joseph's reminder that forgiveness and tolerance were good, Christian traits.

Bishop couldn't remember the last time someone had felt the need to defend him. Certainly no one had done so since he reached adulthood. The idea that

Lila might feel he was in need of defense was ludicrous. She didn't even *like* him, for God's sake. Still, the thought lingered in the back of his mind, reminding him that marriage was a great deal more complicated than he'd ever imagined.

Neither of them noticed Gavin giving his father a thoughtful look. Seeing the blatant hero worship in his friend's eyes had made him see Bishop in a new way, as someone with an identity completely apart from his family.

# Chapter 16

Since there was no formal school in Paris—teachers being in short supply west of the Mississippi—Gavin joined the lessons Joseph Sunday taught his own children. With Gavin gone a few hours each day, Lila was left with only Angel to care for. The little girl was remarkably self-sufficient for her age, content to play by herself if she had no other companionship.

Of the four of them, Angel was the one who'd most easily adapted to the cataclysmic changes in her life. Gavin still regarded both his father and Lila with the wariness of a young wolf, but Angel simply accepted them both with the same ease with which she seemed to accept everything else in her life. Lila envied the little girl her equanimity.

Still, a few weeks after her arrival in Paris, Lila was surprised to realize that she was not unhappy. She liked Colorado, liked the raw newness of it, the feeling that something startling might happen at any moment. While she still didn't see the dangers that Bishop insisted lurked behind every corner, she had to concede that it was nothing like the sleepy town where she'd grown up.

In Beaton, saloons did not jostle elbow to elbow with more respectable businesses. Bearded miners did not swagger down the street, shouting that they'd hit the mother lode and offering to buy drinks for anyone who cared to join them. Bishop told her that the mother lode generally turned out to be nothing more than a tiny pocket of gold and the miner would spend a winter's earnings within his first forty-eight hours in town and then spend a night or two in jail sobering up from the celebration.

In Beaton, ladies of dubious character did not boldly enter a store and shop next to more respectable citizens as if they'd every right to do so. Nor did those same ladies lounge on the balcony of their house of ill repute, dressed in scandalously cut garments and calling out invitations to men passing by on the street below.

Naturally, Lila deplored such behavior but she had to admit, even if only to herself, that after a few weeks in Colorado, Pennsylvania was starting to seem quite dull.

Certainly that term did not apply to her life these days. Turning over in bed, she stared up at the ceiling.

She was restless. It was late and she should have been asleep hours ago. The mantel clock in the parlor chimed midnight, its soft tones adding to her restlessness. Spring fever, her mother would probably have called it, Lila thought as she sat up and swung her legs out of bed. Perhaps it was the warming weather and the increasing hours of daylight that had inspired this sudden attack of restlessness. Or maybe it was the fact that Bishop had not yet come to bed.

Though she certainly didn't welcome his presence in her bed, she'd grown accustomed to it. She might fall asleep alone, but when she woke in the middle of the night, he was always there. Though she was loath to admit it, there was something comforting about having his large frame lying next to hers. It gave her a sense of safety, of being protected. Tonight, when she woke and found him gone, his pillow untouched, she hadn't been able to go back to sleep.

She pulled on her wrapper, smoothing one hand absently over the slight swell of her belly. It wasn't that she was worried, she told herself. Bishop was certainly well able to take care of himself. And it certainly wasn't the fact that, in thinking about those bawdy ladies and their softly voiced invitations, it had suddenly occurred to her that Bishop might be tempted. An argument could even be made that, if he were tempted, she'd have no one to blame but herself. But there was no reason to think that he'd succumb to their charms only after midnight. As he'd so vividly demonstrated a few weeks ago, lovemaking was not an activity limited to the hours of darkness.

Lila slid her feet into a pair of soft slippers. No, she wasn't worried about him and she wasn't concerned that he might be, at this very moment, breaking his marriage vows. She was just thirsty. That was why she was having trouble sleeping. A sip of water and she'd be able to go right back to sleep.

Moving quietly so as not to wake the children, Lila left the bedroom. After tiptoeing down the hall, she came to an abrupt halt when she saw the flicker of lamplight coming from the direction of the kitchen. So Bishop was home after all. Relief washed over her, leaving her almost weak in its passing. It was frightening to realize how much she'd come to depend on him.

She started to turn and go back to bed, her thirst forgotten, but something made her hesitate—a scrape of sound, a hiss of indrawn breath. Her slippers silent on the polished wooden floor, she crept toward the kitchen.

Bishop stood near the dry sink, naked to the waist. Lamplight flickered on the taut muscles of his back and shoulders, creating rippling highlights that, at another time, might have put her in mind of statues carved in ancient times. But at the moment, her eyes were riveted to the wad of bloody cloth he had pressed to his side. On the floor at his feet was a lump of bloodstained white cloth that she guessed must be the remains of the shirt he'd been wearing. For an instant only, shock held her frozen in the doorway, and then she was hurrying toward him.

"What happened?"

At the sound of her voice, Bishop spun toward her. The sudden move pulled on his wound and jerked an oath from him. The color drained from his face, leaving him ashen, the thick blackness of his mustache standing out in vivid contrast. He swayed and Lila was beside him in an instant. She started to slide her arm around his waist but he warned her off with a single word.

"Don't!" He braced one hand against the edge of the sink and she saw immediately why he'd warned her away. His right side was covered in blood from the middle of his rib cage to the waist of his trousers.

"Oh, God." The whispered words were a prayer as Lila fell back away from him, the room tilting around her. It was like seeing an old, old nightmare come to life. How many times had she dreamed of Billy's death, seen the hot rush of his blood as he died?

"If you faint, I'm not going to catch you."

The harsh rasp of Bishop's voice shook Lila out of the grip of memory. She shook her head to clear it and drew a deep, calming breath. "I'm not going to faint. But you may if you don't sit down."

"I'm all right," he said.

She pulled a chair away from the table, spinning it with a twist of her wrist and settling it behind him. "Sit."

He obeyed, sinking carefully into the chair. Droplets of blood fell from his side to spatter against the polished planks of the floor. He cursed under his breath, cupping his hand over the injury. "I'm bleeding all over the floor. I'm sorry."

Lila gave him an incredulous look. "You're sitting there bleeding to death and you're worrying about the floor?"

"The floor was clean," he said as if that explained his concern. "And I'm not bleeding to death."

"The floor will wash and, if you're not bleeding to death, you're doing a damned fine imitation of it," she said sharply. "What happened?"

"I'm shocked by your language," Bishop said, raising one brow in mocking disapproval. Given his pallor, the effect was not what it might have been.

"I doubt that." Lila set a bowl of clean water and a towel on the floor and knelt down beside him. "What happened?"

"I didn't move fast enough." He leaned back in the chair and let her pull his hand away from the injury. "It's a knife wound. It's not as bad as it looks."

"It couldn't be, or you'd be dead by now," she said bluntly. After moistening the towel, she began to wash the blood away so that she could get a look at the injury.

Bishop felt almost removed from what was happening. The pain in his side seemed a distant thing, a minor annoyance. He recognized the feeling as a symptom of mild shock and loss of blood. He'd underestimated how badly he was bleeding and had delayed returning home until he'd dealt with the aftermath of the barroom brawl he'd been trying to stop when he was wounded. While it was true that he was in no danger of bleeding to death, he'd lost more blood than he cared to think about.

Ordinarily he would have insisted on taking care of the injury himself. He'd handled worse, including once removing a bullet from his own leg. He'd never liked other people near him when he was hurt. Like a wild animal, he preferred to crawl away to lick his wounds and live or die on his own. He didn't know if it was the blood he'd lost or if he was getting soft in his old age, but, for the moment, he was content to watch Lila work.

Her hair fell in a thick braid down her back, gleaming like a banked fire where the lamplight caught it.

He thought lazily of wrapping that braid around his hand, using it to pull her close. The towel dabbed gently against the slash across his ribs and he sucked in a quick pained breath, jerked out of his hazy state. Fantasies of that sort were going to have to wait for another time.

"It's not as bad as it looks," she pronounced once the worst of the gore had been cleaned away.

"I told you it wasn't." Tilting his head, Bishop studied the long, shallow wound that started in the middle of his rib cage and cut down and in until stopped by his belt. He'd bled like a stuck pig but it wasn't a life-threatening injury.

"What happened?" Assured that he really wasn't going to bleed to death, Lila sat back on her heels and looked up at him, her green eyes wide and dark with concern. "And don't tell me that you didn't move fast enough."

"That pretty much sums it up," he said. "There was a fight at the Lucky Dragon. One of the participants objected to me breaking it up. It was nothing personal."

"Nothing personal?" Lila's brows rose. She turned the towel to a clean corner, then washed a little more of the blood away. The wound was still bleeding but not nearly as much as it had been just minutes before. "It looks pretty personal to me. If this was much deeper, you wouldn't be sitting here."

"Considering the fact that he was trying to gut me like a Christmas goose, I think I got off pretty lightly." He saw her blanch and immediately regretted his casual description. Reaching out, he touched his fingertips lightly against her cheek. "It's not that bad."

"It's bad enough," she said huskily. "You should have seen a doctor right away."

"I told you before, we don't have a doctor in Paris."

"You said the barber was also a doctor."

"I said he was the closest thing we had to a doctor," he corrected her, trying not to wince as she cleaned the wound.

"Then why didn't you go see him?" she snapped, her voice quivering on the edge of angry tears.

"Zeke was in the saloon when it happened—passed out in the corner." His mouth twisted in a rueful smile. "I suppose I could have had someone throw him in a horse trough to wake him up, but I'm not sure his medical skills would have been up to their usual high standards."

"It's not funny," she snapped, tilting her head back to glare at him. "You could have been killed."

"I could have been but I wasn't." He could have asked her why it mattered to her, but he wasn't sure he'd like the answer.

"So you just decided to come home and bleed all over my clean kitchen?" Her hands were a gentle contrast to the snap in her voice.

"I thought you didn't care about the blood on the floor."

"That was before I realized that this was all a joke to you. Why didn't you wake me?"

"I thought I could take care of it myself."

"Then you're not only slow, you're slow-witted. Any idiot can see that you couldn't possibly clean and bandage a wound like this yourself. You should have woke me up immediately. Even Gavin would know that much. And he's only twelve. It isn't a deep cut but it certainly needs to be taken care of. How did you think you were going to put a bandage on it?"

"I hadn't thought that far." It had been a long time since anyone had scolded him, but there was no mistaking the tone.

"Even if you could have cleaned it, you'd probably have made it worse by trying to twist around to get a bandage on it. You should have awakened me right away. I'm your wife."

"Sometimes that's hard to remember," he said softly.

Lila's head jerked up and her eyes met his. He saw the color come up in her face and knew she was thinking of the bed they slept in without touching, of the intimacies they weren't sharing. Seeing her discomfort, Bishop regretted his words. He'd agreed to their bargain. It wasn't fair to reproach her for it now. Especially not when she was still pale with fear. Fear she'd felt for him.

He had no right to expect her to be afraid for him, he thought as she bent her head to her task again. He'd torn her life apart and had done little enough to put it back together again. He was lucky she didn't take a kitchen knife and finish what Jack Michaelson had started.

Lila forced herself to concentrate on the task at hand. All that mattered now was taking care of his injury. She could think about everything else later. The kitchen was quiet as she finished cleaning the cut. Awareness crept into the silence, as soft and subtle as a morning mist. She was suddenly conscious of the solid male muscle beneath her hands. With every breath she took, she drew in the faint, musky scent of him. A mixture of sweat and blood and an underlying odor that she could only identify as Man.

"I have to get something to use as a bandage," she said. She rose and dropped the bloodstained towel into the bowl of water. "Stay here and don't do anything to open that cut up again."

"Yes, ma'am," he promised with a meekness she didn't trust for a minute. But she could hardly tie him to the chair in her absence. She'd just have to trust that he had the sense to stay where he was.

It was a misplaced trust. When she returned a few minutes later, Bishop was kneeling on the floor, dabbing at the spots of blood that marred the polished pine. He looked up when he heard her enter and, for an instant, he looked as guilty and almost as young as Gavin did when caught in mischief.

"You haven't the sense the good Lord gave a turnip," Lila said, setting her hands on her hips and glaring at him.

"I haven't opened it up again," he said, sounding so defensive that, despite herself, she felt her lips twitch.

"No thanks to your common sense," she snapped, refusing to soften her expression. "Get up from there and let me put a bandage on that cut before you do yourself some further damage."

After crossing the room, she bent to put her hand under his elbow, offering what support she could as he rose to his feet. Straightening, he caught his breath in a quick gasp of pain.

"Serves you right," she said heartlessly. She bent to examine the wound. "What made you think you were up to mopping the floor, anyway?"

"I wasn't mopping it. I just thought I'd get some of the bloodstains up."

"Why are you so caught up in worrying about the floor?" she asked, her tone not quite so sharp when she saw that he hadn't done any fresh damage. "Lift your arms a bit."

"I don't want the children to see the mess," he said as he obeyed her order and lifted his arms away from his body. "I may not be much of a father but I'm the only one they have. They've known more than their fair share of loss. I don't want to scare them."

Lila didn't say anything for a moment. She couldn't. Just when he'd annoyed her beyond all bearing, he had to go and say something like that. She cleared her throat.

"I'll clean it up," she told him, her voice a little huskier than usual. "You just do as you're told. If you open up this wound and start bleeding again, you'll wind up flat on your back in bed, and that's not going to do you or the children any good. Now, hold still."

"Yes, ma'am."

There was no bite behind the soft mockery of his acquiescence. Lila gave him a halfhearted look of disapproval. She put one end of the soft cotton against the small of his back. Holding it in place with the flat of her hand, she leaned forward so that she could wind it around his uninjured side. Because of the position and length of the cut, the only way to bandage it was to wind the bandage around his lower torso.

Standing so close and all but embracing him, Lila's senses were filled with him. Her vision was filled with the solid wall of his chest. Every breath she drew filled her head with the scent of him. She reached around him and, for a moment, her face was practically pressed against his skin. She could hear the steady beat of his heart—a solid, reassuring sound. When she drew back, winding the bandage as she went, her breathing was not quite steady.

"What are you using for a bandage?" he asked.

"I tore up one of my petticoats."

Out the corner of her eye, she saw his eyebrows go up. Though she knew it was a mistake, she looked at him. "First you use strong language, then you mention an article of intimate apparel. Next thing I know, you'll be chewing tobacco and carrying a gun."

The laughter in his eyes was irresistible, particularly since she could see the pain that lay under it. She sniffed and gave him a haughty look. "It's a good thing for you that I don't have a gun. Your life might have been in danger a time or two."

His laugh ended on a soft huff of pain as she snugged the bandage tight to hold the edges of the wound together.

"Sorry." Lila's teeth worried her lower lip. She hated knowing that she was hurting him.

"I'll live," Bishop told her. "Next time, I'll move faster."

"I think that would be a good idea."

As she leaned forward to circle the bandage around his waist, her braid tumbled over her shoulder, falling in the way of her hands. Before she could toss it back, Bishop's fingers closed over it. Lila froze in place, her arms half around him. She could see his hand wrapped around the thick length of her braided hair. There was something strangely erotic about the sight of his tanned fingers against her hair. His hand shifted and the heavy braid curved across around his wrist in a thick auburn bracelet.

Lila was chained to him, her own hair the shackle that bound her. Hardly breathing, she lifted her eyes to his. His eyes were a pure, clear blue, heavy-lidded and hungry, stealing what little breath she had left. She felt an echo of that hunger deep inside her, a pulsing heat low in her belly. His thumb stroked across the braid he held, and Lila seemed to feel the caress as if it were against her skin.

For the space of several heartbeats, they stood together, their eyes locked, their hearts beating in rhythm. Lila felt spellbound, aware of nothing but Bishop and the sharp hunger in his eyes.

It was Bishop who broke the spell by taking her braid and easing it over her shoulder so that it lay across her back. "It's late. Maybe you'd better finish up and get back to bed," he said quietly.

"Yes." The word was hardly more than a sigh. Her fingers were not quite steady as she turned her attention back to the task of bandaging his side.

In those few, still moments, she'd been forced to admit, if only to herself, that she wanted her husband on a purely carnal level that had nothing to do with the sweet, tender emotion she knew love to be.

# Chapter 17

By the end of a week, Bishop's wound had healed to the point where it was no longer necessary for Lila to change the bandage. Though he'd carry a scar, he'd actually been very lucky. Despite what he'd said about not moving fast enough, his speed had been enough to keep him alive. Lila was furious when she found out that the man who'd tried to kill him had received no punishment other than spending a couple of nights in jail.

"He tried to kill you!" she protested, when Bishop told her he'd already released the man.

"It wasn't personal. He was liquored up and looking for a fight. I just happened to get in the way. Jack's not a bad sort unless he's drinking."

"He's a menace to society and should be locked up," Lila snapped. Bishop had come too close to death for her to be in a forgiving mood. If this was an example of the ways in which things were different in the West, she much preferred the more civilized East, at least in this one area.

Bishop's injury served to shift the balance of their marriage in ways neither he nor Lila could have anticipated. It created new bonds and fostered a new intimacy between them. Each time Lila changed the bandage for him, she was forced to acknowledge her attraction to him. And each time, when the task was done and she stepped away from him, she found herself questioning her decision to keep him at a distance.

It was true that *The Lady's Journal of Home & Hearth* said that it was a woman's duty to help a man control his baser instincts. But they hadn't made any mention of her own baser instincts. And did not having relations with one's husband fall under controlling baser instincts, or was it in the category of refusing to do one's marital duty—a sin of mammoth proportions, according to the editors of the magazine?

Lila wrestled with her conscience, seeing questions in every direction and no clear answers. If she were to tell Bishop that she'd changed her mind—and she couldn't even begin to imagine how she'd go about doing *that*—would she be doing it because it was the right thing to do or because of the wicked desire he made her feel? And did marriage, even without love, justify the sin of lust?

On Bishop's part, not even the discomfort of his injury could mask the sweet torture of having Lila touching him. Each time it was an exercise in self-control for him. He wanted to reach for her and pull her into his arms, knife wound be damned. He wanted to feel her mouth soften for him, feel her body melt beneath him.

The damnable part of it was that he could have her without a whisper of protest on her part and they both knew it. She wanted him as much as he wanted her. It was in her eyes when she looked at him, in her touch as she smoothed the bandage around his waist. He could all but smell the hunger in her.

Maybe she was even hoping he'd make the first move. Then she could submit gracefully and not have to answer to her own conscience. But he was damned if he'd give her that out. If she wanted to change the terms of their marriage, she was going to have to say so.

With neither of them willing to make the first move, everything remained status quo, much to their mutual frustration.

Bishop wondered if there was another woman alive who could make kneading bread look seductive. He stopped in the kitchen doorway, feeling the familiar clench of hunger in his gut. Unaware of him, Lila continued with her task, leaning her upper body into the job, her hands working the mound of dough in a rhythmic motion that made Bishop think all kinds of thoughts he'd be better off not having.

She was wearing a plain cotton dress in a dusty shade of rose, the sleeves pushed up halfway to her elbows and a white apron wrapped around her waist.

With her hair caught up in a heavy knot at the back of her head and a smear of flour across one cheek, she was the picture of domestic endeavor. And he wanted her.

Though he made no sound, Lila seemed to sense his presence because her head came up abruptly and her eyes met his. They stared at each other, awareness strung between them like a tautly drawn rope. It was for a moment only and then Lila looked away.

"I'm making bread," she said, as if he might not have noticed. "Bridget gave me the recipe."

"Did she?" He walked farther into the room. He hung his hat on the back of one of the chairs and ran his fingers through his hair. He was aware of a feeling of homecoming, an unfamiliar sense of belonging.

"Bridget says yeast bread is easier to make than biscuits," Lila said as she continued kneading the dough. "You should be glad of that."

"Should I?" Bishop cast her a cautious look. He hadn't said a word about her biscuits, which were either rock-hard lumps or doughy lumps with nothing in between.

"I know perfectly well that my biscuits aren't always quite right," she said. She glanced at him out the corner of her eyes. "You and Gavin have both been kind enough to eat them anyway. Angel isn't old enough to have developed that much diplomacy. She very kindly informed me that she didn't think she liked biscuits anymore and that I didn't have to make them for her sake."

Bishop brushed one hand over his mouth to conceal a smile. "Maybe she just doesn't care for biscuits."

"And maybe I make the worst biscuits this side of

St. Louis," Lila countered. She punched the dough a couple of times and then gathered it up in both hands, shaping it into a neat ball before placing it in a white earthenware bowl and covering it with a clean towel.

Bishop started to say something consoling about her biscuits but his attention was caught by a movement outside the window. A half step to the left gave him a better view without putting him directly in front of the window. The area behind the house had been cleared of trees when the place was built, apparently with the idea of putting in a garden. The garden had not yet come to pass, though Lila was nurturing a cutting of that rosebush of Bridget Sunday's that she seemed so fond of. At the moment, the backyard was nothing but dirt and weeds backed by a ragged line of pines and aspens.

Gavin stood near the back of the yard, the light blue of his shirt visible against the dark-green shadows of the pines. Assured that the movement he'd seen had been nothing to worry about, Bishop started to turn away from the window but he hesitated and looked at Gavin a little more closely. There was something odd about the way the boy was standing.

"You're not usually home this early," Lila said, turning toward Bishop. "Dinner won't be ready for—" She broke off, startled, as he walked past her as if she weren't even there. "Bishop?"

He didn't seem to hear her as he reached the door and jerked it open with enough force to smack it back against the wall. Lila caught a quick glimpse of his expression and felt her heart leap into her throat. He looked as if he were on the verge of murder. What on earth? She hurried after him, nearly stumbling off the porch in her haste. Bishop was halfway across the yard, his long legs setting a pace she couldn't hope to match without breaking into a run.

"What the devil do you think you're doing?" The question was asked in a near roar.

Looking past Bishop, Lila saw Gavin turn, his expression startled. His blue eyes widened and his face paled when he saw his father. Remembering the fury she'd seen in Bishop, Lila could appreciate the boy's look of fear. She lifted her skirts indecently high to hurry forward over the uneven ground. She didn't know what had set Bishop off, but she was suddenly afraid to let Gavin face him alone.

"Give me that!" Bishop reached out and snatched something from Gavin's hand just as Lila reached them. "Where did you get this?"

"Bishop, don't shout at hi—" Her protest trailed off when she saw what it was he held. It was a revolver, blue-black steel gleaming dully in the late-afternoon sun. "Good Lord! Gavin, where did you get that?"

"I—I found it," Gavin stammered. His eyes darted to Lila and then back to his father.

"You expect me to believe you *found* this?" Bishop demanded, his fingers knotting around the wooden grips. His free hand shot out, catching Gavin by the shoulder, jerking his son a half step closer to him. "Don't lie to me, boy."

"I'm not lying." Lila hadn't thought it possible, but Gavin's face paled even more. His mouth set as he looked at his father, his eyes holding a mixture of defiance and fear. "I found it in the alley next to the Lucky Dragon."

"Just lying there?" Bishop asked in a tone of deep sarcasm.

"Just lying there," Gavin repeated, his voice shaking a little but his eyes steady. Lila had to admire his courage. She wasn't sure she could have been as calm in the face of the black rage in Bishop's eyes.

"Bishop?" She set her hand on his arm. His muscles were iron hard beneath her touch. "I think he's telling the truth."

He shook her hand off his arm without a glance in her direction, but she was relieved to see him release Gavin. Not that she thought he'd hurt the boy. Or she was almost sure he wouldn't.

With a quick flick of his wrist, Bishop snapped open the pistol. Though she was no longer touching him, Lila could feel a slight easing of his tension. "The firing pin is broken," he said, apparently speaking to himself as much as to either of them. "And it's too old to be worth fixing. Somebody might have just dumped it."

"I told you I found it," Gavin said, resentful that Bishop hadn't believed him without further proof. "I don't lie."

"What were you doing with it?" Bishop demanded without offering any apology for having doubted his son's word.

Gavin shrugged, his eyes dropping to the ground between them.

"Nothing."

"You don't do 'nothing' with a gun," Bishop snapped. "What were you doing?"

"Practicing," Gavin admitted sullenly.

"Practicing what? You don't have any bullets and this gun wouldn't fire them if you did. What were you practicing?"

Lila couldn't understand his interest in exactly *what*

Gavin had been doing. What difference did it make? The important thing was to make sure that the boy understood that guns were not something to play with, even guns that didn't fire. She shuddered to think of what could have happened if the firing pin hadn't been broken.

"Bishop—"

"What were you doing?" he demanded, deaf to her interruption.

"I was practicing my draw," Gavin said finally, the words seemingly dragged from him. He lifted his head and looked at his father, his blue eyes, so like Bishop's, holding something that might have been a plea. "I want to be a shootist when I grow up. Like you. Willie Smythe says you're the best ever, that you've never killed anybody except in a fair fight, and that nobody's faster than you are."

Bishop felt as if he'd just been kicked in the gut. His lungs were suddenly empty of air, and he saw Gavin through a red haze of pain. He was oblivious to the hunger for approval in his son's eyes. All he could hear was the echo of the boy's words. *A shootist. Like you.* It was like something out of a nightmare.

Most men dream of seeing their sons grow up to follow in their footsteps. Farmers hope their sons will share their love of the soil. Bankers try to instill a respect for money and the management of it into their offspring. Ranchers pray for a son to inherit the land and finish building the dream they've started.

If Bishop had been asked what he wanted for Gavin's future, his only answer would have been that he wanted the boy to find whatever happiness the good

Lord might have intended for him. The last thing he'd have wished was for his son to follow in his footsteps.

His skill with a gun had both kept him alive and cost him his life. A man with his reputation had few choices. Unlike other men, he couldn't simply live his life and let people assume his honesty. He had to come down firmly on one side of the law or the other. He could be a peace officer or he could be an outlaw. There were no other paths open to him.

If Bishop could give his children nothing else, he wanted to give them choices. And here was Gavin, standing in front of him, telling him that he wanted to throw those choices away, that he wanted to walk the same lonely path his father had taken. The thought created an anger in him like nothing he'd ever felt before. Something of what he was feeling must have shown in his face because he saw the last traces of color drain from Gavin's face, leaving his eyes almost painfully blue in contrast to the pallor of his skin.

"You're a damned fool." He spoke low and hard, each word coming out with the force of a blow. "The last thing in the world you want is to be like me. Guns aren't toys for little boys to play with. If I ever catch you with a gun again, I'm going to put you over my knee and take a switch to your backside until you can't sit down for a month. Do you understand me?"

Gavin nodded. His body was so rigid that it seemed to Lila a miracle that he could manage that much, but it wasn't enough to satisfy Bishop.

"I want to hear you say it!" he snapped, his tone so harsh that Lila felt herself flinch away from it, even though it wasn't directed at her.

"I understand," Gavin said, barely moving his lips.

"Go to your room." Bishop's voice didn't soften at the boy's acquiescence.

Lila caught a glimpse of Gavin's eyes as he turned toward the house. Though his expression remained rigidly controlled, there was no mistaking the sparkle of tears in his eyes. It was the first time she'd seen him even come close to crying, and her heart broke for him. She rounded on Bishop as soon as the door shut behind him.

"Don't you think you were a little harsh with him?"

"Stay out of it," he ordered her shortly, not taking his eyes from the gun in his hand. His peremptory tone struck sparks off her temper.

"I will not stay out of it! I am as close to a mother as that boy has and I will not stand by and let you terrorize him."

Bishop lifted his head. "Terrorize him? I'm trying to keep him alive. Or do you *like* the idea of him playing with guns?"

"Of course not! But I don't think it's necessary to scare the life out of him, either. He was trying to impress you. Didn't you hear him say that he wanted to grow up to be like you? Doesn't that mean anything to you?"

"It means he's a fool," Bishop said with a snarl. His hands tightened around the old gun until his knuckles whitened and Lila almost thought the steel might bend with the force of his grip.

"It means he looks up to you," she said sharply. "Most men want their sons to look up to them."

"Well, I'm not most men." He thrust the gun into the top of his belt and turned to look at her.

"What's wrong with him wanting to follow in your

footsteps?" Lila demanded. "You're an officer of the law. It's a perfectly respectable profession."

"He didn't say he wanted to be a lawman. He said he wanted to be a shootist. He'd be better off dead," he said flatly.

"Don't say that!"

"You don't know what it's like out here. You don't know what it's like to spend your whole life wondering when someone is going to come along who's a little faster than you are or maybe they'll catch you with the sun in your eyes. You don't know what it's like. Things are different—"

"If you tell me again that things are different here than they are in Pennsylvania, I'm going to scream," she snapped, interrupting him without apology. "Maybe I don't know what it's like and maybe things are different here but one thing I do know. If you're not careful, you're going to drive Gavin away forever."

"Better that than see him live my life," Bishop said coldly.

Without waiting for her response, he turned on his heel and walked away, effectively ending the conversation. Lila stared after him, her mouth half open in disbelief. She was still staring when he disappeared around the corner of the house. He'd just walked away in the middle of a conversation! Her breath leaving her on an infuriated huff, she stalked across the yard, her petticoats rustling a furious accompaniment to her stride.

While she was no happier than he was about Gavin playing with the gun, it hadn't been necessary to be so harsh with him. Bishop had overreacted to a ridiculous degree. It was perfectly natural for a boy to want to follow in his father's footsteps. Bishop should have been pleased, not furious. It was all very well and good for him to say that he was concerned for Gavin, but she hadn't seen any evidence of outlaws lurking in the underbrush, anxious to prove themselves faster than Bishop. She was starting to think that one of the ways the West differed from the East was in the inhabitants' propensity for exaggeration.

She shoved open the back door and walked into the kitchen, her heels creating an irritated tattoo on the wooden floor. And to think she'd been starting to wonder if she'd been wrong to keep him at a distance. Hah! She'd sooner kiss a rattlesnake.

# Chapter 17

Bishop glanced up from his desk in time to see Lila and the children walking down the boardwalk across the street from the jail. His fingers tightened around the pen he'd been using to scratch out a report. It struck him, just as it did every time he saw her, what a beautiful woman his wife was. She carried herself like a queen, all pride and grace.

She paused to speak to Dot Lyman. Seeing her smile at the other woman reminded Bishop of how rare that particular expression had been for the past few days. Ever since the incident with Gavin, the atmosphere at home had been decidedly chilly, and Lila's smiles had not been turned in his direction. It wasn't until it was gone that he'd realized how much he enjoyed the warmth that had been making its way into his relationship with his wife. But if she expected him to grovel and beg her forgiveness, she was in for a surprise. If he'd been harsh with Gavin, it was for the boy's own good.

Not that Gavin appreciated that any more than Lila did, Bishop thought, looking at the boy. Gavin had treated him to an exhibition of sullenness possible only in a twelve-year-old boy. He hadn't been talkative before but now his conversation was reduced to monosyllabic answers given only in response to direct questions. Bishop remembered Lila's comment that he was going to drive the boy away and wondered if maybe he'd already done just that. Gavin's body was still in sight but his spirit seemed to be somewhere else.

The only member of the family who was still speaking to him was Angel, Bishop thought, his expression softening as he looked at his daughter. While Bishop didn't blame Gavin for the resentment he so obviously felt, he had to admit that Angel's easy acceptance was a welcome relief.

Across the street, Lila and Dot finished their talk and she and the children continued down the boardwalk. They disappeared into Fitch's and Bishop returned his attention to the report he was trying to finish. He hated paperwork. He'd damned near rather dodge bullets than have to pick his way through the bureaucratic mess of forms and reports that accompanied even the simplest arrest. He might have considered making paperwork part of his deputy's job, but Bart Lewis had never made it past second grade and could barely read and write his own name.

He stared at what he'd already written, but his mind was elsewhere and no matter how many times he read it, it didn't seem to make sense. He dropped the pen with a disgusted oath and glared out the window at Fitch's. He'd never, in his entire life, known anyone who could cut up his concentration the way his wife could. When he'd been married to Isabelle, he'd never had any trouble putting her out of his thoughts and concentrating on whatever task was at hand.

Irritated with himself, with Lila, with the world in general, Bishop pushed his chair back from the desk and stood up. Life had been a hell of a lot simpler when all he had to worry about was getting killed.

Bishop was reaching for his hat when the door opened and Bart Lewis came in. "Afternoon, Bishop."

"Afternoon, Bart. Everything quiet?" he asked, half hoping to hear a denial. Quelling a brawl would go a long way toward improving his mood right about now.

"Pretty much." Bart set his battered hat on one of the hooks and ambled over to the stove. After lifting the battered enameled steel pot, he poured himself a cup of coffee, black as ink and thick as molasses from having simmered most of the morning. "I was at the station when the train came up from Denver."

"Anything interesting?" Bishop made it a habit to keep an eye on who came and went in the town. Sometimes it was possible to stop trouble before it got started simply by making his presence known.

"John Sinclair come back from seein' his kinfolk in Virginia."

"Yeah?" Bishop turned his hat between his fingers and wondered if he should go across and say hello to Fitch. He hadn't seen the old man to talk to in a while, and now was as good a time as any.

"He spent a night or two in Denver and said he heard tell of a fellow asking round about you. Fellow name a Dobe Lang."

Bishop had been looking out the window, but now his eyes jerked to Bart's face. "Lang?"

"That's what John said." Bart's thin face looked worried. "Didn't I hear tell of you havin' a run-in with some fella named Lang somewhere in Kansas awhile back?"

"Dakota Territory," Bishop corrected automatically. "I guess you could say we had a run-in. He braced me and I shot him."

"Self-defense?"

"So they said." Which didn't make Augie Lang any less dead.

The two men were silent a moment.

"You reckon this Lang fella askin' about you is some kin to the one in Dakota?" Bart asked, articulating the question in both their minds.

"Odds are."

"There's quite a few folks know you're sheriff here in Paris," Bart pointed out.

"Then I guess he'll find me sooner or later, won't he?" Bishop felt the familiar mixture of anger and frustration at the thought. When was it going to stop? All he wanted was to be left in peace, but apparently that was too much to ask.

Six months ago, Augie Lang had been on the losing

side of a poker game. Bishop had been lucky—which had made him the obvious target when Augie was looking for someone to blame for his losses. There had been a moment, when the other man found out just who it was he'd accused of cheating, Bishop had thought his reputation might work in his favor for once, might convince the kid to back off. But Augie was young and far more conscious of his pride than his mortality. Worse, some fool had probably told him that he was faster than most and he'd seen a way to save face and achieve fame, all with one bullet. Unfortunately for him, the bullet that found its mark was not his.

Lang had been a belligerent young man who'd seemed unlikely to endear himself to anyone, but Bishop supposed that even the most obnoxious man had family who objected to someone shooting a hole in him. Leastways, it seemed Augie Lang had someone who'd been interested enough to look up his killer. A brother maybe? His father? Someone intent on revenging his kin's death. And maybe hoping to grab hold of a little of the fame that had slipped through Augie's cold, dead fingers?

"There was a couple of fellas got off the train that I didn't recognize," Bart said, looking worried.

They looked at each other. Either of the men could be Lang. Or he could arrive on tomorrow's train or the one the day after that. Bishop felt the familiar tension settle between his shoulder blades. Everything that had happened these past couple of months had almost made him forget who and what he was. He'd been so busy getting used to being a family man that he'd stopped looking over his shoulder quite so much.

"You see where either of these fellows went?" Bishop asked as he set his hat on his head.

"One of them went to the hotel. I didn't see what the other one did," Bart said apologetically.

"No matter. If it was Lang, he'll find me soon enough. I'm going to go take a look around."

"You want me to go with you?" Bart asked as he pulled open the door.

Bishop glanced back at him, surprising a look of genuine concern in the younger man's eyes. Damned if the kid wasn't worried about him. "Thanks but I think you'd be better off holding down the fort here."

The last thing he needed or wanted was for Bart Lewis to end up caught in the line of fire. He stepped out on to the boardwalk, pausing to allow his eyes to adjust to the bright sunshine. If Lang had come to kill him, he'd certainly picked a nice day for it, Bishop thought as his eyes scanned the street from under the brim of his hat. It had rained the day before, a light, early-summer shower that had served to settle the dust without leaving mud behind. Today the mountains shouldered their way up to the pale-blue sky, only a few tattered remnants of clouds catching on their peaks.

Assured that there were no unfamiliar faces among the people he could see, Bishop stepped off the boardwalk and into the street. If Lila and the children were still in Fitch's, he was going to send her home. No doubt she'd argue. She argued about damn near everything, but this was one argument she was going to lose. If Lang was one of the men Bart had seen get off the train and if he was looking for a fight, which seemed a near certainty, he wanted his family well out of the way. Whatever the outcome, he needed to know that they were safe.

He was almost across the street when he had the sudden sensation that he was being watched. Slowing his stride, he brushed his coat back from the butt of his gun in a casual-seeming gesture. His every sense was tuned to trying to locate the source of his uneasiness. If Lang *was* watching him, would he make his move now or wait for a time when there were fewer witnesses? The answer might depend on whether the man wanted to avenge Augie's death or make a reputation by being the man to outdraw Bishop McKenzie.

"McKenzie!" The voice came from behind him, loud and booming, holding a blatant challenge, demanding attention from all within earshot and answering Bishop's question in a single word.

Lila and the children had been on their way out of Fitch's when she'd seen Bishop crossing the street toward them. She'd hesitated a moment, not anxious to see him. She was still annoyed with him. It wasn't just his harshness with Gavin, though she certainly thought he'd been rougher on the boy than circumstances warranted. But she was also still angry over the way he'd ended their conversation. She was *not* accustomed to peoplesimply walking away from her without so much as a by-your-leave.

But, annoyed or not, she could hardly avoid him forever, and she certainly didn't want to give the children the impression that she was angry with their father. Bridget could say it was a good thing for children to know that their parents sometimes disagreed, but it went against everything Lila had been taught. Pinning a cool smile on her face, she reached for the door. Before she could open it, she heard someone call Bishop's name, the voice coming easily through the door.

Something in the tone as well as the way Bishop's shoulders suddenly stiffened had her hesitating again. She saw him turn slowly, his hands held slightly out from his body. Voices carried easily in the still, clear air, making it easy to hear what was said.

"I'm McKenzie," Bishop said, his voice cool as a mountain lake.

"Thought you might be." Lila located the speaker as he stepped off the boardwalk in front of the Red Lady Saloon. he was shorter than Bishop but had the kind of barrel-chested build that generally denotes a man of considerable physical strength. He wore blue denim pants that looked as if they could use a good wash and a faded blue shirt. A red kerchief was tied around his throat and a battered tan hat was pulled low over his face. Two guns sat low on cither hip, and she could see that he had the holsters tied down to his leg. He looked tough and dangerous, and Lila felt a twinge of uneasiness. There was something about the way he was walking toward Bishop . . .

"I'm Dobe Lang," he announced, his tone making the name a challenge. "I understand you killed my brother up Dakota way."

"Could be." Bishop shifted toward the middle of the street and the other man followed suit.

"I heard tell you cheated him in a card game and then shot him down when he called you on it," Lang said This time, there was no mistaking the taunting tone of his voice. Lila's hand dropped away from the doorknob. She didn't completely understand what was going on but she was suddenly afraid.

"Your brother's death was of his own choosing," Bishop said. He was now standing in the middle of the street, facing his opponent. "He had a run of bad luck and thought killing me might change it. He was wrong. You don't have to make the same mistake."

Lila thought the other man looked less sure of himself, but if he did, it was only a momentary doubt. His teeth gleamed white beneath the brim of his hat. "The only mistake Augie made was thinking he was faster than he was. I always did say he was going to get hisself killed one day."

"You were right. There's no reason for you to do the same." Bishop's voice was level, quiet, and almost soothing. "Just walk away and we'll forget this ever happened."

Whatever hesitation he might have felt earlier, Dobe Lang was clearly set on his chosen path now. "I don't reckon I'll do that. I figure your luck has done run itself out, McKenzie."

"It's your funeral," Bishop said, sounding more weary than angry.

Still only half comprehending what was happening, Lila pulled Angel closer against her, turning the child's face into her skirts. She reached for Gavin but the boy was just beyond her grasp, his nose all but pressed against the glass on the door, completely absorbed in the drama taking place in the street outside.

Fitch spoke from behind her. "I'd move away from the window, if I was you, Miz McKenzie. Bullets ain't always real precise about where they land."

His words gave a name to her fear, made her realize what was happening outside. Bishop and the other man were about to start shooting at each other. Though it seemed incredible that such a thing could happen in the middle of the street in broad daylight, there was no doubt that that was what was happening.

"Gavin! Come away from the window." She didn't know whether he chose to ignore her or whether he was so absorbed in the drama about to take place that he didn't hear her. Without taking her eyes off the men outside, she reached for the boy again, intent on pulling him out of harm's way, but it was too late.

Dobe Lang's hand dropped to his side, coming back up with a pistol in a move so fast, it was almost a blur. Expecting to see him fire and then see Bishop fall, Lila cried out. Or she tried to. No sound made it past the knot in her throat. She took a half step forward, the danger forgotten, her only thought to stop what was happening.

Bishop hardly seemed to move but there was suddenly a gun in his hand. Lila saw the weapon jerk, heard the solid report as he fired. Dobe Lang froze in place for a long, slow moment, his pistol raised but silent. Lila had the ridiculous thought that the sound of Bishop's gun had frightened him into stillness, that this was all going to end right there and then without bloodshed. A red stain suddenly blossomed on Lang's shirt front, turning the blue fabric an odd shade of purple. He stared at Bishop with an expression of shock on his face, as if amazed to find himself dead, and then his knees buckled and he dropped to the dusty street, silent and unmoving.

Lila stared at the body through the wavery glass of Fitch's front window. Her mind refused to absorb what she'd just seen. It was the first time in her life that she'd been witness to violence. It didn't seem possible that a man was dead and she'd watched it happen. Even more impossible was that her own husband had been the one to kill him.

Lila pulled open the door of Fitch's and stumbled out onto the boardwalk, only half aware of Gavin following her out. Her attention was all for Bishop, who was kneeling next to the fallen man—the man he'd just killed.

Bishop heard the bell over Fitch's door ring, the cheerful jangle harsh in the unnatural stillness that had descended over the street. He lifted his head and saw Lila standing on the boardwalk, her face stark white, her eyes wide and shocked. Angel clung to her skirts, looking uncertain and scared. Gavin stood beside his sister, staring at Lang's body, his face as white and shocked as Lila's.

"Look long and hard, boy," Bishop told him as he stood. He gestured to the body at his feet. "This is what you think you want. And this is where you'll more than likely end up."

Gavin swallowed hard, his complexion turning slightly green. Angel, frightened by the tension in the air as much as by the shooting, which she only half understood, began to whimper and turned her face into her stepmother's skirts. Lila shot Bishop a look of loathing before scooping the little girl up. Balancing Angel on her hip, she put one hand on Gavin's shoulder, pulling him with her as she all but ran from the scene.

Bishop stood and watched them go, aware of a hollow emptiness in his chest.

\* \* \*

It was late afternoon when the shooting took place. It was long after dark before Bishop made his way home. There had been arrangements to be made and reports to fill out. Half the people in town had felt it necessary to give him their versions of what had happened, just in case he was unclear on any of the details.

He'd listened to each and every one of them, nodded in the right places and thanked them for their insights. And all the time, he was thinking about the horror in Lila's expression, the loathing in her eyes. Despite all his warnings about the violence that was often a part of life on a frontier that was barely even half tamed, it was obvious that she'd had no real comprehension of what he was telling her. She'd still believed that Paris was just a slightly rougher version of Beaton. The shooting had given her a painfully graphic demonstration of how wrong she was. He'd have given a great deal for her to be able to hold onto her misconceptions.

Bishop let himself into the house through the back door and stood in the dark kitchen for a moment, absorbing the quiet. He hadn't had a moment alone since the shooting and his head was filled with the babble of voices, all of them saying the same things. *It was self-defense, Sheriff. Seen it plain as day. You didn't have a choice. Man musta wanted to die something fierce, bracing Bishop McKenzie like that. Damned fool.*

Damned dead fool, Bishop thought. He reached up to take off his hat, his movements slow. Damn Dobe Lang and all the fools like him. He dropped his hat on the table and thrust his fingers through his hair. He was tired—bone-deep weary, a weariness of soul more than body. It wasn't the first time he'd killed a man and it might not be the last, but each time it happened, he felt a little less human, a little less alive.

Dobe Lang hadn't been a particularly appealing example of humanity. Nor had his brother. And both men had walked into their own deaths with their eyes open. They had, as had been pointed out to him repeatedly, given him no real choice. It had been his life or theirs. He sure as hell couldn't pretend that he'd rather be lying in a pine box in the back of the blacksmith shop, awaiting burial tomorrow. But that didn't mean he didn't resent the fact that he was left to live with the results of the choices they'd forced on him.

"Hell. I'm getting too damned philosophical in my old age," he muttered. Thrusting his fingers through his hair again, he left the kitchen, moving quietly through the house. The children had probably been in bed an hour or more ago, but he was a little surprised that Lila had gone to bed, as if nothing had happened. The way she'd looked at him this afternoon, he found it hard to believe that she had nothing to say about the shooting.

A glimmer of light beneath the bedroom door told him she was awake. Bishop hesitated a moment, half tempted to turn and go back the way he'd come. He was in no mood for yet another postmortem. He didn't want to hear that the shooting had been his fault or that it hadn't. He just wanted to put the whole blasted incident behind him. On the other hand, if he'd learned one thing about his wife, it was that she was not easily discouraged. If she had something to say, she'd say it, if not tonight then tomorrow. He might as well get it over with.

When the door didn't open, it took him a moment to realize that she'd locked him out of their bedroom.

Anger rolled through him and his reaction came without thought. He took a step back and, without a second's hesitation, slammed his booted foot into the door just above the latch. The wood splintered but held, and it took a second kick to complete the job. The door slammed open with force enough to send it careening back. Bishop stepped into the opening, putting out one hand to block the door as it bounced off the wall.

Lila stood next to the bed, tall and slender in her white cotton wrapper, her hair falling over her shoulder in a thick, flame-colored rope. With the lamp behind her, her face was in shadow, making it difficult to read her expression. But he didn't need to see her face now. He'd seen it this afternoon, seen the loathing in her eyes. His anger disappeared as quickly as it had come, leaving him unbearably tired.

"I told you once before that I won't tolerate locked doors between us," he said quietly, reminding her of their wedding night.

Lila started to speak but before she could say anything, Gavin was there, darting past Bishop and into the bedroom. He placed himself between them, facing his father, his eyes bright with a mixture of determination and fear.

"Leave her alone! I won't let you hurt her."

There was a moment of stunned silence, broken by Lila's shocked exclamation. "Gavin!"

She hurried forward and put her hand on the boy's

shoulder. He was rigid with tension, his attention never wavering from Bishop. Father and son, they confronted each other. Bishop looked as if he'd just been kicked in the chest, all the air knocked from him.

"I . . ." He shook his head slightly, like a fighter who'd just taken a solid punch to the jaw. When he spoke, his tone held a deep weariness that went straight to Lila's heart. "Go back to bed, son."

"Leave her alone," Gavin said again. Beneath her hand, Lila could feel him trembling. She had to put an end to this confrontation before irreparable harm was done to his relationship with his father.

Stepping between them, she forced Gavin to look at her. "Your father would never hurt me, Gavin."

"He broke the door." The boy's eyes darted to the shattered lock.

"That was my fault for locking it. He had every right to be angry." She realized as she spoke that she'd wanted to make Bishop angry because dealing with his anger would be easier than dealing with the wild tangle of emotions that churned inside her. "He would never hurt me."

Gavin shot Bishop an angry look past her shoulder. "He murdered that man today."

"No, he didn't!" It would have been difficult to say which of the three of them was most surprised by Lila's quick defense of Bishop. "He acted in self-defense. That man wanted to kill him. It was a terrible thing that happened, but it wasn't your father's fault. You saw what happened. What do you think he should have done?"

Gavin looked at her uncertainly. "I don't know," he admitted slowly, suddenly looking very much like the boy he was rather than the adult he so often seemed.

"It's been a long day for all of us," she said softly. She dared to reach out and brush back a lock of silky black hair that had fallen onto the boy's forehead, her smile tender. "Go back to bed now. Things will seem clearer tomorrow."

Gavin hesitated a moment longer, glancing uneasily between her and his father.

"Go on, son," Bishop said tiredly. "I won't lay a hand on her."

Contradictory as it was, his father's words seemed to be the final reassurance that Gavin needed. With a last uncertain look at Lila, he slid past her and Bishop and left the room. Lila turned to watch him go. The barely audible *snick* of his bedroom door closing seemed unnaturally loud in the silence he'd left behind.

# Chapter 19

A lone with Bishop, Lila's voice deserted her. She wanted to explain Gavin's feelings, but how could she when she didn't understand her own? Every time she closed her eyes, she saw Dobe Lang's look of surprise when the bullet found him, the horrible boneless way his body had fallen to the dirt. And Bishop's cold, still expression as he watched him die.

She hadn't believed any of the stories she'd heard about her husband. She'd dismissed young William's awestruck admiration as a case of somewhat misplaced hero worship. The boy's father was a banker. While it was a perfectly respectable profession, it wasn't the kind of thing that was likely to excite a young boy. But a dark and dangerous lawman was something else entirely. She'd assumed that William had simply exaggerated Bishop's reputation to fit his own notion of excitement. And when other people had alluded to the same things, she'd shrugged it off as part of the peculiar need that westerners seemed to have to emphasize the differences between the "wild" West with the more civilized East. The idea that she was married to a . . . shootist was just too ridiculous to entertain.

Yet today she'd seen the lethal speed with which he'd drawn his gun; seen him kill a man in less time than it took to draw a breath. It had frightened her. But what had frightened her nearly as much was the relief she'd felt when she saw Lang fall. When she'd realized what was happening on the street, it had hit her that she might be about to see Bishop die. Hard on the heels of that thought had been a gut-deep feeling of panic. Despite her resentment of his occasionally high-handed ways, he was important to her, an integral part of her life. She could no longer imagine her life without him, could hardly remember what it had been like before she knew him. When the shooting was over, there had been one terrible moment when she'd actually been glad that Lang was dead. Glad because his death meant Bishop's life. The realization that she'd offered up a prayer of thanksgiving for a man's death had filled her with self-loathing. And she'd hated Bishop for making her feel that way, for bringing her face to face with a part of herself she'd rather not have seen.

Perhaps Bishop read something of that in her face now because his expression grew even more distant.

"I'll sleep at the jail tonight," he said expressionlessly.

He started to turn away and Lila knew, on some deep, instinctive level that, if she let him go now, it would be an end to any chance they might have of making something real and lasting of their marriage. The ties that bound them were too new and too fragile to draw them back together. If there was any chance of creating the kind of marriage she'd always dreamed of having, a marriage based on trust and respect, and, God willing, love, they had to get past this.

"Don't go."

Bishop turned to look at her, his expression still and waiting. Lila stared at him, at a loss for words. Her emotions were tangled and confused. A part of her hated him and everything he represented. She'd seen a side of him today that had frightened her. She'd seen a man who could kill with frightening ease. Yet she also remembered the sometimes awkward gentleness he showed to Angel, his patience with Gavin, his concern for her own comfort and safety. Pulled in too many directions, she felt tears start to her eyes.

Bishop saw her eyes fill with tears and felt something pinch tight and hard in his chest. He'd never seen Lila cry. She always faced life—and him—with her chin thrust out, ready to take them both on without giving an inch. Though her stubborn spirit and her temper had, more than once, exasperated him beyond all bearing, he'd much rather have dealt with her anger than her tears.

He started to reach out to her and then realized that he was probably the last person from whom she'd want to take comfort. But a ragged sob broke from her as she came into his embrace. His arms closed around her automatically, drawing her close, feeling the soft warmth of her body against his like a gentle balm to his soul.

"It's going to be all right," Bishop murmured against her hair. He'd rather have faced a band of marauding Apaches unarmed than listen to Lila cry. The sound of her tears tore a hole inside him. "Don't cry. Everything's all right."

But his whispered reassurances had no affect. She continued to cry—slow, painful tears that dampened his shirt front and burned like acid against his skin. At another time, he might have recognized her tears for what they were—a much-needed release of tension. But all he could think of was that he couldn't bear the sound of her unhappiness.

Winding his hand around the thick rope of her hair, he tilted her head back. He caught a quick glimpse of the tear-drenched green of her eyes and then his mouth was closing over hers. He tasted the salt tang of her tears against his tongue, swallowed her soft gasp of surprise. He kissed her as if he could somehow take her pain into himself and make it his own.

He had no thought except to comfort her, but then Lila seemed to melt against him, her fingers clinging to his shirt front, her mouth opening in an invitation Bishop had neither the strength nor the will to resist. The hunger he'd been suppressing for weeks was suddenly a clawing need in his gut. As he opened his mouth over hers, deepening the kiss, tasting the answering need in her, a hunger to equal his own, the last traces of his control shattered.

But he was not alone in his lack of control.

His fingers speared through her heavy braid, loosening her hair until it spilled over his hands and arms in a thick silken curtain. Lila's fingers were impatient with the buttons on his shirt, tearing one loose in her rush to bare his chest. Bishop shrugged out of the garment and pushed her wrapper off her shoulders at the same time she was reaching for the buckle on his belt.

Somewhere, in the back of his mind, Bishop recognized what was happening. Death had brushed against them today, laying ghostly fingers on his shoulder, revealing a grim, unsmiling mask to Lila. If he'd been a half second slower or Lang a half second faster, Death could have swung his scythe in a different direction. The elemental hunger that gripped them both now was, in part, a need to affirm life in the most basic of ways—by touch and sight and taste.

But the reason it was happening was not important. All that mattered was the feel of Lila's skin heating beneath his hands, the moist warmth of her mouth, the gentle yielding of her body beneath his. He had no memory of pushing the ruined door shut behind them and sliding a chair in front of it, no memory of easing her back on the bed. His hands raced over her body, exploring the changes in it. Her breasts were fuller now, filling his hand like the most exotic of fruits, and they'd grown more sensitive. When he bent to taste the pouting darkness of her nipple, she cried out softly, a keening sound of pleasure that went straight to his gut. His fingers gentled as they traced the solid bulge of her stomach. There was something strangely erotic in the thought that his child was cradled inside her, a child created in one night of passion that was like nothing he'd ever known before. Until now.

He wanted to explore every inch of her, to savor the feel and taste of her. But his pulse was beating in his ears, deafening him to everything but the need to sheath himself in her, to feel her body take his into the most intimate embrace possible between a man and a woman. He raised himself over her and Lila's thighs parted in welcome. A tiny, unwelcome flicker of sanity made Bishop hesitate. He wanted no regrets, no recriminations thrown at him in the morning. If he took her now, this would be the end of all bargains between them and the beginning of a real marriage.

His eyes met hers, electric blue clashing with smoky green.

"Tell me this is what you want," he said, his voice raspy with need. The feel of him pressed against her was a sweet torture for them both.

Lila stared up at him, seeing the hunger that burned in his eyes, the need that tightened the skin across his cheekbones. She saw, also, the same crossroads Bishop had seen. After this, there would be no going back to the way things had been. He wasn't going to let her pretend to be swept away by passion. She was going to have to admit that she wanted this as much as he did. Her hesitation lasted no more than a heartbeat.

"This is what I want," she whispered.

It was all Bishop needed to hear. He completed their union with one slow thrust that sheathed his aching hardness in the yielding warmth of her. Lila arched to take him deeper still, her hands clinging to the thick muscles of his upper arms. She hadn't realized how empty she'd been until this moment when the emptiness was filled, until she felt herself completed by their joining. This was what she'd been waiting for her whole life.

The hunger was too great to allow for soft touches and gentle sighs. It was hot and hard and fast. They moved together, their bodies in perfect rhythm, one with the other. Lila found herself spiraling upward at dizzying speed, desperate to find the fulfillment she knew awaited her, the pleasure only he could give her.

Though she thought she knew what to expect, she was caught off guard by the power of her own completion. It was like standing in the middle of a Fourth of July fireworks display, lights and sound exploding around her, inside her. Her body arched beneath his, delicate muscles contracting around him, pulling him into the vortex of her pleasure. There was only Bishop, her husband, the father of her child, the man who'd taught her how to live again. Only the two of them alone in all the world.

As she floated slowly back to earth, Lila suddenly remembered the words of the wedding ceremony, words that had filled her with terror a few weeks ago. *Whom God hath joined together, let no man put asunder.* Listening to the ragged beat of Bishop's heart against her ear, feeling the heavy weight of his body over hers, she found the words comforting, a promise for the future.

The first pale-gray fingers of dawn were sliding through the muslin curtains when Lila woke. Her eyes still closed, she stretched out one hand in sleepy inquiry and found Bishop gone, the linens on his side of the bed cool. She opened her eyes to confirm what her touch had already told her, but before she could decide whether to feel relief or disappointment, she saw him standing near the window, the curtain pulled partially open as he watched the sun edge its way over the shoulders of the mountains. Though the air carried a distinct chill, he was shirtless and barefoot, his only concession to modesty and the temperature a pair of half-buttoned pants that rode low on his hips.

Blinking sleepily, Lila let her eyes linger on the corded muscles of his shoulders and back, the rumpled thickness of his dark hair. Her fingers curled into the cool linens. She knew how those muscles felt beneath her hands, knew the surprising softness of his hair sliding between her fingers. She'd never realized it was possible to know another person's body better than you knew your own. Certainly Bishop's hands had mapped her body with a thoroughness that made her blush to remember.

As if sensing her gaze, Bishop turned away from the window, his eyes meeting hers. "Good morning."

The prosaic greeting surprised her though she couldn't have said why. It wasn't as if she'd been expecting a declaration of undying love.

"Good morning," she responded, pleased that she sounded just as normal as he had. If he wanted to act as if nothing had changed, that was fine with her. She sat up, careful to keep the sheet pulled over her breasts. He might be comfortable standing about half naked, but she had been reared to believe that modesty was an admirable trait.

She watched uneasily as Bishop moved toward her. Surely he wasn't thinking about climbing back into bed with her. True, it was barely even dawn and there was no reason for either of them to be up so early, but there was something downright scandalous about the idea of him getting back into bed. His hands dropped to the waist of his pants and Lila felt color flood her cheeks.

"I'll make some coffee," she said, turning her head away and scooting toward the opposite side of the bed. But before she could get her legs untangled from the covers, she felt the mattress dip beneath Bishop's weight and then his fingers closed around her arm, tugging her gently but inexorably back into the middle of the bed. Though she sensed that, if she resisted, he'd release her, Lila allowed herself to sink back against the pillows.

"Running away?" he asked quietly. He leaned on one elbow, next to her, his expression shadowed and difficult to read.

"From what?" There was less scorn and more uncertainty in the question than she would have liked.

"From me." He brought his hand up and brushed a lock of hair back from her face. His fingers brushed across her mouth, touched lightly on the pulse at the base of her throat, and then, in a move that stole her breath, slid beneath the sheet to boldly cup the heavy globe of her breast. "From this."

"Bishop!" She gasped in shock. "You . . . We can't . . . It's morning!"

"I don't know of any laws against a man making love to his wife in the morning." His thumb brushed across her nipple and Lila felt her bones start to melt. "And if there are, I promise not to tell the law," he whispered as his mouth closed over her, smothering her already weak protest.

\* \* \*

The morning was somewhat more advanced and Lila lay snuggled close against Bishop's side. She told herself that she should get up and get started on the morning's chores, but she couldn't seem to find the energy to move. She felt pleasantly tired and drowsy with contentment. Her head on Bishop's shoulder, she slid her fingers through the thick mat of hair on his chest.

She considered the idea that she was becoming a wanton, but at the moment she couldn't seem to get up much concern about the possibility. Here it was, with daylight definitely creeping into the room, and she was lying wrapped in Bishop's arms as if it were the most natural thing in the world, which was how it felt.

"No more talk of separate beds," Bishop said quietly. It wasn't a question but Lila answered as if it were.

"No." The word came out on a sigh. She'd been so sure she was doing the right thing, so sure she needed time to get to know him, time to . . . To what? She didn't know anymore, she admitted to herself, though she'd certainly never say as much to him.

They lay without speaking for a few minutes. A sunbeam found its way between the curtains and painted a bright arrow of gold across the floorboards. If she shifted her head an inch or two, she could see the chair that held the door closed and the splintered wood of the frame where the latch had broken. Lila didn't move. She didn't want to think about Bishop kicking in the door. Or about the stunned disbelief in his eyes when Gavin rushed to her defense. For a moment he'd looked utterly vulnerable, something of a shock considering he'd just stood in the middle of a dusty street and killed a man.

Like it or not, the memories were there, spoiling her fragile contentment. Lila stirred restlessly.

"The children will be up soon," she said. "I should get breakfast started."

Bishop heard the tension that threaded through her voice and knew, as surely as if she'd spoken out loud, exactly where her thoughts had turned. It had, he supposed, been foolish to think they could just forget everything that had happened the day before. Not with the broken door staring them in the face, not to mention Dobe Lang's body cooling at the blacksmith's. And then there was Gavin. He'd done a particularly good job of not thinking about his son.

"It's time I was up and about," he said. As he eased his arm out from under Lila, he sat up and swung his legs over the side of the bed. Staring at the bright slash of sunlight on the floor, he spoke without looking at her.

"I didn't go looking for Lang. He brought the fight to me." He had never before felt the need to justify himself to anyone, unless it was the law in whatever town he happened to be in. But he couldn't get the image of Gavin's face out of his mind.

"I know that." He felt the bed shift as Lila sat up. "And Gavin knows it, too," she added, as if reading his thoughts. "He was thrown off balance by what happened. We all were. He knows perfectly well that you would never hurt me."

"Does he?" Bishop turned to look at her, one knee crooked on the bed. "What about you?"

"Me?" Lila looked at him in confusion.

How many times had he imagined her just like this? Bishop asked himself. Her hair tumbled over her shoulders like a fiery waterfall. Her green eyes soft and smoky, her mouth slightly swollen, and her skin flushed pink in the aftermath of their lovemaking. He could crawl back between the sheets and pull her into his arms without her offering so much as a whisper of protest. Her surrender had been complete, without reservations. There would be no more talk of separate beds and waiting until after the baby was born. She was his wife in the fullest sense of the word. No more sleepless nights. No more indulging in daydreams more suited to a boy of Gavin's age than a grown man. He had what he wanted.

So why wasn't he happier about it?

"Do you think I'd hurt you?" he asked her.

"I know you wouldn't." Lila's response came with reassuring speed. She reached out and set her hand on his arm. "I trust you, Bishop."

From the look in her eyes, Lila was nearly as surprised as he was by the soft admission. Bishop stared at her, caught off guard by her worried look on her face. Was she actually worried that she might have hurt his feelings? He tried to remember the last time someone had worried about hurting him, but he couldn't think of an occasion. He started to say something, though he didn't know just what, but before he opened his mouth, Lila sucked in a quick, startled breath. Her hand left his arm to press against her side.

"What is it?" Fear made his voice harsh. The baby. Obviously there was something wrong with the baby. Even as he was reaching for her, easing her back down against the pillows, his mind was presenting him with a dozen ghastly scenarios, all ending with, at best, her losing the baby and, at worst, Lila's still, white body being lowered into a grave. And all of them his fault. He shouldn't have made love to her this morning. He shouldn't have made love to her last night. Seeing Dobe Lang killed had upset her so much that she was going to lose the baby. He'd frightened her when he broke down the door.

"I'll go get Zeke."

"Bishop." Lila caught his arm before he could leave the bed. Her grip was surprisingly strong for a woman on the verge of death. "I don't need Zeke. I'm all right."

"You gasped." The fact that his heart was still racing made the words an accusation.

"The baby moved. It startled me. There's nothing wrong."

"You can feel it move?" His eyes dropped from her face to her stomach, his disbelief plain to read.

"Yes. The first time it happened, I thought something was wrong, but Bridget told me not to worry. She says it's a sign of a strong, healthy baby."

"Does it hurt?" Bishop was still staring at her stomach.

"Not really. At first, it was a little like a butterfly fluttering its wings, but it's gotten considerably stronger than that the last couple of weeks. Would you . . . if you'd like, you can feel it yourself."

"Me?" He shot a disbelieving look at her.

"If you . . . put your hand on my stomach, you can sometimes feel it push against you." Color tinted her face and he knew she was embarrassed at having suggested that he touch her. He suspected she might prefer it if he declined her invitation, but the idea of actually being able to feel his child move inside her was too fascinating to resist.

Easing his hand beneath the sheet, he set his palm against the soft swell of her belly. Lila's blush deepened but she took his hand in hers and moved it to the right a few inches. Almost immediately Bishop felt a flutter of movement. It was so subtle that he might have thought he was imagining it. But then it came again, a weak pushing against his hand, there and then gone in an instant.

"He moves quite a bit. Bridget says it's a good sign, that the more he kicks, the healthier he is."

"It could be a girl."

"Would you mind if it was?" Lila asked.

"Mind?" Bishop lifted his eyes from where his hand still rested on her stomach. "Why would I mind?"

"I thought men preferred sons," she said diffidently.

"If I was a farmer, maybe, and was hoping to raise a crop of field hands." The baby was still now and he reluctantly slid his hand out from under the sheet. "My father was a farmer and he managed well enough with just two sons."

"Your father was a farmer?" Lila couldn't have been more surprised if he'd said his father could breathe underwater. Bishop arched his brows in acknowledgment of her reaction and she flushed. "I just never pictured you as a farmer."

"I wasn't. But my father and brother were."

During the journey from St. Louis to Denver, she'd asked him about his family, thinking that it might be nice to know something about the man she'd married. He'd told her that his family was dead and then got up and walked to the other end of the car, effectively ending the conversation. But he seemed in a more talkative mood now so she risked another question.

"What happened to them—your family, I mean?"

"Cholera. I left home when I was sixteen. I hated farming. Hated every clod of dirt that went under the plow and every stalk of wheat that came up after the field was planted. When the war broke out, I was among the first to join up." His mouth twisted in a bitter smile. "I'd like to say it was because I wanted to preserve the Union, but the truth is, I thought going to war would be the quickest way to get away from the farm and find myself some excitement. I guess you could say I found it. After the war, farming didn't sound like a bad occupation. But my parents and brother had been dead for almost two years. The house was gone and someone else was farming the land."

His flat recitation gave the story an impact that a more dramatic telling could never have matched.

Lila sought for words to express her compassion but could only come up with the most banal. "I'm sorry."

"It was a long time ago," Bishop said, as if time had erased the pain of loss. But Lila knew that, while time might heal the wound, the scar was always there, a permanent reminder of what was lost.

"The ache never quite goes away though, does it?" she said, speaking half to herself. Her parents, Billy— their deaths had left a gap in her life that could never be filled. Lately added to that ache was the fear that, through her own reckless disregard for society's rules, she might have lost her brother, also. "Nothing can replace your family."

"Thinking about Douglas?" Bishop asked, reading her thoughts with disconcerting accuracy. "Have you heard from him?"

"No." Admitting as much made her brother's silence seem that much more final. Holding the sheets to her breast, she sat up and reached for her wrapper, which lay across the foot of the bed in a tangled jumble. She didn't allow herself to think about Douglas very often. It hurt too much.

"You've had letters from Susan," Bishop said. She felt his eyes on her as she pulled the sleeves on her wrapper right side out.

"Yes, and Douglas always sends his love. Or so she says." She didn't believe that for a minute.

"He just needs time," Bishop said, but the words were hollow comfort.

"Does he?" Lila swung her legs over the side of the bed, allowing the sheet to drop as she pulled her wrapper on. It was silly to worry about modesty, considering all that had passed between them, but old habits die hard.

"Douglas knows who was really to blame for what happened."

She felt the bed dip as Bishop rolled off the other side. Glancing over her shoulder, she caught a glimpse of his lean body as he bent to pick up his pants. She looked away quickly and slid off the bed, tugging her wrapper snugly around her body.

"I'm the one who came to your room that night," she said quietly. "Much as I'd like to believe otherwise, the blame isn't all yours."

"I should have sent you away," Bishop said as he stepped into his pants and pulled them up around his hips.

Lila kept her head lowered, her fingers twisting restlessly in the loops of the bow at her waist, her hair falling forward to form a thick auburn curtain around her face. She thought about how different her life would have been if he'd sent her away. He'd have been gone the next morning. By now she might have half forgotten him. There would have been no baby, no marriage. She'd still be at home in Pennsylvania. Trapped in the same, safe little box in which she'd spent the last few years of her life. Grieving fiancé, loving sister—watching her life drift away on a sea of social events and meaningless chatter, desperate to find a way out of the confines of her life and lacking the courage to do so. If Bishop had sent her away that night, she wouldn't be wondering if Douglas would ever speak to her again. She'd just have to wonder if she was destined to grow old and die without ever having a life of her own.

Lila lifted her head and looked at Bishop. He stood across the bed from her, his shirt half buttoned. A thick lock of dark hair fell onto his forehead, an oddly boyish contrast to the beard that shadowed his jaw. Sensing her gaze, he lifted his head. His eyes were a deep, clear blue, and it suddenly occurred to her that she wanted their child to inherit those vivid blue eyes.

"I'm not sure you *could* have sent me away," she said softly, speaking as much to herself as to him.

Bishop's eyes widened in surprise. He opened his mouth as if to question her statement, but Lila didn't want to continue the discussion. She couldn't have explained her words to herself, let alone to him.

"I have to get breakfast started," she said. Giving her belt an unnecessary tug, she moved toward the door.

"Lila—" Bishop moved as if to intercept her but Angel's voice—bless her sweet innocence—came from the hallway.

"How come the door's broke, Gavin?"

Pushing aside the chair that had been holding it shut, Lila slipped out the door to join her stepchildren.

Hours later, Bishop glared at a pale swath of sunlight that had dared to make its way through the window and trace a path across the stone floor of the jailhouse. He guessed that there were bigger fools than he was, but he'd be hard-pressed to name one. For weeks, he'd endured the torture of sharing a bed with Lila and not touching her. He couldn't count the number of times he'd stuck his head under the pump and sluiced ice-cold water over the back of his neck in an effort to drown his hunger for her. A hundred times or more he'd called himself a fool for agreeing to give her the time she thought she needed. They were married. What the hell difference was time going to make? But he'd promised her time and that was what he'd give her.

Last night, all the waiting and cursing and douses

of cold water had ended. Lila had given herself to him, fully and completely. No more lying awake at night, listening to her breathe and aching with the need to touch her. It was exactly what he'd wanted. Only a complete fool would be less than completely happy.

So what did that make him?

Before he was forced to try to come up with an answer to that, the door of the jailhouse opened and Bart came in. Bishop welcomed the interruption to his thoughts, though he promised himself that, if Bart brought up the Lang shooting again, he was going to lock the kid in one of the cells and leave him there until he turned old and gray. Yesterday Bart had felt compelled to assure him repeatedly that it had been a clear case of self-defense. It wasn't that Bishop didn't appreciate the younger man's loyalty, but he was more than a little tired of everyone telling him about the shooting as if he hadn't been there himself.

Luckily for him, Bart had other things on his mind. "Couple got off the train today," he announced as he hung his hat on one of the hooks near the door. Interpreting Bishop's grunt of acknowledgment as a sign of interest, he continued to talk as he headed to the stove to pour himself a cup of coffee. "Real fancy. Man wearing a store-bought suit and a fancy hat like he was goin' to take a stroll down some street in San Francisco or New York City or someplace. Woman looked like she stepped outta one of them lady's magazines. Her hair was all gussied up and a fancy dress and a hat like you wouldn't believe, all full of feathers and ruffles and such-like."

Bart paused long enough to take a sip of coffee,

cursing when the scalding liquid burned his tongue. But the injury didn't slow him down. "Pretty little thing."

"The hat?" Bishop asked absently. He'd picked up a two-week-old Denver newspaper and was perusing an article about the efforts of a local lady's group to close the town's plentiful saloons.

"Not the hat!" Bart corrected him with a touch of indignation. "The gal wearin' it. She wasn't very big but she was real pretty. It'd be nice if the fella with her was her brother but, from the way he was treatin' her like she was made out of china, I don't guess that's the case." Bart sighed over the unfairness of a world in which pretty women all too often came with husbands already attached.

"Anybody else get off the train?" Bishop asked. He didn't share Bart's interest in the well-dressed couple.

"Nope. They was the only ones. They went right to the hotel. I watched to make sure."

Bishop didn't need to be a mind reader to know that Bart was reassuring him that there would not be another repeat of the day before when a stranger had arrived in town and Bart had failed to pinpoint his location. Bishop considered pointing out that, if another glory hunter showed up looking to make a reputation by killing Bishop McKenzie, his choice of accommodations wasn't going to make much difference to the outcome of his visit, but he decided to say nothing. If it made Bart feel better to keep an eye on new arrivals, it couldn't do any harm.

"Can't figure what folks like that would be doing here in Paris," Bart said, following his own train of thought. "Ain't much here by way of entertainment. You suppose they got off in the wrong place?"

"Only if they got *on* in the wrong place. Paris is the only stop the train makes," Bishop pointed out dryly.

"They might have got on the wrong train. They're city folks, for sure." As far as Bart was concerned, being "city folk" was a reasonable explanation for even the most extraordinary acts of stupidity.

"Maybe they're thinking about buying a mine," Bishop suggested. "Or maybe they just like mountains. Unless they plan on shooting at me or someone else in town, I really don't care why they're here."

He was to remember those words a few hours later when he walked through the kitchen and stepped into the parlor to find not only Lila and the children waiting for him but two people who could only be Bart's mysterious couple.

"Look who's here, Bishop," Lila said with forced good cheer. "Isn't this a wonderful surprise?"

Bishop looked from the anxiety in Susan's soft blue eyes to the implacable hostility in Douglas's gaze and thought that "wonderful" wasn't exactly the word he'd have chosen.

# *Chapter 20*

O nce again, the dining room at the Lyman Hotel was filled to capacity. Word had spread that the sheriff's in-laws were in town and there was considerable interest in seeing what they looked like. A gunfight in the street yesterday and fancy visitors from the East today—life in Paris hadn't been this interesting in months.

No one was surprised to find that the newcomers were elegant and refined, clearly members of the privileged class. "Stands to reason," Dot Lyman told her husband. "It's plain as the nose on your face that Lila McKenzie is a real lady. Not that she's uppity. She doesn't put on any airs, no matter what Sara thinks, but manners like hers don't grow on trees."

Clem grunted his agreement. Ordinarily, there was nothing he enjoyed more than discussing the townsfolk with his wife. It was one of the joys of their married life. But, at the moment, he was wondering if he should run across to the Lucky Dragon Saloon and see if he could borrow a table. If they arranged things just right, they might be able to wedge another four diners into the corner right next to the kitchen. Of course, the door might hit the back of one of the chairs now and again, but no one was likely to care much as long as they had a clear view of the sheriff's table. The McKenzie's certainly had been good for business.

"Is the hotel always this busy?" Susan asked, glancing around at the crowded dining room. "The food must be exceptionally good."

"Dot is a wonderful cook," Lila said. "But I'm afraid you and Douglas are more of an attraction than her roast beef. Other than miners and gamblers, we don't get many visitors in Paris. You know what small towns are like."

"Yes, we do," Douglas said, his bland agreement seeming to carry an accusation.

Lila flushed and Bishop's jaw tightened. If it hadn't been for the fact that anything he said or did would add to her embarrassment, he would have taken great pleasure in punching his brother-in-law on the nose.

"I guess some things don't change, no matter where you live," Susan said lightly, as if Douglas hadn't made his dour comment.

"That's true." Lila's smile was forced. "Bishop kept

telling me how different things would be from what I was used to, but I've found more similarities than differences. People are much the same everywhere."

"Not quite. I can't recall the last time Beaton was privileged to have a gunfight in the middle of the street," Douglas said, addressing the remark to no one in particular.

There was a moment of dead silence, broken by Susan. "I don't know, dear. Occasionally, the meetings of the Ladies' Aid Society become so vituperative that I'm afraid disagreements can only be settled by pistols at dawn. At the last meeting, I thought Ethel Jane Cranston and Eugenia Stevens were going to come to blows over what to serve at tea."

Bishop didn't know the women she'd mentioned but he assumed that the image evoked must be fairly unlikely, since both Douglas and Lila were momentarily struck dumb. Then Lila laughed and even Douglas was startled into a genuine smile, and the tension was eased, at least for the moment.

Leaning back in his chair, Bishop let the conversation flow around him. It was mostly Susan and Lila talking. Douglas spoke occasionally but his mood was such that neither woman sought to bring him into the conversation. Sitting next to Lila, Bishop could feel the tension in her. She was nervous as a one-legged man at fanny kicking, and the careful way she avoided looking at her brother made the source of the her tension obvious.

Bishop hadn't needed their conversation this morning to tell him how much the estrangement with Douglas bothered her. Though he'd spent only a few days at River Walk, it had been enough for him to see how close the two of them were. Of all the things he regretted about what had happened between him and Lila, the rift between her and Douglas was one of the deepest. And one that he, of all people, could do nothing to correct.

"It just seemed like such a perfect opportunity to come visit, what with my brother getting married in San Francisco next month," Susan was saying. It was a measure of her own uneasiness that this was the second time she'd felt obliged to explain how it was she and Douglas had come to be in Paris. "We probably should have written to let you know that we were coming, but I thought it would be more fun to surprise you."

"It was certainly that," Bishop said, smiling at her to take any sting out of the words.

"It's wonderful that you're going to be able to be at your brother's wedding," Lila said.

"Yes, I'm—"

"They've been engaged for almost a year," Douglas said, interrupting his wife. "No need for a hurried wedding."

"Douglas!" Susan kept her voice low, but there was no mistaking the reprimand.

Out the corner of his eye, Bishop saw Lila's fingers tighten around her fork until the knuckles turned white with the force of her grip. He leaned toward his brother-in-law. "One more crack like that, Adams, and you can spend the rest of the evening picking your teeth up off the floor. If you have something to say, say it to me. In private. But I won't tolerate you upsetting my wife."

"Your wife?" Douglas's eyes, as clear and green as Lila's, flashed with anger. "She's my sister."

"If that wasn't the case, I'd already have fed you your teeth."

"Douglas." Susan's tone was less a plea than a demand, and her usually soft mouth was tight with annoyance. "If the two of you want to brawl like a pair of children, you can go outside. But I don't think it's too much to expect a little civilized behavior at the dinner table."

"The choice is yours, Adams," Bishop said, deliberately baiting the other man. He couldn't think of anything that would give him more pleasure than to bury his fist in Douglas's face.

"Bishop." Lila set her hand on his sleeve, her voice pleading.

The light touch reminded him that his main concern was her peace of mind. And, much as he hated to admit it, it probably wouldn't make her feel any better to have him punch her brother in the mouth. A pity, really, he thought wistfully. Reluctantly he sat back in his seat. Lila's hand still rested on his sleeve and he set his own fingers over it.

It was hard to say just where the evening might have gone from there, had the four of them been left to their own devices. It was perhaps fortunate that Sara Smythe chose that moment to sail up to the table. Wearing a deep-blue dress adorned with ivory lace and a four-inch ruffle at the hem, she looked every inch the successful matron. Her husband trailed behind her, with his usual look of vague surprise, as if, even after all these years, he wasn't sure how he'd come to find himself married to the forceful woman at her side.

"Good evening, Sheriff McKenzie. Mrs. Mc-

Kenzie." She nodded at both of them, like a queen acknowledging her subjects, Bishop thought as he pushed back his chair and rose courteously.

"Mrs. Smythe. Franklin." He made the introductions, amused to see Sara's reaction to meeting Douglas and Susan, two people obviously and comfortably ensconced in the level of society to which Sara so blatantly aspired. Some women might have treated them with deference but not Sara. Typically, she reacted by becoming even more overbearing.

"I do hope you'll forgive me for interrupting your family dinner," Sara said, looking as if she didn't particularly care whether they forgave her or not. "But I felt I should take this opportunity to express my concern about your son, Sheriff."

"Gavin?" Bishop raised one brow in question. "What about him?"

"I'm afraid he's encouraging my son, William, in this ridiculous fantasy of his."

"What fantasy?"

"This idea that he's going to grow up to be a . . . a shootist such as yourself." Sara made the word an accusation. There was a moment of silence, broken by Lila.

"William is very young, Sara. He'll change his mind half a dozen times before he's grown."

"That's easy for you to say." Sara waved one hand in a gesture that dismissed Lila's opinion as being of absolutely no importance. "But *your* stepson is the one who's encouraged William in these ridiculous notions. Not that I blame the boy. When his own father seeks out gunfights in broad daylight in the middle of the street, it's not unexpected that he should admire such behavior."

And now they got to the real point of the conversation. Bishop wondered idly what had taken her so long to get to him. From the moment Dobe Lang hit the dirt yesterday, a visit from Sara had been inevitable. She'd never made any secret that she disapproved of the town hiring him. Her contention from the start had been that a man of his reputation would bring trouble with him. In this case, she'd been dead right.

"From what we were told, the gentleman who was killed brought the fight to Bishop, rather than the other way around." Surprisingly, it was Douglas who spoke.

"Conflict can always be avoided if one is sufficiently motivated to do so," Sara said, speaking with the complete confidence of someone who'd never done anything to avoid conflict in her life. "But that's neither here nor there. I'm not concerned with that poor, unfortunate man who perished in the street yesterday." Her tone made Dobe Lang sound like an innocent bystander. "I'd like to know what you plan to do about your son, Sheriff."

"I'm not sure I follow you, ma'am." Bishop raised both brows in inquiry. "Just what is it Gavin has done?"

"I told you. He's encouraging William in this ridiculous notion that you're some sort of hero."

Despite his annoyance at her bullying attitude, Bishop couldn't suppress a twinge of amusement. His mustache twitched as he suppressed a smile. "That *is* a ridiculous notion," he murmured.

"I seem to recall that William was the one who'd been cutting out newspaper clippings about my husband long before he met Gavin," Lila said sharply, not sharing Bishop's appreciation of the moment. "From what I've heard of their conversations, William doesn't need any encouragement."

"I'm sure William would never have come up with this ridiculous idea on his own," Sara said, her face flushing with annoyance. "I've forbidden him to talk about it anymore yet I overheard him speaking to your son about guns just this morning. William has never disobeyed me before."

"I don't know your son, Mrs. Smythe, so I can only speak in the most general terms, but, as a teacher, it often seems to me that the brightest children have the most active imaginations." Susan's smile was filled with sympathy and understanding. "And often, the most intelligent among them are the most high-spirited. I've always thought it was the Lord's way of offsetting the blessings of having a gifted child. Blind obedience is only for the slow of wit, don't you think?"

Sara stared at her a moment. From her expression, it was clear that she saw the trap yawning in front of her. If she agreed with Susan, she was admitting that William's fantasy might not be Gavin's fault. If she disagreed, it was going to imply that her son was slow-witted, which was most certainly *not* the case. The silence stretched as everyone waited for her response.

She settled for a noncommittal and not entirely ladylike "Humpf." Which, Bishop guessed could be interpreted anyway you pleased. "I must be going," she announced, as if she'd just remembered a terribly important appointment. She departed on a wave of rustling blue silk, Franklin trailing somewhat apologetically in her wake.

She left behind a thick silence that lasted until Bishop and Douglas had both taken their seats. It was left to Douglas to sum up the encounter. "What a thoroughly unpleasant woman."

"She reminds me of that governess I had when I was eight," Lila said. "The one Father fired after you put a snake in her bed. I'll never forget the way she screamed."

"Lord, I thought the house was going to come down around our ears before she shut up." Douglas grinned reminiscently. "I think old Thomas threw a pitcher of water in her face finally."

"And then she stood there, soaking wet, and cursed us both up one side and down the other, using language that would have made a sailor blush. And Father fired her on the spot."

"Why did you put a snake in the poor woman's bed?" Susan asked, looking less than amused by the thought that the childish prank had resulted in the woman losing her job.

"Douglas found out she'd been taking a belt to me," Lila said. "Not that I could blame her, I guess. I was, on occasion, a bit willful."

Douglas snorted. "You were impossible." But there was affection rather than condemnation in his voice.

"Willful," she insisted. "Miss Gillyflower had come so highly recommended that Douglas wasn't sure Father would believe him if he told him what was happening so he decided to force her to quit."

"I thought it might take weeks." Douglas picked up the story. "But it turned out she was terrified of snakes and that she had a shocking vocabulary, so we

were rid of her the next morning. Father was so upset
over her language that he never even questioned how
the snake had come to be in her bed."

The silence this time held a different quality. The
anger was gone and in its place was the warmth of
shared memory.

"I could always count on you," Lila told her
brother softly.

Douglas's eyes shifted from her to Bishop and
abruptly his expression became shuttered and cold.
"Not always."

Beside him, Bishop felt Lila sag back in her chair
as if her brother's rejection had been a physical blow.
He knew what Lila wanted—to make peace with
Douglas and repair some of the damage that had
been done to their relationship. He only wished he
could be sure that Douglas wanted the same thing.

If idle hands were the devil's playground, then Sa-
tan must certainly be playing somewhere else today,
Lila thought the next morning as she stirred together
the ingredients for a batch of bread. Her hands hadn't
known an idle moment all morning. From the moment she got up, she'd been cleaning or cooking. She
couldn't fool herself about the origins of this sudden
burst of domestic energy. It had nothing to do with
wanting to get ahead on her chores and everything to
do with Douglas's sudden arrival in Paris.

It had been such a shock to open the door and see
him and Susan standing on the porch. For a moment,
she'd half believed they were an illusion conjured up
by her talk with Bishop. Hard on the heels of the
realization that they weren't a figment of her imagination had come the realization that, whatever their

reason for being there, it wasn't to tell her all was forgiven. Douglas's cool greeting had made that abundantly clear.

Then, before she'd had a chance to do more than absorb the reality of having her brother here, in Paris, in her home, Bishop had arrived and the atmosphere—not exactly cozy to start with—had taken a decided turn for the worse. And then Susan had insisted that they all have dinner together at the hotel where she and Douglas were staying. Lila had jumped at the invitation, thinking that nothing could be worse than having them all sit down to stew and bad biscuits in the kitchen. Not that her brother would turn his nose up at eating in the kitchen. Snobbery was not one of Douglas's flaws. But she thought the hotel might lighten the atmosphere a bit.

"If that was a lighter atmosphere, I shudder to think what it would have been like if we'd stayed here," she muttered to the mound of dough into which she was working flour. And, as if the evening hadn't already had more than its share of unpleasantness, Sara Smythe had to show up, worried that Gavin might be corrupting her precious son. "As if having a mother like that wouldn't be enough to drive the poor boy to a life of crime all on his own."

Before she could finish mulling over the list of the evening's disasters for the fiftieth time, someone knocked on the front door. Douglas. The fact that he'd used the front door told her who it was. Everyone else knew to come around to the back of the house. Besides, Bridget was the only one likely to come calling, and when Lila had taken Angel to visit Mary not more than half an hour ago, Bridget had settled the little girls at the kitchen table so they could "help" her bake cookies. Just the thought of the mess that was sure to result was enough to make Lila shudder with sympathy.

Her hands immersed in the sticky dough, she drew a deep breath and then yelled for her visitors to let themselves in. "I'm in the kitchen," she called when she heard the door open. Moments later Douglas and Susan appeared in the doorway.

"I'm sorry to greet you so informally," she said, forcing a bright smile. "But as you can see, I'm up to my elbows in bread dough. If you don't mind waiting a few minutes, I'll put some water on for tea."

"I can put the water on if you'll just tell me where everything is," Susan said as she reached up to unpin her hat.

"What are you doing?" Douglas asked by way of greeting.

"I'm making bread." Lila dusted more flour over the end of the table where she was working and rolled the dough into it. The dough was starting to get that smooth, satiny feel that made kneading one of her favorite things to do. She leaned her weight into the task, pushing on the heels of her hands as she rolled the dough away from her.

"I recognize the task," he said irritably. "What I don't understand is why you're doing it. Shouldn't you be resting?"

Lila glanced up from her task. "We weren't out all that late last night," she said, surprised by the question.

"That's not what I meant." Douglas glanced at Susan, but she was busy getting cups off the shelf and didn't meet his gaze. "Is it wise to be doing things like this in your condition?" he clarified, his eyes touching momentarily on her stomach. It was the first time he'd referred to her condition, which was certainly not something one could overlook.

"I'm fine, Douglas." Lila lifted the dough and slapped it back down on the table before continuing to knead.

"Don't you have someone who can do this sort of thing for you?" he asked. "A maid or housekeeper perhaps?"

"Maids and housekeepers aren't exactly a common item around here," Lila told him. "Besides, I don't really need one. The house isn't that big and there's only the four of us. Gavin is good about helping out, and even Angel does what she can."

Glancing at her brother's face, she saw that he looked less than convinced. He was clearly uncomfortable with the idea of her doing manual labor. A few months ago she might have felt much the same way Lila thought, but she'd changed a great deal since her marriage to Bishop. She'd discovered that she enjoyed doing things for herself. She enjoyed the feeling of accomplishment that came with pulling a golden loaf of bread from the oven or making the bed with sheets she'd just taken down off the line.

She couldn't deny that she missed some of the creature comforts she used to take for granted. Most especially she missed being able to take a hot bath whenever she wanted with no more effort needed than requesting that it be prepared. Just thinking about it was enough to make her feel wistful. But she was, she realized with some surprise, happier than she'd ever thought possible in this new life.

"I still can't get used to the idea that you're mother to two children," Susan said as she set the tea kettle on the stove. "They seemed very polite and well spoken when we met them yesterday, don't you think, Douglas?"

He made some noncommittal noise that could have been agreement or indifference. He moved restlessly around the room, picking up a spoon and setting it down again before moving to look out the window. Lila watched him out the corner of her eye. She knew him well enough to know that he had something on his mind.

"Gavin and Angel are wonderful children. It took Gavin a little while to accept me. I think he was afraid that I might try to replace his mother. But we came to an understanding. And Angel is just as sweet as she looks. I can't imagine a more loving child."

"You're very fortunate," Susan said.

"I think so." Lila poked her fingers into the dough, gauging whether she'd kneaded it enough.

"I want you to come home with us," Douglas announced abruptly.

"What?" Lila's head jerked up, her eyes wide and startled.

"You heard me. I want you to come home with us. Immediately."

"Douglas, you promised me you wouldn't bring this up," Susan said, looking distressed.

"I can't very well stand here and watch her work like a servant for him and listen to her talk about raising his children as if they were hers and not do something about it," Douglas protested. He took a quick, agitated step away from the door, as if he might sweep Lila up and carry her to safety immediately. "You don't even have to bother to pack. I'll send someone to do it for you later. If we leave now, we can be in Denver tonight and on our way home tomorrow."

"This is my home now, Douglas," Lila said carefully. She wiped her hands on the apron she wore and caught hold of her temper. He was speaking out of concern for her, she reminded herself. He didn't mean to sound so incredibly overbearing. "And I think of Gavin and Angel as my children now. I can't just walk off and leave them without a word. I'm married to Bishop. You have to accept that, whether you like it or not."

"I don't like it," he snapped. "I don't like it at all. You should never have married him. I should have insisted that you stay at home."

"As I recall, you didn't give me much choice about marrying Bishop," Lila pointed out in a dangerously calm voice. "I seem to remember that you simply informed me that you'd arrange for the ceremony to take place as quickly as possible."

"I was wrong," he said with a snarl. "I should have given it more thought. And even if you married him, you could have stayed at home. I should at least have insisted on that."

Lila leaned across the table toward her brother, her eyes bright green with anger. "It wasn't your place to insist on anything at that point. It was my choice to come West with Bishop."

"Fine." Douglas glared at her, every bit as angry as she was. "You made your choice and you came West. Now it's time to come home."

"This *is* my home," she said, raising her voice.

"Don't be such an idiot!" Douglas's voice climbed to match hers.

"You're coming home with us and that's final."

"No."

"You are pigheaded as a mule. Why can't you just admit that you hate it here?"

"You're stubborn as an ox and about as bright. I am staying right here. And if you can't accept that, you can . . . you can go to the devil," she finished, her voice climbing to something near to a shout.

"Fine. I'm leaving but I'll be back. I'm going to talk some sense into you if it's the last thing I do."

"It very well may be."

Ignoring the threat implicit in her words, Douglas looked at his wife, who'd sat silently observing the battle of will between brother and sister. "Are you coming?"

"Not right now," she told him calmly. "I think I'll finish my tea first. But you run along, dear, and I'll see you later at the hotel."

The dismissal in her tone made Douglas grind his teeth together. For a moment, Lila thought he might snatch his wife up and carry her off, but then he spun on his heel and stormed out of the kitchen. A few seconds later the front door slammed behind him.

"Would you like some tea?" Susan asked as calmly as if the scene had never happened.

"Thank you." Lila attacked the already kneaded dough, pummeling it viciously, working out her frustration on the resilient lump. At the other end of the table, Susan poured her a cup of tea, added a spoonful of sugar to it and stirred it, all without the least sign of agitation.

"As you may have already guessed, this visit was my idea," she said when Lila had ceased abusing the bread dough. "I know how much Douglas hates the idea of there being any sort of gap between you."

"He doesn't seem to have much interest in closing that gap," Lila said sharply. She shaped the mound of dough into a smooth ball and settled it in a greased bowl to rise.

"This has been very difficult for him," Susan said.

"It hasn't exactly been easy for me," Lila snapped. She covered the dough with a towel made from a flour sack and turned to look at her sister-in-law. "I'm the one who had my whole life turned upside down. Douglas didn't have to move thousands of miles away and leave behind everything he knew. Douglas didn't find himself stepfather to two children he didn't even know existed. Not that I'd trade Gavin and Angel for anything in the world," she added quickly. "I have no regrets about them."

"I can understand that," Susan said. "They do seem like very nice children. We were surprised when you wrote to tell us about them. Bishop had never mentioned being married before."

"The first I knew of it was when he showed up with the children in tow."

"You must have been furious." Susan took a sip of tea.

"I was upset," Lila admitted. She was faintly surprised to remember just how angry she'd been. Gavin and Angel had become such an integral part of her life that she couldn't imagine life without them. She took off her apron and draped it over the back of a chair. Choosing a seat, she settled across the table from her sister-in-law and picked up her cup. "Bishop didn't plan on bringing them with us to Colorado, you know. But when he saw how unhappy they were, he wouldn't leave them with their grandmother."

"Admirable."

"He cares a great deal for them, though I'm not sure Gavin has figured that out yet," Lila admitted, thinking of the tension between the two of them. "I think the main problem is that they're both as stubborn and strong-willed as mules."

Susan smiled fleetingly. "A trait they share with your brother."

"And their father." Lila brushed a lock of hair back from her forehead, suddenly aware of being profoundly tired. She hadn't slept much the night before. Instead, she'd watched the moonlight paint drifting patterns across the ceiling and thought about the many twists and turns her life had taken lately. Sometime after she heard the mantel clock chime midnight, Bishop had reached out, sliding one arm beneath her and pulling her against him. She'd curled into his hold, her head on his shoulder, her body pressed to his, drawing such comfort from his nearness that she forgot all about her disapproval of his lack of sleeping attire.

"Douglas just wants you to be happy," Susan said, interrupting Lila's thoughts.

"I know that," Lila admitted with an unhappy sigh. "I suppose, after everything I've done, I should be grateful that he cares at all. But I'm not a child for him to order about. I'm a married woman with a home and two children who depend on me. I can't desert them, even if I wanted to."

"And Bishop?" Susan probed gently. "What about Bishop?"

"Bishop." Lila stood up and went to check on the rising bread as if the yeast might suddenly have sprung to mad, impetuous life and caused it to overflow the bowl in a matter of minutes. It hadn't done anything of the sort, of course, but she needed a moment to gather her thoughts. *What about Bishop?* Such a simple question but she didn't know the answer.

"Are you happy, Lila?" Susan asked when Lila didn't respond to the first question.

"Yes." She was surprised by how easily the answer came. Turning to look at Susan, Lila smoothed one hand over her stomach, unconsciously seeking reassurance from her unborn child. "Yes, I am happy. I suppose that's hard for you to believe, considering the circumstances."

"No." Susan reached for the teapot and refreshed her cup. She smiled at Lila, her eyes gleaming with an endearing touch of mischief. "I know it's bad manners to remind you, but I did tell you that I thought you and Bishop could have a good marriage. He's a good man."

"Yes, he is," Lila said, and knew it was true. "Though he certainly can be very annoying."

Susan waved one hand dismissively. "That goes without saying. He's a man, and they can't help but be annoying sometimes."

Laughing a little, Lila sat back down at the table and reached for her lukewarm tea. "I'll keep that in mind next time Bishop makes me so mad that I want to forget all about being a lady and kick him in the shins."

"His shins are bound to be harder than your toes. You'd only hurt yourself."

Lila's laughter came more easily this time. "You're probably right."

Susan's smile faded and she reached across the table, touching the back of Lila's hand. "All Douglas

wants—all we *both* want—is to be sure you're happy.
And if Bishop makes you happy, I'll see to it that
Douglas doesn't cause any trouble."

If *Bishop* made her happy? Lila stared at Susan,
struck by the other woman's assumption that Bishop
was responsible for her contentment. It was a ridiculous idea. She'd only be happy because of him if she
loved him. Which she didn't. Of course she didn't.
Did she? Good heavens, she couldn't love him. Not
when she had no clue at all as to what he felt about
her.

Bishop wasn't at all surprised when Douglas strode
into the jail like a man bent on starting a war. On
some level, he'd known this confrontation was inevitable. There was too much left unsaid between them.
Bart Lewis had been dozing in a straightback chair
tilted back against the wall. Douglas's entrance startled him awake, and the chair's front legs hit the floor
with teeth jarring suddenness. He blinked blearily at
Douglas, looking like a sleepy bird surprised in its
nest. Bishop took a moment to hope that Bart never
found himself in a situation where his life depended
on quick thinking.

"It's almost noon," Bishop told his deputy. "Why
don't you go get yourself some lunch?"

"You want I should bring you back something?"
Bart asked as he rose and slouched his way to the
door.

"Thanks but I think I'll go home for lunch today,
say hello to my wife." This last was added solely for
Douglas's benefit, and he immediately regretted giving into the childish impulse to pour salt in what was

obviously still an open wound. Bart looked vaguely surprised but didn't comment, for which Bishop was grateful. The deputy nodded to Douglas and left, picking up his hat on the way out the door.

"What can I do for you, Douglas?" Bishop asked, rising from his chair and circling the desk. "You're not hear to report a crime, I hope?"

"I'm taking Lila home with me," Douglas said, ignoring the baiting question.

Bishop went still as he considered the implications of Douglas's statement. Had Lila said she wanted to go back to Pennsylvania? A few days ago that might not have surprised him, but he thought things had changed between them. Last night she'd turned into his arms as if there were nowhere else she'd rather be.

"Lila *is* home," he said quietly.

"No, she's not. This dusty collection of shabby buildings is no place for a lady. I know it and Lila knows it. She's just too pigheaded to admit it."

So this wasn't Lila's idea. Bishop felt as if a great weight had been lifted from his chest. She hadn't gone to her brother and begged him to take her back to Pennsylvania.

"You didn't come here to ask me to insist that Lila leave with you, did you? That doesn't seem a real likely thing for me to do, does it?" he asked.

"No, I guess it doesn't," Douglas said with undisguised bitterness. "I had the wild idea that I might appeal to your better instincts. I should have known better."

Bishop's jaw tightened but he refused to rise to the bait. "She's my wife."

"I know that," Douglas snapped, biting off the words as if they left a foul taste in his mouth. "And I know you've every right to keep her here."

"Keep her here?" Bishop thrust his fingers through his hair and tightened his grip on his temper. "You make it sound like I've locked her in one of the cells back there."

"She might be safer there!" Douglas strode to the window and glared out at the quiet street. "This is no place for a lady, Bishop, and you know it. Look at it. It's nothing but dirt and false front buildings. This isn't the kind of life she's used to."

"She seems to be adapting pretty well," Bishop said stiffly. Damn him for knowing just where to strike. How many times had he seen Lila walk down that same street and thought that she looked like a hothouse rose plunked down in a bed of cactus?

"Lila's stubborn. She won't give up easily. But do you honestly think she'll be happy here?" Douglas didn't wait for an answer but continued, digging the knife in a little deeper. "You said yourself that there's not a decent doctor within reach. What if she needs medical care?"

Bishop had no answer. It was one of the realities of life on a frontier where doctors were few and far between. When Bishop didn't say anything, Douglas's temper snapped. "My God, man, isn't it enough that you treated her like a whore? Must you put her life in danger, as well?"

Bishop was across the jail before Douglas finished speaking. He caught a fistful of the other man's shirt, jerking him forward until only inches separated them. "If I ever hear you use that word in connection with my wife again, I'll kill you with my bare hands, brother or no."

Douglas flattened his hands against Bishop's shoulders and shoved him away. His eyes were bright with fury, his fair skin flushed with it. "Fine words from the man who ruined her," he said with a snarl. "I invited you into my home as a friend and you seduced an innocent girl and then just walked away. Didn't it occur to you that there were obligations that went along with taking her virginity?"

"It occurred to me but I thought she'd be better off without me."

"I can't argue with you there," Douglas said bitterly. He jerked his clothes into place with quick impatience.

"There's no point in going over this again," Bishop said tiredly. "What's done is done."

"That's what you said at the wedding. It covers a lot of ground, doesn't it? Is that supposed to make what you did all right, just because it's done?"

"If I could change things, I would." But even as he said it, Bishop knew it was a lie. He wouldn't change anything if it meant that Lila would no longer be a part of his life.

Perhaps Douglas recognized the lie for what it was because his expression took on a new edge of contempt. "Everything worked out very nicely for you, didn't it? You married a lady, got a mother for your children, someone to clean house and cook meals. Oh, yes, and someone to warm your bed. You certainly did get quite a bargain."

Bishop wondered if Douglas would feel better if he knew just how chilly his bed had been until recently, but he wasn't about to discuss the intimate details of his marriage with his brother-in-law.

"I'm not keeping Lila a prisoner here" was all he said. "But I'm sure as hell not going to hogtie her and put her on a train with you."

"I can see I'm wasting my time," Douglas said.

"I guess you are."

Douglas started to say something more but, before he got a word out, they both heard the unmistakable report of a gunshot. Bishop was moving before the echo had faded. When he first came to Paris, stray gunshots were not uncommon occurrences. He'd soon put a stop to the casual dispensing of bullets. Other than his encounter with Dobe Lang, it had been months since anyone had fired a gun in town.

"Stay here," he told Douglas on his way out of the jail. Douglas ignored him, of course, following him out onto the boardwalk. Bishop didn't have to guess as to where the shot had been fired. People were gathering at the far end of the street, surrounding a figure lying on the ground. Cursing under his breath, Bishop lengthened his stride. Just what he needed. Some damned fool had probably shot himself in the foot, which would just serve to add fuel to Douglas's arguments . . .

His stride faltered, his thoughts fragmenting momentarily when he caught a glimpse of pale-yellow cotton spread across the dusty street. Lila had a dress just that color. Every time he saw her wear it, he thought that it looked as if the cloth had been woven of pure sunlight. There must be a hundred dresses that color, he thought. It couldn't be Lila—

Even as he broke into a run, he heard Angel's voice rise on a shriek of pure terror. "Mama!"

# *Chapter 21*

Bishop offered no apologies as he shoved his way through the small crowd. As he stepped past the last person blocking his view, he saw his worst fears realized. Lila lay on the street, her skirts pooled around her like a spill of sunshine. He wanted desperately to believe that she'd just fainted. But the ominous red stain that had crept across her shoulder made that impossible.

Bishop dropped to his knees. Angel knelt on Lila's other side, her small hands tugging at Lila's arm, her voice rising on a shrill crescendo of fear, repeating the word "Mama" again and again.

"Oh, my God." Douglas's words were more prayer than blasphemy.

"Take Angel," Bishop ordered without looking at him. He set his fingers against Lila's throat, seeking a pulse. He found it, reassuringly steady and strong. He was only vaguely aware of Douglas stepping over his sister's body and scooping Angel up into his arms. She struggled against him, screaming hysterically. Douglas tightened his arms around her, stilling her struggles with gentle force, murmuring meaningless words of comfort that had no effect.

"I need a knife," Bishop said to no one in particular. Half the town carried knives. As soon as he voiced his request, several were proffered. He took the nearest one, a hunting knife with a wickedly sharp blade. Bishop hooked the tip under the front opening of Lila's gown and slashed the fabric open all the way to the arm. She stirred, murmuring something indistinguishable as he peeled the fabric away from her skin as gently as possible. Her shoulder was covered in blood, making it impossible to determine the nature of the wound itself.

He was reaching for his handkerchief when there was a stirring in the crowd. Suddenly Gavin was there. He stood frozen for a moment, staring down at Lila's still figure.

"Is she dead?" he asked, his voice unnaturally calm. But when Bishop looked at him, he saw his own fear reflected in the boy's eyes.

"She's not dead," he said shortly. "And she's not going to die." He wouldn't *let* her die. He pulled his handkerchief out and shook it open. "Take your sister to the Sundays' and ask Bridget to come to our house. She's tended a bullet wound or two in her time."

"Who'd want to shoot Lila?" Gavin asked, bewildered.

"I don't know but when I find him, I'm going to kill him," Bishop promised. "Now take your sister and do what I asked."

Gavin hesitated only a moment longer before turning to where Angel lay sobbing in Douglas's arms. She went to her brother without protest. She was no longer crying hysterically. Instead, her tears were soft and hopeless. Bishop forced himself to tune out the sound of his daughter's fear, concentrating instead on mopping the blood from Lila's shoulder. He didn't want to move her until he had some idea what kind of damage the bullet had done.

"How does it look?" Douglas knelt on the other side of Lila's body and watched Bishop work.

"Her pulse is strong." Bishop took the handkerchief Douglas offered when his own became too blood-soaked to be of any use.

"There seems to be a lot of blood," Douglas said. "And she's unconscious."

"That might just be the shock of being shot. The wound doesn't look too bad," he announced, his voice shaky with relief as he uncovered the bullet hole near the top of her shoulder. "I think the bullet went through and the bleeding is already slowing down. The wound needs to be cleaned and bandaged. Let's see if we can get her home before she wakes up."

Lila woke to the feel of someone driving a red-hot poker through her shoulder. She cried out and tried to bring her hand up to push away her attacker, but her arms were apparently bound to her sides. She would have struggled but she heard Bishop's voice over her head.

"Lie still, sweetheart. I'll have you home in a minute."

*Sweetheart?* The endearment was enough to force her eyes open. Her view was limited to the expanse of his shirt and the solid thrust of his jaw above her. He was carrying her, she decided. That was why she couldn't move her arms, because they were held against her body. But that didn't explain the knife-sharp pain that stabbed her with every step he took. She bit her lip against the need to cry out again and the sound emerged as a smothered moan.

"I'll get the door."

That was Douglas. Lila was rather pleased with herself for identifying his voice. It seemed quite a feat considering the pain that seemed to be oozing its way downward from her shoulder to encompass her entire body. She heard the click of the latch and then the light changed as Bishop stepped into the house—their house.

"What happened?" In her mind, the question was clear and strong, yet her voice came out weak and thready.

"You've been shot."

Shot? The idea bounced in and out of her head in rhythm to the sound of Bishop's footsteps on the wooden floor. She couldn't seem to make a connection between herself and the word. But if she'd been shot, that would explain the pain.

"The baby?" She would have put her hand to her belly if she could have moved.

"That baby is fine," Bishop said so firmly that she believed him instantly. He couldn't sound so sure unless he really knew.

"Don't put me in the bed," she told him. "I'll get blood on the sheets."

"The sheets will wash," he said shortly, and lowered her to the bed.

Lila forgot all about the sheets and concentrated on not screaming as pain shot from her shoulder outward until every inch of her ached.

"Scream if you want to," Bishop said softly.

Lila felt his fingers against her forehead as he brushed back her hair. She opened her eyes. Was it a trick of the lighting or her imagination that made his skin look gray?

"Where's Angel?" she asked, bits and pieces of memory floating back to her. "She was with me. Is she all right?"

"She's scared to death but she's not hurt. I had Gavin take her to Bridget's and asked him to send Bridget over here."

"Gavin will take care of her. He's a good boy. You shouldn't be so hard on him. You're going to drive him away if you're not careful."

"I'll be careful," he promised. "Now just lie still until Bridget gets here."

His fingers felt pleasantly cool against her forehead, and Lila wondered if she had a fever. Maybe he was mistaken and she hadn't been shot at all. She'd been very sick with fever once when she was little, and she remembered how cool her mother's hand had felt on her skin. But she didn't remember the fever hurting this much. Nor had their been any blood and, from the sticky feel of her torso, she'd lost a considerable amount of blood.

"Am I going to die?" she asked calmly.

"No!" Bishop's answer was quick and sharp. "I'll be damned if you will!"

"Watch your language." The pain was starting to recede, leaving behind a not-unpleasant numbness. "A gentleman doesn't curse in front of a lady." Her eyelids felt very heavy and she let them drift downward. "Are you sure I won't die?" she asked dreamily.

"No!"

She heard Douglas's denial but it was faint and far away, unreal and unimportant. She drifted further away from the pain as if floating on the glassy smooth surface of a broad river. It was so peaceful. So . . .

"Lila!" Bishop's voice was sharp and angry. His fingers caught her chin in an ungentle grip, dragging her back into the real world. Lila's eyes opened and stared into the painfully vivid blue of his. "I'm not going to let you die."

"It's really not your decision," she told him, her voice weak but unmistakably cross.

"You're not leaving me. I'll follow you to the gates of hell if I have to and drag you back by your hair."

From the look on his face, she believed he meant it. He looked as if he'd take on the devil himself, and she wouldn't have been willing to take bets on who'd win the battle.

"No one's going anywhere near the gates of hell." Bridget's acerbic voice preceded her into the room. "What kind of a way is this to behave in a sickroom, shouting at the patient as if she were one of your prisoners? Get yourself out of my way."

With a last, commanding look at Lila, Bishop stepped back. As he straightened, Lila heard Douglas speak from the other side of the bed. "You're in love with her, aren't you?"

For a moment, the pain ceased to matter. Lila held her breath, waiting for Bishop's answer. When it came, his voice was so low that she had to strain to hear him.

"Yes."

"Here now," Bridget said. "A swallow of this and you'll sleep right through me tending to your wound."

Lila turned her head away, pursing her lips in refusal of the bottle Bridget held to her mouth. "I have to talk to Bishop," she shouted, only the shout came out as little more than a whisper.

"Later," Bridget promised soothingly. "You can talk to him later."

"Now," Lila insisted. Despite all their reassurances to the contrary, she wasn't convinced that death wasn't hovering just out of sight. "Now."

"What's wrong?" Bishop's voice came from behind Bridget.

"She says she has to talk to you." The minister's wife clicked her tongue in exasperation as she moved back. "See if you can get her to take a swallow or two of this laudanum," she said, thrusting the bottle into his hand.

"Drink this, sweetheart," Bishop urged.

Lila ignored the bottle, her eyes searching his face for some sign of his feelings. Certainly the words "I love you" were not emblazoned across his forehead, but why would he look so worried unless he loved her?

"I'm not going there," she whispered.

"Not going where?" From his expression, it was clear he thought she was delirious.

"To hell. A gentleman would never suggest such a thing to a lady."

"Then I'll follow you to the pearly gates." With a deft twist of his wrist, he got the laudanum bottle to her mouth and tilted a healthy swallow down her throat. "And I never did claim to be a gentleman."

Lila closed her eyes. She was adrift on that gentle river again, the pain floating somewhere far away from her. "Bishop?" Her tongue felt thick and clumsy, but there was something she had to say. With an effort, she forced her eyes open, staring up into his face for half a heartbeat.

"What is it?" His fingers were cool against her forehead again and she let her eyelids fall shut, thereby missing the impact of her words.

"I love you too."

**Five months later**

She wasn't exactly grateful that she'd been shot, Lila thought as she carefully sprinkled water over what she hoped was going to be a perfect batch of biscuits. And certainly she'd never dare even hint at such a thing in front of Bishop. The one time she'd suggested that her injury had had some benefits, he'd become irate and it had taken her some time to calm him down.

It was just that there was always sunshine behind even the darkest of clouds, and she was inclined to think—if not say out loud—that the sunshine behind this particular cloud had more than made up for the rain it had spilled into their lives.

If she hadn't been shot, it might have taken months or years for Bishop to admit that he loved her, even to himself. And she'd been so busy telling herself that she couldn't be in love with him that she might not have come to her senses any sooner. That alone was worth one small bullet wound, particularly since, other than a certain stiffness in her shoulder, she hadn't been left with any permanent physical damage.

Bishop's vow to kill whoever had shot her had gone by the boards when young William Smythe came forward and confessed the deed. He'd taken a gun from his father's study and was playing at being a gun fighter when the weapon went off. He'd made his confession despite his mother's loud insistence that he say not a word to anyone. There had been no doubting the boy's contrition, and Bishop had accepted his apologies. When William told his father what he'd done, Franklin said it was past time the boy went away to school, where he'd learn some discipline. Sara had refused to hear of it but the banker had surprised everyone by overruling her. William had departed for military school in Virginia.

Later Lila had overheard Bishop tell Douglas that it was a shame William had turned out to be the villain—he would have felt a great deal better if he could have bashed someone's face in. She frowned a little as she stirred the water into the dough, careful not to mix it too much. Her brother and Bishop were still far from best friends, but at least they'd come to some sort of understanding. Susan had been right— once Douglas was assured that she was happy, he'd stopped insisting that she go back to Pennsylvania.

At least the rift between her and Douglas had been patched up—another good thing to come of her being shot, she thought as she turned the soft dough out onto a lightly floured section of the table and kneaded it quickly—just a few strokes, enough for it to hold together but not too much or the dough will toughen, Bridget had told her repeatedly.

The back door opened as she was patting the dough out. Bishop and the children entered, bringing a rush of cold air with them.

"Pa says it looks like we'll have snow before morning," Gavin announced as he took off his coat.

"I hope it lasts until Christmas next week," Lila said.

"I want to make a snowman," Angel announced. She tilted her chin up to allow her father to get to the top button on her coat.

Looking at the three of them, Lila felt a foolish lump come into her throat. Though she couldn't say for certain that it was her getting shot that had welded them into a family, it certainly hadn't done any harm. Afraid that he was going to lose her the way he'd lost his mother, Gavin had looked for something solid to hold onto and had found his father there for him. Not that they didn't butt heads as often as not, she admitted. But at least the boy knew Bishop cared about him.

A thin wail from the parlor made it clear that the newest member of the McKenzie family had awakened from her nap and was not pleased to find herself alone. In the six weeks since her birth, she'd grown accustomed to being the center of attention. Named Margaret Ann, after both her grandmothers, she was well aware of her own importance in the universe and had a healthy set of lungs to announce her displeasure if things didn't go the way they should.

Lila had just picked up a glass to cut the biscuit dough and she glanced unhappily at her flour-coated hands. "Bishop?"

"I'll get her," Gavin volunteered before his father could respond. Though he pretended a manly indifference to his baby sister, Lila knew he was as enamored of her as the rest of them were.

"Me, too," Angel said. "Maggie likes me."

"Maggie likes anybody who pays attention to her," Gavin said with cheerful cynicism. "She's too little to know better."

"When he gets older, he'll figure out that adults like people who pay attention to them, too," Bishop commented as he shrugged off his coat and hung it on one of the pegs by the door. Crossing the room to where Lila was carefully cutting out biscuits, he slid his arms around her waist and tugged her back against him.

"Careful. I'm making biscuits and they're going to be really good this time. Bishop!" His name was a muffled shriek of protest as he buried his cold face against the side of her neck.

"You wouldn't want me to get frostbite, would you?" he asked innocently. His hands slid upward, gently cupping her breasts.

"I suppose you're just warming your hands," Lila said, suppressing a shiver of awareness.

"What else would I be doing?" Bishop nibbled her ear.

"A more suspicious woman might think you were making improper advances," Lila suggested breathlessly.

"A gentleman would never even think of such a thing," he protested as she turned into his arms.

"That's just one of many reasons I'm glad I didn't marry a gentleman," Lila said as his mouth closed over hers.